REVOLUTION
ON THE
ROCK

KARREN ABLAZE!

REVOLUTION ON THE ROCK

First published in 2022 by Mittens On Publishing,
145 - 149 Cardigan Road, Leeds LS6 1LJ, UK

British Library Cataloguing-In-Publication Data. A catalogue record for this book is
available from the British Library

ISBN 978-0-9574270-6-8

Disclaimer: The characters and businesses depicted in this story are fictitious, with the
exception of the bands, and well-known political figures and events. Additionally, certain
public offices and institutions are mentioned, but the characters and events therein are
quite imaginary.

This book is dedicated to the memories of:

Simon Morris
Ingrid de Leeuw
Nila Kamol Krishnan Gupta
Paul 'Candiflp' Blackwood
Louise Woodcock
Jo Cox

Chapter 1 – All Roads Lead To...

How do you know you're home? Is it the noise of the street, grime flows banging from makeshift sound systems – or the sight of your neighbours slumped merrily on their steps, cans of Red Stripe in their hands? Could it be the air, so curiously warm this evening, with its signature blend of curry spices, spliff and laundry detergent – or the view through the front door, wide open to a dishevelled living room, from which four sneaky pairs of eyes are looking back out at you?

What are they all doing here?

In that moment of startlement, the final rays of sunlight glint in Bunty's bunched hair as the smiles and cries of her friends beckon her to come quickly inside. It's a moment she will replay later, and often, in times and places that confine her, when barriers slam down to dam her powerful momentum, forcing her to glance back for the first time in her young, rushing life.

"We're your going away party!" Sofia whoops. She'd jump from her seat but for Marie, her two-year-old daughter, who's nestling between her legs.

Bunty laughs, kissing them both in turn. "I'm only off for a fortnight, daftie!"

"Sixteen days," corrects Meg, Bunty's housemate. "I made pizza!"

"I'm so gonna miss your cooking." Bunty drops down next to Sofia in the space that DJ Shock/Horror has made by budging onto the arm of the chair.

He leans towards her to whisper. "I know you've gotta try this cruise ship gig, but just remember the rest of the world isn't like Leeds."

"Umm, vote of confidence much? I'll be fine!"

"Just remember your fam is always here for you."

Bunty sighs. "I'll be back in time for the stupid referendum, I'll get the Jobcentre off my back, *and* I'll be able to pay my rent." She kisses him on the cheek. "Just don't have any killer gigs while I'm gone."

"You'll get to see places!" chimes in Meg.

"And you'll get free food," adds Shock/Horror, looking hungry. Tantalizing smells of tomato, oregano and olive oil are pervading the room; Meg passes them slices while the smog-blurred sun slips behind red brick terraced houses across the street.

Sofia rips hers into pieces to share it with Marie. "Bunty, you know that kid said we were like The White Stripes?"

"No! He knows Jack White plays bass, right?"

"I told him and he was like, 'Oh!'" Sofia stretches her eyes into a look of mock astonishment, then quickly resumes her usual expression, the one that says *I know you, don't mess.*

Bunty sets her plate aside and jumps up to grab her guitar. She contorts the fingers of her left hand into an impossible-looking chord and strikes the strings with her right. The result is quiet without amplification, but suitably discordant. "We're like... Heavens To Betsy!"

"They're too obscure, and ancient!" Shock/Horror hoots in derision.

Sofia contemplates the matter. "We should just say who we are."

"'Fuck off, we're The Vagilators' – that should be the name of our record."

Sof's eyes sparkle. "Write it down!"

Bunty takes a Sharpie from the shelf, scrawls on the aquamarine body of the Stratocaster copy, then lowers the instrument back against the wall. "Bye you. Be good," she tells it quietly, hoping no-one can hear. "I'll be home soon."

Her dad insists on carrying her case into the coach station even though it's got wheels and weighs much less than one of the monitors she regularly lugs on and off stage – or did, till she lost her job. He's fussing.

So's her mum. "Here's some soul food for the ride," Precious says, handing her a warm Tupperware box that she won't be allowed to open on the coach. "It'll remind you to come home soon."

Bunty can hardly speak by the time she hugs her dad goodbye. His "God bless" is echoing in her ears as the driver puts the bus into reverse, and in an instant she's lost sight of them both.

The coach slips from the city onto the dark motorway. It's the first time she's been away from Leeds, on her own, for more than a night or two, and she hadn't anticipated just how sharply that farewell would cut her heart. She doesn't care if the driver can see her rubbing her eyes with her sleeve, just as long as he sees her; she's chosen a front seat for that wide-windscreen enhanced viewing experience, and also cos she's in no mood for the creeps who might be lurking further back.

The trip would be so much quicker by train. This, though, is the option she can afford. The bus will detour into half the cities in England as they weave through the night, but the heating's on, the lights are low, and the other passengers have the same chill vibe. She puts her latest playlist on shuffle.

She hadn't realised how many Leeds bands are on it, and it's making her homesick already. Gang of Four – woah, this song's older than I am, but I love it so much. She leans back into the headrest for the exquisite feedback of the intro, then reflexively rocks forward with the pitter-patter heartbeat drums and duelling male vocals – one sung tersely, the other mumbled, both pissed-off – and lonesome droning guitars. "Love will get you like a case of anthrax / And that's something I don't wanna catch."

Then it's 'Hail Seitan' by Milk Crimes, ramshackle choppy guitars and a boy's unselfconscious yelping. She sings along with him under her breath: "This time I won't fall / Cos we won't commit at all." Maybe she really does need a break right now, and not just cos she's broke – this could be the perfect opportunity to get over Katrina. She gazes ahead at the tail lights of cars and lorries as they speed away from Leeds, and her heart aches to see the headlights of the vehicles on the other side, going back there.

2

"Morning all. This is Southampton. Please take all your belongings with you when you disembark."

She yawns, rubs her eyes some more, and surveys the area as the coach rolls into the station. It looks kinda Lego – all hypermarkets and multi-storey car parks, and nothing like the romantic picture she'd invented of a pretty town on the south coast of England. With her trainers and wheels on the ground she assesses grim skies and scraps her plan to explore. She feels like shit on toast, and all she really wants is a bit of a lie down before she starts this new job.

Hoodie up to hide drizzled frizz, and with Google Maps as her guide, Bunty drags her suitcase along stagnant high streets. Between boxy port buildings she spies the low line of the sea, then rounds a corner to face her new home, vast and looming: The Odyssey of Wonder.

Oh my fuck, would ye look at the size of that?

She tries to count the ship's floors but the vibration of her case throws her vision off. For weeks she's been fantasising about this luxury liner and the hours she'll spend lounging in her cabin, Disney fishes peering in through a porthole, and now here it is. She says goodbye to damp grey England, and steps into the terminal.

Chapter 2 – Unsettling In

The turnstile swallows and regurgitates her ticket, and the ramp leads her to the embarkation point. Bunty walks in and keeps walking until a woman in the vestibule asks her to stop.

"Name, please?"

She lets go of the handle of her case and it clatters to the floor. "Maguire".

"Mog wire?" The receptionist's brow gathers into a vertical line.

Bunty spells it out.

"Cleaning team?"

"Sorry, what?"

The woman runs a manicured nail down the list and, when she finally locates Bunty, crosses her out.

"Okay. I see. Sound engineer. Your cabin is 212. This is your key. The induction meeting is in the Trojan Horse lounge at 9.30."

There's something about that combination of blatant racial profiling and the total absence of welcome that leaves her feeling dazed, but she checks the time and it's only fifteen minutes before the meeting starts; so much for getting some sleep. She trundles to the stairwell, and after long moments of sniffing eau de carpet – air freshener with a hint of vomit – an electronic chime announces the arrival of a lift. It's empty and she gets in, case in tow. Before her fingers can even jab at the controls, an accusatory bark sounds from behind.

"You new?"

Bunty turns to face a short bald man. "Erm, yeah, I just got here?"

"Aye, I can see that!"

She takes a breath. "Just... what?"

"You're in the lift!" he spits.

"Yes, I'm in the lift. How is that a problem?"

"Everyone makes that mistake on their first day. You just don't know. Staff don't use lifts."

She blinks, trying to process the implications.

"Lifts are for t'passengers!" he continues. "It's in the handbook. You'll be getting yours soon, I suppose."

"I guess? I'm on my way to the induction meeting now. But there aren't any passengers on board yet..." She looks down at her case.

He narrows his eyes. "Alright. Don't let anyone see yer, and I won't tell." This pronouncement is sealed with a wink that makes Bunty feel ill at ease, or maybe just ill. She clocks his name badge for future reference – Dave Hedges. Seconds drag, and she risks being hypnotised by the way his florid complexion clashes with the electric blue of his jacket before the doors meet and seal with a mechanical crunch.

She falls back onto the mirrored wall, pushes all the air from her lungs, and gazes at infinitely receding versions of her suddenly very sad face. When the metal doors part she emerges with the newly acquired caution of a cat, into a labyrinth of narrow, dimly lit corridors. An almost sub-aural Gary Barlow tune oozes from speakers set in carpeted walls. She winces, scrutinises signs loaded with ranges of cabin numbers, and hastily navigates to her new room. A key card pressed into a slot makes a door jerk inward. She pulls her case across a metal curb.

It's tiny, like the room she grew up in. She looks at the place where the window should be, but a beige plastic wall stares blankly back at her; the Disney fishes are nowhere to be seen. Her chest tightens. There are bags and a jacket on the upper berth, so she drops her case by the lower bunk and backs out of the room. The meeting starts in five, and there are ten flights of stairs in the way.

Bunty's more breathy, sticky and stinky than she'd ever really want to be as she pushes open the doors of the Trojan Horse lounge. Seventy faces look up at her. She drops onto the nearest seat, and a tapping of the mic signals the meeting's start. That piece of timing's good at least; most of the eyes have turned to the speaker.

"Welcome on board The Odyssey of Wonder. I'm Jeff Saunders, the staff co-ordinator on this voyage." Thus begins a speech in which the finer points of health, safety and etiquette are covered in mind-wounding detail. Bunty tries to concentrate but can't penetrate the smug delivery or the well-rehearsed monotony of the thing. Her mind drifts, eyelids close, her head drops forwards.

Everyone's laughing, but she's missed the joke. She checks her face for drool and starts to survey the room to try and remain conscious. It's a sea of whiteness. Then she spots some people of colour, Filipinos maybe? and a couple of guys she would guess as being British-Pakistani. No-one looks like her. Something about being the only black girl here makes her think of her mum, back when she first met Dad's family. "I know you love them, Bunty, but they were not welcoming to me," she'd told her. "When your grandma and grandad Ireland first came to stay I put some music on for them. Just a bit of Bob Marley, you know, something I thought they'd enjoy. They were like, 'What's this monkey music?'"

Bunty shudders at the memory, and a twist of anxiety in her stomach keeps her alert for the rest of the meeting. As soon as it ends, most of what she's already thinking of as the Filipino contingent leave together. They're lively, catching up after a break from work, and introducing new colleagues to each other with kisses on both cheeks. Wow, if they're anything like the Filipino nurses who looked after mum in hospital, I'd love to hang out with them... But right now I just need a bit more shut eye.

Her feet drop down the ten flights – so much easier with gravity at her back – and when the cabin door swings open she finds a girl sitting on the top bunk with a mirror propped against her knees.

"Hi! You must be my new roommate! I'm Chelsea!"

"Oh, hi Chelsea, yes I'm..."

"Hot, isn't it?"

Bunty wonders if tiredness has rendered her speech inaudible.

"God, did you see that manager at the meeting? He looks totally gay! I was soo bored, I had to walk out. There were a few hotties there though... what's your name sorry?" The girl looks up quizzically, holding a can of hairspray above her long blonde hair.

"...Bunty," she coughs, gazing longingly towards the place where a window should be. Light buzzes from softly humming fittings on the ceiling, and the pumped-in air has a slight sibilance to it. She crawls onto her bunk.

"You're in the entertainment team, right?"

"Technical – I'm a sound engineer."

"Oh really? They normally put all the entertainment staff together. We're up for a laugh all the time." She laughs. "By the way I LOVE your hair! How do you get it like that?"

"I need to sleep."

"Well, we'll hang out loads, and I'll introduce you to all the girls. And the boys." She intones the last word more deeply, and laughs some more. Bunty wonders whether drinking starts really early on the ship. But Chelsea does pipe down, and she feels herself start to drift.

Ten minutes later the smack-squelch of the closing door brings her back to the cramped cabin. Her dream of sleep crushed once more, she gets up, opens her case, and starts to unpack.

Chapter 3 – Oh, The Booty Duke

The ship is a miracle of food – there are all these restaurants, and you can have just about anything you want. She locates one, The Olympian, and settles into a corner seat to scope the place out. Chelsea sees her before she has time to throw herself under the table.

"Bunts! Mind if I call you Bunts?"

As she opens her mouth, Chelsea continues. "Sit with us! We're over there."

Too knackered to think of an un-rude reason why not to, Bunty gets up and follows Chelsea to the large table by the window where a group of entertainment staff are lounging.

"Hey everyone, this is Bunty, she's my roommate, and she's got amazing hair, look!"

Everyone looks up at Bunty and her now-tatty looking bunches. She responds awkwardly to their greetings and scans for somewhere to sit. A boy with a mostly-shaven head shuffles his chair aside to make room for her.

"Hi, I'm Bryan!" he says brightly, holding out a hand. "I'm sorry about Chelsea, she can be horrific. How are you doing? Is this your first voyage?"

"It is. I'm feeling a bit out of place."

"Well, don't take any notice of anything they said at the meeting. This is your real induction." He gestures towards his friends.

She looks around the table, then at the rest of the room. The demographics are not in her favour.

"Penny for 'em."

Bunty's eyes widen. But if he's really offering to give her the lowdown...

"Okay then. In the meeting I saw a bunch of people who looked like they were from the Philippines maybe, but I haven't seen them since..."

"Oh, you won't."

"What d'you mean?" She stares at him.

"They're below deck staff. They're not allowed above deck." He takes a mouthful of steak.

"When?"

"Hmm?"

"When aren't they allowed upstairs?"

"At all. During the voyage. They stay below deck, working on maintenance and stuff."

What the...? Bunty feels like she might fall off her chair, but she needs to get to the crux of this.

"So it's pretty much only white people allowed above deck?"

"No, no, it's not like that." He reaches for the ketchup. "It's not a racist thing, it's just that's their job. Have you met any of the managers yet?"

Bunty blinks, trying to catch up. "I've only seen that guy, Jeff."

7

"He's harmless. But there are some real pieces of work here. I shouldn't be scaring you though. You would make mincemeat of them anyway."

Bunty's not sure what she will make of them, or why he's said that. She looks around the group; Chelsea's laughing with two friends in the corner.

"No, but did you see that Jeff? He was like, 'Oh I'm too weak to move this table,' and then he was eyeing up the janitor guy. So funny!"

"Chelsea, stop being such a homophobic bitch." It's a lad sitting opposite. He's slender and pretty, sporting a long fringe and eyeliner.

"Oh, you're alright, Tarqs. I didn't mean you."

Tarquin puts his head in his hands, then shakes it while looking across at Bryan. Bryan stretches a hand over to him. "Only two more weeks, mate."

"Right." He sighs, stands up and announces dramatically: "Fuck you all! Back to the grindstone."

Bunty decides to leave too; she needs time to process this crazy system, and she's still jonesing for sleep. After muttering a quiet goodbye to Bryan, she walks away and hits the stairs at the same time as Tarqs. He's decent company for the eight flights down, and it's enough time for them to exchange news on their respective underground music scenes. He's from London but has heard of her old haunt, The Booty Duke, and is full of envy. "Loads of bands went on about it. I really wanted to go. I'm gutted it's closed now. What happened?"

"Oh god, there was this one single noise complaint, and the council upheld it and fined us out of existence. Funny cos then it got turned into a high street clothes shop straight after."

"Weird that. Gentrification one, live music nil, yet again."

"That's about right," Bunty acknowledges sadly, as they go their separate ways. And now here I am on this bizarre water bound microcosm of... what, exactly?

Card, click, in. She flops onto the lower bunk and her muscles immediately start to unwind on meeting the flat horizontal surface. Her mind drifts to another world, a peaceful space, with the feeling of the faces of her friends...

Four minutes later Chelsea bursts in. Bunty wakes to see her roommate tossing her hair in front of the wall-mounted mirror.

"Bunts, is it better like this, or like this?" She demonstrates her hair down, then pushed forward into a 1940s-style roll.

Jesus, Mary and Joseph. Bunty sits up and considers how to give a meaningful reply, one that isn't totally dripping in exhaustion-fuelled contempt.

"I don't like the roll, but that's cos of the housewife implications..."

"What do you mean?" Chelsea asks, looking perturbed.

"Erm. It just reminds me of those 'We can do it!' posters where the woman has her hair up in a headscarf. I know it's a positive message, but I don't see why women should wear the uniform of pre-war housewives in 2016. Y'know what I mean?"

Chelsea shakes her head slowly, her face a picture of confusion. "Are you... a feminist or something?"

"Course. Aren't you?"

"Well no. I like men!"

Fuck! "So do I."

"You don't sound like you do."

"When don't I? You've only known me for a couple of hours."

"Just now, you were talking about housewives and uniforms and stuff."

Bunty lets out a breath. "Being a feminist just means you want equal rights for women. Equal chances."

"But we have those already. We can vote and go to work. What is it you actually want?"

"Try walking down a street at night. Try walking down a street during the day! Try getting a job in a male-dominated field..."

Chelsea's face has twisted into a puzzled grimace, and she looks close to tears.

Bunty gives up. "It looks fine either way."

Chelsea moves to the door, saying she's going to ask someone who'll give her a sensible answer, and Bunty shrugs, retreating back into the shelter of her bunk. Sleep claims her once more.

She wakes with a start. It's five past six, and her shift's at half past; just enough time to wet her hair, tie it up and get changed before climbing up the ship. It's the first time she's had to put on a uniform since school. A Fred Perry-style shirt with 'Elite Entertainment' embroidered on the chest, and black trousers that she'd been instructed to bring – when she slips into them she feels gross and owned, and her heart resonates with a whole new tone of regret for the job she lost.

The nylon's hot and prickly against her skin by the time she reaches the Poseidon Suite. She strides to the desk to prepare for soundcheck. The show's kicking off at half seven, and she might need time to get acquainted with some of the equipment, though she did request the specs in advance and what they're using is similar to the state-of-the-art desks she worked during her degree course. She locates the list of performers and their requirements, and is flicking through it when a stubbly man in his forties approaches the desk.

"So, when's he here?"

"Who, sorry?"

"The sound guy."

Bunty gathers her strength, and looks into his eyes. "I'm Bunty Maguire. Sound Technician. Who are you?"

My grandma would be proud of me, she thinks, for leaving "the fuck" out of that question. Maybe I am learning some nice Jamaican manners after all.

"Ah. Erm. I'm Tony, the entertainment manager. Do you need any help, luv? I've worked these before," he offers, gesturing at the array of controls.

"So have I. So, no thanks."

Tony grunts and walks away. She gets on with her job with gritted teeth, setting the levels for the artists who appear, fortunately, on time and in sequence. After a while she relaxes into the familiar rhythm of the work.

When the show – a faux-X-Factor-type charade – is underway, nostalgia for The Booty Duke hits her even more. Every shift at that city centre venue was a joy. Like that Saul Williams gig – she can recall every detail, from the moment she arrived and dropped her bag on the tatty wooden floor and started to set up. Tiredness and

9

the heat of the room are making her drift to that other venue, months into the past and hundreds of miles north...

Saul had greeted her with a handshake that turned into a hug. A warm guy. Kinda hot, actually. He was in black jeans and a customised t-shirt with a bunch of strings and things around his neck, and shiny silver bangles on his wrists and cute dreads protruding around his head at various angles. He introduced her to the person looking after his music, Thavius Beck. Oh my god! Shock/Horror will go nuts when he finds out! It turns out Thavius is gonna be sitting adjacent to the sound desk operating a laptop, so she gets the cabling ready for this underground hero. There's not much for her to do, it turns out, with just Saul on stage – one mic is all he needs.

Her mum and dad are in attendance, which is kind of weird. Her dad, Jimmy, knows Saul from when Peel used to play his stuff, and Precious knows him from her own DJing days, though he was mainly doing slam poetry back then, but somehow word got round. They've both sworn to leave her to get on with her work, but she's promised to mind her mum's bag so she can dance unencumbered.

The place is quiet when Saul gets on the stage. There seems to be three different crowds, a small group who have his records and are excited, poetry nerds, and people here cos they've been told they should be. And overall that makes the room a cool one. Leeds is not a place for being cool though. Love it or fuck off, is how Bunty feels.

He walks on wearing a cape, rhyming his poems, and from a standing start the words are flying out of him:

...I am that nigga
I am a negro!
Yes negro, negro from necro meaning death
I overcame it so they named me after it
And I be spitting at death from behind
And putting 'Kick Me' signs on its back
Because I am not the son of Sha-Clack-Clack
I am before that, I am before
I am before before
Before death is eternity, after death is eternity
There is no death there's only eternity
And I be riding on the wings of eternity
Like HYAH! HYAH! HYAH!...

She looks around. People are edging forward, some looking astonished, others confused. A semi-circle forms in front of the stage, the vibe's warming up, but some have their arms crossed over their chests – there's still a fear of vulnerability.

Then Thavius hits play and launches the music for 'List of Demands'. About seven people start jumping up and down to the frenetic beat; others don't know the song but their heads are bobbing. Bunty wishes she could race to the front and join in the pogoing, but she's got a job to do.

The vibe changes again with the symphonic keyboards of 'Burundi', and for this Saul jumps down to the floor. It can be a bit of a pop star wanky move, but Bunty watches as the quiet ones shuffle forward and dance with him. He seems to be broadcasting on more than one level, as waves of what she can only think of as empowerment sweep through the room. Fuck it. She smiles at Thavius as she steps from behind the desk and into the crowd.

Saul's in the centre of a circle. Bunty takes a place in it, and shakes and sways while laser beams of connection shoot across the room. He's a shaman, guiding her in a dance with the ancestors, accessing their profound knowledge, inviting a release of fear, and insisting she embrace the power at her essence. She goes deeper into the rhythm, into his energy, and he in hers. Later, when she sees photos of that night they show nothing of what really went on.

The set ends and she scarpers back to the desk. Luckily the levels have been even enough; she got away with it. The encore includes "Coded Language," and it pins her to the wall in awe.

Her dad swings by, wide-eyed and swearing in wonder, her mum looking blissed out at his side. She hugs them both at once. What a fucking show.

Bunty puts the settings back to zero. With her hands on the controls she lets out a long yawn as the memory recedes. The static-y Elite Entertainment shirt crackles against her chest, and the sound of ten-year-old belting out a grimly determined rendition of Robbie Williams' 'Angels' brings her fully back to the present. She clutches the bangle on her wrist.

Christ on a fucking blood clart, she curses inwardly. I miss music.

Chapter 4 – Breakdown (A Nowhere Wolf)

It's Day Two on The Odyssey of Wonder, and Chelsea's doing her hair again.

"Bunty, where are you from?" she asks from behind her mirror.

"Leeds. You?"

"Nantwich. But I mean... where are your parents from?"

"Huh?" *Where am I really from? This bullshit again.*

She glares at Chelsea, who isn't looking up from her fascinating reflection. "My dad's from Ireland and my mum's from London."

Chelsea does look at her then, and the expression on her face is priceless.

Bunty twirls round and grabs the door handle. "Off to work. Later."

She leaves out the three words "small-minded bitch," that should naturally complete the sentence.

I'm too fucking polite for my own good. Just like Grandma.

Her first shift is a matinee – a pantomime for the small screaming passengers. Their shrieks and demands penetrate deep into her skull, planting a headache there. The show seems like it's running over schedule, but it's just a cruel trick of perception.

Afterwards she visits the bathroom. Two guests are on their way out; a woman and a girl of perhaps seven years. The woman's eyes spark at Bunty, and she speaks quietly but urgently to her charge.

"Keep hold of your purse!"

Bunty knows from long and tedious experience that this is about her, or rather their fear of her. She feels a familiar combination of sinking heart and rising rage – a rage that she cannot speak, as to do so would only seem to confirm their warped perceptions. *That woman doesn't know me. She probably never will, with an attitude like that. But what about the kid, what's she going to grow up believing?* She stares straight ahead as they walk past. The weird vibe leaves with them, but Bunty's stuck with the same old fury and sadness that she's been trying and failing to navigate for most of her life.

She can smell the aromas of lunch as she walks past the restaurants, but her stomach's too scrunched up to be able to think about partaking. She flows down the stairs and straight to her bunk where she sits, hugging her knees and feeling homesick. There's little time to dwell on anything though, and maybe that's for the best, cos pretty soon she has to get back up the stairs for the afternoon show.

Damn, I'm hungry. Better remember to eat something...

The stairs are more challenging now. Usually she can climb four flights before her legs get heavy; this time she's struggling on the first. Is it the heat, or just tiredness? She feels light-headed, and is swaying a little. Then her legs buckle. *Shit.* She swerves into the wall, heart hammering. *Is this what a heart attack feels like?* Clear liquid pours from her forehead, and her thighs and belly are clammy too. Her chest's so constricted she gets the urge to take off her bra. *In public!* No-one's in

12

sight; she reaches under her top and unhooks the clasp at the back, tugs the strap off her left arm and whips the thing out of her right sleeve. That feels better, but she isn't. She hears herself moaning slightly as a couple with a young boy walk past, eyeing her suspiciously. Maybe it's cos she's stood there clutching a bra. She shoves it in her pocket.

I need help.

Here – a bar. She swerves in, lurches towards the wooden counter, and holds onto it. A girl approaches. "Hey, what's up with you?"

"Uh, not well," Bunty grunts.

"Let me get you something to drink. Water?"

She nods, and the bartender fetches her a bottle of water and a glass.

"Maybe you need to eat something? Some chocolate - shall I get you some?"

With her head on her hands, Bunty tries to lift it up to say yes please, but it doesn't come out very loudly.

The bartender is proffering a Mars Bar. Bunty takes it soundlessly, tears the wrapper off and downs it almost in one. In a minute or two the sugar's hit her bloodstream, the lights are switching back on in her head, and she no longer feels like she's dying.

"You might have low blood sugar," the girl behind the bar says. "If you're not eating properly? I see it a lot with the entertainment staff. They just drink and then try and walk up all the stairs."

"Yes, but I've not been drinking, booze anyway. Just coffee. Lots of coffee."

She can sit up straight now, but still feels the need to hold the bar down. And she can focus on this girl, enough to see that she's really cute in a gothy way, with blue hair and a pierced eyebrow.

Bunty smiles at her. "You might be right. I feel a bunch better."

"There you go!"

"You're like a doctor!" She's all big eyes and gratitude.

The gothy girl grins back at her.

"You're breaching etiquette young lady. Y'can't lie about like that!"

Uh, Dave fucking Hedges. He's looming over Bunty like a malignant willow tree.

The bartender faces him off. "This member of staff's been feeling unwell. I'm helping her out."

"Well, if she's ill she has t' get t' t'doctor! She can't be lolling around in full view of t'passengers."

"She just needed something to eat. She'll be alright now."

Bunty can't work out why this girl is sticking up for her, but she appreciates the support.

Dave Hedges glares at them through narrowed eyes. "Well, yer'll know fer next time," he mutters, before wandering away.

"Thank you!" Bunty smiles weakly at her new ally.

"You're welcome. You can do without dicks like him."

"You're telling me."

When Bunty stands, she's pleased to discover that she can walk in a straight line. So she goes to work.

Chapter 5 – Ship of Fools

I cannot be fucked with this anymore.

She pulls her hoodie closer against the cold night air. The Atlantic extends endlessly and she gazes into its blackness, yearning for the artificial lights of civilisation – for something like home.

This is going to take too long. I need to get off this thing.

The liner lurches and she stumbles, her trainers squeaking on the spray-covered deck as she mentally replays the last few minutes – the comedian's cocky pose as he reeled out one of his favourite gags.

"What do you do when your wife is staggering?"

A pause; some raised eyebrows.

"Hit her again."

The red-faced old fellas in the audience had started to guffaw, their cheeks moving up and down in delight, beer sloshing in glasses held aloft. Their partners, in lipstick and pearls for the evening's entertainment, seemed oblivious to the hatred behind the laughter, but Bunty saw how some of them had lowered their eyes in a way that suggested submission. All part of the fun.

She'd stepped out from behind the sound desk and bolted for the door, blurting to Tony that she felt sick as she passed him. It wasn't a lie.

Now she clutches the rail and takes deep breaths, hoping to quell the nausea, trying to work out what to do next. This whole thing's too much; I need an out.

The advert had made it seem so appealing: free board and food, travel built in. But clearly she hadn't thought it through. In light of her economic situation, jumping ship isn't an option, and jumping overboard wouldn't help anything either. She hears footsteps approaching along what she thought was a deserted deck and looks up to see a man in a blue uniform. It's Tony.

"Are you alright, darlin'? We were worried when you ran out like that."

"I'm okay," she lies, certain he wouldn't get what she's going through; she'd seen him laughing along with all the others. "Just not got my sea legs yet."

"They have pills for that in the office, you can pick them up there anytime. Neck a few of those and you'll be reet."

"OK. Thanks." She's trying to think what to say to make him go away. "Look, Tony, I don't feel well. You can manage without me for the rest of the shift, right? It's all set up..."

"We're going to have to be. Don't want you throwing up all over the mixing desk, that thing cost a fortune."

"Alright." She gulps fresh air in relief. "See you tomorrow." Bunty starts to move towards the door. She doesn't really want to go inside, but needs to bring the conversation to a close.

"Just come to me if you have any problems." As he says this he reaches for her hand, giving it a little stroke.

She jerks back and her eyes widen as a brand new feeling of horror slams down on top of the mess of emotions she is already struggling with. "Oh. Okay," is all she can manage before she pulls open the heavy door and trips inside, desperate to escape him. She races down a mountainside of stairs, tears of fury clouding her eyes.

I gotta get off this ship before I...

Before I what?

Chelsea isn't home. Thank fuck for small mercies. Their shared table is cluttered with make-up and hair care paraphernalia. Bunty pushes most of it to one side so she can have some space to lean on, so she can think.

The first stop will be Gibraltar. If I get off there, I can get back to the UK; it's a British colony so they must have flights to London. I've got about £70 – that should cover the flight. And if I can't afford the coach back to Leeds I can always hitch. It's doable.

The door squelches open and Chelsea appears, so Bunty retreats into the two cubic metres of darkness that is her bunk. She can't take anymore right now, and the duvet is all the protection she's got.

"I just saw Tony," Chelsea announces accusingly. "He said you didn't work your shift tonight."

"Not well," Bunty mumbles. A.K.A. please fuck off.

"Well, he says he thinks you're faking it and you don't have any team spirit. That you're a quitter, and how he would personally call your Jobcentre and tell them if you leave before the end of your contract."

Bunty feels fury rising once again in her chest. Murmurs, "The fucker."

"That's not very nice, Bunty. Everyone thinks you've got a chip on your shoulder, and you've got no sense of humour."

Bunty sits up and glares at Chelsea, unable to believe what's coming out of her mouth.

Yet she continues. "He called you a sour-faced... well, I can't repeat what he said exactly." Chelsea snorts in a satisfied kind of way.

"What did he say? Say it!" Bunty's chest is tight, but her voice is big with righteous rage.

Chelsea looks at her, wide-eyed. "Fucking hell, Bunty. No need to be so aggressive. I'm going to see Bryan." She storms out of the cabin.

Fucking... fuck you!

Bunty doesn't know what to do. There's no outlet. If there was signal she'd be on the gram declaring the cruise ship gig to be one great big pile of nope, but that disappeared with Southampton's skyline. She could pay £1 for five minutes on the on-board computers...

Or she could go and see if that girl's still in the bar...

But her legs won't play, and she can't risk being seen out right now. She lies back in her bunk, tormented by frustration and loneliness; exhaustion pushes her into feverish sleep.

Chapter 6 – Should I Stay or Should I...?

For a few moments she doesn't know where she is. She feels peaceful, soft and light. Then it hits her: the steady drone of the engines, the faint hiss of the air conditioning, and all that's gone before. This is day three; did all of that really happen in just two days?

And tomorrow it's Gibraltar. I need to be ready, and keep it together, and act normal. What's normal round here though?

Her mind turns to planning. A salve; the illusion of control. How long would it take to pack? Minutes – I never unpacked. I'll do it when Chelsea isn't around, and leave some stuff here – a t-shirt, a toothbrush. I don't want them to come looking for me.

Her first job of the day is a children's talent contest. Arriving early to set up, she finds the ballroom quiet with no dickheads around, and the show is reasonably diverting despite the tedious material some of the kids have chosen – or had imposed on them. A ten-year-old boy breaks the mould with a Clash song, and she flashes him a grin as he bounds past her towards his proud punk mum.

But just before the matinee shift wraps up, Tony taps her on the shoulder. She jumps, fully allergic to him by now. He clears his throat.

"Love, admin have asked me for your passport. They didn't process all the details they needed at the commencement of your contract, so they have to do it now."

As if nothing happened last night. As if he never said all those things to Chelsea.

"Uh. W-when can I have it back?" Trying not to sound alarmed. Failing badly.

"Straight away love, if you run and get it for me I'll bob it over to them now."

Run. Bob. Love. She's seething, but if she refuses him suspicion might be aroused. The timing's too obvious, and it can't be a secret that she's unhappy on this stupid racist boat.

The sixteen flights of stairs consume her break time. She masks her fury as she hands her passport to him.

"Glad to see you're feeling better."

Cunt.

"Cables!"

"Sorry?"

"I gotta go and sort out some cables." She marches off. So much for normal.

In her next break she looks for him; he's notably absent from his office, and no-one seems to know where he is. She tries the secretaries' office, but they're saying that they haven't even received her passport, and know nothing about returning it to her.

"You've got your disembarkation card though, haven't you love?" asks the head secretary, looking up from her computer screen. "That's all you need for your shore leave."

Bunty nods and forces a smile. "I have that."

The secretary checks down the list and confirms that Bunty does in fact have shore leave for Gibraltar. "We'll be able to get your passport back to you by the end of your contract. To be honest we usually have them all in safekeeping anyway. Is there any reason why you're worried about it?" she enquires, gazing at Bunty over her glasses.

"No reason." She feels she's given too much away with this enquiry, and that maybe the woman can pick up on her anxiety. She ducks out of the office.

This. Is. Fucked. I can't leave without my god damn passport. They have me.

A loud gurgling in her gut reminds her that she's omitted to eat again, so she climbs two more flights to reach a restaurant. There's a table by the window where she can lurk, slightly out of range of the nearest Euro-pop-spewing ceiling-mounted speakers.

There's that girl from yesterday!

"Hey! How are you feeling now?"

"Apart from having a completely shit time?"

The girl laughs. "What's your name, by the way? I'm Tallahassee."

Bunty tells her.

"Welcome to the weird name club! Where did you get yours?"

"From my mum – she used to read Bunty comic when she was little, and it was like her idea of what a 'proper' English girl was like. So she called me that, kind of ironically, I guess." Bunty grins. "What about you?"

"I named myself when I transitioned. It's a mouthful though – you can call me Talla."

It's good to meet another comrade from the queer world. "Was that a while ago?"

"Two years. And now I'm on this fucking ship!"

"Jeez, how do you cope? You've done this before?"

"Third voyage. It's hell, but it pays for stuff. I've had to learn to keep my tongue sharpened, and keep the fools at bay. It's no fun though, always having to be on your guard. It's lonely!"

Bunty has every sympathy. "I was gonna ask you for survival tips…"

"Well, you gotta get the basics down. Eating, drinking, sleeping."

"Even that's not easy," Bunty confirms glumly. "My shifts are split all over the place and after you've gone up and down all those stairs there's no time left for anything else."

"Alright Smurf?" It's a male voice from behind Bunty's head.

"Fuck you, Tony." Talla sneers.

"You'll get pulled up for using language like that in front of the public. I'll have to make a report you know."

"Yeah, whatevs."

He's still behind Bunty's head. She doesn't want to look at him, preferring to watch Tallahassee's barefaced defiance, but she has been trying to track him down. She starts to turn towards him.

"Tony, I need to…"

That's when she feels his hands in her hair.

"Always wanted to do this," he says, sounding pleased with himself. His fingers are right in there, stroking her scalp. "Feels alright…"

"Get OFF me!" Bunty shrieks. People at the table opposite look around. He pulls his hands away, staggers a few steps back, turns and scarpers.

She shudders, and hugs herself.

"Shit, are you alright?" Talla leans across the table, extending a hand.

"I want to be sick. I feel gross. I fucking hate him."

"That is fucked up. I need to report him for doing that."

"Are they going to believe you though?"

Talla gets up and approaches guests at the tables around theirs. "Did anyone see what just happened?"

But the diners are shaking their heads. There are some anxious looks, and the rest are mumbling into their soup. She turns back.

"That was so blatant. Fuck! And no-one's bothered." She puts her hands through her blue hair. "Wanna get out of here?"

Bunty nods, and they walk out arm in arm. Talla has a cabin to herself – "I think this is the secret to my survival actually," she admits – and they settle into her bunk to share an assortment of bar snacks that she has squirrelled in there. "Yeah I know I said that thing about eating properly…"

Bunty laughs and spits flakes of cheesy puffs over herself. "This is *my* survival plan – I'm planning to fuck off when we get to Gibraltar. But you've gotta not tell anyone."

"Sure. It's been done before. But then I won't have anyone to hang out with." She makes a sulk face.

"Come with me?"

"I'd love that." Talla grins. "Gibraltar adventure!"

"The only thing is, Tony has my passport."

"It's hard to get it back you know, they normally keep them in a safe."

"I know, but they don't even have mine in the office. I think he's got it on him."

"We're gonna have to kill him."

They high five on that.

"Wanna give it one more try at the office? I'll come with you cos I want to report that shit."

"Okay. He did more of it last night as well. Touching me."

"Oh, fuck. Come on then."

They head out of the tiny cabin and back up the stairs. It's only two floors up. Rounding the corner of the overheated corridor they see that the main door to the admin section is shut and locked.

"Weird – they said there would always be someone here."

"Ah, you believed the hype they told you at the induction."

Bunty blinks at the sound of male voices and laughter nearby. A cabin door is slightly ajar.

"I've got my eye on that bitch."

"Oh her – well you know what they say about them."

"Been watching too many rap videos, mate."

"Awful attitude. Nice hair though, I had a feel of it earlier."

Fucking Tony.

Talla and Bunty are frozen outside the room. They glance at each other, then dash back the way they came, sharing an instinctive need to avoid these guys. They're down a flight of stairs before they can even speak.

"Christ." Bunty slumps against a wall.

"Fucking jerks." Talla shakes her head. "Back to my cabin?"

But Bunty can barely move.

"I know what would help." Talla calls the lift. The bell pings and the doors part; she beckons Bunty inside.

"But we're..."

"Fuck 'em. This is an emergency."

The lift moves up rather than down. When they emerge Talla takes Bunty's hand and guides her round the corner into her bar. "I have a tab here."

She orders shots.

Bunty slams two of them back, and starts to come round. "That was so fucked up," she confides in Talla. "I feel... hunted."

"I'm not surprised. What are we gonna do?"

She shakes her head. "Back to plan A. Man overboard?"

"It's definitely an option." Talla laughs.

Bunty smiles wryly; it helps to pretend that she has some power in the situation. She hears a gaggle of voices, a garrulous group entering the bar.

"Buntyyyy!" Chelsea's drunk. "I'd recognise that hair anywhere!"

Bunty looks at her like she's just added Chelsea to the death list too.

"Ooh, what's wrong with you?"

Talla starts to tell her what they just heard outside the open cabin door.

"Don't, Talla!"

But she's too late, the essence of it has already been blurted. Bryan's here too, listening.

"Oh, don't worry about that – it's just a bit of banter."

Talla eyes him. "Thanks for explaining that to us, random guy."

"I'm Bryan." A smile spreads across his face and he offers his hand to Talla forcefully, causing himself to stumble.

Talla just looks at it.

"Oh! Friendly!"

"Bunty's found a friend she can be sour-faced with!" laughs Chelsea. "Tony said she doesn't have a sense of humour," she repeats to no-one in particular.

"I'll tell you a joke then," Talla almost shouts. "A straight middle-class white guy walks into a bar."

Bryan and Chelsea look at her expectantly.

19

"Nothing happens!"

"I don't get it?" Chelsea looks disappointed.

"Fuck off!" Bryan's not impressed either. "C'mon Chels. You're right about these two." They stagger away together.

Bunty's been silent throughout, her mind shut down. She takes another shot and it helps, just enough to tell Talla she *will* take her up on the invite back to her cabin. Talla puts an arm though hers and waves goodnight to her colleague behind the bar.

"I just fucking give up," Bunty says when they're by themselves again. "I hate all that 'banter' crap. It's basically telling you that you don't have the right to say you're being hurt by abuse. Or even have the right to how you feel about it…"

"I know – it's comedy uber alles." She hands Bunty a drink.

"It's like we're on the HMS Bernard fucking Manning."

Talla splutters beer and gives Bunty another high five. "If you don't laugh along with them – and remember I've seen this from both sides – you're like the killjoy, the over-strict mother."

"That's it!" Bunty sits up, animated now. "It's all about being infantile, about being naughty…"

"Yep. This is what you see from behind the bar. Their right to make a mess, to crap themselves. It's like they're still mentally fighting against their mums for the things they had to do to take care of them. Still not wanting to tidy their rooms. As long as someone else cleans the shit up."

"And the cleaners…" Bunty looks up.

"Always women. Usually women of colour."

"And they totally believe they're entitled to our bodies…"

They gaze at one another. "This shit needs blowing out of the water," Talla declares. "Are you in?"

Bunty shakes her head. "You're talking about the entire patriarchy."

"Yep."

"I'm all in, but I just don't think I can…"

Talla leans over and takes her hands. "It's okay…"

"You know the weird thing is, I was worried about how badly it might affect them if I leave. But Tony *has* told me he can operate that desk as well as I can…"

"Fuck 'em. You don't owe them anything."

"Alright. Fuck the fuckers."

Talla's acceptance is making her feel secure enough to dare to feel what she's been steeling herself against. There's the weight of the tears behind her eyelids, and the pressure in her chest, like she doesn't have her usual lung capacity. Could this be a reaction to trauma, to all the racism and misogyny she's absorbed over years, all her life, now reactivated by Tony and his sympathisers? A torrent of adrenaline has been flooding her system since she got on the ship.

"I don't think I can deal, here. I feel like… my mind's grey, like something's got on top of me, and it's crushing me. I know I need to fight them, but the fight's hurting me. Everything I do seems to give them more fuel, and they come back stronger."

Talla nods, sadly, and wraps her arms around Bunty. "I get it if you need to go."

Chapter 7 – Prepare for a Second from Now

Bunty stretches, and swings her legs over the side of the bed.

"You're gonna do it, really?" murmurs Talla, looking at her blearily.

"Yep. For my mental health." And now I have the sadness of leaving you, and there's no time to even say it…

Talla sits up. "Then fly. Fly, my pretty!"

"Fuck them up for me, won't you?"

"I'll poison their drinks and spit on their bar snacks!"

"Promise?"

Talla nods solemnly, and pulls her in for a final hug.

Bunty walks dimly-lit corridors and unlocks the cabin door as stealthily as she can, her phone on flashlight. There's a muffled sound coming from the top bunk and it takes her a moment to realise what it is: Chelsea's crying in her sleep. Bunty's heart responds with a twinge of pity, but can't alter her plan. She gathers the few items that weren't already in her case and zips them in, sacrificing a t-shirt as a decoy, and in a moment she's out the door, catching it as it closes so it barely makes a click.

Now she needs to be invisible. She could avoid detection by taking one of the passenger lifts, as long as she doesn't meet Dave Hedges or some other jobsworth on the way. She calls the lift and dives in. It's empty, as she'd expect on this deck, though as it ascends it picks up guests on their way to breakfast. They're too busy talking about what they're planning to eat to take any notice of her.

"There'd better be enough smoked salmon to go round, not like yesterday. It was a disgrace!"

The husband nods. "Considering we've paid an arm and a leg for this holiday."

Bunty wishes she could relax and have breakfast rather than being in sweaty scary escape mode. But this is her chance. She exits at level 12, walks towards the disembarkation point, then dives into the toilets. She pisses anxiously, then leans against the cubicle partition until her phone says it's 8.00 am. And then she waits a bit longer, feeling for the ship's final lurch as it meets the port. Right – now.

She steps out of the bathroom and turns towards the exit. Queues of passengers have assembled for their excursions, moving into teams under the leadership of tour guides, and half a dozen staff are lined up to check out for their shore leave via the woman with the clipboard. They're all clutching paperwork. She has hers too, but she also has a suitcase…

The coast is clear, the exit wide before her. Picking up a brisk pace just short of running she moves past them all. The clipboard lady looks up, and almost jumps, recognising her. "Excuse me! You must show your pass!" she calls.

"See ya!" Bunty yells, flashing her pass in the woman's direction. "Those souvenirs aren't going to buy themselves you know!"

"But, you…" The woman flaps around a bit, but can't leave her post.

"Laters!" She throws the word over her shoulder and it seems to appease the lady, who sighs and turns back to the queueing staff. Bunty maintains her pace, not wanting to meet another gatekeeper. She steps into the white light of the port building and doesn't turn back. Her eyes are focused on doors marked 'exit'.

That's when someone grabs her shoulder.

Chapter 8 – So this is Gibraltar

"Excuse me, miss."

"What?" Bunty snaps, anxiety imploding in her stomach.

"You're in a hurry!"

She reels; the ground's no longer moving, but nausea's rising. She's looking at a uniformed man.

Fucking amateur cop. Umm – say something normal.

"Just... seizing the day!" It's her best impersonation of cheery but she suspects it comes over more like demented.

"You dropped these." He holds out her shore leave papers.

"Uh, thanks."

He retreats, and she turns back towards the automatic doors under the exit signs, blaspheming under her breath. Stepping outside, she's immobilised once more.

What the Bejesus is *that*?

There's a great grey jagged thing in the sky – a sudden mountain, rearing from an otherwise horizontal world, looking mean and weird and mighty all at the same time. Green on top, it has grey cliffs hanging down the side, and there's a low-rise town snuggled at its base.

Passengers are surging past, shoulder bags slung diagonally across chests, cameras around necks, selfie sticks aloft. Some sniff the air, others stare, like her, at the geological spectacle up ahead. Bunty catches fragments of lunch plans and gift shopping lists as she gives in to the momentum of the crowd forcing its way around the port's car park. Stumbling forward, she fears she might get carried off with them on their tourist missions. No-one seems to notice she's toting a suitcase, and folk keep tripping on it as they try to claim the seemingly empty space behind her. Despite the collisions, she can't take her eyes off that... thing.

Then the smell hits her. The fresh sea air she'd tasted on the ship seems compromised here, tainted, somehow. She picks up the acrid lurch of crude oil, but there's a lower note too that she can't quite place. Whatever it is, it's not good.

They're coming up to a checkpoint, with barriers across the road. The crowd's surging around both, squeezing through bottlenecks, and she can tell by the relatively unhindered communal movement that no-one's checking anyone here.

Then she's out of the port. I've made it!

But what have I made? I have no fucking clue, and no plan...

Her chest feels tight. She veers towards a brick wall but can't lean on it – the crowd's too strong, and no-one notices she's having an asthma attack. There's a bench coming up ahead; she lunges towards it, triggering the seething impatience of ferocious daytrippers who force their way past, regardless. Once seated she tries deep breathing but can't seem to do it right. She hauls the case up next to her and fishes around for an inhaler.

The crowd river's flowing so thickly around the bench that there's no room even for her knees. She pulls them up and sits with them tight to her chest, though this doesn't help her breathing or subdue the consternation of the entitled travellers as they power past. She puts the blue inhaler in her mouth, presses the canister down, sucks in the little cloud of medicine it releases, and in a minute or two she can breathe again. Thank fuck.

Bunty squints in the bright sunlight, scanning for information about this place, as her phone starts to buzz. Network messages – "Welcome to Spain". With the Rock looming straight ahead and land to both sides, she guesses she's facing east, so that must be Spain across the bay. She knows this much about Gibraltar from school geography lessons – it's that tiny shard of land, a thorn jutting from Iberia's belly, pointing straight at Africa. Maybe she should explore a little before she turns right round to go home again…

More buzzing, as texts pour in from her mum, Sofia and other friends back home. There wasn't much signal out at sea, yet she'd somehow assumed everyone had immediately forgotten her and just got on with their own busy stuff. She starts to think about explaining this new course of events to her folks, but can't work out how to in a way that won't worry them half to death. The joyless urgency of the procession continues to push around her, and a white-haired old woman trips over, landing first on her knees and then her hands. Her probably-husband bends to pull her up, and two others stop to ask if she's alright. The rest of the freed inmates swirl onwards, inclining their heads to gawk at the accident, and the couple make their way gingerly to the bench. Bunty puts her things away and slides her case down onto the paving slabs below.

She thinks how uncomfortable the injured woman must feel with so little space to buffer her grazed limbs. It turns out that she's well-equipped, at least, with wipes and plasters at the ready.

"We have to be back on the ship by 4 pm," the woman tells her.

"Are you going up the Rock?" Bunty gestures at the crazy mountain that's lurching ostentatiously above the Mediterranean, as if there was some other rival rock in the vicinity.

The woman doesn't answer, but beckons a security guard who's resting on a lamppost by the booth. "Excuse me love, which way is Williamson's?"

The guard turns towards them and responds in sentences flecked with Spanish, while waving his arms widely to indicate where she should turn off the road.

Williamson's? Is this a displaced piece of Britain, Bunty wonders, a fragment of the mainland that got seriously lost? Is it full of the same high street shops that typify every English town she's ever visited? Her mind is equally boggled by the limitations of the traveller's ambition. After three and a half days of confinement, and with a mere four hours to spend on land, does she really only want to go to a supermarket – and a fucking Williamson's at that? It's everything she'd heard and feared about the British abroad – they just want the sun, The Sun, English breakfasts and Tetley tea.

Her own concerns, though, are more immediate. She checks her breathing again: it's clear. She gets up from the bench and merges back into the people-river. The

24

flow is denser now and it's even harder to get anywhere; she's going to have to get out of the way until it thins out. To her left she sees business units and two-storey blocks of flats, and behind them a low wall of roughly-chopped concrete blocks protecting the land from this corner of the bay. She veers into a side road and walks freely towards the water's edge; the sudden solitude feels pristine.

The concrete blocks look as though they've been dropped from some great ice cube tray in the sky. Beyond them, in the bay, teenage boys are racing speedboats, and further out industrial ships float, anchored. And along the wall Bunty sees a woman, also gazing out to sea. She's wearing a blue flowery dress and a floppy hat with dried flowers on the rim, pulled down to shield her from the sun's glare. So carefree! Is this what the locals are like?

When the woman – who is walking slowly in her direction – gets close enough, Bunty ventures a smile. At that moment an all-encompassing roar blasts from the eastern sky, and both turn to see a metal tube launch upwards, the words 'Royal Airlines' painted along its side.

"Wow, the airport's close!" Bunty exclaims as the noise subsides.

"Everything's close in Gib," says the woman in a Liverpool accent. "You'll get used to it."

"Do you live here?"

"I used to; I'm here to see a friend, and for a trip to Madrid with me fella."

She tells Bunty of her trajectory, from Liverpool, to here, to the capital. "I don't know why I couldn't stay. I had a great job here, an easy life. I'm working as a nurse in London now and it's wearin' me down, but I don't think I could stay here."

Why would it be so hard to stay? wonders Bunty. But that's not my concern; I'm only here to go home – and I'd better get on with it. "Are there any cafés round here?"

"Nothing here, but town centre's not far, I'll point you in the right direction if you like."

"Awesome, thank you."

When they reach the corner the woman holds out her hand. "I'm Stephanie, by the way. Maybe see you round?"

Bunty bids her goodbye and steps back into the crowd-stream. It's diminished to a trickle now, and she quickly loses the cruisers to shops and taxi drivers offering trips to the Rock's summit. She trundles along the pavement, sighing in relief, then jumps when she hears a scream.

The sound's coming from the doorway of a kebab shop. She turns to see something furry struggling under the flapping wings of a massive seagull. The gull's pecking at the little creature in vicious jabs, while it – whatever it is – claws back at the body of the bird, whose shrieks are no match for tiny thing's piercing wail. When the seagull ascends in order to dive-bomb its prey, she sees a patchy, grubby and very upset-looking monkey left behind on the ground. The bird makes one last lunge, then exits the scene vertically. The monkey scans the street with fearful eyes, runs to a low wall, and disappears over it.

Bunty steadies herself and keeps on walking towards whatever the fuck this place is.

Chapter 9 – It's an Imperial Outrage

Bunty finds the place Stephanie told her about – a square, called Casemates, lined with pubs and cafés – and walks around its periphery looking for somewhere that might serve decent coffee. Café Genoese looks old, and is more appealing than the adjacent Burger King, or Al Dente's across the way. She takes the last remaining table by the ice cream fridge and sits looking out onto the square, hoping that the shade and the fridge's chilled air will bestow something like the sweetness of a sea breeze onto her already-too-warm skin.

Espresso is the cheapest drink on the menu. Bunty orders one with ice, leans her elbows on the table and rubs her temples to ease the stress-buzz in her head. She can just about hear the radio behind the bar playing upbeat Spanish pop, as sugary as the café's wares. A polite man brings her drink. She pours the thick foamy coffee from the cup onto barrel-shaped ice in the accompanying glass and swishes it around. The bitter liquid cools her throat and settles her nerves a little.

She tunes into the voices around her. On the ship she was surrounded by a largely British crowd; lots of south-eastern accents, outspoken and grumbling, and some more softly-spoken older couples, middle class and relaxed – the sounds of relatively stress-free lives. Now the cruisers have merged and dispersed amongst the local population she's hearing other tones, and a lot of Spanish being spoken. Of course there are Spanish people here, she thinks, in a land that was once theirs. But their language is interspersed with English words in a seemingly haphazard way. Maybe her curious listening looks like friendliness, cos the next phrase she hears is "Excuse me, is this seat free?"

A scruffy-looking woman startles her from her eavesdropping. She's in her seventies perhaps, smiling and gesturing at an empty chair. Bunty nods and the woman sits down, positioning a wheeled shopping bag beside her. "On holiday?" she asks, pointing to Bunty's case.

"No, I just quit my job."

Admitting it makes her feel weird and deflated, without the victorious glee she thought she might feel.

"Oh, are you a programmer or some such, at one of these gambling firms?"

"I'm a sound engineer. I was on a cruise ship – until this morning."

"You jumped ship?!" The woman looks impressed.

"I guess I did." She looks up at the deep blue sky, still processing the turn of events.

"How exciting! What are you going to do now?" She shuffles forward in her chair and leans on the table, ready for a story.

Bunty smiles, and takes a sip of her drink. "I don't know; it's been less than an hour since I left. I'm still getting my bearings." She looks around the square. "What about you – do you live here?"

"I suppose you could say that," the woman tells her, scratching her nose, "inasmuch as I don't live anywhere else."

Bunty bypasses the cryptic answer. "Well, what are you up to here?"

"I'm doing some research, I suppose you could say. The thing is I don't have anywhere in the world that I exactly need to be..."

"So why Gibraltar? This research...?"

"It's family history. My mum was Gibraltarian, evacuated to London in the Second World War, and she never really came back. She had me in London and I grew up hearing tales about this place. So I'm retracing her steps, you might say, but the lie of the land has changed, everything's changed..."

"Have you found much out?"

"Well, I've seen the house where my mum grew up, and I've managed to find a cousin, but he's not much help, he's old and doddery now. So I'm picking up a bit of the general colour and trying to picture what it must have been like back in her time."

"How's it working out for you, being here?"

"I'd say it's quite a healing journey, overall. It's not always easy – I'm essentially homeless, staying in a hostel cos it's the cheapest place in town."

"That sounds tough."

"It is a little, but I'm friendly with the manager now, and he makes sure I'm comfy."

"I think I might be homeless soon as well; I can't pay the rent on my room in Leeds..." Bunty frowns. "And I gotta find somewhere to stay here too. It's good to know there are hostels."

"Actually, this great nation has a sum total of one. It's not far from here, you just go along the side of the square by the icy sea." She points across the plaza towards a shopping centre.

"But we're inland? I just walked from the port!"

"The ICC. Sorry. International Commerce Centre. A very grand name for that seventies monstrosity."

Bunty sees it then, an unimposing white and grey concrete building with a multi-storey car park on top.

"Ah, okay! But..." She tries to keep up. "You said this is a village and a great nation. Is it a British colony?"

"More or less. A British Overseas Territory."

"It's part of the UK, right?"

"Yep, but with its own government."

"My passport's on the ship," Bunty blurts. "They took it and kept it..."

The old lady's wrinkles deepen in the centre of her forehead. "You can't get anywhere without that, dear. You're stuck. There's not an awful lot of room for manoeuvre."

"I'd be able to go into Spain though, wouldn't I? Gibraltar's in the EU, isn't it?"

"It is, indirectly through the UK, but no you can't, for various historical reasons. There's a hard border, and you need your passport to get through it."

Bunty grimaces, her system flooding with a new feeling of claustrophobia. "But there's an Embassy here, right?"

"Not as such, but there is an office that deals with consular matters..."

"Where is it? Is it far?"

The older woman sketches a map on a napkin. They swap numbers, and Bunty learns that her name is Nancy. After paying for her coffee, Bunty sets off up a steep road to the hostel.

She drags her suitcase, sweating in the morning heat, and thinks about this piece of land. Small states always interested her; odd places where everything's played out in miniature – and this one's especially weird. But the smallness, with its sense of confinement, is getting her in the throat like she's being strangled. She stops and takes a few breaths, and is relieved to see the sign for the hostel across the road.

Up close, the exterior is deserted and the front door's locked. She knocks a couple of times, and eventually a young man in a t-shirt and combat trousers appears. He greets her with a supercilious "Hello, yes?" as though she's interrupted something important and shouldn't really be there.

"Can I book a bed for tonight?"

"Come back after two," he says. "We have plenty of space, so don't worry. You can leave your bag here if you like."

Bunty looks down at her cumbersome suitcase, and with an independent traveller's instinct for survival calculates that without it she'd be royally screwed. She shakes her head and turns away.

She walks back towards the square with her stomach growling, and remembers Talla's advice to eat sometimes. On the way up she'd passed a café that looked like it might be vegetarian, so she retraces her steps and bundles her body and case through the establishment's stiff door. The place has faux seventies décor and a kitchen along one side. A short, chubby fella appears behind the counter. She can't quite hear what he's saying over the kitchen noise, but somehow they establish her food order.

It seems that lunchtime stresses him out. He's bellowing at everyone in the kitchen; a customer mentions that she doesn't like parsley, and he's outraged. "I'm from the Middle East! Parsley is standard!" He keeps up his half-polite, half-aggravating banter with his customers, and when her food arrives with dirty cutlery she senses there's no point in mentioning it.

Mum would hate this!

As she eats he keeps on at customers and staff alike, and makes it known that he doesn't want anyone lingering at the tables after they've finished their meals. She takes the hint, and within minutes is back out on the pavement. She finds a bench and rests with her eyes shut, soaking in the heat of the sun and the strange linguistic patterns that flow around her until it's time to try the hostel again.

This time the door's open, and the cat-like young man is reclining languorously behind his shabby reception desk. She repeats her request.

"A bed? Sure. ID, please."

She blanches, and pulls out a bank card.

The chap isn't impressed. "An ID card, like national ID? Where are you from?"

Bunty tells him.

"Then your passport please."

"Can I stay here without one?"

"Not really, no. It's a legal requirement."

Tears prick her eyes. "I don't have anywhere else to stay..."

"I'm sorry, I can't help you."

This is something she could not have anticipated. In the UK you can check into hotels and hostels without ID. It hits in the gut that she is suddenly paperless, without rights, unable to leave, unable to stay. The receptionist is fixing her with a testy look; she picks up her case and turns to go.

Nancy's nudging her way through the door, an array of plastic bags dangling from her wrists. She addresses the desk boy loudly. "I see you've met my daughter!"

He looks startled.

"She's staying with me tonight," she adds haughtily. "Please add it to my bill." She grabs Bunty by the arm and pulls her along the corridor, turning only to wink. Bunty follows her to into a room with a tiled floor and two sets of bunk beds inside.

"I think I bamboozled him," Nancy says, now they can't be overheard. "He's scared of me because I won't take his condescending manner and I get on really well with his boss. I heard your conversation through the door – we can't have you out on the street."

"Mate!" Bunty puts her case down and hugs her new friend in delight.

Then, while Nancy goes to the bathroom, Bunty gets into her new bunk, stretches out, breathes, and assesses the situation. It's not looking good. Even with papers it would cost £15 a night to stay here, and she just doesn't have that kind of money. She barely has enough for a flight home, let alone replacing her stupid-ass passport. Everything needs to be sorted, like, yesterday.

She looks at her phone. It's 2.15. She shouts her plans to Nancy through the toilet door.

"Good luck," Nancy shouts back. "Keep me informed."

Chapter 10 – Summer Times

Bunty sets out, napkin-map in hand. She strides from Casemates onto Main Street, a pedestrianised channel edged by three- and four- storey buildings lined with familiar chain stores, but with a lot more tacky tourist outlets, jewellers' shops and cheap offies than the high streets back home. Old people clack their sticks on the cobbles and younger locals saunter around in the mottled sunlight. Everyone seems to observe the same protocol as they move down the street: wander, stop, smoke, chat. She swerves around them all, dodging clouds of tobacco fumes and sticky mists of chemical droplets that billow from perfume stores.

Main Street streaks on for a mile until it hits a roundabout bisected by an ancient wall bringing the whole thing to an abrupt conclusion. She turns a corner that takes her down the lower banks of the Rock, and finds the right door: number three.

But it's closed. Bunty pushes it and rattles the handle, but the thing won't budge. She scrutinises the gold-plated sign on the adjacent wall: "Governor's Office. Opening hours: Monday to Friday, 8.30 am – 3 pm."

Her phone says it's 2.39. And this is definitely Friday – she isn't going mental. She leans on the wall, shielding her eyes with her hand, and waits for someone to come back. This could be her chance to appreciate the caress of warm air on her bare arms, but the nerve endings in her gut are starting to prickle; what if no-one shows up? At 3.01 she kicks the door in frustration; she's not getting home this weekend.

The mid-afternoon sun drops its rays deep into the narrow streets, and she would love it so much if she had the smallest clue as to what she's doing here. But she really fucking doesn't. She trudges back along Main Street, eyes on her shoes. Then she recalls her promise to Nancy, and stops to taps out a quick text. A few seconds later a response pings back.

Oh no! Too bad Monday is bank hol!

Fuck!!! That's four days before she can even start to sort this mess out...

She dials a UK number, and Sofia picks up.

"Bunty, are you okay? What's wrong? Are you on the ship?"

She catches her friend up on the events of the last few days in phrases punctuated by sobs.

"What a bunch of tossers!" Sofia's aghast. "I'm glad you got away though! What are you gonna do?"

"I don't know... Sof, I should have stayed where I was. Talla could have helped me... But... I couldn't... And now... I... Nothing's working. I'm not working. That cruise ship was so messed up, and now I'm in this... place... I don't know anyone here. I mean I've met Nancy, but I can't lean on her, she has enough problems already."

"Oh, Buns!"

"I feel so stupid," she sniffs. "Why didn't I fight to get my passport back? I can't afford to make mistakes like this. Sof, am I too impulsive?"

"Maybe a bit, but you gotta have the impetus to get out of a situation like that..."

"What a waste of time though. I'll be worse off than before and I'm going to have to explain it all to my advisor, and they probably won't believe me, and they'll sanction me for leaving anyway. And I'm stuck here..."

"Yeah, and that ship job seemed like the perfect solution, didn't it? Getting paid to travel."

Bunty's sobs get louder.

"Shh, don't worry, you'll be home soon!"

"What home do I even have though? I can't afford to keep my room on."

"There's your mum and dad's place..."

"So I tried to move forwards and ended up moving backwards... I shouldn't have let my passport go! I can't even afford to buy a new one, and I bet they probably won't even pay me anyway."

"They sound well shoddy."

Bunty looks in the direction of the port. The ship's scheduled for a four o'clock departure. She could still go back.

"Sof, hang on. The ship is still here. D'you think I should...?"

"I dunno, love. You hated it on there."

Bunty turns and tries to walk in the direction of the port, but her feet won't play.

"Can you go back and grab your passport and get off it again?"

"No... I don't think so." She feels a heavy groan in her guts. "They weren't releasing it when I asked them."

"Where's the next stop after today?"

"Sicily, in three more days."

"Could you deal with that? And then travel back from there?"

"No," Bunty admits. "I can't."

Sofia sighs, and Bunty feels the love and concern flowing down from the satellite that's bringing the signal.

"Okay. Listen. It might all seem like a big mistake now, but something could happen that changes all that. You might be there for a reason."

"I dunno. I don't..."

The call dies. Bunty stares at the screen. £0.00. That credit was meant to last the whole trip.

She keeps walking, and lets the tears go free.

Chapter 11 – The Magical Power of Bookshops

She swerves into a tiny park and takes custody of a secluded bench. No-one else is here, so she gives in to exhaustion, gazing up at branches sparkling in mottled sunlight. Beyond is a sky bluer than she's ever seen. It's suffused with a yellow-gold that she can't quite see but it's definitely there, somewhere in the mix. Small birds hop on the ground around her, looking for sandwich crumbs, but she has nothing for them and that makes her cry even more. A bloke in a suit comes and sits on the next bench along, and Bunty decides to get out of his way.

She trudges back onto Main Street, and spies a diminutive bookshop she didn't notice on her way up to the Governor's Office. Her curiosity takes over – what kinds of zines do they have here? The door creaks open and she stares around the place. All the up-front shelves seem to be full of books about military history. She searches for something less violent but can only find romances, detoxes, and how to do your make up like a reality TV star.

Fuck's sake. Mainstream much?

A face emerges from the other side of a stack of books and grins at her.

"Did I say that out loud? Shit, I'm tired!"

He laughs, and she notices he's cradling a copy of Clothes Clothes Clothes... by Viv Albertine.

"I've got that. It's amazing!"

He lifts it up and examines the back of the jacket. "I think I might have to get it. I can't believe they have it here!"

She appraises him. His straight black hair is falling into his eyes and he's wearing a Sleaford Mods t-shirt. There is life on this planet after all!

"I like your shirt."

"Oh!" He looks down. "I made it myself; no-one seems to have to heard of them in Gib. Are – are you based here?"

She summarises her situation, and his expression changes. "That's rough!"

"A bit."

He hesitates, and then asks "I don't suppose you have time for a drink? There's a pub just opposite here..."

"Time is what I have plenty of right now," she blurts. After the week she's had, some booze might not go amiss. Should she really hang out with this dude though? Who is he even? But it's not like she has anywhere else to be...

They walk across the cobbled street and into a bar called Case Dismissed. She orders whisky and coke, and he gets a coffee. Uh, he didn't mean that sort of drink! She gazes around the place. They're at a table next to some oak shelving laden with antiquated law books and a collection of fancy old hammers. Her fingers creep in their direction, but she resists the urge to drum with them. Don't want no police cops coming and finding me without papers and stuff. So she focuses on this guy; he's looking at her expectantly.

"What are you going to do now? Do you have any plans?" he asks, stirring demerara sugar into his coffee.

"I have pretty much exactly no plans, so I'm going to have to work a few things out until next week when I can get into that there Governor's Office." She swishes the ice around in her glass. "What about you though – what are you doing here?"

"Umm, well, I'm a programmer..."

He looks like he's checking for approval, or its opposite, but she's just pleased he's accepted her deflection. She doesn't want to start crying again like she did at Sofia earlier.

"What's wrong with that?"

He winces slightly. "Some people find it... a bit geeky?"

She smiles. "Some of my best friends are geeks! You're not from Gibraltar though?"

"No, I'm from Sheffield. What about you? Somewhere up north too, I think, by your accent?"

Before they can zoom in on each other's Yorkshire neighbourhoods, they're interrupted. Someone's turned the TV above the bar up way too loud. It's blasting out BBC News 24, and there's an item about the Queen. It seems she's been offended by some foreign dignitary's manners, or lack thereof.

"I can't believe they still have a monarchy," he mutters.

"Me either!" Bunty scrunches her beermat at the very idea.

"They're really into it round here."

"Really?" Bunty slams down her drink in shock.

"Yeah," he laughs. "It's all the portraits of the Queen, GR pillar boxes. It's like the 1950s!"

"I saw stuff like that but thought it was just tourist overkill."

"No, they really like it!"

"Shit! What's it like living here?"

"Gibraltar's an incredibly weird place that has become incredibly normal to me, cos I've been here for, like, two years. I might have acclimatised to things I shouldn't have." He laughs ruefully, though Bunty doesn't understand why.

"Do you miss the UK?"

"Yeah. But not the weather. I miss the people, and gigs and stuff."

"You know what I saw today in the street? A monkey! Fighting a seagull!"

He grins in recognition. "Those apes are badass! What were they were fighting over?"

"I've no idea! Territory?"

"Ha! Yeah, maybe the seagull was Spanish."

It's Bunty's turn to laugh, and his turn to come up with a monkey story.

"We had a problem with the barbary macaques here for a while, they were getting a bit out of hand. They were nicking jewellery out of people's apartments!"

"I didn't know monkeys liked their bling."

"Yeah! And junk food, they're addicted to that."

Bunty sniggers at the idea of apes in gold chains walking down Main Street eating bags of crisps.

"Anyway, the Gibraltar government decided to do something about it. They rounded up the naughtiest troupe, about twenty of them, and shipped them off to Scotland!"

"Scotland? No freaking way! Why?"

"Yes way! It was like a monkey ASBO. And I have no idea..." He laughs, but it turns into a yawn. "Sorry."

"No, you're tired. Should we call it a day?"

He looks disappointed. "Oh, okay. I am a bit... I can walk you to the hostel if you like?"

"If it's not out of your way?" Bunty's wiped out too, but wouldn't mind more of this guy's company.

They set out along Main Street, strolling in the warm evening air. Again she hears people speaking two languages at once.

"Everyone here seems to be speaking Spanish and English together – are they workers from across the border?"

"Those are the Gibraltarians! It's their language, Llanito."

"Oh, cool!"

"It's a bit of a mix, Spanish, English, some Italian and some home-grown words..."

"Do Gibraltarians see themselves as Spanish or British?"

He guffaws. "Not Spanish, hell no! Gibraltarian first, and then British. I mean, how do you see yourself?"

"Well, British, but also Irish, and maybe Jamaican. What about you?"

"British, cos I was born there, but my folks came over from India."

"It's funny how many people would say we're not British."

"I know right." He furrows his brow and swings his bag in front of him. "Daily Mail readers!"

"Do you remember those posters that Theresa May put on the sides of buses in London the other year?"

"Yeah! 'Go home.' I was like, what, are they gonna send me back to Sheffield? She would have done me a favour cos the train fares are extortionate."

"I don't suppose if I rang that number from here they'll send me home..." Bunty gazes wistfully at the clear evening sky.

"It would be alright if they did something useful like that..." He grins at her. "But you should stay! Have a holiday."

She looks at his excited face and can't tell him she's shit broke.

"Look, in case you're bored and want to meet up again..." He scrabbles in his bag, pulls out a pencil and a bit of paper, scrawls something on it and hands it to her.

Bunty sprints past the snooty receptionist and bursts into the dorm. Nancy's propped up in her bunk, a large book on her knees.

"Oh, hello you! Where have you been?"

"Umm, wandering about!"

"Drowning sorrows?"

34

"Yeah, a bit." She unfolds the piece of paper in her hand and reads:

AS IF. 00350 500 7158

Underneath is a drawing of a cat holding a placard bearing the words "FIGHT THE POWER."

Chapter 12 – Gizza Job

The lively acoustics of the hostel's plumbing wake Bunty around seven, and her bunk bed answers with a creak as she turns over to go back to sleep. Later the sun's rays, unimpeded by thin curtains, get right up in her face. She goes to the window to try to sort it out and gasps as the Rock fills her vision, jutting ominously into the azure sky.

She showers, dresses quickly, and rushes downstairs with damp hair frizzing freestyle; she just needs Nancy to still be here. Turning a corner, she finds her in the courtyard, lounging in a plastic chair, eating breakfast with fellow residents.

"Bunty! Join us!"

She doesn't need to be asked twice. Yesterday she only had lunch, and before her is a pile of toast with little packets of butter and Nutella and jam. She grabs a plate and loads it up.

A clean-cut white guy pours her some tea. He's observing her keenly, though Bunty can't work out why. She accepts the drink with a gruff "ta," and turns to her friend.

"Nancy, that *Rock* – is it like a volcano or something?"

"Aha! No, my dear, it came from the sea! It's a big old slab of prehistoric life..." She sips her coffee. "What are you doing today? I could walk up there with you."

"That sounds cool, but I've got to find a job," Bunty tells her between bites of toast. "I'm almost fully broke. I'm thinking in a restaurant or something – I don't suppose you have any leads?"

"You could try The Jolly Sailor. I'm friends with the owner there, Jasandra. If you go, tell her I sent you."

Bunty wraps the rest of her toast in a paper napkin, downs her tea in one and gets up to wash her plate. The tea-pouring fella stands up too, and another of the guests, an older, bearded man who had been sitting nearby. She can feel them circling behind her while she's at the sink, and turns to see what they're up to.

"Would you be interested in taking Jesus as your Lord and Saviour?" the clean-cut guy asks, with a hopeful grin like he's offering her a free sample of something in a shop.

Bunty looks him straight in the eyes. "No, actually. Not right now, and not later either."

She gets enough of this in Leeds. Nice people until you refuse to modify your sexuality for them. She's almost out of the room when his friend pipes up:

"Do you have any brothers or...?"

Nancy finds her in the corridor. "Are you sure you don't want me to try and wangle you another night here, Bunty?"

"You've been so good to me, but I'll sort something out." Now she knows it's infested with evangelicals she can't get away fast enough.

She wanders over to The Jolly Sailor. It's on a street called Irish Town, not far from Casemates square. Bunty checks the business hours on the door; it opens in half an hour, at ten. She sits on the front step and munches the rest of her toast as people along the street pull up shutters and set out signs on the sun-mottled cobbles. The street's just about wide enough for a vehicle, but the only wheeled things moving along it are hand-pulled carts full of fruit and veg and trolleys loaded with building materials. It's comforting, somehow, to watch all this analogue activity.

The door behind her opens from within and a woman lurches over her. Bunty jumps up.

"What's all this then?" the woman asks, curling her lip.

"I'm looking for Jasandra?"

"That's me. Can I help you?"

Her voice is quick and sharp. She has long black glossy hair, brown eyes and butterscotch skin. In her calf-length turquoise and green dress, Bunty thinks she has an almost mystical quality, but there's a look in her eye that suggests that you wouldn't want to cross her.

"I met your friend Nancy, and she said you might have work for me. I'm just looking for something temporary?"

"You are in luck," Jasandra replies as she starts to pull open a series of wooden shutters that line the front of the pub. "We're looking for someone at the moment. If you bring your CV in, we can see."

"I'm actually looking for something straight away, and for not very long at all..." she blurts.

As she explains her circumstances, Jasandra lifts chairs from the pub out to the street. Bunty takes a stack of them too, eliciting a grunt of thanks.

"Can you wash plates?"

"Oh yeah! I used to do that all the time in my mum's café."

They place a table in position and go inside to fetch another.

"Then you've passed the test; we're short of a dishwasher in the kitchen. Can you start tonight, six o'clock?"

"Sure!"

Jasandra winks at her. "Don't be late, chica!"

Now she can afford to top up her phone credit. She sorts it, and taps out an SMS: *Sof I got a job already! Gonna be washing dishes again! How are you and Marie?*

Her phone buzzes. *We're great hon. Sitting here in the rain waiting for you to come back. Good for you with the work. You going to be there long? And you got a place to stay?*

Nah, a few days max. Not sure about accom. Hotels etc want to see a passport...

Remember in France, we stayed in that Airbnb and they didn't ask for passports? Any of them there?

Sof, you're a genius!

She finds a bench and gets the Airbnb app up. In a few minutes she's found a listing for a room – a bit scuzzy looking, and not cheap either, but she can't fuss cos she needs it for tonight. She taps the reserve button, inputs her card details and straight away gets a message back about it.

How is it that I just sorted a job and a place to stay? And it's not even freaking lunchtime! I'm killing this Gibraltar thing.

She turns her face up to the clear sky, and her gaze extends to the summit of the Rock. What's *up* with that crazy mofo?

Chapter 13 – T'Top o't'Rock

Bunty dials a long number; Nancy picks up.

"I'm sorted on the job front so I've got time to go up that Rock thing, if you're still into it?"

"Jasandra fixed you up then? Good lass!" Nancy sounds cheery, but tired. "Actually, my knees are shot today – let's go on the cable car!"

"I've never been in one before. Is it scary?"

"Relatively safe, I'd say."

Bunty waits for Nancy in Sanguinetti's, a café that's been going, if the signs are to be believed, for over a hundred years, so they must know how to make a good cup of tea by now. A thin, blondish girl with a big smile and large steel clips in her hair greets her cheerfully in a heavy Spanish accent. Her face becomes gravely thoughtful as she pours a giant pot of tea, and Bunty returns her change as a tip. It's cooler inside the café, but the fake leather seats are sticky when they meet her legs. She admires the old green tiles on the floor, and the Tintin figurine in the window. He stands, hands in pockets, looking pleased at the vista he beholds; maybe life is easy for a young man round here.

Nancy limps in and drops onto the seat beside her.

"You look knackered! Are you sure you wanna go?" Bunty asks.

"The walk will do me good. It's not that far."

When they reach the cable car station there's a line of tourists wrapped around the building like a jittery snake, its tail trailing along the edge of the car park. Bunty admires the adjacent art deco fire station while they wait, and Nancy tries to screen out the noise of screaming kids.

"My nerves!" she declares. "Summer holidays are a bit of a trial for me. I did my time, raised three kids. I could do without being deafened by everyone else's."

"Hmm," says Bunty. "You could get some ear defenders."

"I need them, around here! Are you planning on spawning young at some point?"

"You know, I'm really not," Bunty tells her decisively. "I've never felt an urge to."

"It's early days though, for you."

"Yeah, but I think I'm sure," Bunty reaffirms, as she narrowly avoids tripping over a five-year-old boy who's attempting to pick up spilt ice cream off floor, while his mother yells at him to leave it alone.

They're right in front of the ticket booth, and Bunty catches a glimpse of the price. "Oh no, Nancy, it costs a fortune!"

"Let this be my treat. You wouldn't let me help you out earlier. And I can afford it, contrary to appearances."

Bunty sees she's not about to relent. "I won't forget this."

"Get away with you," Nancy laughs, and buys their tickets.

They file round the corner to wait for an empty car. When one comes clanging in, they enter the cabin along with a dozen others. The doors close, and it begins its ascent over the car park. Then the container is dragged up the side of the rock-mountain by creaking ropes and pulleys, swinging over apartment blocks and stony slopes scattered with scrubby bushes. In minutes they've been cranked up to the summit and are released into a concrete station; Bunty gasps at the brutalist grimness.

Nancy nudges her, and she glances down to see a tiny brown ape in her path. Bunty squawks, but the monkey doesn't even return her gaze. He scratches himself impassively, unfazed by the influx of humans arriving in sky boxes. When she looks up, they're everywhere, perched on fences like sentries.

"Got any food on you?" Nancy asks.

"Nope..."

"Then you're safe. These buggers will eat anything. They keep the chocolate and ice creams under lock and key in the gift shops up here," Nancy mutters as she guides her up to a viewing platform.

That's when Bunty sees the point of this place. They're facing a long ridge that rises up towards Spain. She can see La Línea, a city on a plain hemmed by beaches and sea, with a backdrop of mountains in the distance. She peers along the coast in both directions; it's glorious.

They stroll around the viewing platform, observing permutations of rock, sea and land in all directions. "Nancy, what is this Rock thing? You said it was something prehistoric... you know about geology, right?"

"I do," Nancy smiles. "Not often I get asked. Well, the massive tectonic plate which became Africa and South America split into two sections. It was a harsh break up, and they drifted a long way apart. The African plate bumped right up against the Eurasian one, and that created the Mediterranean, down here." She points at the sea to the west of them, then turns to face south. "The crash almost shut the Med off from the Atlantic, but when it didn't it made this bottleneck" – she indicates the strip of sea between them and Morocco – "Then, under the water, a thick limestone bed formed out of squashed down prehistoric critters..."

A monkey walks on all fours along the fence next to them and distracts Bunty from her geology lesson. "Hello you! Aww, cute!"

Nancy smiles. "Hello little fella!"

"So, this limestone bed...?"

"That's what we're stood on now, basically. It got caught up between the two plates as they collided, was crushed between them and buckled inwards, with both ends sticking up. We're on one end, and there's the other." She directs Bunty's gaze towards the Moroccan coast, just across the water. "That's Gibel Musa – Musa's mountain. And this was known as Tarik's mountain, Gibel Tarik."

"Gibel-tarik..." Bunty tries it on her tongue. "Gibeltarik... Gibraltar!" She beams in delight at the linguistic turn.

"They were also known as the Pillars of Hercules. Imagine what they look like if you're in a boat down there, sailing towards this narrow gateway. They used to think this was the end of the world..."

"Erm, maybe it is?"

Bunty is staring at a small monkey that's appeared on the platform next to them. It's tearing up a nappy and eating the white fluff from inside it.

"Oh!" Nancy covers her face with her hands.

"Eeuw!!" squeals Bunty, as the monkey turns towards them, its face streaked with dark dirt. She backs away as another tiny ape leaps over to fight for the prize of the nappy.

"That might be our cue to leave," Nancy suggests.

"Uh. Yeah. And I'd better not be late for work."

"Not when you're working for Jasandra."

They make one last survey of the magnificent panorama of rock, land and ocean, and head back to the cable car station.

Chapter 14 – Wash Pig

They walk back to the hostel, Nancy for a nap and Bunty for a shower before work, even though she's outstayed her illegal one-night residency.

"Do you think they'll let me?"

"I'd like to see them stop you! You're sure you don't want to stay tonight?"

Bunty can't put on her friend anymore, fearing the older lady could end up properly homeless if she pushes her luck with the hostel owners. "I've got something sorted, I'll be fine."

They hug goodbye and, feeling fresher, Bunty trundles her case along the cobbles of Irish Town to report for her first shift.

"There you are," says Jasandra, with a tone that suggests Bunty's done something wrong already. "Wait here a minute."

Bunty looks around. The wooden floorboards are warped, but the bar's topped by marble slabs. Two one-armed bandits are tucked in the corner like naughty cowboys, and a large flat screen high up on the wall plays nineties music videos. Waiting staff bustle around in black t-shirts with Jolly Sailor logos on them. The atmosphere is chattering with boredom.

Jasandra's back. "Put your things in here, and I'll show you the kitchen." She gestures to a small room by the side of the bar, and Bunty pushes her case inside.

"Where are you staying?"

"I've got a room on Airbnb."

"Well good luck to you. I've heard tales about them."

Bunty thinks this strange; there are millions of Airbnb listings, and Jasandra can't have heard tales about all of them, but she senses it would not be a good idea to mention that. She follows her new boss into a large room filled with condensation-covered stainless steel.

Jasandra hands her a hair net, and peers at her trainers disapprovingly. "Not the right shoes for the job. Can you wear something harder on top?"

"These are all I have with me," Bunty answers, as she crams her hair into the net.

"Well, this is Graeme, the head chef. Graeme, this is our new girl, Bunty. She's going to be washing pots tonight."

Graeme grunts a greeting without looking up. He's doing something complicated with tomatoes, and wearing a white smock smeared with what she hopes is tomato juice.

"This is Javier, the assistant chef."

A skinny guy in his late twenties greets her with a smile and a "Buenas tardes".

"Now this is where you will be working; Javier will show you everything that you have to do."

The sink is piled with pans. Javier indicates a large industrial dishwasher. "You put the plates and glasses in here." He pulls the door open and steam gushes out.

"Then you put them over here," and points to piles of crates under a long steel worktop. "The rest go in the sink."

She gets to work, running hot water and plunging rubber gloved hands deep into burnt, greasy pans. This way the plates get a few minutes to cool down, she reckons, before she extracts them from the dishwasher.

A female voice comes from behind: "You gotta get these in the dishwasher." She turns and sees a petite girl with buttery blonde hair. "Oh, perdon, you are the new girl?"

"Yes," she answers, uncertain what to do in greeting. Spanish kisses? In the kitchen? She decides against it. "I'm Bunty."

"I am Inmaculada. That's Nerea," she says, pointing to a girl who's pushing through the doors with a loaded tray in her hands. "I have to go – see you later maybe." And with that Inmaculada dashes off to collect the plates that Javier is pointing out to her, whilst singing her name to a tune Bunty doesn't recognise.

She unloads the dishwasher, puts the new load in, and returns to the sink. The floor is slippery with splashed water and she's glad of her grippy trainers, despite Jasandra's safety concerns. She'll be fine as long as she doesn't drop big knives on herself.

Her stomach gurgles at the smell of frying things. She makes a mental note to eat more often; sustenance hasn't exactly been at the top of her agenda.

"Javier, do you think there'll be something we can eat later on?"

"I will get you something, what do you want?"

Bunty requests chips and salad, and he departs with a wink. She gets stuck back into the sink and Javier returns with food for her which he puts up on a shelf, away from the splashing soapy water. She eyes the plate, but she'd better not break off just yet.

When Inmaculada returns, Bunty peels off her gloves and chances a few bites.

"Where are you and Nerea from?" she asks, stuffing a handful of chips into her mouth.

"She is from the north, the Basque country."

"And you, are you from round here?"

"Yes, de La Línea." She bites her fingernail and looks sad.

Bunty can hardly hear her over the churning of the dishwasher and the slamming of oven doors. She leans forward. "Are you okay?"

"No. Yes." She shakes her head. "Okay."

Jasandra appears just in time to see the two of them talking, and Bunty with a plate of food in her hand.

"This is what I am paying you for, to talk and eat my food?"

Her eyes narrow at Bunty, who shoves the meal back up on the shelf and turns to retrieve her rubber gloves.

Inmaculada slips out of the kitchen, and Jasandra goes to speak to Javier. Progress report on her new employee, Bunty guesses, fearing the worst. She resolves to keep her head down.

Later she risks a bathroom break and checks for messages from her Airbnb host. It's bugging her that she hasn't heard back from him to arrange her check in. Nothing still. She sends another message.

Back at the sink, she amuses herself by memorising the Spanish phrases that Graeme is barking, though they're usually limited to the name of a food item followed by 'pronto' or 'ya!'. His pet name for Javier seems to be 'hijo de puta,' which he spits when his assistant doesn't fulfil his orders quickly or accurately enough. She also hears Graeme calling him a 'coño', and asks Javier what that means.

"It means... woman's parts," he answers awkwardly, lowering his eyes.

Bunty's jaw drops; back home that would be a grave insult.

"Don't worry, he says it in a good way. I explain later!" And Javier dashes off with a tray of chipped potatoes, ferrying them towards a steaming vat of oil by the opposite wall. She hears the chips splash and sizzle as he tips them in, and a few minutes later the room is pervaded by waves of greasy heat.

Around ten the flow of plates starts to slow, and by half past she's washing the last of the pans. Then she and Javier go around cleaning surfaces, and he shows her where the rubbish bags go. There doesn't seem to be any recycling going on; she decides to ask about that another time and not when they're trying to escape the kitchen.

Bunty brushes the floor and Javier follows her around with a mop. It's half past eleven when they finish up. They find the others in the bar dividing up the tips for the night; Jasandra puts a beer in front of her, and tells her she'll get paid at the end of the week, in cash. Nerea, with one arm around Inmaculada, passes Bunty her share of the gratuities. It's a tenner; better than nowt, she thinks, tucking it away in her jeans pocket. She checks for messages from her host for tonight; still nothing. Maybe this is what Jasandra was talking about. Her stomach lurches.

Nerea guides Inmaculada out of the bar, shouting "Adiós" on her behalf. Bunty watches their departure and wonders what's happening with Inmaculada. Jasandra, presumably reading her thoughts, sits down opposite and leans towards her.

"Be careful of that Inmaculada."

"What?"

"She is very delicate. Her mother has cancer, and all her mother's sisters had it too. They died."

Okay, that kind of careful. "Oh Jeez, that's fucking shit luck." Bunty's too tired and distressed by this news to remember not to swear.

Jasandra looks at her directly, and raises an eyebrow. "Not luck, chica. It's the refinery. You know it? Too many people dying round here and it never stops." She raises a drink to her lips and puts the glass down with a sigh.

"Why is no-one doing anything about it, if it's killing loads of people?"

The landlady turns to wave to Javier and Graeme as they shout goodbye from the door. "That's something for the politicians to understand." She pushes her chair back and steps around the bar, returning with Bunty's case.

"Venga. I close up now."

Bunty says goodnight to her boss, steps out onto the street, and stops to check her phone again. Still nothing from the host. Fuck. There's another message from her mum though, and she's feeling terrible cos she still hasn't worked out what to tell her, but this sitch is much more urgent. She considers her options. Nancy's at the hostel, but she mustn't get her into trouble. Asif's number is in her pocket, but calling him doesn't feel right. Turning up at his place is not how she wants to start anything... if there is anything to be started...

She rounds the corner and drops onto a bench. Couples are heading home after nights out, and besuited guys with skewed ties stumble on the cobbles. Well, at least it's not cold. She props the case beside her and leans her head on it for a moment. So tired...

Chapter 15 – Amigos o Enemigos

"Bunty?"

She opens her eyes. It's Javier from the kitchen. He's towering over her, looking worried.

"Oh! Hi." She sits up and blinks at the orange streetlights.

"What are you doing out here?"

"Just getting a bit of shut-eye." She yawns. "I didn't manage to sort out a place to stay for tonight." And you woke me up, she thinks, grumpily. "What time is it?"

"Half past two." He regards her steadily. "What are you going to do? Bunty, you can't stay here..."

"It seems safe enough, so far anyway." She looks around; there are fewer people now, and the ones that are left are disproportionately male, and out of it. Then she notices a man leaning on a wall opposite, watching her, and wonders how long he's been there.

"Erm..."

"Yes, I saw him. Come on, you can stay on my sofa."

"I'm, erm..."

How can she decide? This could be one of those devil-and-deep-blue-sea scenarios. She's only just met Javier. He seems alright, but how can you tell? The fact that they work together provides some security, but she can't rely on that. He's looking at her intently, but not in a creepy way.

Fuck it, she's going to have to take the risk.

"Thanks Javier."

"Of course. I live quite close to here."

"In Gibraltar?"

"Yes, near Ragged Staff Gate."

Bunty breathes a sigh of relief, realising the offer would have been academic if he'd been staying across the border. She gets up, stretches and grabs the handle of her case. They turn the corner onto Irish town.

"So here we are, the ragged staff..."

"¿Qué?"

"Ah, it's nothing. You've been out?"

"Yes, meeting friends."

He seems sober, and that reassures her too. They walk in a silence that comes from exhaustion. His flat is up two flights of stone stairs, and they enter a front door that leads to a corridor with several doors on each side.

"Do you live alone?"

"No, with two amigos, but they won't bother you."

Bunty is bothered, but doesn't say so.

He sets her up in the living room with blankets and cushions on the sofa, and explains where the bathroom and kitchen are. They say goodnight, and when Javier closes the living room door Bunty collapses onto the sofa, which reeks of cigarette smoke and dust, but she's too tired to care.

The 'amigos' are on her mind though. There are two of them, and they could both be male. She remembers from her Spanish studies how the masculine plural ending is always applied to groups even when some members are female; there only has to be one male for the whole group to be counted as masculine. Logically this means that there is at least one guy she doesn't know here, who doesn't know she's here, and could come in at any moment. She doesn't want to think about what could happen, but can't help planning how she would escape if it did. She tries to keep her eyes open...

She wakes up coughing. The sun's beating through an uncurtained window, and there's someone in the room, on the armchair at the end of the sofa. It's young man, fair-haired and skinny. He's smoking a cigarette, and watching her. She pulls her feet away from him.

"Did I disturb you? I'm Trent." He reaches forward to shake her hand.

"Umm. Didn't know you were there..." She rubs her eyes, ignoring the proffered limb.

He takes it back and raises his eyebrows. "And why, pray, are you here?"

"I work with Javier..."

"Oh, Javier, the sly dog. Why are you on the sofa then?"

"Because..." Bunty doesn't like Trent, or his insinuations. "That's where I am."

"Steady on! I see you're a feisty one." He licks his lips. "You'd have to be, to wear an outfit like that."

Bunty glares at him.

"What you don't realise, Bunty, is that my dick is much more comfortable than that sofa."

"What the...?" Bunty gasps. "Fuck you!"

"Well, you're very welcome to! My room's just next door."

She stands up. "For some weird reason, Trent, I'm just not feeling it." She picks up her case. "Next time you're online, google Wankers Anonymous. They might be able to help you."

Trent's spluttering into his tea when Javier walks in. "Bunty, did you sleep well?" He looks around the room uncertainly. "I see you have met Trent?"

"Yes, thank you, and yes, unfortunately." She walks past him to the bathroom.

In the shower she tries to wash away the emotional grime of the exchange with Trent, and her rage dissipates a little. Javier's in the kitchen when she comes out.

"Would you like a coffee? Some breakfast?"

"Coffee would be good, thanks." Her stomach's too scrunched up to be able to eat.

"I am sorry about Trent. I think he is what you English would call a 'deek-head'?"

"That is exactly what we would call him!"

"He tries to learn how to meet with women by doing a course online. To me, is sad."

"To me too."

47

Yeah, Javier's alright. She sighs, tries to let it go.

"You working tonight?"

"Yes, I think so. But here, take my number, and if you are in this kind of problem another time..."

Bunty knows she'll never come to this flat again, but taps the digits into her phone anyway. Javier walks her down to the street.

"I'd lose that flatmate," she advises him.

He looks shamed. "I will try."

"Cheers Javier. In a bit."

"Hasta luego, camarada."

She walks back towards the town centre in the late morning haze, trying to process her fury. Along the way she describes the abuse on her Insta, and the hearts and supportive comments start to appear. She feels less alone, but she's still stuck on one side of a screen. Maybe she should see Asif...

While the networks process his number, she gets a twang of anticipation in her chest. That's interesting...

But there's no answer. Huh, fake number. The twang breaks loose and plummets downwards, landing with a thump of disappointment in her gut. She keeps walking; what else is there to do?

Chapter 16 – Exploration Sunday

Five minutes later her phone rings.

"Erm, hello – I missed a call on this number just now?"

"Asif?"

"Bunty? Oh, great to hear from you! Sorry, I had the ringer off."

"No pasa nada. What you are up to?"

"Well, I have an exhilarating day of nerding around ahead of me... unless you have any suggestions?"

"I'd quite like a guided tour of this fair micro-state if you can drag yourself away from... what are you playing?"

"Very perceptive! Umm, Minecraft," he admits, ruefully. "But, yeah, I can do that! I could meet you in an hour? Hang on, where are you staying?"

"I'm of no fixed abode right now, but how about Casemates – Café Genoese?"

"Awesome. See you in a bit!"

She goes via The Jolly Sailor to dump her case. Jasandra's drinking coffee behind the bar, and raises a finely shaped eyebrow at her.

"What's going on with you, chica?" she almost growls. "Are you a tramp like that Nancy?"

Bunty bristles at the way she talks about a supposed friend. "I need to sort out somewhere to stay, that's all."

"Well, mi amiga Pandorina has a spare room, she says she wants to rent it to a girl. You want me to give her a call?"

"Oh – yes please, if it's not too expensive."

"You get what you pay for in this world, nena," mutters Jasandra as she taps at her phone.

Jasandra's judgemental manner is rubbing Bunty up the wrong way, but she can't afford to burn any bridges right now – especially not this one.

"Pandorina, tengo una empleada – yes she works for me, fregando platos – quién necesita a place to stay... sí, sí, una guiri, English, muy guapa..."

In a moment her boss is off the phone and writing down an address and phone number.

"You can go here. She'll sort you out."

Bunty takes the paper, thanks her boss, and heads back out into the glare. Despite the shower she's sticky with sweat already; it's fuckin' scorchio. Outside Café Genoese she picks a table facing the square, orders her usual espresso and ice, downs half of it and calls the number.

"Hola?"

"Hello... Pandorina?"

"Ah, you the one Jasandra called me about? What time you coming?"

"Can I come over after my shift tonight? About eleven?"

"Sure reina. I see you then."

49

Bunty sips the cold bitter drink and contemplates her fortune – a job, a room, even friends, after only two days in this place. She lets the muscles in her shoulders relax, and starts to appreciate the Mediterranean vibe in the square. No-one's going anywhere fast, everyone has time to stop and talk. And there's Asif! He's also moving slowly, trailing two bikes and trying to avoid collisions with the Sunday morning crowd.

"I've brought transport," he calls from a few feet away.

"So I see!"

"This place may look small," he tells her as he reaches the table, "but we're not going to get round the whole thing in one day on foot. Be my guest," he offers, holding one of the bikes towards her, an old yellow Raleigh. She gets up, scrabbles in her pocket for a couple of coins which she leaves on the table, and grabs the handle bars. She climbs on to test it out.

"I've got a spanner on me if you need to adjust the seat."

"No, it's about right."

She wobbles around a bit while her brain locates the bike riding neurons.

"Follow me!"

He pushes off, and starts swerving towards a corner of the square she hasn't inspected yet. The wheels whir beneath her and she struggles to catch up as he disappears down an alley between two pubs.

"Wait up Asif! Shit, this is a bit medieval..."

In a moment they've passed through the thick stone walls and are back out in the sunlight, but the landscape is something else. They're surrounded by deciduous trees and stone walls; it's like an English village. They slow to pass a couple trailing several young kids, and Bunty sees some stray but actually quite chubby cats. She stops to stroke an attentive tabby.

"These look well fed!"

"They're the town's pets. Those and the monkeys."

Bunty and Asif cycle on, and the idyllic scene vanishes as they reach the edge of a busy road. They navigate a roundabout by a pair of petrol stations run by companies she's never heard of before. Then they're zooming across a vast expanse of concrete.

She shouts into the wind. "Where are we going?"

"As far north as you're permitted to go," puffs Asif, battling the gale that's sweeping over the unsheltered terrain. "To the border! I want you to see what commuters have to deal with every day."

But they don't get far – there's a loud alarm, and a pair of level crossing barriers come down just ahead of them. Asif pulls in and lifts his bike onto the pavement.

"We might as well sit down; this is going to take a while."

"Why? What's going on?" Bunty's staring all around, trying to work it out.

"It's either a plane taking off, a plane landing, or both."

"Oh shit, this is the runway?"

"Yeah, you can usually go across it, but they have to do this a few times a day."

"No way!"

She walks to the barrier and stares across the expanse of tarmac. "Are you sure?"

50

Bunty can't hear his answer for the noise of the jet coming down. It lands to their left and taxis around smoothly.

"It's amazing how they manage not to end up in the sea," Asif observes.

Then the barriers are raised and they're back out onto smooth tarmac, buffeted by the stiff Mediterranean breeze.

Asif leads her to a point where the road's blocked by several more barriers and checkpoints. They both dismount. Bunty's making a mental note to be careful what she asks for in future; after the time she's had recently she'd probably have been better chilling out today. But here they are, at the border, facing Spain. She's never seen anything like this before.

"Here we are at the frontier," declares Asif in his best tour guide voice. "On that side you can enter Gibraltar through Spanish and then Gibraltarian border controls, and going into Spain it's the other way round, over here." He is waving his arms as he speaks, dividing up the air. "Locals describe this spot by its dimensions, these four corners. They call it 'focona'."

Bunty laughs.

"Going through to Spain, you pass through a hefty customs operation."

"What's that about?"

"Ah, Gibraltar's famous for its cheap fags and booze," he explains.

"But I thought Spain had all of that already?"

"They do, but not as cheap as here."

He swivels round. "See over there, where it's marked out for all those traffic lanes? That's for The Queue."

"There's hardly any cars there."

"Wait till rush hour. It takes anything from thirty minutes to four hours to get out of here."

This isn't helping Bunty's sense of claustrophobia. "Erm, kind of serves them right for driving?"

"Kind of does. It's no fun though if you're trying to get home to your family, or if you've got some kind of emergency. Or if you need to pee."

"Oh Jeez. What about if you're walking through?"

"Sometimes you can go straight through, but there are usually queues at passport control. That's unless the Spanish decide to close the border for a bit – then you could be stood here for an hour. It's tough when it's forty degrees and there's no shade."

"Why... why would that happen?" The rituals of this border – and even the fact that it exists – seem crazier the more he explains them.

"Customs can initiate a go-slow. I gave up and moved to Gibraltar to avoid the stress."

"You used to live in La Línea?" she asks.

"For a while, yeah."

"How was it?"

"There's a lot of poverty; it's an interesting place. Do you know about the history of the area?"

Bunty shakes her head. "Only what I've been picking up today."

"You probably do know that Gibraltar's a heavily contested piece of land – people have been nicking it from each other for centuries. Spanish regional kings, northern Africans, the Spanish state, the Dutch, us lot..." He furrows his brow. "It will be stolen again, it's just a matter of time. My money's on Spain, of course. The cycle repeats every few hundred years, and what Franco started the current government is continuing."

"What do you mean?"

"Have you seen those chimneys across the bay – the oil refinery?"

"Jasandra talked about that... Maybe it's what I could smell when I got off the boat?"

"Yeah, it stinks! Franco put it there in the seventies, after he closed the border. For the past thirty or forty years it's been belching out illegal levels of toxic crap."

"What is it there for, what does it do?"

"Turns oil into plastic."

"Like we need more of that right now..." Bunty shakes her head.

"I know. The only trouble is, the wind doesn't just blow in one direction. It tends to go west as well as south, and they've had all these cancer clusters right across this side of Andalusia."

Bunty thinks about Inmaculada. Asif stops talking when he sees she's crying.

"Oh no, I'm sorry!"

"It's okay. I've just been feeling a bit stressed." She wipes her tears away with her hands. "Umm, so when Franco closed the border, it was right here?"

"Yep. It was a different set up then, there was a big gate over there by the road, and another barrier here, both locked, and apparently people would go to the gates to wave and shout to their family members on the other side. It only opened again in 1982."

More tears squeeze out of her eyes. "How could they hear each other?"

"I dunno..."

Bunty gazes across the border, past the point where cars enter and exit Spain, to the billboards and tower blocks of the town beyond. She takes in the pedestrians filtering through, the cars entering at tortoise speed. She thinks of people separated from their loved ones and their work.

"Almost five thousand Spanish workers had to leave; it really did a number on La Línea's economy," Asif tells her.

And it hits her again that she can't pass either, the border's closed for her too now. She needs to go north, across Spain and France, but right now she's not going anywhere except for this tiny scrap of land.

"Bunty, you okay?"

"It's just the thought of people stood here calling out to their relatives like that..." She doesn't want to tell him everything she's feeling, the panic and claustrophobia, and how she can't even work out how to communicate with her own mum and dad.

"I know. It was all they had left after Franco cut the phone lines and stopped the postal service."

Bunty gazes at the shiny red phone box by the passport control building. It's an analogue anachronism, a remnant of a Britain past, but it's real – maybe it even works. She feels the warm plastic of the mobile phone in her pocket. She has options; she's not cut off like people were here in the seventies.

Asif's still looking at her. She rubs her eyes. "I'm fine, honestly!"

"I feel like I keep making you cry!"

"It's not you," she tries to assure him. "Go on, I want to know more!"

Asif holds the door and she follows him into the dark wooden hall that houses Gibraltar's passport control and customs operations. He points out a poster declaring that heroes are welcome in Gibraltar; next to it is another, advertising the dates of the heats for the Miss Gibraltar contest.

"I heard about this. Nancy says they're obsessed with beauty contests."

"Yes, someone from here won Miss World in 2007, and it's been a constant preoccupation ever since. The newspapers are full of beauty contest reports all the freaking time, and the TV station puts the competitions on repeat."

She shakes her head. "It's like the fifties or something!"

"I know, it couldn't be more gender-polarised. Look at this one." Asif points to yet another poster, this one well-lit and prominently displayed, featuring a woman holding a gun. Bunty moves closer to take it in. She looks glamorous in bright red lip gloss. The rifle lies heavily in her hands, and she supports it uncertainly, as though she's not sure that she knows what to do with it. Yet the sparkle in her eyes suggests amusement – the photographer's making her laugh.

"Ugh, that's sinister!" she gasps. "This place is like a Daily Mail wet dream!"

A pair of border guards walk by and take a good look at them, and their bikes. "Let's get out of here." Asif urges. "I feel bad showing you this when you can't even go to Spain. Do you think you'll have your passport soon?"

"I hope so. And when I get it I'll be straight out of here," she blurts, and sees Asif's face sadden. "I wanna see everything here first though," she adds more softly.

"Well, allow me to be your guide!" He brightens up again, and they turn the bikes back towards the runway.

They stroll past the bus stop where two London-red buses chug diesel fumes into the air. Bunty notes the bus company's slogan, decal-ed onto the windows: 'Possibility in every direction', and points it out to Asif. "Are they going to reclaim more of the sea then, or try to invade Spain?"

"That would be a battle and a half," he grins. "Spain's pretty keen to get its Rock back, so I can't see them giving up another centimetre. This section – the isthmus from the border and up to the town – is even more disputed even than the rest of Gib. It wasn't supposed to be part of Gibraltar at all, but as you can see they built an airport on it and all those housing estates." He waves his left arm. "Technically Gib is supposed to be the area covered by the length of two cannon ball shots from the top of the Rock..."

"Erm, how far's that?"

"I know right? But the British have claimed this bit on the basis that they used it quite a lot..."

"So that's double the reasons for Spain to be pissed off."

They get back on their bikes and forge their way back across the choppy runway. At the end, Asif slows and puts his trainers on the concrete in front of a large monument.

"You have to see this."

He waves at its base, which is inscribed with the words 'Gibraltar, cradle of history'.

"Wow – actual *history* came from here? Who knew!"

Asif mutters something about a skull in a cave but she can't hear him through the noise of the wind.

"I'll tell you in a bit!"

They ride on. Line Wall Road circumvents the town centre and takes them in the direction of the southern tip of the peninsula. After a mile or so Bunty recognises Javier's street on the left. Various fortifications appear to their right, and suddenly there's an amazing view out to sea.

"Let's stop here!" Bunty shouts excitedly. She pulls in and jumps off her bike to get a better look at the bay, with its array of ships and tankers, Algeciras port in the background, and the Atlas Mountains glimmering a little further out.

She takes it all in, and then looks down at the promenade. Kids are racing around on bikes and skateboards, or jumping into swimming pools and screaming. Asif sees the ice cream van and suddenly he's like a kid too; he races off to get them one each.

He returns with a pair of old-school 99s dripping with sticky pink sauce, and they sit on a wall, enjoying the sugar, vegetable fat and whatever it is that the sand-coloured cones are made of. A group of lads have appeared and are yelling a lot. Bunty can't follow the Spanish part of their speech, but the English words of the guy getting on his motorbike suggests he's planning to settle a score with a touch of tyre-slashing. Nothing fits together here, it's a swirl of contradictions: nature and industry, sunshine and violence...

"Does this place make sense to you?"

"Make sense?" Asif muses. "I don't think it's supposed to. It's a clash of too many things."

"Like the tectonic plates..."

"Hmm?"

She relays what Nancy told her about how The Rock bust out of the earth.

"Right! And the first Homo sapiens liked it here, apparently."

"You what?"

"Oh, this is mad. You know how Neanderthals are named after a place in Germany where they found the earliest known skull of a humanish guy? Well, a few years before that, someone found the skull of a woman from the same era, in a cave up on the Rock. They put it in a cupboard. If they'd realised what it was at the time, Neanderthals would actually be called Gibraltarians."

"OMG!"

"Hence the cradle of history thing."

"It actually makes sense!"

"You have to dig a bit, but yes."

Bunty takes photos of the bay, the tankers, the mountains on two continents, and then they start off again, hurtling down the road through a tunnel chipped out of cool jagged stone – "Welcome to The Rock!" yells Asif – only to surface a moment later and enter another, longer one. It's scary without a cycle lane. Cars and vans barrel along beside them, and Bunty's relieved when they emerge back into open space.

"This is it – the end of Gibraltar!" Asif declares, gesturing towards a large car park with a concrete-built café in the middle.

Asif chases her as she zooms to the headland, marked by a stubby lighthouse. They lean on a cast iron fence, staring out to sea once more, this time facing Morocco. The air is refreshing after the sweatiness of their journey. Bunty takes deep breaths and dissolves into the view. She's fascinated by details she can just about make out on the far shore; the glint of sunlight on the windows of the port buildings, the rippling mountains.

"Is this the southest bit of, erm, not Spain...?"

"It's almost the southernmost point in mainland Europe, but not quite. That's at Tarifa over that way," he tells her, pointing to the west.

She twirls round to take in the 360-degree vista of sea and land and rock. "I'm glad I'm getting to see all this before I go. Oh, what's that?" She points to a building set a moment away from the tips of the toes of the Rock – a tall, white, elegant structure with a tower, laced with gold. "Is it a mosque?"

"Aye! Maybe the Moors did prevail after all!" winks Asif.

"It looks beautiful... do you want to go in?"

"Nah, I don't feel like it. You can probably tell I'm not very religious."

"Okay! Can we go around the other side of the Rock then?"

Back on their bikes they race one another to a road that skirts the eastern face, and then ride single file into another cold tunnel that goes on for miles, or feels like it does. They emerge at the foot of a vast escarpment that falls steep and dark and forbidding. In the shadow of the Rock everything suddenly feels serious. "I don't like this side so much," Bunty tells him.

"I was going to suggest a picnic, but you're right, this isn't the spot. We're about a mile from where we started, so we could just complete the circuit?"

Bunty's into that, so they hasten around the side of the peninsula, past a couple of small seaside settlements and into a shadowy industrial zone called Devil's Dyke Road. Bunty laughs at a shop named Pollos Hermanos – "Chicken Brothers!" – but finds the rest of the street a bit grim.

"I know," answers Asif. "It reminds me of some parts of Sheffield!"

Bunty suggests they have their picnic with the cats, so they return to that medieval corner and perch on a grey stone wall. Asif passes her fruit, crisps and cheese. It's the most welcome meal ever. "I seem to be relying on other people to feed me right now."

"Oh! I can cook, sort of!" Asif exclaims, with an eagerness that make her heart melt. He describes the curries he's mastered, and Bunty wonders if he could be any more perfect.

He cycles with her to The Jolly Sailor; Bunty stumbles when she dismounts.

"Have I worn you out?" He looks worried. "Maybe it was a dumb idea?"

"It was ace. Thank you for showing me around." She reaches up and circles her arms around his neck.

Asif hugs her back, his eyes sparkling. "See you soon, yeah?"

Chapter 17 – Shiftwork

Bunty beholds a scene of chaos. Babies crying, men shouting at a football game blaring in bright greens and reds from the widescreen TV, women leaning over tables yelling at one another, and Inmaculada and Nerea rushing around with plates of chips and burgers, trying to keep them all happy.

Bunty's glad to retreat to the comparative quiet of the kitchen. Javier greets her with a wave and a wink, and Graeme keeps his head down – not even a grunt today. She pulls on rubber gloves and gets stuck in at the dishwasher, next to which piles of plates and towers of glasses are waiting to be scalded clean.

During a lull Javier informs her she has fifteen minutes' break. She doesn't smoke, but the only place to get time out is round the back, by the bins. Inmaculada's there already, halfway through a cig.

"How's it going?" Bunty doesn't want to pry, but she can't ignore what she saw and heard yesterday.

"Yes. Going okay," Inmaculada tells her between puffs, the tension in her face easing slightly as she draws in the chemical cocktail.

Bunty gives her a smile and wishes she could offer more – anything.

Nerea appears and embraces her friend. "You have to go back in, Jasandra say," she tells her gently.

Inmaculada sighs, stubs her cigarette on the wall, and goes back into the pub.

"It's a hard time for her." Bunty grimaces at her understatement of the obvious.

"You tell me. But this happen very much. Many people get sick and die with cancer here."

Bunty shudders. "Because of the refinery?"

"We think so. No-one tell us. No-one help. And no money for when it happens to you, for your family to live."

"What about the law?"

"The system is not for us. It cares for the businesses. Not for people, no hay justicia..."

Bunty shakes her head. "I know it's been tough in Spain since the recession..."

"La Crisis? Sí. Not so much work now. Forty porciento without jobs in my town." Nerea turns away. "I go inside; I have to keep this job."

Bunty peels herself from the wall and follows her inside. It's a warm evening, and next to steaming dishwashers is the last place she wants to be. "I'm trying to think of it as a free sauna," she tells Nerea, which makes her smile at last.

Javier approaches her while she's attacking an oven tray with a knife, hacking away at baked-on cheese. "Bunty, where do you stay tonight?"

"Jasandra's fixed me up with a friend. Don't worry."

"I am happy to hear it."

The sleepy Sunday night street echoes with the din of suitcase wheels on cobbles. Bunty stands outside number 5 Jyske Hill. She presses the bell and examines the old wooden door, the red paint peeling off its scarred surface, until it opens and a woman appears.

Pandorina shouts "Hola" and kisses Bunty on both cheeks, then picks up her case and turns to climb the stairs. "Pasa, pasa," she calls. "Put the shoes down there."

She unlaces her trainers and climbs the stairs bare-footed. The walls are decorated in pale violet and yellow, exuding a cloying femininity that gets up Bunty's nose like her host's heavy perfume. She follows her into the kitchen.

"So," Pandorina begins, pulling up a wooden chair for her to sit on, "You need a place to stay? How long?"

"I'm just here while I get a new passport – a few days."

"What happened to your passport?" Pandorina's tones of authoritative concern are softened by her Mediterranean accent.

"I left it on a cruise ship..."

"That was silly. Where did you cruise from?"

"Southampton, in the UK."

"Yes, Jasandra says you're English. How many days you gonna be here?"

"Hopefully less than a week. How long does it take to get a passport?"

"Oh, weeks. Maybe six or eight. But it could be different if you have an emergency. You ask in the Governor's Office."

"I went there on Friday but they were closed, it was before three o'clock..."

"Summer hours. You know – we finish early in the summer."

You don't say, thinks Bunty bitterly. "I'm going back in the morning so I might know more then."

"Okay, you tell me tomorrow."

The kettle has boiled, and Pandorina pours Bunty some herb tea. "You like manzanilla? Camomile?"

Bunty thanks her and accepts the cup. "How much are you charging for the room?"

Pandorina strokes her sleek hair contemplatively. She's wearing feather earrings and blue eyeshadow that matches them, and her long hair is somewhere between dark brown and blonde, depending on the light.

"Well, it's normally £45 a night."

"I'm only making £28 at Jasandra's, and some tips. Could you do it any cheaper for me?"

The landlady furrows her brow. "There's nobody else coming in this week or next. You can stay for..." She sketches out a few figures on an envelope, "£25 a night." She stabs a full stop into the paper to emphasise the end of her calculations.

Bunty nods. She's not sure how she will afford to eat as well, but this is her only option – apart from staying on a sofa with one eye open, or threatening Nancy's security, or making things really weird with Asif.

"Okay. I show you your room."

She gives Bunty a tour of the house, and when they reach the bedroom on the second floor, Bunty finds it's small but sweet, with a single bed and a skylight. Pandorina leaves her there and she collapses on the bed. Finally, she has space to herself. Maybe now she can start to process everything that's happened in the six long days since she left Leeds. Does she want to, though? The gnawing uncertainty of her situation, broke and stranded in a weird micro-colony thousands of miles from home, is overwhelming. She thinks of her dad, who always finds ways to make things seem brighter. He'd call this an adventure. Could it be?

With that more favourable possibility in mind, she shuts her eyes. Sleep swallows her whole.

Chapter 18 – Happy Birthday QE2

The sun glares in through the skylight. She's fully clothed, and too hot. This room, this bed, the window, everything seems familiar. But… no. For a moment there she thought she was home.

Bunty sighs, then stretches, catching stiffness in her calves from all the cycling. Today should be easier, she thinks, with safe walls around her, as long as she can find the money to pay for them. But that sense of restriction hits her again, tightening her chest. How am I gonna get home? And what will happen when I get there? Maybe don't think about that bit…

Shit, what time is it? 10.30. Good, she can walk to the passport office and get everything sorted. She re-does her bunches, which have been responding badly to the humidity, and pounds down the stairs. Picking up her shoes from the hallway, she sits on the third step to lace them up. The front door opens and Pandorina pushes inside with plastic and paper bags crunching around her. "¡Buenas dias chica! ¿Qué pasa? Where you going?"

"Morning! I'm just off to the passport office."

Pandorina drops her bags and waggles a finger. "Not today you're not! No passports for you!"

"Uh?"

"It's a fiesta, a holiday today. You go tomorrow. Today you party with the rest of us."

Shit. Of course. Nancy had told her on Friday. And Pandorina didn't bother to mention it last night; she must have been preoccupied with negotiating the rental arrangement.

"Venga. Have a rest. You look tired."

"I'm going for a walk."

"Okay, suit yourself." Pandorina goes upstairs with her acquisitions. "Hasta luego."

Bunty steps into the street and grimaces as the sunlight stings her eyes. She strides down the steep cobbled street, swearing inwardly. And now she's hungry too.

Rounding the corner, she spots a stone doorway with a crate of black grapes propped on a wooden stool outside. She lowers her head as she enters. The room inside is tiny, and no-one's about. There are boxes of fruit and veg on the floor, and a high up shelf holds olive oil and other provisions. She calls "Hello," and a large scruffy man emerges from the back.

"Sí, guapa, yes?"

"Can I have some of those grapes, outside?"

"You want I mix them with the green grapes?"

"No, thanks." She passes him a pound coin that is warm from her jeans pocket, and he keeps the change, if there was any.

"Adiós, señorita."

She slopes down the street, popping grapes in her mouth and spitting out pips. The fruit sugar only seems to give her more energy for worrying. She dodges the path of a motorbike revving up behind her, then sticks to the side of the narrow alley. What am I doing here? Because... I have no choice. I've got to sort this out, I can't stay here and work in a kitchen and be semi-homeless. But when I get home there'll be so much more grief from the Jobcentre. As though I wanted to be out of work. Like I needed to be shit-broke...

She DMs Sofia. "What am I doing here, Sof? This place is stupid."

Ten minutes pass before her phone buzzes back. "Cos you don't got your passport, dum-dum. Any news?"

":(NO! Everything is shut cos it's bank hol."

"It's not a hol here. You got one and I don't?!"

She asks an old lady sitting on a bench at the side of the street, who answers between puffs of her cigarette. "Queen's birthday, pet."

Bunty grimaces.

"Any excuse for a fiesta," the lady winks.

"QE2's bday :/" Bunty DMs to Sof.

Sofia's right back at her. "OMG. Have a nice day off in the colony!"

Bunty's trying to. But on top of anxiety she has the guilt from not messaging her folks; she can't do it till she has good news. Her legs hurt, yet she keeps wandering the lower slopes of the Rock until she's much too hot, and really hungry. A Japanese café tempts her. It's cooler in than outside, but their air con is not providing the powerful blast of icy air she was hoping for. She sits on a sticky chair and inspects the shop's interior: the two types of fake wood on the walls, a bit like her mum's café, but here the Formica tables are mucky. The waiter brings her what little vegetarian sushi they have, but no chopsticks. When she asks for them he misunderstands, thinking she's asking for the WiFi password, so she eats with her fingers, whilst trying to block out the autotuned synthesised candyfloss sounds oozing from the radio. She's the only customer. This place makes her miss Leeds more, where she can eat well for cheap, and go to gigs, and see friends. But she'll be home soon enough.

She whiles away the rest of the afternoon in a park, messaging and posting on Instagram, but it only makes her feel more lost. Bashing away at the screen like a baby with a Fisher Price toy, the sliders and dials and wheels that spin look like they'll do something if you hit them hard enough, but they don't take away the pain, not really.

At quarter to six she ambles to The Jolly Sailor and arrives early for her shift. Jasandra greets her; she seems more tense than usual.

"Bunty, come over here. You wanna beer?"

She shakes her head. Beer at the start of her shift? She follows her boss to a corner table.

"The fella who had your job before you, Jorge. We thought he'd gone away to Spain for good, but he's back. His father is sick, so he needed some shifts."

"Are you getting rid of me?"

"No, I told him share. He works the week, you get weekends."

61

"But..." She's about to reiterate that she won't even be here for that long, then realises that isn't going to help. "I don't know how I'm going to pay Pandorina."

"You must have some money with you? You didn't come here with nothing in your pocket?" Jasandra looks at her scornfully.

"I had to leave my job on the ship. You know." She's starting to scowl, and knows that's not her best communication technique. "I'll get started anyway."

"Not today – Friday you can come in. Fridays Saturdays, those are your nights."

Bunty blinks and nods. Pushes her chair back, stands up.

"See you Friday, chica. Chin up!" Jasandra commands.

She steps out into the street. Into intense sunshine, now with added Spectre of Homelessness.

"Bunty?"

She looks across the street. It's Inmaculada.

"Where are you going? You no work tonight?"

"Jasandra doesn't need me. The guy who worked there before has come back..."

"¡Oh, Jorge! Qué hijo de puta..."

"She says his dad is ill."

Inmaculada's face darkens. "Okay. I no beat his ass today then." Almost a smile. Then she looks straight into Bunty's eyes. "Jasandra tell you – about my mother?"

"She did, I'm sorry to hear about it." Bunty stretches an arm towards Inmaculada, but her British reserve stops her short of an embrace. "I don't know what to say..."

"It's okay, you don't have to say something."

Bunty wishes she could help, wishes she could make this suffering go away. She puts her arm on the girl's shoulders and Inmaculada accepts the hug. She holds her slight body, feels her chest quaking. Surely she shouldn't be working in this state? But what else can she do, if the rest of the family are unemployed?

When they separate Nerea is there too, her face full of concern. She immediately embraces Inmaculada. Bunty moves to go, but Nerea looks confused.

"Where you go?"

She explains again.

"Mierda. I know you need the money."

"Yep, just to pay my rent..." Bunty's brow is creased.

Nerea rummages in her bag and pulls out a pen, and a receipt. She writes on the back of it.

"This is my number. Call me tomorrow. We have to go in now." She starts to guide Inmaculada to the front door.

"Thanks Nerea..." Bunty doesn't know what this is about but appreciates the gesture from someone she barely knows. Turning to Inmaculada, she speaks softly. "Take care tonight."

Inmaculada nods, and the girls disappear into the pub.

Bunty stands for a moment, unsure what to do next. She can't think of anything at all, so she begins a slow walk back to Pandorina's, her heart so loaded with concerns it weighs her upper body down. Sadness for Inmaculada mixes with her own hopelessness and homesickness. She needs solutions, or simplicity, or even just some idiotic optimism that could make it all okay.

Chapter 19 – A Date with The Governor

She's on top of it this morning. On it like a bonnet. Awake since sunrise after the most boring night in history, hanging out with her phone and crashing out by nine, Bunty's all showered, hair washed, oiled and dried, and striding down Main Street to the Governor's Office before it's even open.

At the corner before the office an unending procession of vehicles – tiny trucks, cars and mopeds – swerves round from a blind spot and forces her to stay on the miniature pavement. When she makes it across the road she turns to admire the old houses painted in blues and greys on the side of the street where she'd been marooned. They look charming but damp, like buildings in a North Wales seaside town – the sort of places she went on holiday as a kid.

In the space outside the Governor's Office there's already a queue. She waits behind people assembled on the disabled ramp that leads to the front door, and tunes into their impatient muttering. She keeps her own frustrations to herself. They're complaining about the office opening late, while she mainly wishes she'd had a coffee first, and something with a bit of sugar in it.

"I've got to go to work," a man puffs into the almost-chilly morning air. "What are they playing at?"

She shrugs. "I'm not from round here."

The wooden door creaks open and is pulled inwards by a young woman with long black hair and glasses. They all file in after her, through a high-ceilinged hallway and into a small, austere room. Bunty looks around and finds a handmade structure hanging on the wall that serves to dispense forms, with peeling labels to indicate what they are, but she isn't sure which one she needs. They all seem to be for people from Gibraltar.

Two of the windows have 'passports' listed in the signs above them, and one of these windows has a woman behind it, the same one who let them all in a moment before, and a couple of people are waiting there already. She looks for some kind of ticketing machine, but it's much more old school than that. The room's too small for actual queues, so she sits on the polished wooden bench that runs beneath the wide-ledged window, pulling her feet in to give more space for those standing. When the passport window becomes vacant, she steps up to it and finds herself facing the tight-lipped, pretty-eyed young woman. It's the moment she's sort-of dreamed of, and she's almost too nervous to speak.

"Hi, I, erm, lost my passport."

"What's your name?" Her accent is the same exotic, soft Mediterranean burr that Bunty's getting used to, but spoken a little more brusquely than usual.

She answers as abruptly as she's asked, but the lady doesn't understand her.

"Write it down please." She passes a small piece of paper and a biro under the partition.

Bunty posts her name back to the lady, who reaches into a drawer for a form which she affixes to a tatty clipboard.

"Fill this in first."

It's a lost and stolen passport form. Bunty takes it and sits down, using the biro tied to the clipboard, and quickly writes out her details. It's clearly designed for Gibraltar residents, so she amends bits of it to make it clear that she's not from here.

Someone else is at the desk. She waits her turn again, and returns the form and clipboard.

The woman doesn't look at it. "Come back in three days with these documents." She pushes another piece of paper under the window.

"Is it really going to take three days?"

"Yes. Or next week if you prefer."

She can't get used to the tempo, or lack of it, that seems to orchestrate life around the ancient Rock. It's as if the geological centre emanates some prehistoric, near-inert rhythm and everyone's tuned into it. But, she reasons as she steps out into the street, in three days she'll have a passport. Is that what the woman said – that she could get it on Friday? She goes back inside to check, but more people are queueing at that window now, and she doesn't feel like being snapped at again. Three days it has to be.

She's a mile away, at Casemates, when she actually reads the list of documents that she must supply: Driving licence. Birth certificate. Previous passport. Utility bills or bank statements to prove her address – all the things she does not have. She can, however, offer a debit card with £36.75 in the account, a used bus ticket to Southampton, and her membership card for The Booty Duke, now defunct. Should she go back and talk to them about it? The woman's forbidding tone keeps coming back to her, and the deadening pulse of Rock-driven inertia slows down her brain.

Bunty looks across the square and sees a crinkly-faced lady on a bench. She's wearing a luminous pink tracksuit with the words 'Live Forever' emblazoned across her chest as she puffs intently on her cigarette. Now there's the kind of optimism I need, thinks Bunty. Against all the fucking odds.

Nancy meets her at Sanguinetti's.

"I feel so lost."

Nancy doesn't say anything – just holds her hand.

"Do *you* feel like that sometimes?"

"Yes, every now and again. But for you this is just a waiting game. Maybe you can even enjoy yourself while you're here?"

Nancy pours her some tea.

"I suppose..."

Bunty takes her cup and looks out at a group of tourists negotiating their way along Irish Town. "Some people actually come here on holiday, don't they?"

"Yep. Some people like this old Rock."

"But I feel wrong here. Is it just me? I *so* don't fit in."

"They'd have to change a lot for you to fit in here. You're a natural boat rocker, and this boat really doesn't want rocking anymore."

"I didn't know I was a boat rocker. I'm definitely a punk rocker."

Nancy laughs.

"But it kind of feels like there's something fixed, kind of in the atmosphere? It's like the whole place is resisting some sort of readjustment..."

"You're right, Bunty. The modern world's looming, and Gibraltar just wants to stay the same, with all its old-fashioned ways."

"Do you think it would be better if it goes back to Spain?"

"That might modernise things a little, but then you've got 30,000 people who don't want to be Spanish, with nowhere else to go."

"So no-one here wants that?"

"They had a referendum in the sixties. Only thirty people voted for it to go back to Spain. And they were not at all popular afterwards..."

"That's kind of decisive." Bunty pours more tea.

"Spain's busy trying to hold itself together. It's fighting hard to keep its parts – Catalonia, Basque country – regions that keep asserting themselves as not-Spain. It's a stressful time for them."

"What about their African colonies? If they let go of those it might give them some better karma?"

"Ceuta and Melilla? No, they're hanging onto those."

"So can't they blame the UK for keeping hold of Gibraltar then?"

"I don't think so, but that doesn't stop them from having a go. I always think it would make just as much sense for them to try and annex Portugal, if they really want the whole peninsula. Oh, look at the time – I should get going."

Nancy gathers her bags and slurps down the last of her tea. "In the big scheme, though, everything will change. It's just the way of things. One day the Rock will crumble into the sea bed it came out of, and then all the arguments will be over."

Bunty pulls a coin from her pocket and puts it on the table, and they leave the café to merge with pedestrians on Irish Town, dawdling under the lapis lazuli sky.

Chapter 20 – A Flying Pig

It's been a week of long, lonely days, and the curious charms of this miniature nation are starting to wear thin. She should reach out, to Nancy or Nerea or Asif, but somehow she can't; something crucial in her has closed for business. Instead she sleeps, and mooches, and waits for Friday.

On Thursday Asif texts her. *Work's doing my head in. Do you have time to meet for lunch?*

I've got all the time! *When & where?*

She finds him at a table outside Masala Memories, nursing a pile of bhajis and samosas. He jumps up to hug her, and when she sits he pushes the plate of greasy delights towards her. But she's not hungry.

"You don't look too good, Bunty. What's up?"

"I'm not dealing with stuff. I need to get back. And I'm not sure I can."

"What d'you mean?"

It all comes spilling out, about the documents she can't supply to support her application, and how she's run out of money, that her shifts have been cut and she can't afford to pay Pandorina for the room. "I don't even know what I've been doing, I'm just freaking out."

"Listen, you've got friends here. I'm sure we can work everything out between us."

"But I need to get home."

Bunty's vaguely aware that she's not making sense, and she can feel the tears pressing behind her eyes. They've been lurking there for days, and now they break out and roll down her face. Why does she do this every time she sees him? She wrenches thin tissues from the serviette dispenser on the table and presses them to her cheeks. Asif leans forwards, protecting her from the curiosity of passers-by.

"Do you want to get out of here? Go for a walk?"

She nods. They head out into the street, and find themselves meandering around a narrow strip of park that lies alongside the bay.

"You know you can ask me for anything you need, Bunty."

She's not sure she can. Why should she? This is the third time they've met. But she doesn't say any of this. She's just trying to keep it together.

"Is it really such a rush to get home, anyway? What difference would a few more days make?"

"You're kidding?" She glares at him.

"No, it's a genuine question. Why is it so urgent?"

She sighs. She can't seem to get angry with him, even when he's being really annoying.

"I've been here for almost a week, and I'm not getting anywhere. I don't belong here, I can't afford to be here, and there are things I should be doing at home..."

"Like what?"

Why's he being so dumb today? "Voting in this stupid fucking Brexit referendum, for a start. It's happening in less than a week! I'm terrified in case it all goes to shit."

"Yeah, I'm worried about that too. A Leave result would be devastating here – the whole economy could fall apart. It wouldn't help the perpetual uncertainty about sovereignty either. No-one knows what Spain would do."

"It's the UK I'm worried about. Everyone I know is voting Remain, it looks really good in my social media bubble. But what if...?"

"It's too awful to contemplate."

They both stare at the rubberised playground floor.

"Can you set up a proxy vote though? Just in case you're not back in time."

"I dunno! What's one of those?" Her turn to be the dumb one.

"You get a friend vote for you, the council sets it up. You just go on their website and fill in a form."

"Oh! Thank fuck you can do that!"

"Do you have someone reliable back home who'd vote for you?"

"Sure, I think so."

"I imagine you have a lot of good friends in Leeds. And I can't see you hanging out with Daily Mail readers."

"Yep. And no, not really."

"Apparently the vibe in non-metropolitan areas isn't so good, like in the south, outside of London. Loads of people are convinced that they're being ripped off by the European Union."

"I know." Bunty gnaws at a nail. "It's like they think leaving the EU would mean no more immigrants."

"They just don't want to see black and brown faces." Asif's brow creases a little. "They'll be gutted when it turns out we all get to stay cos we're actually British, and our ancestors aren't from the EU, just the countries that England fucked over in its empire days."

They stop at the swings and Bunty squeezes herself onto one of them. Asif slides more easily into the one next to her.

"They've got a big problem with white people from the rest of Europe too. Who gets to stay? What about The Queen? Should she go back to Germany?"

This makes Bunty guffaw.

"It's just, like, which wave of immigration every person has come from. Or, waves, really. Anglo-Saxons weren't from Britain."

They dodge out of the way of two small boys racing for the swings, tiny skullcaps atop their heads. Asif and Bunty continue their stroll.

"Wouldn't it be easier to DNA-test all the xenophobes and find out what they're really made of?"

"They'd still be in denial," Asif sighs. "This isn't about what's true."

"They want to put up barriers. My mum says it's been going on for decades." Bunty jumps up and walks along a small wall. "When she was a kid they all used to play out in the street, and people would be round each other's houses. Then bit by bit everything closed down, like when they clamped down on the dole and got everyone working shit jobs. She said people stopped going to the cinema when they

67

all got their own video players, and the paedophile scares meant we didn't get the same freedom they had, growing up…"

"Where I lived you could see the garden fences getting higher and higher…"

"The whole thing about the sharing economy," Bunty continues, animatedly, "it makes you think how much STUFF could be shared, apart from anything else. Like you could club together on your street and share tools…"

"Lawnmowers! Not every house needs one!"

"In your leafy suburb, yeah!" Bunty smiles. "In Chapeltown we're more likely to share sound systems. Did you get yours sorted out, by the way?"

"Huh?"

"Your vote."

"Yep, postal. All done."

"Mister Organised!"

He laughs, and glances at his phone. "Shit!"

"What is it?" Bunty's taken aback by the sudden change of tone.

"It's a text from my mate at work. You're never gonna guess – David freaking Cameron is in Gibraltar right now! There's a rally in Casemates at five, apparently he's speaking at it."

"Eeuw."

"Looks like he's come over to reinforce the anti-Brexit message."

"Cameron's gonna 'splain it to the Gibraltarians…" Bunty's shaking her head – the thought is really grossing her out. "This whole thing is his fault in the first place!"

"I know right. Are you gonna go?"

"Umm. I guess? Maybe we could throw stuff at him."

"Good plan. I gotta get back to work, but I'll look for you there?"

He hares away, and she wishes he didn't have to. Now she's alone again with her gnawing anxieties about her own life, the future of the UK, Europe, and the whole fucking world.

Chapter 21 – The Death of Democracy

She meanders back to Casemates in a daze and gets there way too early. The square is busier than usual, but not by much. It's partly cordoned off and there are loads of police, sweltering in their navy blue uniforms and domed hats. A film crew is training cameras and mics on a stage in the north east corner of the square.

"It's all been a bit spontaneous," she hears a policeman tell a woman in a wheelchair. "We didn't have time to set up a platform for disabled seating. You should be alright here."

She observes the work in progress, and something about the ordered civic activity in the square reminds her of *Camberwick Green*, a kids' TV show from the 70s that her dad used to play her on YouTube.

Asif rushes over, breathless.

"Hey!"

She turns and smiles. It's good to see him twice in one day.

"I thought there'd be more people here," he comments, looking around at the rows of old ladies squeezed together on wooden benches. "Shall we find somewhere to sit?"

Bunty sees a café that has lots of vacant chairs outside. The sign above it reads 'Al Dente's Hygienic Fish & Chips'.

"We could try there? I could murder some chips. But I'm not sure about the hygienic thing…"

"Umm, yeah. Maybe let's just get a drink."

There are around twenty people in situ, enjoying greasy food and cans of pop. Bunty and Asif are about to sit down when a woman in a grimy apron appears. "Eet's closed!" she declares, with an aggression that seems out of place.

"Oh! Okay! Is it alright if we sit here to watch the speech then?" Bunty asks.

"Eet's closed!" the woman repeats, through gritted teeth.

Bunty and Asif look at each other, and turn to leave. They pick their way past dozens of empty chairs, and the people who are allowed to stay.

"What was that about?" Asif looks forlorn.

"Maybe she was having a bad day?"

They scan the terraces of the cafés and bars and eventually locate two seats at a table where a man and woman are drinking cocktails. "This one has a good view of the stage," Bunty suggests.

"Mind if we join you?" Asif asks the woman.

"No, sure," she responds. She seems friendly enough.

Bunty looks around, but all the waitresses are busy. She can't afford a drink anyway. "I never thought I'd want to see this guy up close. It's weird, him being here…"

"Yeah, it's proper historic – it's the first time a British prime minister has bothered to come here since 1969."

"Wow, that's ages!"

They look around expectantly. Bunty chimes in again.

"For some reason I've always thought of him as a pig. I'd never normally call a human that, but the very first time I ever laid eyes on him on TV, I just thought, 'You little pig!' It was like hate at first sight."

Asif rocks forward in his seat, laughing. "I know exactly what you mean! But I wish I'd used this opportunity to do something. I could have got some eggs from Williamson's."

A microphone squeals into life, and everyone looks towards the stage, at a man who isn't Cameron. He speaks with clear, received pronunciation.

"I'm sorry to announce that David Cameron will not be appearing today."

There's a general shuffling and a bit of huffling. "What? After all this?" the woman next to Bunty complains. Her accent suggests she's a Brit on holiday.

"His speech has been cancelled because a Leeds MP has been shot and is now in hospital."

The man leaves the stage abruptly, and everyone looks at one another.

Shit. Bunty thinks about the MPs she knows of in Leeds. She starts biting her nails, and Asif gets on his phone to load up a news site, but the signal's poor. A few minutes later the same bloke returns to the stage.

"Prime Minister David Cameron's appearance has been cancelled due to the shooting of West Yorkshire MP Jo Cox. Because of this incident, all referendum campaigning on both sides has been suspended for 24 hours."

Asif has a news site up; Bunty leans towards him and they read together.

"Is he one that wanted to stay or go?" the Brit-lady asks.

"She's a woman. And Labour, so she would have been campaigning for Remain," Bunty tells her, as Asif scrolls through the story. "The guy got it wrong about Leeds in his first announcement; she's the MP for Batley and Spen."

Bunty reads how Jo Cox was kicked, stabbed and shot outside her surgery in Birstall that afternoon. An ache grows in her cheeks and the pressure of tears rises up behind her eyes once more. She puts both hands over her face; Asif puts his arm around her shoulder.

"This is unbelievable," he says. "She's a really strong anti-racism campaigner. And the reports are saying that the guy who did this was shouting 'Put Britain First.'"

Bunty hugs Asif back and swears under her breath.

After a while they relax their hold on each other. His hands go on the table, like he's not sure what to do now. Most of the crowd has dispersed, and the couple they'd been sat with have left too. "Let's go," Bunty suggests.

They walk slowly, heads down, through the thick walls of the square, and stop to gaze blankly at the well-fed cats.

"Where are we going?" Asif asks.

Bunty's shoulders fall. "I don't know."

"There is one place I'd like to go."

"Yeah?"

"The mosque," he says quietly.

"Of course." Bunty squeezes his hand. "Can I come too?"

"Sure."

They turn around and walk south, back through the square where the stage is being dismantled, and along Main Street. They talk quietly.

"I know it's stupid to put too much faith in institutions like the government, but it's what we're supposed to believe in," Bunty sighs, "and I feel like that's been smashed up. To attack an MP like her... She's like everything you'd want to be."

"It wouldn't even have happened without this stupid referendum. No wonder Cameron's keeping out of the way today."

It's a long walk. When they finally reach Europa Point, it's drenched with light. Just sky and sea, and those Moroccan mountains across the water.

The mosque, when they get up close, is huge. They enter at ground floor level and walk the corridors, passing offices, a library, a waiting room. They can smell someone cooking dinner, and through one door they spy a little girl sat in a big chair playing a game on her phone.

"You've not been here before, have you?"

"No – I'm lost!" he whispers back.

They leave through a different door and climb an external staircase which takes them to the top floor. The large wooden door is open, and inside they find a hallway lined with pigeonholes, which she guesses are for shoes, and next to these, long shirts hung up on hooks.

"Do we put these on?" she asks Asif.

"If you want to. No-one's looking anyway, so it's up to you."

She picks one up; it feels kind of clammy, like it's been worn a few times, so she decides to go without. They step into a large hall where the air is much cooler. Asif walks to the centre of the room, sits down on the carpet and closes his eyes. Bunty stands by the door and takes everything in. At the far end of the room there's a wooden throne with a green cushion on it, and behind it the wall is lined with wooden panels. In the centre there are four pillars, and above them a glass dome rises up. To the left and right, stained glass windows with green and clear panes let in sparkly light, and all around the floor are little stands with books and boxes of tissues on them. In the back corner two barefoot surfer dude types are lounging on the floor, talking quietly.

She steps to the front, helps herself to a tissue, and blows her nose, ruining the silence.

Asif stirs and gets up. He smiles at her and they walk to the atrium and retrieve their shoes. Once outside in the sun, Bunty asks how he's doing.

"Better, thanks. More settled. I had a chance to pray for her. How are you?"

"I think I'm okay. I don't even know."

They walk to the southernmost tip of land and sit on a bench facing the sea. Asif checks his phone, and his expression changes.

"Bunty, I've got bad news."

He turns to her, and the colour's gone from his face.

"Jo Cox is dead."

Chapter 22 – Even The Governor Can't Stop Me Now

She wakes in the early hours, her mind steeped in a blissful dream of a gig, a beautiful song, and her friends. Then it all floods back – the abject horror of what happened yesterday. A woman who devoted her life to benefit the people around her, kicked, stabbed and shot in the street, her healthy body destroyed in a matter of minutes. The details replay themselves unbearably: what it must have felt like to be booted down by a man emitting so much hate, and have a blade forced into her, and what she must have seen when his hateful face turned to hers and pointed the gun.

Bunty writhes for what feels like hours, sweating and feverish. Daylight brings relief – the awful visions subside, but the facts don't fade. Jo Cox represented so much of what she believes in, and the fascists got her...

She sits up in bed, hugging her knees, feeling so very sad – for Jo, for her husband and their kids. And somehow she gets herself up and dressed and makes her way down to the Governor's Office.

A woman calls her name.

"You can't get a passport here."

"I'm sorry?"

"Normally we could issue you with an emergency passport," says the lady, slowly and firmly, "but your passport is not lost."

"But I can't get it..."

"But you can't say it is lost if you know where it is." The woman makes some notes.

"They wouldn't give it back to me."

"You have to contact them. Ask them to post it to you."

"But that'll take ages! I need to get home!" Bunty tries to keep her voice steady, but seismic waves in her gut are causing it to tremble. "Can't you give me an emergency passport so I can get home, then I could ask them to send it to me in the UK?"

"That's not what an emergency passport is for. Just because you leave your passport somewhere, you can't just come here and get one of those till you get it back. You need to get your passport."

Don't I know it, she thinks but holds her tongue. They glare at one other through the glass.

"I am sorry, there is nothing I can do for you."

Bunty gathers her bag and turns to leave. She doesn't know if she has any resilience left. She feels sick and dim, like everything she tries gets fucked up, and what's the fucking point.

Europa Point. That's where she ends up, again, as though pulled by a magnetic south. Leaning over the wall that limits further movement in that direction, she looks down at the cliffs.

I could jump, and stop all this.

No, I'm not going there...

She scrolls for a tune, and 'Borders' by M.I.A. blasts in her ears, the perfect soundtrack to all this geopolitical fuckery. Recognition helps her sit back, and breathe. She lifts her head to take in Morocco, and the Mediterranean. How many people have drowned in this sea, trying to escape war and violence? All the journeys that people, children, old folks had to take, leaving their homes, families, lives. And look at me. I'm privileged. When I do get it back, my passport means I can go almost anywhere. I'm not living through those awful things. I'm safe here, I think, even with almost no money... even if I ended up on the streets, it wouldn't be so bad. And when I get home... yeah, there's more hate there than ever, and I have no money, but eventually I'll get a job. Worst case scenario, I move back into my folks' place. It's not what I wanted, but it's not the end of the world...

She hits shuffle, and 'Because of Whirl-Jack' by Cocteau Twins emerges. Golden guitars swoop in the air before her, and a woman sings words that Bunty can't quite make out, in a voice that's sky-bound, mesmerising. Glimmering guitar-light swirls as she squints in the sunlight, and her heart leaps and swings over the shimmering water of the strait. The bassline gallops with a palpitating drumbeat cracking at its back, and piano hammers strike like momentous teaspoons in Moroccan tea cups. Everything visceral in her goes taut, yearning to move into the ether where her spirit has already flown. It doesn't matter that her body's rooted to the ground, cos she's fractured and blended in the music as it crashes along in joy.

When it gives way to the next track, 'Tinderbox of a Heart,' her soul returns to sway on a rope swing over long grass. The sighing, oscillating vocal tones soothe her on a deeper level, letting her know that she will survive these crazy challenges. The song makes her feel giant, as though she can step over all hurdles, stride across the sea and rearrange those pillars to mess up Hercules' crazy scheme. She's bigger than Hercules. She can stride home.

Chapter 23 – Scare B&B

Bunty feels happy, somehow. It's a weird sensation, given that there's no real reason for it; it settled on her when she let go of her impatience to get home, and the despair that went alongside it. Something in her has relaxed, and she's content to mooch about the house in t-shirt and shorts, listening to music and talking to Pandorina's cat. She's started cooking – a healthy move after those spells of accidental malnutrition. And she even feels better about her landlady's attitude, which tends to be on the cooler side of friendly.

"Pass me the tipa," Pandorina demands from her position near the sink.

"Huh?"

"Tipa!" Pandorina snaps, looking at her like she's super-dense. After another blank look she walks to where Bunty's standing, picks up the teapot and returns to the sink, snorting with derision and muttering about 'guiris.'

"So tipa is teapot?" Bunty ascertains. "What's a guiri?"

"You know – guiri guerros. Foreigners."

On Saturday Bunty comes home late from work, and she's hungry, again. She grabs a few items from the fridge, knocks a salad together, and moves to the front room. It's almost midnight and her mouth's full of lettuce when she hears a thud out in the street. She jumps up and peers through the window. There's a man in a checked shirt standing there; she doesn't know him. Craning, she sees a pair of legs on the pavement, and they look like Pandorina's. She starts to open the door.

"Don't let me in! I'm too drunk!"

Really? She doesn't know what else to do but take the order at face value, so she gently pushes the door back into the frame.

"Let me in!" Pandorina bellows.

Bunty opens it again. Her landlady clambers into the house, lurching precariously.

"You had a good night?"

"Estoy un poco listo!" Pandorina announces. "I drank ALL the whisky!"

"Okay..."

She's not sure what to say. But Pandorina doesn't care what Bunty has to say because she's on the sofa, fighting with her boots and emitting a stream of incoherent swearing.

Her man-friend, who followed her in, slurs an introduction – "I'm Steve" – and holds out a hand in front of his swaying body. Bunty allows him to take hers, and then wishes he hadn't when he lifts it to his stubbly face and mock-regally kisses it.

He's not exactly an impressive catch. Surely her landlady, so confident and full of herself, could do better than this grubby-looking guy?

"TAKE MY BOOTS OFF!" Pandorina growls.

74

Steve does as he's told, and Pandorina hurls one boot, followed by the other, across the room, narrowly missing the cat. Bunty dodges it too, and then sees Steve murmuring to Pandorina with his hand on her arse. Erm. Time to get out of here.

"Just give me a minute, you two," Bunty tells them, as she quickly shovels the last bits of salad into her face and gathers her stuff from the table.

Pandorina acknowledges this with a grunt, and Steve leaves the room.

And suddenly she's shouting again. "Oi! Wanna fuck?"

Bunty's mind spins. Pandorina's lying across the sofa with her legs splayed and she's murmuring hazily: "Mmm, I like it when you touch my tits."

That's it. "Night, Pandorina."

Pandorina doesn't reply, but reaches a hand to where her skirt's rucked up to her hips and caresses herself through her lacy thong.

Bunty bolts upstairs like she's being chased by hell dogs. The living room's been transformed into a bedroom scene but the players aren't in the right places. From the landing she spies Steve, stood over Pandorina's bed, rummaging through his bag. He looks up at her guiltily. The dogs chase her to her own room, where she twists the lock that she's never even thought to use before. Then she tests it. Would it hold, if someone tried to hammer it down? She's at the window scoping out escape routes when the action begins downstairs.

"Uh! Uh! Uh!" goes Pandorina, her low voice transforming, with each grunt, into an animalistic bellow.

And then they start in earnest. The sofa – at least she's guessing it's the sofa – is banging repeatedly against the living room wall, and the noise reverberates up to Bunty's room, almost drowning out the pounding of her own heart. She stares at her wall as though she might see it shake. Steve joins in with a chorus of enthusiastic noises which she finds even more disturbing than Pandorina's. She's heard female sex noises before, but not the eerie sound of a man being so vocally expressive. When he comes there's a sound like a twisted metal structure, pointed down, drilling.

In the silence that follows, Bunty sits on the edge of her bed, feeling sick. If Pandorina can behave like this, what else will she do? Normal rules have gone out the window, and maybe she should too. In practical terms, though, she'd have to exit through the living room – where she imagines they're nakedly entangled – and she really doesn't want to see any more than she already has.

She lies down but stays awake, alert for noises that could signal someone approaching. When Pandorina and friend eventually make their way up the creaking staircase, Bunty's eyes are pinned on her door, scanning in case any of it moves. She hears them shuffle into Pandorina's room, and starts to breathe. The coast is clear.

But she's so fucking tired.

Stay till morning.

Stare at the ceiling.

Make a plan.

There might have been some thin sleep, but it was brutally extinguished by the trilling of her phone. She fumbles, grabs it upside down. "Hi?"

It's Asif. That honeyed voice. The line's crackly; maybe it's windy. She can just about make him out.

"What are you saying – a mystery trip?"

"Yeah, today, if you're up for it. There's a bit of a practical matter though..."

"A what?"

"A practical [crackle]. It would involve going to Spain. We'd be sneaking you in and [crackle], easier in the car."

A slow bomb explodes within her, as the events of last night flood back. She feels like she's dying in some way. Those two are in this house. It's not her home. How could she have ever thought it was?

"It's probably a stupid idea though, I just wondered what you [crackle]."

Calculations speed through Bunty's brain and the answer is FUCK IT.

"Yes!" she whispers. "Perfect." This is her ticket out of here.

Asif's not getting it. "No seriously? I was going to say maybe I could borrow a passport to get you back in, but I wasn't sure how you would feel about [crackle, crackle, crackle]."

Breaking the law? Whatevs.

"No – just – yes. I'm in." And hoarsely, but she hopes, not too desperately, she adds "How soon can you get here?"

"Brilliant!" Asif exclaims, and Bunty imagines him waving an arm in the air. "An hour?"

"Yes. Please. Thank you."

She lies back on her side and looks under her eyelids for the last little bit of sleep. The room dissolves into a dark ripple. And when she comes back, she knows what to do.

Everything back in the case. Drawers that spoke of a sort-of home are quietly pulled open, emptied and pushed back with equal care. She just needs to put a whole bunch of space in between those two people downstairs and this body, this being, that she's trying to preserve here on the side of a crazy rock, so far from home.

She takes her keys from her jacket and lays them on the bedside table, then watches by the window. When she sees Asif approach the house she leans out and loud-whispers "Don't knock!"

"Okay!" he mouths back. He looks amused, happy, and wide awake.

She seizes her case and tiptoes down the stairs. Her trainers are already on so she can get straight out the door. But there in the kitchen stands Steve. He's wearing jeans, no shirt, and he's buttering bread on the counter. He looks up at her, his face a hateful kind of blank. Bunty holds her breath, points herself forwards and walks out the door.

She feels cold and wrung out as she steps into the street, but Asif is full of light as he moves towards her. She flings her right arm round his neck, and he squeezes her – they've moved past Spanish kisses already. But there's no time to wonder where they're going, or even where she's going all by herself today. All she wants is a quick getaway.

Asif takes in her pale face and the bag by her side.

"Are you alright, Bunty? What's going on?"

"I will explain," she answers grimly. "Just not right now."

"Okay. Come on then." He jerks his head towards the corner. They walk round it into a road almost completely filled with a battered old Ford Cortina. It's parked illegally, but it's not as if there's any other traffic on the tiny, cobbled Sunday morning street.

"This is yours?" she gasps. It's lime green, gorgeous.

"Yep – a guilty pleasure..."

She circles it, inspecting it from every angle.

"It's a bit bad really, I mean in terms of emissions. It's on its last legs."

"I love it!"

"Bunty..."

She unglues her gaze from the car and brings her attention back to her friend.

"I'd better talk to you about going to Spain. You might not get back in unless we plan something." His brow is crinkled in contrition. "I feel like, this is bad of me, I shouldn't be putting you in this position. It was a dumb idea." He bites a nail on his left hand.

"This is the perfect day for me to go. And if I never come back, that's fine."

"How can you say that?"

"Look Asif, this is my choice. I'm up for it. I'm so glad you called. And I seriously don't care – as long as I can get into Spain."

"Well, that bit's easy. They don't really check. You could wave a crisp packet at them and they wouldn't notice."

"Great. Then, shall we...?"

"Okay." He spends a long time on the second vowel. "Can I ask what's going on with you?"

"It's going to take a while."

"You're going to keep me hanging on, aren't you?"

Bunty's eyes say yes, so he opens the boot and she chucks her case inside.

"Did something happen with your landlady?" Asif asks as they climb into the car.

"That's very perceptive!"

"Really? What?"

She's checking out the seventies dashboard with a fascination that makes it easy to ignore his persistent line of questioning. "This car is ace!"

He sighs and turns the key in the ignition. The engine coughs unhealthily and the Cortina starts to edge its way along the narrow grey street.

"I'm so glad to see you, Asif."

Her smile seems to reassure him, and anyway, he has to concentrate on negotiating these alley-like thoroughfares until they reach the traffic-choked main road. Then they're zooming across the breezy plain of the runway. In the absence of aircon all the windows are down. Bunty sticks her head out and inhales sea breeze laced with something chemical, that by-now familiar olfactory cocktail.

They get diverted around a chicane by the airport terminal.

"No queues today – we're in luck."

At the border they go slowly past a Spanish guard. He stands and stares, but his eyes don't seem like they're focusing on anything in particular. Asif holds his passport up while Bunty keeps her head down and rummages through her bag. He keeps driving, and once they've passed the guard Bunty looks back to see him gazing into the distance still.

"See, he wasn't bothered," chuckles Asif.

Bunty exhales heavily. "You're right! I didn't show anything..."

"But I still don't know how we're gonna manage on the way back in, unless we..."

"Seriously, I don't want to get back in. I'm in Spain! Yay!!" She sticks her arms out of the window, greeting the nation in triumph.

"Yep, welcome to La Línea."

Chapter 24 – Jumping with Both Feet

They're on the outskirts of a scrappy looking town. Bunty sees cabins by the side of the road that function as diners and car hire offices, all closed up and shut down. Layers of drab tower blocks extend behind these structures, up to the deep azure sky. On the other side, the bay. Asif points to a small beach.

"That's Western Beach, it's part of Gib."

"Nice."

"I wouldn't recommend it."

"Why?"

"It's very close to where La Línea's sewage gets pumped."

Bunty shrieks. "Eurgh, no!!"

"Just another little environmental issue..."

The Rock slowly shrinks behind them. The bay's full of tankers, and they get a hazy view of the Moroccan coast. Directly ahead is the rugged landscape of Algeciras city. The red and white striped chimneys of the refinery stand in the foreground, towering over the outskirts of the town.

"So, where are you taking me?"

"It's not far actually... hang on, you'll see..."

Asif flips on the indicator and they turn into a residential street. Sticking out of the road ahead of them, between rows of white and yellow flat-roofed houses, is an architectural anomaly – an old stone bridge. It rises from the middle of the road, reaching a sharp point at its centre. They admire it while waiting for the red light to change.

"What in hell is this?"

"It's Roman. There used to be a huge Roman city right here."

"No way!"

The light turns green and they drive across the artefact.

"Yep, it was called Karpeia."

"So..." Bunty looks around at the houses and apartment blocks. Apart from the bridge, everything seems like it's sprouted up since the sixties. "What happened?"

"The fall of the Roman empire?"

"I know that!" Bunty elbows him.

"Well, there *have* been some local developments you might be interested in..."

In a moment they're beyond the town on a section of coast road. The bay lies to their left, laden with tankers, and to the right there's a massive wall. Each section is covered in a mural painted in alluring greens and blues, depicting nautical and natural scenes. It goes on for about a mile. Asif drives slowly to allow Bunty to take it all in.

"It's beautiful, but..."

Above the wall, candy-striped chimneys spew clouds of gas. Blazing towers are interspersed by storage tanks and chrome pipelines. It's all tucked behind a no-man's land lined with barbed wire and rolls of razor wire.

The contrast between the cute images and the dystopian reality couldn't be sharper.

"All these paintings are of a different world."

"A happy, healthy world," Asif adds, grimly. "The artists must have signed an oath of apoliticality."

"I suppose this must be how a lot of art works, to hide the grimness of stuff. But I've never seen anything as blatant as this."

"Yeah. If they were commissioned to do this to distract from the refinery, the money people shot themselves in the foot. A bit of realism would have given it so much more credibility."

They pass the entrance of the plant and yet another section of the refinery. Evidence of industry is endless in all directions, even in the sea.

A kilometre later they turn away from the bay and Asif pulls into a driveway that has a car park at the end.

"What's here?" Bunty asks, staring all around.

"Roman stuff!"

"Ace!"

Asif leaves the car up on the gravel and they walk towards the gate. A young man with dark hair and a beard comes out to greet them.

"He looks like he's in a Spanish indie band," whispers Asif.

"Which one?"

"Pretty much any of them."

Bunty hides her smirk as the boy is here now, and he seems really friendly.

"Is it okay if we have a look around?" Asif asks him.

"Sure, but I must go with you," the boy responds in soft Andalusian tones. "I can give you a tour if you like? I am Pedro."

Bunty and Asif agree that that would be awesome. Pedro guides them past a series of excavated ruins, to the point where the tour officially starts. Along the way he explains that the Roman city was preceded by a Carthaginian one and that there was a Phoenician city further inland. He tells them how the mouth of the nearby Guadarranque river used to be much nearer to the site but gradually shifted out over centuries. They gaze around, trying to imagine ancient landscapes, but every view they turn to is dominated by steaming towers and flaming chimneys.

Their guide takes them to the remnants of a building that has steps up through the middle, and says it might have been the entrance to a big temple. Pedro lets them climb the remaining stairs, and as they do so Bunty notices him getting short of breath, which seems kinda strange for someone so young and seemingly fit. Then she spies a well that looks like an igloo, and skips over to photograph it.

She turns back, but stops in her tracks at the sight of a chimney throwing out a huge orange flame. It looks so intense against the sky. None of the other colours in the landscape are as bright, despite ubiquitous blue skies. She takes a snap, then hears Pedro saying something about photography.

"What was that, sorry?" She steps over ancient stones towards him.

"I am supposed to say to you at first that it's okay to take photographs, but you have to check it with us if you want to publish them on your blog or something like that."

Bunty agrees, though she's not sure why she should, and Asif has a question.

"Is it true that most of the city is underneath the refinery?"

"Yes – everything inside the city walls is here, but the rest has been lost."

"Do you know what got lost?"

"We understand there was the city's main gate, a Visigoth necropolis, and many other buildings."

They all gaze sadly in the direction of the plant.

"If you have time I show you the Roman theatre?"

They follow him along a grove of tall trees through which the sun is throwing dappled light onto the rough roadway, and emerge in front of a huge excavation.

"They estimate this seated six thousand people."

Asif's walking along next to Pedro, but Bunty's straying; she's at the fence that separates the site from the refinery. It must be so easy to get in from here...

She has a good look at the huge metal structures on the other side of the twenty-foot fence, takes a few photos, and then returns to the other two.

"Why did you say you have to accompany us everywhere?" she asks the guide.

"For security, I think."

She nods – his answer's in the ballpark she'd anticipated.

"And for safety," he continues. "Something could happen at the plant, an explosion, and it would be my responsibility to get everyone out of here. I can't do it if I don't know where you are."

Bunty hadn't thought of that, and before she can process it she starts coughing, and can't stop. It's like something's clawing at her lungs. Asif moves next to her, concerned and questioning, as she bends double, trying to force whatever it is out of her chest. When she straightens up her eyes are streaming.

"I'm okay, don't worry," she gasps. It's like she's always trying to reassure him. Asif rubs her back, and when the stars around her head subside they walk slowly back towards the entrance.

Bunty asks Pedro about himself. The top of his shirt is open a little and she notices a small plaster across the base of his neck. It runs in a straight horizontal line, as though his throat's been cut by a neat and delicate pirate.

"I see you have a plaster?" she asks, pointing to her own neck.

"I had an operation," he says, a little sadly. "They removed a node from my thyroid."

Bunty hesitates a moment, before proposing the obvious. "Do you think it's because of the fumes – from the refinery?"

"It might be," he admits ruefully. "I have been working here for three years."

Bunty wonders why he doesn't relocate, but doesn't say it. Jobs are hard to come by round here, she knows that. He smiles bravely, and they exchange cheek kisses and thanks.

81

Walking out along the gravel to the car, Bunty suddenly realises. "Maybe that's why he was out of breath..."

"What's that?" asks Asif, as he reaches in his pocket for the car keys.

"Oh, nothing." She doesn't want to burden him with her concerns, and changes the subject. "I have to tell you though that I am very, very hungry."

"It so happens that it's lunchtime," Asif responds with a smile. "Shall we get something to eat? And maybe you can tell me what's happening with you?"

"Maybe," Bunty blanches. "But I don't think I can talk about it while eating."

Asif frowns. "That bad?"

"Yep."

He circles the car back into the village that's close by the archaeological site.

"I think there's a good place around here. And by good, I mean local, and cheap as chips."

"Mmm, chips!"

They pull up in a narrow street of run-down low-rise buildings. The sun's overhead; it's getting hot. A young man in shades is striding past as they get out of the car. When he sees Asif, his mouth opens in a snarl: "Fuckin' Paki!"

Bunty's eyes flash with rage, and she moves towards him.

"Bunty, no!" calls Asif. But it's too late, she's tapping the guy on the shoulder. "Hello! Excuse me?"

The man keeps walking. Bunty keeps up with him. Asif's still calling for her to stop, and he's by her side when the racist finally turns to face her.

"Can't you leave me alone? I'm allowed to walk down the street," he blusters, looking more sulky than anything else. An overgrown kid in grown up clothes, out all by himself.

"No, you're not allowed to walk down the street and talk like that," Bunty tells him.

"Who says? It's not illegal."

"I say."

He turns and starts to walk away.

"Oi!" She's still after him.

Asif grabs her. "Leave him, Bunty!" He looks freaked out.

"Coward. Fucking racist coward," she spits at the racist coward's rapidly retreating back. "Asif, I can't believe it, I'm really sorry."

"It's not the first time I've heard things like that, Bunty," he tells her, sadly. "I've been alive a few years now. I don't think it's something you can stop."

"I *can* stop it. He's not going to say that again in a hurry!"

"He will, but it will be among friends – whatever kind of friends he has."

"But he won't say it in the street. Did you see, he couldn't look me in the eye?"

"True..."

"If enough people confront them, the racists will get weaker."

"I think they're getting stronger now."

Asif's statement hits her hard; it's only been three days since Jo Cox's death. Bunty grabs a lamp post to steady herself, emotionally as much as physically.

"Come here." Asif reaches out to her. "You massive warrior."

"I should be comforting you, Asif. I didn't just get racially abused."

"But you stood up for me. I don't know when anyone ever did that." He squeezes her, and then looks into her eyes. "Dangerous though – seriously Bunty! Don't you have a concept of that?"

"I don't know. If I did, I don't think I'd be here..."

"You're right. Again." He smiles. "Come on, let's eat."

"Are you sure you're okay?"

"Yeah. All in a day's... whatever."

Bunty hugs him again and feels even more tenderness for him. Don't get all complicated, she warns herself, as they walk along the street towards the bar. I'm not here for long, and I've only just broken up with Katrina. Just... don't.

They find somewhere to sit on plastic garden furniture that's set out haphazardly in the yard outside the café. This place is rough-looking but busy, which must be a good sign. A waiter swings by. He's dressed in a grubby sweatshirt, and asks them in a thick Andalusian accent, "Hola, buena. ¿Quiere una bebida?"

Asif tells him they do want drinks. They want drinks very much. Pretty soon beers are in front of them, along with menus printed out on tatty pieces of paper. They choose some tapas, and Bunty drums the table excitedly. "I can't wait for the fried things!"

It takes a while but the guy eventually returns with the goods, and they munch on chickpea and spinach stew, patatas bravas and tiny dishes of ratatouille with fried eggs on top.

"I think I like Spain."

"This is your first time here?"

"Yep!"

"Wow! What an introduction. The rest of it isn't like this..."

"If the rest of it is as good as this food I am definitely in."

After lunch they walk around the village, then onto the beach, where Bunty finally tells him what happened last night. Asif shudders. "That's fucked up. I get it now, why you were so keen to leave. But what are you going to do now? Where are you going to go? I can't just leave you out here."

"It's okay. I have a plan. I just need to make one call."

Asif waits on the sand while Bunty wanders off, somewhat secretively, to talk to someone on her phone. When she comes back she gives him an address, Aurora 50. He looks alarmed.

"I'll be fine," she tells him firmly. "It's a friend."

Chapter 25 – I Walk La Línea

The sky darkens as she sits with Inmaculada at the living room table. Neither get up to turn on a light, so the room's lit only by streetlight shining in through the windows. They drain cups of coffee; Inma has a lot to tell.

"I didn't say you – my father, he die when we are young. When I am thirteen. Him, only 28. Since then his five sisters die too..."

Bunty gasps.

"All of them," she continues. "All cancer. All young – less than fifty años. My older brother had a cancer taken out, and my mother had it taken out three times. And now it is in her brain..."

"Inma, I'm so sorry, I didn't know all of this. It's terrible..." She reaches across the table and takes Inmaculada's hands. The girl cries for a few moments and then looks up.

"Where is your brother now, is he near here?" Bunty asks her.

"He go to Madrid. He say it is not healthy to be here – peligroso, dangerous. He come back soon though, to see our mother."

Bunty agrees with Inma's brother. She wishes her friend could get away from this place before the same thing happens to her. They sit in silence, Bunty with her eyes on her amiga in case she needs to speak, or cry some more. Inmaculada sighs, long and deep, and pushes her dark hair back from a forehead lined with worry.

"You gonna stay here, no? Be my sister." She squeezes Bunty's hand.

"Only if it's okay for you? Just let me know what I can do."

"Just – tranquila. Rest here. It is good to have a friend."

"Do you see Nerea very often?"

"Sometimes, yes. But she has her own problems."

Bunty hopes it's nothing like what Inma's going through.

"You can sleep on the sofa, is okay for you?"

The furniture that she points to looks comfy enough. "I so appreciate your kindness. Hopefully I can sort out my passport soon and then I'll be out of your hair."

"I like you in my hair," Inma responds with a smile. "I get you some covers."

Bunty wakes with the sun. She calls the cruise company in the UK and listens to a message that says their office is closed until nine – another two hours, with the time difference factored in. As she lies sprawled on the sofa wondering what to do till then, a teenage boy walks into the room.

"Oh, hi! Are you Carlos?"

Inmaculada had mentioned her younger brother. He seems shy and glum, muttering only "Sí, hola," as he passes through to the kitchen where she hears him running the tap and switching on the stove. She clears up her blanket, and goes to the bathroom to get dressed. When she returns he emerges from the kitchen with a tiny cup of coffee and offers it to her, asking "You want...?"

She accepts and they sit in awkward silence, Bunty on the sofa and Carlos at the table.

"Do you go to school?" she asks him.

"Sí," he responds, defensively, as if she had just questioned his fledgling sexuality. "At eight and a quarter."

"That's early, compared to the UK," she observes.

"UK people are lazy!" he laughs.

"Some are, some aren't. What kind of music do you like?"

He surprises her. "Rock. Queen. Slipknot. AC/DC. Muse."

"You don't look like a rocker."

"I have to have long hair? That's not good for a boy, here."

"I guess not!" She's seen little evidence of non-conformity among the locals.

Carlos leaves for school and she tidies up the kitchen, looking for things to do to help out these siblings. But she can't find much – the place is so clean already. She hears Inma moving about, and brews coffee for her. She had been unfamiliar with the Spanish way of making coffee, but last night watched in fascination as Inmaculada put grounds and water in the metal device before placing it on the stove-top. Inma comes in and kisses her, and Bunty tells her about the chat with Carlos.

"You get on very well with him! He usually talk to no-one!" laughs Inma. "Now, I am sorry, I have to go and visit my mother in the hospital..."

"Do you want company?"

"No, you take a rest. I want you to enjoy your time in Spain," she tells her guest. "Maybe I need support later."

When it's nine o'clock in London she redials and speaks to a receptionist who is able, after a long wait with torturous Coldplay-type hold music, to put her through to someone who knows what she's talking about. Sort of, anyway.

"So, you left the ship during your contract?" The woman on the other end sounds sceptical.

"Yes, and my passport is still there. I need them to return it to me."

"What they will do is keep it until the end of the cruise and then return it to our offices here in the UK. You can then collect it from here."

"But I can't! I'm in Spain!" It's as though the woman isn't listening.

"In that case you need to go to the Embassy there. They will give you an emergency passport so you can get back to the UK, and then you can collect it."

"It's quite difficult to do that!"

Bunty wants to smash her phone.

"We aren't allowed to send passports through the post. I'm sorry."

Bunty hangs up.

Okay. Start again. Deep breaths. She googles 'British embassies in Spain.'

"You're kidding," she mutters under her breath as the results comes up. She's going to have to go to Madrid.

So she searches for timetables from La Línea to Madrid. There are no trains, but she finds a bus company website and enters the departure and arrival points. The results page takes ages to load, and then it's a 404. Fuck, how can the bus company site be broken?

Google tells her that the station's only ten minutes from here by foot; maybe face-to-face will work better. She pulls on her trainers, grabs the key that Inmaculada has told her to use, and pounds down the stairs to the street where she negotiates uneven pavements in the bright morning sun.

Bunty gazes around the station. It's not just the bus company's website that's broken; the ticket hall is shabby and buzzing with tension. She walks past the vandalised windows of a disused shop, the promise of soft drinks and snacks long since destroyed by blades, lighters and whatever they used to smash in the glass. In the centre of the room a twelve-deep queue has formed at the only attended ticket desk, so she takes her place at the back. Judging by the time it takes for one person to be seen, she could be there a while, so she wanders out to where the buses are. One has 'Sevilla' printed on a board at the front. That could get me closer to Madrid, maybe. The driver's standing by the open door, dragging on a cigarette.

"I want to go to Madrid," she tells him.

He simply points his finger indicating that she should go back into the ticket office hall, so she returns once again to the back of the straggly queue. The air is still. They're out of the sun, but it feels hotter in here under the yellowing plastic roof. She watches as police, locals and tourists mingle in the hall, forming a kind of abstract theatre performance which keeps her amused until she finally reaches the window.

She asks the man behind the glass about routes to Madrid, and for timetables. He tells her about buses to Malaga, and then a connection that could take seven hours. As she waits for him to print out the timetable, she's startled by a sound like a whip being cracked. She turns to see the driver of the Seville bus pulling a glasses cleaning cloth through his fingers, extremely close to her head. He returns her gaze dismissively and starts talking with the man behind the counter. They share jokes she can't understand, and the man hands the driver a printed list of the passengers booked in for his journey. After that she can't seem to get any more information out of him. "What if I went via Seville?" "Lo mismo," he answers – the same – whilst waving her away. She steps from the counter feeling dazed. What just happened? A glance at the timetables shows her that it would be quicker to travel via Seville. And she hasn't even found out the price of the ticket. Could she go back? But the queue is still long, and she doesn't have it in her now to go through that again.

She hits the bathroom for a stand-up piss; it's the kind of place that smells like you don't want to touch anything, not even the tap. Then there's nothing to do but return to the apartment, which means getting lost in the city's skewed grid...

"¿Dónde está la calle Aurora?"

"¿Aurora? No sé..." an anoraked youth tells her. "Ask in the bar on the corner."

Bunty taps the address into Google Maps, but even that draws an error message. So she enquires with a taxi driver, who tells her "el GPS no funciona" around here. Has the place even been mapped? But he knows the way, at least.

Three flights up, she guzzles juice from the fridge and pushes off her trainers so her soles can drink the coolness of the floor tiles. Then she pores over timetables and tries once more to find travel information online. A site designed for American tourists throws up useful price info and confirms that it's quicker to go via Seville, but only just – and that it's much cheaper to travel direct, on one bus without changing. She looks at the length of the journey and shudders. But it has to be done...

It's Carlos's lunch break. He slopes in and gets on the sofa, leaning into it and looking sad. Bunty does her calculations in the blare of his daytime TV. The bus leaves at half nine at night, arrives at six in the morning. She'll have enough time to find the Embassy, be there in time for it to open, get everything sorted, and then get the next bus back, which leaves at 9 pm and arrives at half five the following morning. That's two nights on buses, but no accommodation costs, and only 37 euros for the round trip. If she eats home-made sandwiches and drinks only water, she can afford to do it.

She's going to have to go back to the station to buy the tickets, but not just now. She gets on the sofa with Carlos and drifts off to sleep in front of the TV.

Chapter 26 – Help Me Find My Way Back In

Bunty wakes up feeling like shit. She's evidently not built for siestas. Carlos has gone, back to school presumably. She downs a glass of water and assesses where she's at. To Madrid, tonight? Tomorrow night? And how will she manage afterwards, cos this trip's gonna eat up most of her remaining funds? She still technically has a job in Gibraltar, but probably can't cross the border now. Or can she? She decides to test her luck, to see if it can be done.

It's a twenty-minute trek to the frontier along the twisted grid, grimy with afternoon heat and exhaust fumes that linger in the grooves of the low-rise city. The final section, across lanes of lazy traffic, starts with a pedestrian crossing and ends with the ingoing traffic queue. She's looking left, looking right, and not falling over; all good so far. In the middle of the final lane a man tries to sell her a carpet, but she shakes her head and moves on. Some decisions are easy.

The only piece of ID she has left is her bank card. She clutches it, but it doesn't feel right in her hand. It looks nothing like a passport, for starters. She is hoping that slack security on the Spanish side can somehow be replicated in the Gibraltar corner too. Or maybe they will understand? There's no language barrier; well, not so much. They might even be able to verify her British citizenship. She has to believe in chances.

There's a guard stationed right outside the entrance of the Spanish passport control unit. Asif told her that the guard always sits behind a desk, inside, and reads the paper. Well, not today. She's in his sights. She walks quickly, past a man and a woman in their thirties lugging bulky suitcases. As she approaches, the guard calls out "Passport please." Knowing she can't satisfy the request, she steps back, letting the couple go first, so she can explain her situation. The man and woman stop, park their extensive luggage, take their passports out of shoulder bags and present them to the man, chatting with him as they do so; she hears the woman telling him that they're from England. That's when a group of Spaniards arrive, getting right behind the English couple and jumping what she'd thought of as a queue. The guard starts flirting with one of them, a girl in a bright pink vest. Laughing, he follows her through the building in order to continue the conversation. Bunty walks in beside them, unnoticed.

The office is bisected by a row of passport checking machines. They have the look of an obstacle about them. But one of the gates is open, the passport checking function switched off, and everyone's going in through that one. The guard bids "adios" to his friend as Bunty slips through the gate in front of her.

Get. In.

Emboldened by the luck that made the first stage so easy, she strolls into the second passport control office. But this one looks a lot more serious. It's old-fashioned in comparison to the first; no fancy equipment, just a guard sitting squarely behind a desk in the middle of the room. There are spaces on either side for people to pass by, but it's very clear, it's understood, that you don't try to run through the gap on the other side. You're to file by the side where he's enthroned, like a dignitary greeting a king. Two people are ahead, showing cards that prove their local status, and by the time she reaches the desk they've moved on. The guard's attention is focused solely on her. Her bank card feels sweaty in her hand, and while she doesn't exactly hold it aloft for inspection, he has clocked it, and is looking at her enquiringly.

He seems Spanish, she thinks, with a complexion that has looks like it has rarely been out of the sun. His roundish face is gentle, not a typically British one, but then neither is hers. She feels inclined to speak to him in Spanish, but that can't be right. Anyway, English is easier right now, and surely more appropriate.

"I've forgotten my passport."

"Then you can't go through."

"I have this..."

"I need to see your passport."

"It's just for a few hours. Could you give me some sort of document please?"

"What sort of document could I give you?" he asks gently, not quite approaching exasperation. The kindness she senses is real; he takes the time to explain what would happen next. "If you go through here without a passport, you will not be able to get out."

Bunty knows that on the other side, the exit route, there are only Spanish checks, so actually it's much easier to get out than it is to get in, but she figures that it would not be politic to argue that particular point with him. Instead, she gives up.

"How do I get back out?"

"The same way you came in."

She turns round and walks against the flow. But how can she get back through the Spanish office, having just sneaked in? She looks at the pavement that skirts the building. Rows of plastic barriers have been set into it, but they couldn't actually prevent anyone from passing; they're low enough to step over. She opts for this route for the sake of simplicity, all the while wondering at the ramifications of bypassing a border control in such an explicit fashion. Sure enough, the border guard is back in position by the entrance, and of course he's noticed her. He turns and watches her tiptoeing around the outside of his frontier office, picking her way through the barriers in her dusty trainers. She looks straight up at him, smiles, and walks right past him.

The guard stays in place. He does not say a word. His feet-wide-apart stance and mildly curious gaze turn out to be backed up by nothing. She wonders if he's scared of confrontation – in which case, this was a strange career choice – or maybe he just can't be bothered. Either way, she thanks the goddess for mild-mannered Mediterranean police.

But that's her job out of the window.

Chapter 27 – Roll Bus, Roll

By the time Bunty reaches the bus station her eyes are stinging, and she doesn't know why. But her sore peepers are relieved to see that the person on duty at the information desk is a woman – she hopes she won't get bullied this time. Her instinct proves right; no-one pings anything at her head, and soon she's out in the sunshine holding her prize, bus tickets to Madrid and back, plainly printed on white thermal paper.

She leaves tonight.

Short term goals always focus her. Six hours to get her shit sorted. Make a tonne of sandwiches... and is there anything else to do? She thinks through the week ahead. Thursday is referendum voting day in the UK. She really thought she'd be back there in time for that; instead she's on holiday in the scuzziest Spanish town imaginable.

She feels a wrenching unease, especially since Jo Cox's murder, about whether she can trust her fellow citizens to vote sensibly, but this fear has been masked by the personal traumas of the trip. Her dad, with his trade unionist background, impressed the importance of voting on her from an early age. "You don't want to let your Suffragette fore-mothers down, do ya?" She searches for Leeds City Council's site on her phone. Unlike the bureaucracies she's been tangling with recently, their system works with ease, and pretty soon her proxy vote has been set up. She texts Sofia.

Are you sure that's gonna be okay?

Of course Buns! It'll be a pleasure. Getting a bit scary here, so the more Remain votes the merrier. How's Gibraltar?

Umm, Spain actually now. It's hot, and poor.

Sounds like home, except for the hot bit. When are you back?

It's hard to say. Still on the trail of a passport. Going to Madrid tonight to the UK Embassy. They should sort it, right?

Fkn hope so! I miss you!

Me too! Big hugs from us! Enjoy Madrid!

Bunty ducks into a small supermarket, negotiates narrow aisles and picks up peanut butter and bread. This leaves her with a five euro note and some small change, which she tucks into a tiny pocket in her shorts. Back in the apartment she's relieved to see Inma, who has an hour spare before leaving for work. They make coffee.

"That's a long journey, Bunty."

"Yup, nine hours!"

Inma wrinkles her face. "I don't like to go."

"Don't worry about me." She looks at her friend's tear-stained face and asks gently, "How's your mother?"

"She is not good. I am scared." Inma begins to cry, and Bunty holds her. Her heart aches when Inma leaves for work. Then she brushes and mops the tiled floors and takes out rubbish and recycling. At least her friend won't have to do that in the morning. Then Carlos shows up. He's been in the hospital since school finished, and he's looking even sadder than Inma was earlier, if that's possible.

"Is she gonna die?" His long-held tears erupt.

Bunty reaches for him, but he's too proud to be held.

"I don't know, Carlos. I'm so sorry it's like this."

"What's gonna happen to me and Inma? Will they take me away?"

"You have all your aunts and uncles..."

"I don't wanna leave here! How can we pay for the apartment?"

"Well, Inma has a job..." She feels terrible, knowing what the wages are like, but has to stay optimistic for him. "You can get one when you're old enough."

"Can I? No-one else has one."

There's over fifty per cent youth unemployment here – but which half of the glass is he in? "You're smart. You can be one of the ones who gets a job. What do you wanna do?"

He shrugs, keeping his eyes on the floor.

"What do you like doing? What are you good at at school?"

"Art. I like painting."

Shit, an artist. She can't sell him a fairy tale; he'd be better off staying in education. "You gonna go to college?"

"I dunno, should I?"

"It's a good idea if you enjoy the subjects. You'll get paid more later."

"I go to college and where do I live?"

"Have you talked to Inma about this?"

Carlos looks stricken, and Bunty sees how much he's trying to protect his older sister.

"Umm, can I help you with anything tonight, before I go?"

"Go? Where?"

"I'm getting a bus tonight, to Madrid..."

"Madrid! I go with you!"

"I'm only going for one day. You have to be at school anyway."

"We go to Madrid when I am not in school?"

"We could try..." Bunty doesn't want to make promises. "I'm going to get my passport so I can go back home, so I'm not sure how long I'll be in Spain..."

"Don't!" He snaps, sulkily. "Stay with us! You and me and Inma can live here!"

Since when did we get so attached? "It's really nice of you guys to let me be here now, but you might be sick of me in a few days."

"No! Not sick!"

She needs to leave really soon.

"Listen, can you help me with something? Can you lend me a bag to take on the bus? I only have my suitcase and I don't want to take it..."

"Un momento." He gets up and goes to his bedroom, coming back with a large shoulder bag. "Like this?" He shows it proudly – the man of the house.

"That's perfect!"

He's pleased. Much better than hopeless, but how long will it last?

"I gotta go now," she tells him, as she darts around shoving things into the bag. "But when I'm back would you show me some of your paintings?"

"Sure. When you back?"

"Wednesday."

"Okay. I wait for you."

Bunty's choked up as she walks to the bus station. How can I, so messed up and broke, make things better for these two? She can't bear the thought of what they're going through, but has to focus on this journey; this bus is her only chance. She sprints the last few streets, gets to the station with seconds to spare and clambers on board, sweating, ticket held aloft.

As she sits down, the door creaks closed and the driver reverses out of the parking bay. The bus is almost empty and she has two seats to herself. She settles in by the window and pulls from Carlos's bag what she'll need for the night ahead: a book, a notebook, phone and earphones, sandwiches, water, chocolate. The sun's low in the west and the bus moves the opposite way, out of La Línea and along the coast. During the first forty minutes there's enough light for her to gaze down at the coastline and up at the silhouettes of mountains, but after that all she can see are the lights of petrol stations, bars and billboards. Still she stares, curious, while the question of how to help Carlos and Inma gnaws away at her. Their pain negates hers, and then her brain cuts off altogether, leaving only the words of a Jeffrey Lewis song to run around her head:

Roll bus, roll, take me off
A rolled sweatshirt makes the window soft
If I fall asleep, don't wake me up
Roll bus roll, take me up.

Chapter 28 – 6 am at Atocha Renfe

About twice every hour the bus pulls into a station. She wakes at each stop and peers through the window, trying to work out what's going on. People get off and on quietly, or usually so, except for the woman who boards at Marbella and talks loudly on her phone for an hour. Bunty turns to her iTunes. Lizzo's latest is too energetic for this hour, so she reverts to Elliott Smith's *Either/Or*, lulled by his sweet, unique chords and soft voice. The songs are sublime; she wonders at the way he transformed frustration, pain and sadness into such heart-rending art.

Around midnight they go into Malaga, but all she can really see is a baked potato seller in a tiny van dwarfed by swathes of desolate apartment buildings. She walks to the end of the bus, clutching at the backs of the chairs for balance, and looks down to where the toilet should be. Up at the front she asks the driver about it. "No hay," he replies. "There is no toilet. We stop in two hours."

That would have been good to know before I got on the freaking bus, she thinks. Okay, no drinks till 2 am. She crosses her legs and hopes for sleep.

There's something about buses that's so peaceful. It's taking you where you want to go, so you don't have to strive – just stay put, and you'll get there. The rhythmic growling of the engine pacifies her, emptying her mind. And somewhere in this placid daze a song appears in her mind. She sings it quietly to herself.

Like a lime (oh-oh)
Green (oh-oh)
Ford Cortina
Great escapin'
Barely scrapin' the ground
Takin' off like a rocket
Exiting the Rock, uh
Holding down
A job or something I gotta do
Before that gets removed too
No doubt
Takin' off like a rocket
I got nothin' in my pocket
Stripped down...

She texts Sofia – *Hey! I started a new song!* – and puts down the phone, not expecting a reply at this time, but it beeps straight back.

That's good. You're up late? Us too, in hospital.

Oh no! What's up?

Marie's ill.

Bunty's heart sinks. She quizzes Sofia for the details about the little one's health. They're waiting for test results, and could be there all night, so they keep each other company via SMS. When the bus does finally stop, Bunty staggers to the service station and dials Sofia's number.

"Can't talk now Buns, I'm in with the doctor."

She heard the fear in her friend's voice. She paces outside the building, barely aware of the night air flowing into her lungs, and waits as long as she can before texting back.

Gonna get my passport today Sof, and be with you as soon as I can.

It's just before six and still dark when the bus docks at Madrid's South Station. The roads are quiet as Bunty starts her walk. The Embassy's a bit more north of the centre of the capital than the bus station is south of it, and Google Maps says it'll take over two hours to get there, but their predictions are for dawdlers. She should be there well before the office opens at half eight.

The air is still cool as she paces the pavements under towering apartment blocks. Rows of parked cars line each street; the shops are closed, and the bars too now. She passes party-goers returning home and outpaces early risers heading into work. A grocery store shows signs of life, but she has nothing to spend. Then she reaches a train station.

Bunty has a thing about train stations. It's not just the architecture. Maybe it's the possibility they represent – all those places you could go, if you can only afford a ticket; they're straight up romantic.

She swerves into one of the entrances and does a double-take. It's a jungle! The concourse is full of plants: palm trees, cacti, flowering things growing right up to the vaulted ceiling, and the air's deliciously rich with plant-exhaled oxygen and loamy earth. She stares about her, and begins to explore.

This could be my favourite train station yet. I'm in love with Madrid already!

When the tropical paradise gives way to a Starbucks she reluctantly makes her way back outside, and continues on her journey along the edge of a large boulevard. As the sun rises she realises she's adjacent to some botanical gardens. Better to walk through it than around it – it shouldn't add too many minutes. She meanders around lush rose beds, spies a reddish-black squirrel in her path, and stares, fascinated by his tufty little ears.

Her phone buzzes with a text from Sofia: *Panic over! Marie much better. We're home now. Happy Summer Solstice!*

Oh thank fuck! So relieved!!! she types back. And looks up the sky. She hadn't known it was midsummer, but here it is, right here, right now, in the very centre of Spain. She returns to the street and walks with more purpose and energy, enjoying the soft light that's gently illuminating the grand old buildings lining the boulevard. The morning traffic is flowing, and more commuters join her on the wide pavement.

"Puta negra."

"What the...?" She stops and turns to focus on an old man who's just sauntered past, seemingly the one who shot the gravelly whispered insult into her ear. He's moving fast.

"Fuck you!" she yells after him.

A motorcyclist removing his helmet looks at her accusingly. She scowls. The old man has gone and she's left feeling helpless and shocked. There's no-one to address, no-one who wanted to be a witness. After that she keeps tabs on all the men that pass, staring them out before they can do anything. She feels tense and suddenly tired, the city's beautiful scenery now just a backdrop for her humiliation.

She spots another park and goes inside to take a rest. A wooden bench lies empty in the fresh sunlight; she puts her bag at one end and reclines, using it as a pillow. She doesn't want to squash her sandwiches, but daren't leave her bag exposed in a city like this. She shuts her eyes.

"Hey! Where are you from?"

A friendly-looking young lad is interrupting her nap. He's with two others; they're unnaturally energised for this time of day.

"What's it to you?"

She feels vulnerable lying down in front of him, so pulls herself up and looks him in the eye.

"I thought you looked interesting!"

Interesting my arse, she thinks, and reaches around for her bag. He seems to take the hint, to her relief. "Well, I will not disturb you!" He and his two friends move on, but so suddenly that it makes her uneasy. She checks her bag. The section where she kept her bank card is unzipped and empty.

Chapter 29 – Mad World

Bunty jumps up and runs in the direction they went, following them into the entrance of a Metro underground train station. She races down the steps into the atrium, reaches the turnstiles and looks all around. There are two ways to go from here – two staircases, two platforms. She vaults the turnstile, ignoring the shouts of the guy whose job it is to stop her doing that, and picks the closest set of stairs. Dodging commuters, she scurries down, hits the platform and scans for the thieves. They're not here, and there's a train pulled in on the other side. She watches helplessly as the three of them board it. The lead guy notices her, prods one of the others, who grins and waves, and the train pulls out. She could chase them, get the next train – but where are they gonna get off? Fuck.

She trudges up the stairs to face the security guard. He seems pissed off, but not as much as she is. "You cannot go in there without a ticket. I must call the police."

"If you would, please, that would be great. Some men robbed me – they got away on that train."

"It is not necessary if you leave now."

"But I need to speak to the police!"

"Then call them yourself." He walks back to his booth.

"Excuse me. Where is the nearest police station?" she asks in her most exasperated phrasebook Spanish.

"Calle de las Huertas. Not far." He shuts the door.

It's over to Google then. Dear Google, what do you do when you're in a foreign country with no passport and very little money and you can't go home and someone steals your bank card so you can't even get the money to get a new passport?

Instead, she types 'Calle de las Huertas, Madrid,' and it dutifully directs her to a street that's a couple of blocks away. At least it's not a big detour from her epic walk. She finds it easily – a bricky building with 'Comisaria de Policia' above the front door in yellow seventies-style block capitals. The windows have serious-looking bars on them; trouble with burglars, maybe?

The front door's shut. She consults the sign marked 'Horario' – they open at ten. That's in... just over an hour. Jesus, Mary and Joseph. She drops down onto the front step and curls up, arms on bent knees, head on arms, and weeps with exhaustion and rage.

When her sobs subside she can feel what it is that's underneath the fury. It's fear. So much bad stuff has happened, and is it going to keep happening like this? How will she get ID, how will she ever get home? She wants to call her parents, but she can't do it. They have their own stress, and no spare money anyway, and she can't bear the thought of them sitting there in Leeds worrying about her.

She thinks of all her friends, wondering who to ask. Not Sofia, Christ, she has enough on her plate. The rest of her mates are broke, and she isn't going to ask Katrina. Of her friends over here, Nancy's living in a fucking youth hostel and Inma and Carlos might be on the verge of destitution. We're all falling through the net together. Except Asif. He has a job, he might have spare cash. But she can't – it's anathema to her to rely on a man because...

Because she has feelings for him. Because she wants to start something. It's the first time she's allowed herself to think that. Yep, he matters to her, more than a friend, and she doesn't want to ruin it. And now this. Maybe she's going to have to ruin it. Hot tears of frustration land on her jeans.

There's a clinking noise, and she looks up to see that someone's dropped a euro coin by her feet. "No, I'm..." she calls to them, but he waves at her with a smile, and carries on.

I'm not homeless.

Shit, is that even true?

I have a place to stay, she wants to tell the kind man. Yes, I'm sleeping on buses for a couple of nights, but I do have a sofa to go back to, a few hundred miles from here.

And my stuff is packed up in boxes somewhere in Leeds...

She squeezes her knees. The front of her jeans are sticky with tears and snot. Maybe she is really, properly homeless. What a thing to realise, alone and broke in Madrid.

She breathes. It's okay. I'm alive. I've got friends. But I'm not gonna call Asif.

Shortly after ten the door behind her opens and a man appears; she gets up slowly up and turns to greet him. He has cropped dark brown hair and is wearing a short-sleeved police shirt.

"I want to report a crime."

He points to the front desk, and she waits there until the same man reappears on the other side a few minutes later. Then she tells him what happened, about the men in the park, and her bank card.

"Wait here," he says, gesturing to a row of plastic chairs by the wall. So she sits, and waits.

Fifteen minutes later an older cop appears and summons her into an office. He shuffles papers; she watches him from across the desk. He asks her name, which he carefully writes down. And her address – she gives him that of her parents – then starts to worry that a letter might go to them. Next, he asks to see her ID. This again. She explains everything, and that she's in Madrid to go to the Embassy. He stops writing.

"I cannot report the crime without identificación."

"But..."

"I am sorry. If you come back after you have been to the Embassy, with your new passport, you can report it then."

She can't even speak. She stumbles from the office and back into the street, tears clouding her vision. Go to the Embassy. And do what, with no bank card?

A voice in her head tells her that *this* is what embassies do – they help citizens who are in trouble in another country. So she must go there. She must keep going.

The walk is a struggle now. The shock and stress of the harassment and the robbery have sapped her energy, and she still has four miles left to go. Elegant buildings and vivacious streets don't charm her like she thought they might: instead she sees dirty gutters and slimy drains. And in place of excitement there's a brick-like weight in her stomach. She's losing her trust in life.

After two tough miles Bunty sees a group of despondent teenage boys on a street corner. They remind her of Carlos, and she thinks of him and Inma. How could I be so selfish? This is nothing like what they have to face. My troubles are temporary. Dismaying and annoying, yes, but they won't go on forever. I'll find my way out of this...

She starts to appreciate her surroundings anew. The late morning sun is shining on the leaves of little trees planted along the pavement, and a café at the corner of the block has tables with parasols arranged in a most tempting fashion, facing a plaza with a fountain. She feels the euro in her pocket, the one the man dropped on the ground for her. Maybe this is what it's for? She chooses a table, the waiter comes by and she orders café con leche, which she loads up with sugar. Sipping it brightens her mind, and it feels good to rest her feet; she needs to pace herself for the long walk back to the bus station later. For a few moments she feels like she could just be on holiday.

Madrid is a cake with so many different flavours: sweetness, light, grand architecture, municipal disinfectant, useless police, over-friendly robbers, abusive old men. And she's only spent a few hours in here; what else could it reveal?

The final stretch is easier. She passes through a newly-built sector in the north of the city and locates the street she needs to be on. It's much later than she intended – one o'clock – but she's here at last. Google guides her to the shiny-twisty skyscraper that apparently hosts the Embassy. In the entrance a security guard x-rays her sandwiches and insists on keeping her phone while she zooms up in a fast lift to the forty-first floor. There she waits on a sofa until her number is called, and goes to face a young woman behind a counter, her dark hair neatly shaped into a bob. Bunty pours out her story, relieved to finally be in a position to get some help. The woman passes her two forms and a sheet of instructions, and tells her where she can have some photos taken.

"I'll bring them straight back," Bunty promises. The woman nods neutrally, and presses the button to summon the next catastrophised Brit.

She's in the lift again before it hits her that without her bank card she can't pay for the photos, and that she should have addressed the matter of money, of having been robbed, while she was at the desk. Fuck! Where are my brains? Sweat sprouts from every pore, and a sudden ache in her gut makes her lean forward. With one hand on her hip she detects something lumpy, something that shouldn't be there. Woah!! It's the emergency fiver! She pulls out the scrunched up five euro note, kisses it, and hopes no-one is watching the lift on a CCTV somewhere.

Adrenaline propels her to the nearby train station where the woman told her she would find a photo booth. She reads the documentation while waiting for the strip of images to pop out of the side of machine. One is for reporting her passport lost or stolen. She's not sure about this – the woman in the office in Gibraltar said her situation didn't fit either of these; she'll check that with them when she goes back in. And the other – the prize – is for a temporary travel document, valid for one journey. This will get her home. The third sheet lists the documents she needs to provide in order to receive the temporary passport. It says she has to show some other ID, like her birth certificate – safely stored in box somewhere with the rest of her stuff in Leeds – or a driver's licence, which she never even applied for; who needs a car when you live in the inner city? It also mentions the fee, 112 euros, which, even if she had her bank card, she cannot produce. There's nothing like that hiding in the pockets of her shorts.

That's a whole lot of understanding they're going to have to do for her to get through this. She prays to the god of diplomatic missions that the staff are feeling very consulary – or even consolatory – this afternoon.

Chapter 30 – Four Photos and a Flying Lesson

Four images – two geeky-happy, two sad-eyed – fall into the slot. Her hair's certainly contributing to her new homeless image; she's surprised she didn't have more coins thrown at her while she was waiting for the pictures to develop. Still, it's only for a temporary passport; she won't have to show it to strange men in airport booths for the next decade.

She dashes the kilometre back to the Embassy, not wanting to lose a moment. Everything has to be sorted out today, and there's a lot to sort out.

Once back in the big shiny swirly building, Bunty marches to the security guard's station, offering her bag for another blast of radiation. He looks at her questioningly.

"I was here before, about my passport."

"Yes, I know – I remember. Did they not tell you to come back tomorrow?"

"They just said come back, with the photos and stuff. So here I am!" Stop playing games, big boy. That uniform must be going to your head.

"You will have to come back tomorrow, I'm afraid."

"Why, what's happened?"

"The office is closed."

He doesn't look like he's messing. He seems sorry, if anything; a tiny crease has formed between his big brown eyes.

"It can't be – I've come especially from La Línea. Has something happened?" A terrorist attack? That would explain all the security...

"Nothing happened, it's just routine. The office closes at thirteen thirty. You can come back tomorrow, at eight thirty."

"But it's open till five – I checked – here..." She clicks on her phone's browser, googles the opening times of the Embassy again, and waves the screen in his face.

"Yes, it's true, the Embassy is open until five in the afternoon."

Thank fuck. "So I can go up then?"

"No. You are going to the Consulate, not the Embassy."

"What?"

She feels faint.

"The Consulate deals with passports, and matters relating to British visitors to Spain."

"And the Embassy...?"

"Is for the ambassadors, for political matters."

"So the Consulate...?"

"Closes at thirteen thirty and opens at eight thirty in the morning."

The woman at the cruise company head office told her she would have to go to the Embassy. It had seemed so plausible.

"I'm not going to be here..." her voice is growing weaker. "I have to get the bus back to La Línea tonight."

"You can't stay tonight?"

"I have no money. All I have is a bus ticket to go back there."

He looks at her kindly. He's not just trying to get rid of her. "You know you could go to the consulate in Sevilla? Or Malaga, I think that is closer?"

She falls backwards slightly and meets the wall behind her. "What the... so I did all this for nothing?"

He is trying to make this okay for her. "At least you have visited Madrid, no?"

She can't even tell him.

Somehow, somewhere, she has to find it in herself to walk the six miles back to the bus Station. But she doesn't have it yet. The metal bench underneath her is stopping her from falling any further. That's something. If she can just stay here, then nothing else will happen. If she can somehow just stop, then nothing else will ever happen, ever. Loud traffic speeds by, and old ladies inch past her along the pavement. The posh ones always seem to have filthy looks on their faces, like they saved them for her especially. Maybe it's a Madrid thing, or maybe this is just me, now – homeless and gross, the one that everyone looks down at. Maybe I should invest in a paper cup and start working my way up to beggar status.

And what makes you above that?

Hmmm – what? Who are...?

Don't worry about that. Just tell me – what makes you the one that it shouldn't happen to?

Cos I'm scared!

And all the other people who are homeless and begging, how do they feel?

I can't think. It must be horrible.

Maybe they feel just like you, as they fly off the end of a helter-skelter of bunk beds and sofas and park benches and find themselves crawling on the floor, dirty and messed up and looking for a plastic cup...

Yeah, that's me, and that's them – but I'm new at it, so I'm more scared.

And you're more safe. You have a place to go.

I can't get back! I can't get home! You know that!

Not yet. But you have a place to go, still.

Yeah I have a place, but how long before Inma gets sick of me, or they lose their apartment and we're all out on the street?

You're a fully-fledged member of the precariat now. Are you up to it?

Why should I be? How can I be? Why should anyone be?

Because this is you now. I don't mean you forever from now on. I just mean now.

Okay, just for now...

There's something else.

What? I can't do anything else. No more nothing else.

It's a good thing.

Is it?

Yes – you'll like it, I promise.

Go on then?

Because you're free of the usual weight of the things that people call security, you have a superpower. You just have to let your mind become lighter; if it gets light enough, you can fly.

I can't fly, they won't let me.

They can't stop you.

For real?

Just try.

Bunty stands, and drops her bag behind her. A small leap, and it takes straight away – she's up. It's that easy – who knew? But can she stay up? She feels like she's going to drop back down, yet somehow, she's still afloat. Wow! Her hands are out in front of her head, Superman style, and she's moving forwards in the air.

Keeping going when you thought you would fall – maybe this is the superpower.

There's a tall fence ahead, it's higher than she is, but when she approaches it all she has to do is adjust her position slightly – and she's over! She experiments with the controls, the angles needed for ascension. But then she looks down and it's actually too much – dizzying, height-sickening – so she points her arms downwards, and sure enough, it works that way too. Up and down both function perfectly, as does side to side. She'll have the journey back to the bus station covered in no time. This is so awesome! But I've left my bag down there. Better go back and get it...

"Hello! Chica! Hola!"

Stop shouting.

"¿Qué pasa? ¿Chica? You okay?"

It's too loud.

"We're gonna need an ambulance 'ere, Jim."

A male voice joins in. "I'm on it. 'ang on. Sí, emergencia. Una chica en la calle... sí, ambulancia por favor..."

Two faces are peering down at her. Did she fall out of the sky? That could be quite dangerous.

"Am I hurt? Did I fall?" She sits up to examine herself, feeling for fractured limbs.

"You fell off the bench," the woman tells her, while the man continues on the phone. "You weren't respondin' for a while there."

"My legs are okay!"

"Well, you only fell a foot or so." Her expression changes to one of recognition. "I think we've met before!"

"In... Gibraltar?" Bunty feels really, really strange. "Stephanie?"

"Yeah! You'd just gorroff the boat!" The woman touches her arm excitedly. "What are you doin' 'ere?"

"British Embassy... I mean Consulate... trying to get a passport, but I can't, and I have to go back to La Línea now, and I thought I could fly there... well at least to the bus station..."

She looks up at the woman, confusion crumpling her face. "Why are you...?"

"I'm on me way home, we're goin' to the airport now. But fancy seein' you!"

"I don't think I need an ambulance, you know."

"Sit down and let me 'ave a look at you."

102

Bunty remembers that Stephanie's a nurse, so does as she's told, allowing her to take her pulse and look at her eyes.

"The only thing I can't check is your blood pressure, but you can gerrit done at a farmacia for a couple of euros. Will you do that for me?"

"Uh-uh." Bunty nods.

"Drink some o' this."

Bunty accepts the plastic water bottle and takes a few mouths full, even though she has some of her own. It feels too complicated to explain that.

"Are you eatin'?"

"Yes, but just peanut butter sandwiches for two days."

"You can live on those. Stand up."

Standing proves to be no problem, and Bunty's pleased to find that she feels entirely stable.

"I think you can cancel that ambulance, Jim," she tells her friend. He gets back on the phone. "But we 'ave to get goin'. 'ang on."

Stephanie goes to the kerb and within a few seconds has flagged down a cab. She asks the price to the airport, and then calls Bunty over.

"Listen love. Where're you trynna get to now?"

"Estación Sur. The south bus station."

The woman turns back to the driver. "And what if you carry on there afterwards to drop off me friend?"

"Quinze," he tells her. Fifteen.

"Right." She summons Jim, and picks up Bunty's bag. "You're comin' with us."

"What? But I don't have any..."

"I know you don't, come on, get in. I 'ave to use of the rest of me 'oliday money somehow." She grins, and once again Bunty follows the nurse's orders.

Jim gets in the front so Bunty and Stephanie can share the back seat. "We've got twenty minutes. Come on, spill. What's 'appened to you these last three weeks?"

"Has it only been three weeks? It seems longer..."

"Almost! So you'd just got off that cruise ship in Gib..."

Stephanie teases the story out of her. Bunty didn't even know everything that had happened until she finds herself saying it out loud. She shudders when she recalls Pandorina's drunken antics.

"You poor love! How're you gonna get 'ome?"

"That's what I thought the Embassy was for! I'm running out of ideas now."

"Well like 'e said, there's always the one at Malaga you could go to."

"I don't know if I can do it all again."

"I know. Listen, give us your phone number, and your email. I'm gonna do some research when I get 'ome."

Bunty wonders what kind of research she means, but the taxi has stopped outside a sign that says 'Salidas'. They're at the airport.

Stephanie takes her purse and pays the driver whilst ordering that he "Take me friend to the bus station now por favor luv," in her warm but forceful manner.

"Oh, and that's the rest of me euros. Spend 'em for us, will yer?" Stephanie winks.

Before she has time to object, the car door has closed and Stephanie is chasing after Jim, who has both their suitcases and is deftly negotiating the crowds. Bunty looks down at three twenty euro notes on the vinyl next to her. The taxi pulls away, and she turns in time to glimpse Stephanie's flowery hat disappear into the departure hall.

Chapter 31 – Australian in Europe

When he drops her at the south station she has four hours to spare. Typical Bunty modus operandi would have her disappearing off for another quick adventure before departure time, but this particular teatime is different. She feels blessed.

Bunty focusses on this new art – of finding things to do near a bus station without getting distracted and missing the bus and getting stranded in Madrid. Is this what being an adult is like? She knows enough psychology to understand that the brain isn't fully formed until the mid-twenties, and she's not quite there yet. Knowing this fact seems to mitigate some of the anxiety that comes from being ever-changing and a little bit daft. So she makes a plan to chill in the station café, and to take walks of no more than two blocks away. Short leash time.

Estación Sur is adjacent to a shopping complex which holds no interest for her; she needs to keep those sixty euros for something special, like survival, and/or escape. She crosses the road, stands at the corner, and notices a white dome in the distance. It magnetises her; that's where she's going.

The first block takes her past cafés and offices, and the next is laden with apartment blocks and trees rooted in the dusty golden earth. So much for the two-block rule – the third is much more interesting, and it isn't a block at all, so maybe it doesn't count. It's a massive futuristic-style expanse – a space park!

The white-domed structure turns out to be a planetarium. This would be such an excellent place to spend her extra hours. But, damn, it's stone cold closed. She shrugs and wanders back along another path. Her head feels itchy, and she wishes she could take a shower. This stone fountain looks really tempting. I could dry my hair in the sun... But maybe the water is yuck...

Bunty scoops some up and examines it. It seems alright. She peels off her Converse and steps in, gasping as each wave of cold kisses the nerves in her aching feet. As her temperature eases, she thinks some more about The Stephanie Miracle. Without her she could have ended up in hospital or something, or trying to walk back – and just as broke as she was.

She looks up, then steps back in shock, almost slipping on the algae-coated slabs underfoot. There's a face, not far from hers, smiling right at her. It's bordered by hair that radiates like sunrays – dazzling, dreadlocks.

"What the...? Erm, hola?"

"Hello there. I hope I didn't disturb you,"

"Well..." She looks down at her feet in the water.

"I've got too many apples. Do you want one?"

She blinks at him. The sunlike man passes her a huge red apple, and she takes it, and takes a bite. It's crunchy and sweet, so she decides to forgive his rude interruption.

"What time is it?" Bunty asks between mouthfuls. "I have to catch a bus."

"Me too. Hmm let's see..." The man stares up at the sky. "It sets at 9.30-ish and it's over there now so, I dunno, eight maybe?"

Bunty looks up uncertainly.

"How long have you been on the road?" he asks her.

"It depends what you mean by road. Two days, or three weeks, if you count the sea as road. And Gibraltar."

He nods.

"You?"

"Fifteen years."

Oh. "Travelling all the time?"

"Yep. I'm writing a book about how to live without money, or without working anyway."

"Amaze! What's the secret?"

"For me? I write poems, and make them into little books, and sell them. This one's for donations, if you're interested."

Bunty thinks of Carlos, the artist, and wonders whether this could be a viable model for making a living. She doubts it.

"I don't have any spare money... I can offer you a peanut butter sandwich though?"

"Done!"

In order to do the swap Bunty has to climb out of the water and reach into her bag. Her feet sizzle on the concrete. She sits on the edge of the fountain and pulls out two sandwiches, passes one to the poet and starts to eat hers as she flicks though the book he hands her in return. It's tiny, barely bigger than an outsize postage stamp, though somewhat thicker. She reads the front cover.

"You're Abbo Reginald? Good name."

"Pleased to meet you. And you are?"

"Bunty."

"Touché!" He grins. "So, Bunty, which direction are you heading this evening?"

"Due south, to La Línea. It's gonna take all night."

"Ooh, where's that?

"On the coast – it's the last Spanish city before Gibraltar."

"What's it like?"

"La Línea? High unemployment, lots of pollution, everyone seems to be getting sick..."

"Great! Can I come?"

"I don't see why not. There was plenty of room on the bus last night anyway. But I thought you already have a bus to catch?"

"I do. I just didn't know which one yet." He leans back on the wall and gazes at the descending sun, chewing his sandwich. They're silent until it slips out of view, and that's when Bunty checks the time on her phone.

"Shit, I've got to go – the bus leaves in ten minutes!"

She pulls her shoes back on and laces them roughly, then yanks her bag from the ground. Together they run across the park and the three blocks back to the station. Once inside they dodge other the travellers in the shiny-floored ticket hall and pound down the stairs to where buses are lined up ready to go. Her heart racing, Bunty speeds along the central platform, not stopping to check the board, just panic-scanning the fronts of every bus parked there. She doesn't see one for La Línea. Shit. Is she stranded in Madrid after all?

The last bus in the line is pulling out. She rushes over to check its destination. 'Algeciras' is printed on the sheet of paper that's stuck to the inside of the windscreen. Forgetting to speak Spanish, she yells "Wait! Please!" whilst waving dementedly at the driver.

The driver shakes his head.

And the bus stops. Bunty runs at the doors. They hiss apart.

Her eyes, just then blazing with panic, are now ready to cry with relief. She could kiss the driver. Instead she pants "Gracias!" and "Muchas gracias!" at him while she clambers up the steps and digs in her bag for the ticket.

The driver isn't happy. He's telling her off in Spanish, and he has a lot to say, something about how normalmente, no, he doesn't stop and you have to be there before the time the bus is due to depart, and a bunch of other things she doesn't understand. This all seems perfectly reasonable to Bunty, and she tells him "lo siento," – I feel it, I'm sorry – but it doesn't stop his monologue. She moves up the aisle so Abbo can get on. He presents his travel pass to the driver, which pushes him from mere simmering rage to fury. "Madre de Dios!" he shouts. Bunty's glad she's no longer the target of his ire. Abbo and the bus driver argue for a few moments, then the driver seems to give up, and Abbo makes his way along the aisle after her. They go as far from the driver as they can, to the back seat.

"What was the problem?" she asks, still catching her breath.

"I've got a Euro pass but I'm supposed to make a reservation. What a good guy – I'll offer him a book when he's calmed down."

The bus leaves the station, taking a left turn away the centre of Madrid and another towards the east, where they catch the motorway to the south. Bunty and Abbo turn to watch the red glow of the setting sun through the back window.

What a fucking day.

Bunty takes off her shoes, puts her legs up on the seat and leans against the window. Abbo stretches out diagonally, his feet in the aisle. She reads poems until she falls asleep, but once they hit the coast every stop jolts her back into consciousness, and in the end she gives up trying. Abbo snores throughout most of the journey; after so many years on the road this must feel like home.

It's still dark when she makes out the Bay of Gibraltar, or is it the Bay of Algeciras? "Depends where you're standing," murmurs Abbo, as if he could read her thoughts. They move past shabby apartment blocks into the semi-circular bus station where everyone has to abruptly remember how to use their legs. A groaning Abbo follows her down the steps onto the pavement where they start to breathe real air, sharp and thinner than the air-conditioned stuff they've been running on.

"Woah!"

He's pointing south, his mouth agape.

"What's *that?*"

"Oh, that little thing?" Bunty yawns. "The Rock of Gibraltar. It watches over us all. So what are you gonna do now?"

"Imma explore!" he grins. "Maybe walk up that thing before it gets too hot."

"You got your passport, right? You'll have to cross a hard border to get there."

"I couldn't have got far without one. Unlike yourself, you international woman of mystery."

"International woman of stupidness, more like," she sighs. They swap numbers and promise to hang out, then Bunty makes her way home along dark streets, treading past closed up shops and tiny old houses, breathing the characteristic smell of malfunctioning drains. It's quiet enough that she can walk in the road, easier than on the tiny pavements where she can barely fit both feet at once. She feels relief when she reaches a road that has working streetlights *and* an open café; she's missing Madrid already. But most of all she's missing sleep. Straight to sofa, or shower first? She debates the merits of each as she rounds the corner to Calle Aurora. Key in the big wooden front door, up the staircase with the tiles hanging off it, one floor, two, and the third takes her to Inma's. She pushes the door open and creeps into the living room, ready to crash. But there's someone there.

Chapter 32 – Home Is Where

"Carlos?"

He looks up from his computer game, startled. "¡Vaya! You are back!"

"Yes I am. Have you been up all night?"

"Yeah yeah. But who's gonna stop me?"

"Erm, me?" Dawn is breaking outside the window; this kid really should be in bed.

"Go on then."

Carlos raises his hands in surrender. Bunty takes the controls from him and guides him up by the shoulders. Of his own volition he shuffles along the corridor to his room, and Bunty hears him close the door. Jeez, how often does this happen?

She gets on the sofa, her feet warmed by the patch where Carlos has been slumped all night. Finally she's on a bus that's keeping still...

When Inma gets up two small hours later Bunty shifts herself and waves, avoiding contact so that her friend doesn't have to smell her – and goes for that long-awaited shower. The hot water makes her feel alive, as though the grime on her body had somehow been cushioning her from full consciousness.

She walks out wrapped in a towel, looking forward to catching up with Inma, but finds a note in the kitchen: "Gone to see mother. You sleep in my room." Bunty munches a biscuit, pours a glass of juice, and considers the matter. A little lie down won't do any harm. She takes her drink and a book into Inma's room and nestles on the sweet-smelling bed. Her eyelids drop before she's read a page.

"I AM IRON MAN!"

WTF? She opens her door to see Carlos stomping around the living room, roaring along to the Black Sabbath track he's playing on YouTube. She shakes her head and checks her phone. It's 2pm – a perfectly respectable time for a person to rock out.

"Not been to school?"

He looks contrite. "No. Don't say to my sister?"

"Okay, not this time. But I don't know when she'll be back from the hospital..."

"She say me it will be more late today."

Bunty makes coffee and they swap YouTube favourites. She wonders if she should be showing him something more educational than cats jumping off cupboards, but decides that what this vulnerable kid needs now, more than anything, is friendship.

Her phone announces an email from Stephanie:

Hola chica!

Me and Jim got back safely to London, you'll be glad to hear, but sadly the weather's completely crap compared to Spain and Gib. I hope you got your bus, and that you're feeling more yourself, and eating something other than peanut butter!

Listen, I need you to write a letter for me. Just copy out what I am going to write next, and sign it, and scan it and send it back to me. I think it's obvious why :-)

Bunty reads the rest of the message, and cries.

"¿Qué pasa Bunty? What's wrong?"

"Nothing, Carlos. I'm happy. I think I'll be going home soon!" She smiles up at him, wiping the tears from her cheeks.

"This is your home now! With me and Inma!"

"Just for a while, Carlos"

"Then we go with you to England!"

"Well, you can come and see me." She's not sure what to say; maybe it's best to focus on the now. "Let's make the most of this time together while I'm here."

She squeezes his hand, and he nods, sadly.

They hang out a lot over the next two days while Inma visits her mum and goes to work, and Bunty keeps an eye on him to make sure he goes to bed and then to school the next day. She takes over cooking duties, though her taste turns out to be too spicy for them and she has to promise to tone it down. What's this like? she asks herself. Some kind of normality, even if it's just for a short while...

Abbo calls the day after their coach journey, and they go for a walk in the afternoon. He's found a really cheap hotel.

"14 euros a night, it's less than most hostels, and you get a room to yourself with a wash basin in it. It smells a bit weird... but then so do I!" He passes her a can of San Miguel from his shoulder bag.

Sounds like heaven, Bunty thinks, cracking the can open and sipping the lukewarm brew. A room. The stuff you can do if you have a passport! But it won't be long for me now, she reminds herself. And in accordance with her agreement with Carlos, now is the time to simply enjoy being here.

"This is the Australian dream," Abbo tells her. "Travelling in Spain, drinking beer in the sun!"

Yeah, what are you moaning about, Bunty Maguire? She high fives Abbo, and they step over the wall onto the beach.

Chapter 33 – San Juan Ain't No Pagan

Bunty and Abbo lie in the dirty sand and listen to Sky Larkin (her choice) through the speakers he carries in his backpack. The sun disappears behind them, cooling the long day into darkness as crowds gather on the sand.

"What time does it start?"

"Midnight, I think. Inma should be here soon, so she can tell us what the fuck's going on."

"Pagan festival, by the looks of it. A couple of days past the solstice."

"Apparently the church moved it from the 21st to make it less heathen."

Abbo laughs and looks around at the unlit bonfires. "I'm not sure they succeeded! Is your other friend coming out, Asif is it?"

"I don't think so. I usually see him at weekends."

"You didn't ask him?"

"I didn't want to pester him."

Abbo looks at her strangely. "Because?"

"Umm, it's hard to say," Bunty mutters evasively. "I've been meaning to ask you more about your name –"

"And so the subject is changed!" Abbo winks at her. "Well, the one they gave me means 'the father of all nations,' which is awkward cos I despise nationalism, so I changed it a bit."

"And here you are being sheltered by a stolen rock..."

"It's all stolen, if you go back far enough. Not many native people still have their land."

"I think you'd hate what's going on in the UK right now. They're having a referendum on whether to leave Europe. Shit, that's today, the vote..."

"Like Greece, right?"

"Yeah, but this happened cos of a stupid far-right party that isn't even in power, and then the right-wing government promised to call a referendum to appease the people who *might* vote for the far-right party. It's been really horrible watching it all, it's such a pantomime..."

"Putting the 'dumb' into 'referendum'..."

"Exactly."

"Britain has a great history of isolationism, and of course colonialism, so I can't say I'm too surprised." Abbo sucks on his roll-up and puffs smoke into the air.

"You know what it's like. There's the usual, umm, everyday racism, but it's all gone up a few notches. An MP was assassinated in the street last week cos she was doing anti-racism work."

"Jeez." Abbo sighs. "So how's this vote gonna go?"

"I've been really worried about it, but the betting shop odds are all in favour of a Remain result. Apparently that's the best indicator you can get..."

"Yep, where the money is." He stubs out his roll-up on a rock. "When will you know?"

"Sometime in the early morning I guess." And then it hits her. By the time they light the fire at midnight the result might be out. The thought chokes her up.

The beach is getting increasingly crowded and Bunty doesn't look round when she hears the sound of feet slapping on the sand behind her. Something heavy lands on top of her, throwing its arms round her shoulders, and a baseball cap lands by her feet.

"Carlos! Oi!" Bunty pushes herself up from the sand and gives him a playful punch, then kisses his big sister who was striding up behind him. Inma has a carrier bag with beers in it, and starts sharing them out.

"Inma, this is Abbo. I've told him you can explain this tradition to us."

"La Noche de San Juan? It is like the New Year for us. To say goodbye of all the bad things we don't like, and to ask for the good things we want to happen."

"You have to burn the bad things in the fire!" Carlos explains excitedly. "And write a list of the good things." He fishes something out of Inma's carrier bag. "We have paper..."

"What are you going to get rid of?"

"Cancer!" he yells, "And chemistry at school."

Inma squeezes him around the shoulders. "And of course we want our mother to come home."

Bunty smiles at her gently, and they share out the paper so they can each make their own lists. She stares down at hers.

Goodbye to -
Racist sexist homophobic fuckwits
Capitalism and poverty
Hello to -
~~*Going home*~~ *Making things better here for Inma and Carlos*
Hanging out more with Asif???

Yeah, why *didn't* she ask him tonight?

Abbo tries to get a look at her list but she pulls it away, laughing, and grabs at his. He's writing a poem.

San Juan, you gotta burn it up
Fuck the pollution, you're gonna church it up
In the sky in the beach in the night
We put our secrets in your flamey sight
Are you angel or devil?
And what did Bugs Bunny ever do to anyone anyway?

She passes it to Inma with a grin.

"Maybe you can answer the question?" Abbo suggests.

Inma looks at their curious faces. "About Bugs Bunny?"

"Yeah – it seems really weird to me, cos in the UK people burn an effigy of Guy Fawkes. He tried to blow up parliament in like the 17th century..."

"Wasn't he a really cool anarchist dude?" asks Abbo.

"Umm, people think that, but actually he was part of a Catholic plot to get rid of a Protestant king." All those hours on Wikipedia have paid off after all.

"Bummer!" Abbo looks highly disappointed at this.

"And the basic conservatism of British culture means everyone just goes on burning him year after year without knowing anything about it. That's why we thought there might be some deeper meaning behind the cartoon characters?"

"No." Inma shakes her head blankly.

Bunty and Abbo crack up laughing.

There are competing sound systems blasting out tacky Spanish pop, so they decide to find a quieter spot where they can please their own musical sensibilities.

"Is reggae okay?" Bunty checks, gets a consensus, and sticks on some Prince Far-I. Abbo starts off the dancing, while Bunty unlaces her trainers and enjoys the feel of soft sand under her toes. Carlos sways, embarrassed at first, but the beer soon relaxes him. Together they dance off the cares of the old season.

It looks as though all the families in the area are here, and in the cooling evening the crowds thicken around the pyres. When firefighters light them at midnight, Bunty's glad of the heat.

"We burn our wishes!" Carlos grabs Bunty and Abbo, and pulls them towards the closest bonfire. The dry wood's going up fast as they run to throw their lists into the crackling blaze of old furniture and bits of trees, then jumping back to protect their skin from the scald of flames. Their upturned faces reflect flickering orange as they witness Bugs Bunny turn to dripping plastic goo, his solvent-based soul hissing and merging with the night sky.

Bunty checks up and down the beach. Some have started smaller fires where they're cooking meat and fish, and there are others that kids are jumping over. "They do it three times," Inma explains, "for good luck."

"The firefighters don't look so sure," Bunty observes. They're standing by watchfully, in case the good luck jumpers aren't so lucky after all.

Inma laughs and leads them to the edge of the sea.

"And now we swim!"

She runs into the water with Carlos in tow. Bunty and Abbo watch the pair splash one another and scream in the shallows.

"Is the water warm enough for that?" Bunty asks Abbo.

"Depends how brave you are. But I don't think anyone's gonna appreciate the fact that I don't wear underwear..."

Bunty splutters her beer and they opt to be spectators for this particular tradition. Inma comes back and gets something out of her bag – an empty bottle – and returns to the water to fill it.

"This is our San Juan water. I will take it to my mother," she explains when she returns. "Now we must go home. Carlos goes to school tomorrow," she sighs. "Normally my mother takes him home and I stay out for the parties."

"Want me to take him? You can stay out," Bunty offers.

"No, is best we go. I visit her in the morning also."

Bunty hugs them both good night, and turns to Abbo.

His face is one huge grin. "Did someone mention parties?"

Chapter 34 – 17,410,742 Go Mad on Brexit Island

The crowds have dispersed and Abbo has lost consciousness; he's snoring blissfully on the sand. Bunty leaves him there and walks back through town to the apartment. The streets are less scary tonight – in fact they feel positively friendly, with drunk San Juan partiers greeting her gleefully in the street.

Compulsively now, she refreshes the news on her phone. It should all be fine – the British public are not really so crazy as to want to leave a situation that gives them so many legal protections, that guarantees peace between member states, allows them to work or retire in amazing countries, and get health care, benefits and pensions while they're at it. Of course they've been baited for months by the deranged denizens of the right-wing press, downgrading refugees to 'migrants' and demonising both groups against all evidence to the contrary. She scrolls down the page, consumed by uncertainty. It can't be a Leave result. But what if...? It's too close for comfort.

Up in the flat she wakes, feverish despite a cool breeze flowing in through the living room windows. She rolls over and checks the news again.

The incoming results for each city and region are represented by an infographic that, as the hours pass, only exacerbates her anxiety. There are two bars of colour, starting on opposite sides of the screen. Remain results are blue, Leave is yellow, and impossibly, horribly, the yellow strip is growing longer than the blue one.

I don't know a single person who thought it was a good idea to vote to Leave, but I don't know anyone who reads those papers either. She flips onto her side and gazes at the looming silhouette of the Rock, imagining it breaking away from Spain, from Europe, and floating out to sea. Raising her phone to her face once more, she stares in horror at the yellow bar nudging the centre of the screen as city after city falls to the Leave. Is she witnessing the start of the disintegration of Europe, the end of peace and prosperity? When Leeds' little sister city, home to many Pakistani communities, votes to leave the European Union, she feels like she's going crazy.

Bradford, what the fuck?

Leeds votes Remain, by a tiny majority, and she cries with gratitude. There's still hope – it could still work out. She slips back into an uneasy sleep, but wakes to feel cold sweat pouring from her neck and chest. And that's when she sees that the line has been crossed.

Bunty leans forward, puts her forehead in her hands, and sobs.

She can't get up off the floor.

Her hair's on the tiles. Normally she'd care, but not now. She feels sick, and rolls onto her side. Visions of her country celebrating xenophobia crowd her mind.

It's not been easy, the past few hundred years, for her family. On either side.

It's not going to be easy, now, for anyone...

She stares at a message on her phone. "Bunty, when are you home from your trip? Did you hear about Brexit? Gutted. Call us. Mum xx."

She lies and listens to the walls closing in. Stone and metalwork scrape the ground, a horrific noise, like on that very early Scritti Politti track, you could barely call it a song; it's fragmented and stuttery, with a vocal like a child locked under the stairs trying to learn to speak in a state of trauma. A discovery from her dad's record collection, it scared and intrigued her as a child. Now the walls are closing on a nation, shuttering it in shadowy ignorance and suspicion, a return to an idealised past of physical and psychological limitation – dullness – a darkness of whiteness.

Her heart bears the weight of a broken society, and it breaks, cos she knows what it's all about. The savage instincts of Anglo Saxons, a race so idiotic they preferred to live in mud than use the buildings left them by Romans...

The grief hits her in waves. There must be times when she sleeps, cos there are moments when she wakes, and everything feels okay for a moment or two. But then she realises she is on the floor because – because of –

Inmaculada's standing over her. "Bunty, you are sick?"

"Inma, no, I just had some very bad news."

"I heard about it, about Brexit..." She kneels down and takes Bunty's hands, as Bunty pulls herself up to sitting. "Your friend is here..."

Hovering by the door is a dishevelled-looking man with very sad eyes.

"Asif!"

He falls to his knees and crashes into her. He's shaking. She holds him, leaking tears and mucus onto his hoodie. They press their crushed hearts together.

Inma folds her legs onto the floor beside them. "What will it mean, for you two?"

Bunty looks up at her. "I'm scared."

Asif is rubbing his hands over his face. "The racism..."

"The everything," Bunty sniffs. "The Islamophobia. The whatever this is going to do to culture, the economy, to everyone's freedom..."

"To everyone..."

"I kind of see people trapped there – me trapped there..." Bunty shudders.

Asif looks at her. "You won't be, but it will make everything harder."

"It makes me scared to go back, cos of that feeling... and last week..." She can't bring herself to talk about Jo Cox's murder, not right now. "It's just, the stupid idiots who called this, who thought it would be a good idea, they're on the ascent now. And what's going to happen to the rest of Europe?"

Inma leans towards them. "I think it doesn't have to happen..."

"No, the result isn't binding..." Bunty gazes at her, feeling some hope. "So maybe it won't."

Asif forces a smile. "My fear is that the UK will end up looking like a parody of itself – like Gibraltar, but with infinitely more poverty and hate..."

"And a lot less sunshine," adds Bunty. "I can't help thinking about the ignorance of most of the people who chose this, and how it will tear everyone apart, and how many couples could be broken up..."

Inma holds them both, as Bunty and Asif cry for the way of life they might soon lose.

Chapter 35 – Viva la Eutopia

"I've thought of something that will cheer us up."

Bunty groans. "There isn't anything."

Asif seems confident despite her anti-positivity shield. "Let me pick you up – are you at Inma's?"

"I am."

"Okay, wait there!"

Blue skies belie the devastation rumbling in her heart. How could those stupid little islands cut themselves off from all this? She looks at the Rock, and the sea beyond. What grief they must be feeling in Gibraltar now, too. Their whole operation could collapse, while the Spanish government bays to take back what they lost so long ago. She drops onto the sofa, emotionally drained, and contemplates once more what her host family are going through. Sadness emanates from everywhere.

The intercom buzzes. "Taxi for Bunty Maguire!"

She picks up her keys and zombies down the stairs. Asif's on the other side of the front door, beaming.

"What's going on, Asif?"

"Well, I know you like surprises..." He glances towards his car, parked illegally in front of the apartment.

"But I'm a mess, I haven't eaten..."

"We can't sort out the UK's problems, but that is a thing we can definitely fix."

He has a gleam in his eye, and Bunty decides to go with it, whatever it is. She gets in the car. They pull out of Inmaculada's street and sail by the mile-long stretch of beach on the east side of the city. The road's lined with fast food outlets and apartment blocks in flaking red and yellow paint.

"We could eat here – look – Jesús Hamburguesería!"

"We could. I have this vegetarian place in mind though. It's not close by – are you up for a long drive, in general? I've got snacks if you want something now..." He rummages with one hand behind his seat and pulls forward a carrier bag containing crisps, fruit and other offerings.

"In general, that sounds like a great idea." Bunty looks through the bag and selects an iced doughnut.

"DJ for us?"

"Mm hm."

With sticky hands she scrolls through her iTunes, cueing up tracks to help them process or forget their pain.

She hits play on Fugazi's 'Exit Only.' Guitars buzz and splinter from the speakers, and the singer spits up a suitably gruff refrain.

"It's sounds like he's singing 'Exeter'."

"You have to imagine he's singing 'Brexit-uh'."

"Ahaha, that works!" exclaims Asif, as he guides the car along a road that cuts between moors of sandy rock and scrubland. They're passing towns of various types: coastal ones built for tourism and northern European migrants, and real Spanish pueblos with whitewashed houses. Bunty gazes at the strips of white or adobe apartment blocks glowing under the brilliant azure sky, and tries to screen out the architecture to focus on the beauty that lies beyond.

And she has to keep her eye on the tunes. Her next selection is 'Cold as Ice' by Foreigner. Staccato piano and staid drumming open a strangely familiar song of alienation about someone who won't take advice, and is willing to sacrifice their love.

"What the...?"

"Give it a chance. You're gonna have to forgive the guitar solos."

"Oh wow, this is perfect. How do you know stuff like this?" Asif turns to look at her. "You're not old enough!"

"I listen to everything. My mum and dad both have massive record collections so that's what I used to play with as a kid. Right," – she scrolls and hits enter once more – "this one is tailor-made..."

It's Billy Bragg's 'Take Down the Union Jack.' They listen in silence, gazing into the distance as the road once more hugs the Mediterranean coast.

Bunty's eyes follow the shape of Andalusia's bays and headlands and she marvels at the way the mountains change colour as they approach. She still feels like she wants to kiss Asif, but she's not sure what this is, and it would be weird to start something when she's about to leave. Holiday romances are bollocks; if anything she wants a real friendship with him. She looks at his face; he seems happy to be here with her, but maybe he's just a happy person? And if he liked her, wouldn't he have done something by now? She promises herself that she'll keep it in her pants.

"No way!"

"Wha'?" Did she say some of that out loud?

"Parking space! Right outside!"

They're in a built-up place, a town or city on the coast, and now she can go outside and see some more of it. They're still surrounded by bland contemporary architecture, but Asif's very excited about something.

"You're gonna love this place!"

It's a vegetarian café. "You don't have many of these around, then? I guess I didn't see any in La Línea... or Gibraltar..."

"There are seriously fuck all. The Andalusians don't really have the concept of vegetarianism. They'll swear blind it's veggie even when there are pork sausages sticking out of it, or it's completely covered in fish."

"I get the feeling tuna's considered a vegetable round here."

"Then you know what I'm talking about."

They choose a table on the pavement outside, and a Spanish lad brings them all the delicacies they could possibly desire. The table fills up with juices and smoothies, salads, stuffed aubergines and coffees.

"This place is heaven!" Bunty tries to say, with her face full of falafel. "I feel like a new human!"

"I know, it's like some kind of spa, but with food instead of massages."

They relax into a state of food-induced bliss.

"You still haven't told me where we're going…"

"Umm, all I can say right now is that it's a long way, but I think you're gonna dig it."

"You're kidnapping me!" Bunty laughs.

It turns out Asif really meant it about the long way thing – two hours later they're still on the road. Bunty's witnessing great swathes of the Andalusian countryside and she's loving it. Huge mountains and small pointy hills, olive groves, olive groves on pointy hills, tiny villages dominated by old churches, and hills with castles on them.

"I actually don't care where we're going, this trip is ace!"

They pass a sign that gives the name of the pueblo. Marinaleda. It looks like a regular village, stretched out along a road. Rows of white houses, and houses-in-progress, ride up from the main carriageway, and there's a large municipal park. Asif pulls the car up by a graffiti'd wall.

"Is this… are we here?"

Asif's grinning, which she takes as a yes.

She gets out and recovers the use of her legs, stamping around on the road and the pavement while Asif stretches, then stands looking a wall.

"We've come all this way to see a wall?"

Bunty joins him in front of it. From what she can tell the graffiti seems to favour socialism, though the circled A's clearly refer to anarchism. "Well, it is a much higher standard of wall-writing than around where we live…"

"Oh yeah – did you see that one in San Roque? 'Rajoy sí'?"

They shake their heads at the notion that someone would go to the edge of town at night with spray paint in order to confirm their approval of Spain's long-standing conservative leader.

"Okay, but…?"

"Wait!" He grabs her by the hand and starts running down the street. "Check this out – excellent village park!" he points to the left. "Massive swimming pool!" To the right. "Loads of houses." He waves his hands in the air in general.

"Erm – still not getting it?"

"Collectively-owned factory!" He's running out of breath and stops for a moment in front of what looks like an olive-canning facility.

"Really?"

"Yes – this is Spain's one and only communist village!"

"No freaking way!"

They walk, and see more graffiti, and people hanging out in groups, or sitting out in the street on plastic chairs – a regular sight in La Línea too, but now the act seems infused with revolutionary potential. They reach a workers' union building adorned with slogans wrought in iron: 'Otro mundo es posible'. Another world…

There's a larger building set back from the road that has a massive wooden sculpture of an electric guitar across the front of the roof, its body in the shape of Andalusia.

"A venue!"

Her pace quickens. There are stalls in the car park at the front, selling records, band t-shirts and badges, books and zines. Bunty and Asif breathe in the alluring aroma of frying veggie burgers.

"What's going on? This is the first time I've felt at home for ages!"

A purple-haired girl answers. "It's a punk rock festival." She's wearing ripped shorts, stripey red and white tights and a Lorena and The Bobbitts t-shirt. "Where are you from?"

"The UK," Bunty answers, sadly.

"Oh, I'm sorry," the girl responds.

"So are we, right now," Bunty tells her.

Another girl has stepped up to the first's shoulder. Her long dark brown hair is held off her face by a scarf, and her burgundy jeans and tatty black t-shirt have badges on them. "They are Brexiters?" she asks her friend.

"No!" Asif and Bunty cry in unison.

Bunty elucidates. "We wanted so badly for that not to happen. You guys must think British people are idiots."

"Maybe just 52 per cent," the girl smiles. "You wanna sit with us?"

Asif and Bunty glance at each other. It's a yes. They climb up wooden steps to a deck outside the front of the venue, and Asif goes to get beers.

They swap names; Martina and Marisol.

"So do you two live here, in the village?"

"She always lived here," Martina tells her. "I moved here two years ago."

"You're not Spanish? I don't recognise your accent."

"I'm from the Czech Republic. Gracias!" Martina accepts a beer from Asif.

"I've read a lot about this place," Asif says, sitting down. "Is it as cool as it sounds?"

"It depends," says Marisol. "What did you hear?"

"Well, that lots of people work for the collective, and when there's less work, everyone works fewer days, so there's no unemployment..."

"There is still some unemployment, but not much, not like the rest of Spain," Martina tells him, looking to Marisol to say more about her home.

"Yes, it's 25 per cent unemployment in Spain, but only ten per cent here," Marisol says. "Our system means we have more time for each other, so it makes a strong community. We share things, so we don't need to buy as much."

"I heard that mortgages are like twenty euros a month?" Asif asks.

"Yes," Marisol tells him, "but you have to work on the houses for one or two days a week. When you are building houses you do not know which one will be yours, so you give the same care to every one."

"We both work for the collective, and we are building houses too," Martina chips in.

"It sounds freaking awesome!"

"Tell us about you," asks Martina. "How come you are here?"

"Asif's working in Gibraltar, cos he's like a tech genius…"

Asif laughs, and she carries on: "I'm basically stuck in Spain cos I don't have ID. I left my passport on a ship."

The girls' jaws drop. "What the fuck?" interjects Martina.

"It's a stupid story. But now I'm staying with a family in La Línea. It's really tough for them cos two of them have cancer; there's a huge oil refinery there, and the pollution is horrific."

"I heard about it," says Marisol. "There was a film about it on television. Many people in that area get cancer, more than in the rest of Spain."

"It's so awful, I wish I could do something!"

"You can always do something." Marisol tells Bunty, looking straight into her eyes.

"But it's run by a huge company, and the Spanish government is happy for them to keep polluting…"

"How do you think this village is the way it is? People fought the government for many years until we got the land. We just kept going. There were hunger strikes."

"Hmmm…" Bunty has recovered from her lunch and is now contemplating veggie burgers. "I don't think I could do that."

"You don't have to!" laughs Martina. "But think about collective action. There is so much you can do. Listen, tell me some things about this company that runs the refinery…"

The Marinaleda girls and Bunty start brainstorming, and Asif goes to the car to fetch a notebook. Before too long they have the makings of a plan.

"Freaking hell!" Bunty exclaims. "I think we can do this."

"Shall we celebrate with burgers and beer?" suggests Asif.

His proposition receives unanimous approval, and they cement their newfound comradeship with buns oozing oil and ketchup.

Later, when other comrades arrive to look after the stall, Marisol and Martina join Bunty and Asif inside the venue, where a Spanish punk band is playing.

"Maybe we should get going back," Asif says to Bunty, over the noise. "It's like a three-hour drive."

Bunty's smile flips one hundred and eighty degrees.

"Stay with us! Stay with us!" shouts Marisol, and Martina nods vigorously, grabbing Bunty's hands and shaking them.

"Well, we could, but I'm supposed to be at work tomorrow…" Asif tells them, sadly.

"On a Sunday, seriously?"

"I was voluntold. Compulsory overtime."

"Sick day! Sick day!" Martina and Marisol chorus.

Bunty looks at Asif, hopefully. "I think they have a point?"

He's outvoted. "Fuck it! Alright!"

Martina and Marisol high five Bunty and Asif, and that's when the dancing starts.

Much much later they stumble through the quiet streets of the pueblo. "Shhh!" Marisol puts a finger to her lips. "Babies are sleeping!"

They reach the girls' house, which they share with two guys. It smells of hash smoke, which makes Bunty wrinkle her nose, but she's tired, and happy to crash out on the sofa. She watches Asif moving about, putting cushions on the floor for his bed. Mm-mm. But she's made a promise to herself.

Chapter 36 – Hangover Square

The morning comes too soon, so they sleep through it. Then Bunty wakes and watches dust motes float in the afternoon sun. Asif isn't there, but his bag is, so he can't have gone back without her. She hears the girls talking and clattering in the kitchen and goes to investigate. The table is laden with coffee, fresh fruit juice – "from the village orchard," they tell her – and toast with olive oil, garlic and tomato.

"You two are amazing!" she tells them, between mouthfuls of toast. "Listen, if I manage to pull off something like what we talked about last night, do you think you'd come along?"

"I gonna ask," says Marisol, her voice still gravelly from last night. "We have a communal bus, but it depends on the mayor and the council and the others in the village. I will try to make a proposal at the assembly."

"You have a village assembly?"

"Yes, every two weeks. Make sure to give me your number and I will tell you."

There's a knock on the door. Martina gets up to open it and Bunty hears Asif's voice. "I got souvenirs – Marinaleda olives!"

He displays a jar. Marisol and Martina laugh, as he sees the spread. "I bought them for breakfast, but I see you have that covered."

"No thanks, Asif," Martina responds wryly. "I'm sick of olives! We bottle them all day."

"You're like the great provider!" Bunty tells him. "You got us all those beers too."

Marisol passes him some breakfast. "It is one of your strengths," she tells him. "But it is important to receive as well. You do not need to adhere to traditional gender roles."

Asif nods and starts munching his toast. "But I have to support the revolutionary women. That's my role, I think."

The girls pat him on the back and laugh. "He is a good ally," declares Martina.

After breakfast Bunty and Asif hug and Spanish-kiss their new friends before wandering back to the car. It's a beautiful journey home. They take a direct, though longer, route along country roads, via a town in the mountains called Ronda. Asif stops the car there and points to an old, fortified stone bridge. "Fancy a walk?"

Bunty goes straight to the bridge and peers down into a chasm between cliffs, to a river a hundred metres below.

"This is incredible!"

"I'm so glad I can show you some of the real Spain."

"La Línea is grim," she tells him, "but it's still Spain. Maybe it's just a reality we don't want to see."

"I stand corrected."

Once more the urge to kiss him overwhelms her, and it takes all her British self-control to hold back. She gazes at him instead, taking in every detail of his adorable face.

"You look hungry," Asif observes.

"Yes, I am," Bunty admits, but she isn't going to tell him how. They wander back into the town and find a small bar that does bocadillos and coffee.

"I love these old man bars," Bunty tells him as she munches her sandwich.

"Yeah, I like that there are millions of independent places here. Much better than all the chains in the UK."

"Oh!"

"What is it?"

"I suddenly had a feeling in my gut like I don't want to go back! That's weird!"

"It's all you've wanted since you got here."

"Weird." Bunty repeats, looking down at the table.

Her head's spinning. Maybe this strange desert place, with its ancient mountains and gorges, has erased her usual frame of reference. Or maybe it's all the booze...

"At least I've not been thinking about Brexit."

"I *knew* I could take your mind off it!" Asif's delighted at the success of his mission. "But yeah..." He looks like he is trying to make himself be more serious again, and can't quite manage it. "Fuck it, Bunty, we're not even there. I know it's horrible, the situation in the UK, but look at where we are..."

He's right. This is something. Bunty smiles at him, and realises she does now have some sort of good news. When he goes to the bathroom she texts her mum back, finally: *I'm taking a holiday in Spain. Will be home soon. Love to you and dad. XX.*

And with that weight lifted from her conscience she finds she can properly enjoy the Sunday afternoon vibe that buzzes lazily around them, like the sweet dusty light flooding in through the wide-open windows of the bar.

They take a languid walk around the town before driving out through the sierra. The roads are so quiet, and at first the only company they have are wild animals – big-eyed hares dancing in the road, and strange birds staring from fences. Back on the coast they stop for petrol and Bunty gets out to look around. There's a shop selling British papers, and the front page of the Daily Mail makes her recoil. Activists from No Borders have allegedly brought a refugee into the UK, and the editorial is describing them as political extremists.

"Hey Asif, shall we form a band called The Domestic Extremists?"

"Yeah! Let's do it."

Bunty's turning the radio dial, trying to DJ with her intuition. It's a method that either works amazingly or totally fails, and it's working now. She finds a station playing 'The Logical Song', and moves to change to another station.

"No, leave it," Asif tells her.

"Why? What is it? It's horrible!" Bunty's blanching at the ragtime keyboards.

"It's Supertramp!"

"Uh. I read David Cameron likes them."

"Just imagine him listening to this."

It's a sickening thought, but she accepts the challenge. She envisages a young Cameron, a lanky sixth former with greasy hair, spots and insecurities, identifying with the words of the song.

"Oh, the poor rich white boy feeling so alone and confused!" she cries.

"I knew you'd get it."

"Maybe he had anarchist tendencies that he had to suppress cos of family pressure." Bunty's almost crying with laughter.

The singer wails off into the distance as they fall about laughing, and Asif swerves to avoid a dog running in the road.

"Fuck!" Bunty yells, twisting round to see the poor hound narrowly evading death on the motorway, then resumes her duties, spinning the dial and landing on Roberta Flack's 'Killing Me Softly.' They both sit there wishing it was The Fugees. They're in the shadow of a huge mountain and on the other side a whole new set of radio channels comes into range. The tuner does a deft mix from Flack to some classical music that rises and falls like the landscape. Bunty lets the airwaves do their thing for a while, then jams her finger on the search button. It skips to a station playing 'Rebel Girl' by Bikini Kill. She turns it up.

"Spanish national radio must know you're here."

"They must know about Martina and Marisol."

"M and M!"

"You only just thought of that?"

"Uh... yeah," he grins goofily. "They came up with some brilliant ideas last night. Do you think you'll go ahead with something like that?"

Bunty sounds doubtful. "God, I don't know how, on my own."

"You're not on your own." He looks at her for a moment, then puts his eyes back on the road in time to brake for a car recklessly overtaking them.

"Argh! Well played!"

"But what do you think?"

"It's a bit scary, Asif. I'm illegal over here as it is. They could get me just for having no ID, let alone if I start taking on the state and shit."

"True, sorry. I'm not always very practical."

"You're great."

Asif's face widens into a grin but he keeps it pointing forward this time. "I'll stop pestering you about it, but you know where I am if you need my support."

They pass the rest of the journey listening to a Devo CD, and Bunty tells him about Cowtown, a band from Leeds. "They're like a cross between Devo and The B-52's, but they're a trio with the economy of, say, Shellac. And they're really sharp and funny."

"I gotta hear those!"

She's daydreaming of being at one of their shows with him when the Rock of Gibraltar lurches into view. The sun has set and dusk is coming down as they descend into La Línea. "Home stinky home," Bunty declares, as Asif pulls the car into calle Aurora and parks it illegally again. "These are always the best spots," he tells her. "But I can't stay. Will I see you soon?"

"I'm not going anywhere. Shout me when you're back on this side of the border."

Bunty hugs him, stopping herself before it goes on too long, and hops out of the car.

She buzzes up to the apartment, and Inma answers, but she sounds weird – weirder even than people usually sound on intercoms. "Are you okay?" Bunty asks her.

"Come up," sobs Inmaculada. "My mother is dead."

Chapter 37 – El Tanatorio

Bunty leans her face on the door frame. What am I gonna do? How can I help her now? By the time she's clambered up the stairs to the apartment, she feels like she's falling apart.

The door is open. Bunty closes it behind her and peers into the living room. Inmaculada isn't there. She stands outside her bedroom calling her name; she's not there either. Then she hears a jagged cry and follows the sound to find Inma in her mother's room, on the bed, facing the wall.

"Inmaculada, I am so sorry. What happened? What can I do?"

"She die in the hospital," Inmaculada gulps. "She never goes home." Inma erupts into more sobs. Bunty falls on the bed next to her, crying too, and holds her. She knew how much Lola had wanted to come back home. And she should have. She was only 45 years old.

"I'm so sorry. Was it today?"

"Today morning. Before I go there." She howls some more. "The funeral is tomorrow."

Tomorrow. Already. "That's really soon. What can I do to help?"

"I come here to get some of her clothes for her to wear. I have to go back to the tanatorio. The rest of the family waits there."

Shit. Inmaculada shouldn't be doing this alone. "Look, I'm here now. Just tell me what you need."

"Can you get her blue dress from the armario? It is like a... virgin blue."

Bunty gets up, opens the cupboard and starts to run her hands along the line of dresses, trying to think what virgin blue must look like. Virgin Mary, presumably. A bright blue dress, almost turquoise – it must be this one. She lifts it by the hanger and turns to check with Inma.

Inmaculada lifts her head, then collapses in sobs once more. The sooner she can reunite Inma with the rest of her family, Bunty thinks, the better.

"Do you need anything else?"

"Her rosario..." Inma can hardly speak, but she points to her mother's dressing table, and there in a glass dish Bunty sees a rosary. She lifts it gently and goes to show it to her friend, holding her shoulder this time as she asks, "Is this the right one?"

Inmaculada cries, but more softly this time, and answers "Sí."

"Shall we go to the tanatorio now? Do you want to take a taxi?"

Inmaculada nods, and Bunty goes out to make the call. As she passes the kitchen she picks up some fruit juice and a small cake, in case Inmaculada hasn't eaten. Then she returns to Lola's room and supports Inma to walk through the apartment, down the stairs and into the waiting taxi. They sit in the back seat together for the short journey and Bunty tries to interest her in the juice and cake, but Inma shakes her head; it seems like it's enough effort for her to draw breath right now. When they reach the morgue Bunty pays the driver and takes Inma by the hand to help her out of the car, and a young man bursts from the main door of the big white building in front of them.

"Inma! Vienes, hermana."

Bunty realises this must be Inma's older brother, Antonio. He takes Inma inside, his arm around her shoulder. Bunty follows them, feeling uncomfortable about witnessing their profound grief when she's almost a stranger. They take the lift and emerge into a large vestibule, and Antonio leads the way through glass double doors to a room where lots of people are gathered around a coffin. Most are holding drinks, and Bunty sees there's a bar in the vestibule. She doesn't want to go to the coffin, doesn't want to intrude on the family's suffering, so she slides her back down the wall and sits on the floor, out of the way.

She watches as Lola's friends and family console one another. There's a lot of crying and hugging, kind smiles and some laughter. Children are being held and patted by everyone in the room, as they go round playing or reaching up to various adults to ask them what's happening. Older women are seated on plastic chairs near the coffin, leaning towards one another, but they don't look shocked. This experience is not new to them.

One person appears left out – Carlos doesn't seem to fit into any of these social configurations. She can read the sheer unassuaged grief on his face as he roams around, tense and alienated. Then he spots her.

"'Sup?" he asks, sliding down to sit beside her. Bunty wonders if he's had too many beers.

"I'm so sorry, Carlos." She looks at him, concerned.

"Not your fault." He gazes back at her, apparently calm, and then brings the palm of his hand down on the floor with a slap. "Fuck!"

No-one looks around to see who's shouting. Either they're used to it, or they're not interested in what this kid is going through.

"It is fucked up," Bunty acknowledges.

"It's fucking fucked up. I want to die." He's quiet for a moment then, as though struggling with what he wants to say. "¿Por qué no yo? I prefer it is me and not her that go to the fire."

"Oh, no, Carlos..." Bunty reaches for him, and he falls onto her, sobbing. She thinks what it must have been like when his father died, a decade ago. He would have been six then.

His uncle Juan, however, has evidently witnessed his outburst, and strides towards them. "Venga, Carlos. You are a man."

Carlos lifts his head and stares at Juan. It's a long stare. Then he pushes his wiry body up from the floor and stands in front of his uncle. "Yes, I am. So I can say this: fuck you." Spittle sprays from his mouth in sheer rage. Then he turns and marches from the room at an almost unnatural speed.

Bunty looks up at Uncle Juan. Well fucking done, she thinks, for grief-shaming your orphaned nephew. Juan seems to grasp something of this as he grunts and turns away. She watches him walk towards the bar.

She's exhausted after the late night, the drinking and the sofa-surfing, and doubts she'd be able to catch up with poor raging Carlos even if she could muster the energy to try. Her heart aches for him, as well as for Inmaculada, who's walking towards her. Bunty gets herself together and stands up.

"Bunty, we gotta go to the house now for to say the rosary." She looks panicky.

"Sure, I'll come with you – just tell me what to do."

"Okay..."

Inma's looking around the room, and doesn't seem completely there. Then she brings her attention back to Bunty. "What happen to Carlos?"

"He left, he was upset..."

"I think he go home. That is best for him."

Inma goes to speak with some women across the room and then returns to Bunty. They walk together down the stairs. She's pale and silent, seemingly empty of words and tears. Outside she presses some digits into her phone and utters four words. "Tanatorio, sí, ahora. Luego." That's all it takes; the taxi appears two minutes later. They ride back to the house, Bunty holding her hand as Inmaculada slumps against her. A time to rest.

Back in the apartment, Inmaculada won't give Bunty any instructions but starts to move chairs around the room. All Bunty can do is try to pre-empt her – it seems she's setting up a circle using the sofa and dining chairs. Then Inma begins to tidy up, so Bunty takes the brush and goes round the floor with it. What happens at a rosary gathering? Bunty doesn't know; Spanish culture is still a mystery to her. She makes coffee just in case, spooning ground beans into the cafetiere and placing it on the cooker. The intercom sounds, and she buzzes them in, whoever they are. Soon there are a dozen women in the living room. It's hard to breathe with so much perfume in the air, or to think amidst the noise of their raised voices as they fuss over Inmaculada, who's now effectively pinned to the sofa by their attentions. At least she's sitting down, Bunty thinks. She asks some of the women if she can get them anything to drink. After a few funny looks and shaken heads, she retires to sit by a table in the corner of the room. An older woman stands and orders "Silencio, ya," and they all settle down in the hush that emerges. A subdued chanting begins, accompanied by the rattling of beads being pulled from handbags. There are a few younger women who don't have beads, but they still seem to know all the words.

Dios te salve, María. Llena eres de gracia...

The prayer is repeated many times. Bunty starts to pick up phrases and joins in when she can. She has no problem with talking to a female deity, and it seems entirely appropriate right now. Please help Lola, she asks the Virgin. And please look after her children... Where are they though? Antonio must still be at the morgue... but where the hell is Carlos?

Chapter 38 – A Wild Nobility

She gets up quietly so as not to disturb the chanting. Inmaculada doesn't see her; she's praying with closed eyes, tears streaming down both cheeks. Bunty feels the gaze of some of the women on her as she tiptoes out of the room. She closes the apartment door carefully, and walks down to the street. Now what – where does a kid hang out in this town? It's midnight but still warm; a teenage boy could be anywhere.

Could he have gone back to the morgue? Surely not, if that dick Juan is still there. She stands at a crossroads, gazes along the roads in each direction, and listens. Dogs are howling and televisions are blaring from the open windows of apartment blocks. There's some music, some yelling – but no clues.

She starts toward the centre of La Línea's sprawl, but she doesn't know where his friends live, or even who they are. A few apartment windows are lit, but many have their shutters down. Gone to bed, gone away, or empty. A cigarette packet and some paper cups tumble along the street in the sea breeze, the remnants of a gathering. It's late, and the deserted streets make her nervous.

I should have asked Inmaculada for his number... but I can't now. I'll go back to the morgue if I can't find him out here...

She peers through the windows of a bar. People drinking and laughing; it seems quite civilised, and there are no underage drinkers to be seen. What would she do if she was in this situation, not wanting to go home, but with nowhere else to be? Of course – the park, that time-honoured sanctuary of disaffected youth. She switches direction.

In a few minutes she's at the edge of the feria ground on the south side of town. Reserved for the annual fair, it's a huge space adjacent to the border. Dusty, scrubby and messed up, unloved most of the year round, right now it's a spooky place with no lighting save for the streetlights on the roads that surround it. She steps between trees onto crunchy leaves, her senses alert, and taps the torch app on her phone to guide her along uneven paths.

There's rustling; something, someone is close by. She freezes. A sudden blow to the back of her jacket makes her yelp in terror and she runs, tripping on tree roots, hands in front to find the way. Whoever it is is chasing her – and barking.

She stops by a tree and a huge, soft-pawed Doberman bounds towards her. "Christ," she greets the hound, panting. "You scared the living Bejeezus out of me!" She leans toward the beast, offering him a stroke, but he flinches and retreats.

"You're scared too, poor thing. And hungry? I ain't got nothin' for you, I'm sorry."

Bunty sets off walking again, her nerves in shreds. She feels for the phone in her pocket, but it's not there. "I must have dropped it when you ambushed me," she chides her companion, who's tagging along with her now. "Come on then, help me find it."

But she can't see it anywhere. And of course, she now has nothing to illuminate the ground with. After a few minutes she gives up; she'll have to return early in the morning to resume the search, and hopes that she can remember where to come back to. Her mission seems increasingly dumb-assed as she roams in the scary dark in a scary park with a massive, nervous stray dog. "This is like Scooby fucking Doo," she tells him – or her – ruefully. But at least she's not alone.

She keeps going, Scooby at her heels, with only a vague dispersal of light from distant streetlights to see with. They reach a clearing, some sort of amphitheatre covered in graffiti and murals. There's a figure on one of the steps. Not so tall, hunched over... could it be? She treads lightly towards him. But what if it isn't...?

He looks up with a start, and shouts. "What the fuck? You fright me, crazy English girl!"

"I found you!"

She hears a metallic rattle, something hitting the ground, but doesn't see what it is.

"I don't go far. Don't worry, I am a good boy."

When she gets close she can see he's been crying. But he's not letting on.

"And what the fuck is this, you got a dirty dog now?"

"He's just helping me, I think." Bunty strokes the hound's head. "How are you doing, Carlos?"

"Well, you know, my father and my mother are dead, so really really great," he spits, banging his left foot on the ground.

She isn't sure how to help this injured young bull. Maybe there's nothing she can do.

"At least I have an English friend," he sighs.

So it's probably okay to give him a hug. She puts her arm around him and he leans his head on her shoulder.

And then he kisses her.

"No!" She sits bolt upright. "Don't!"

"I thought English girls like it," he tells her sulkily, banging his foot again.

"You thought wrong." She glares at him. But as furious as she is at this insult, her heart is crumbling to see him this way. "Look, I *am* your friend. But it's not like that. I had to come and find you, to find out if you're okay. I didn't want Inma to be worried, so I didn't tell her. I left her saying the rosary."

"Catholic cunts."

"Well, that's as may be..."

"Maybe, maybe..." He's singing. The beers at the morgue haven't worn off, or perhaps he's had a few more.

Damn. She's stuck in a park in southern Spain at night without her phone, with a stray dog and a drunk and grieving teenager. How does she get into these situations?

Scooby's sniffing the steps they're perched on.

"Come here, dirty dog."

Scooby scoots backwards.

"He seems so frightened."

"They all are. People hurt them."

"That's crazy."

"It's a crazy world."

"I can't argue with you."

She thinks how hard it is to be a teenager even if you don't lose both your parents. He's too young to have to know this pain.

"Got cigarettes?"

"No."

"I will come to England with you, okay?"

"Okay." Her head's spinning, but he's had enough harsh reality for one day.

"Where did you go yesterday?"

"Marinaleda."

"Where?"

"Communist village. Sevilla province."

"Cool."

Silence. Then, "That man you went with – he your novio?"

"No, he's a friend."

"Then why you no want me? You are a gay girl?"

He's scuffling his feet in the dirt, head down, while Bunty faces the eternal dilemma about whether to come out as bi.

"A bit, yes."

"Ahaha, my gay English friend! I tell my friends!"

"Okay, you tell them." She sighs. "Walk back with me?"

"Pretend I am a girl?" He makes a kissy-face.

"No. Come on, stupid. Let's go home." She stands up and holds out a hand for her hormonal and messed up charge. "I'll make you something to eat."

"Sí?"

"Sí. Venga."

At this he stands up, and they begin a winding stroll back to the apartment.

"Fuck you, dirty dog!" Carlos shouts at Scooby, but only after the hound has escorted them safely through the scariest part of the feria ground.

The dog hangs back then, at the edge of his territory. "Hasta luego, Scooby," she calls. "Thanks for protecting us!"

When they get back, the apartment is quiet. Inmaculada's door is closed; hopefully she's asleep. Bunty pours Carlos some juice and makes him a sandwich, which he laughs at ("English bocadillo!") and eats anyway. She fires up the computer in the living room and they trade some more YouTube links. Eventually the proliferation of rabbit videos does its job. He goes quiet, then she hears him snore. The sun is rising, and she only has one more job to do.

She slips out of the apartment once more and returns to the park. Scooby's nowhere to be seen, and it takes her a while to find the spot where the beast had ambushed her, but when she gets there she can see the device's black plastic cover amongst leaves and twigs, followed by the battery and the front of the phone. The screen is cracked, but when she snaps the battery into place the light comes on.

Something still works.

She walks back in the yellowy glow of dawn, and starts to text Asif: *You would not fucking believe...*

And then realises she can't tell him. She can't summarise that night, and she doesn't want to.

Chapter 39 – I Can't Breathe

Carlos must have woken and gone to his room, so the sofa's free. She literally crashes onto it, tumbling headlong into sleep.

An hour later Inmaculada is up. Through the tiny gaps that appear between her eyelashes Bunty watches her cross the room, but she can't abandon the quicksand of dreams, not now. She turns over to snuzzle the sofa cushions. But warm hands are pulling at her back.

"People are coming here," Inma loud-whispers. "You have to move."

Bunty groans. "Can I get in your bed?"

"Yes. But it's the funeral now."

"Now, like now?" Noooo.

"In one hour..." Inmaculada sounds stressed. Bunty's sleep time is over. She sits up, levers herself off the sofa and staggers to the bathroom for a pirate wash; she looks like hell. She looks how Inma probably feels.

Bunty undertakes the job of buzzing in relatives and ushering a sorry-looking younger brother out of bed. He must remember what he did last night because he can't look her in the eye as she hands him toast and coffee. She takes a few mouthfuls herself whilst helping Inmaculada set up the living room for the reception afterwards, then they all vacate the apartment. A series of cars wait down in the street. Bunty ends up in a back seat with people she's not met before, and they don't seem happy to have her there – although it's possible that passing out on the short journey to the church doesn't help her case. In the church she can barely stay awake, and the funeral goes by in a haze. She dreams of Lola smiling and waving goodbye, and wakes with tears in her eyes. She feels peaceful, and wonders if she could or should tell Inmaculada about it.

During the reception Bunty claims a corner of Inmaculada's bed, somehow managing to screen out the sounds of garrulous relatives. And then it's evening; she peers groggily into the living room and sees that the rosary service is about to kick off. When she goes to pee her reflection still looks rough; surely the Virgin Mary won't mind?

The gathering isn't exclusively female this time as the priest is in attendance along with some male relatives and friends. She finds a space in the corner and prays simply for Lola's kids; Lola is free now. When Bunty looks up, Uncle Juan is staring at her. What does that jerk want? Best not to think about him right now. After an hour of chanting the session wraps up; Bunty exchanges a few words with some of the guests, and offers to make the coffee.

She's steadying the coffee pot on the stove when Juan barges in. He backs her into a corner – his white-shirt-sleeved arms lean on cupboard doors, forming bars at either side of her head.

"My family does not want a foreign whore here," he snarls, and she can smell his beery breath. "You have to go."

Her fight or flight response is flickering on and off. I don't think I can push him… I could bite his fucking elbows off though? But he's too big, and horrible. So I gotta go. Flight it is.

He got no wings, but he says he gonna fly.

Prince Far-I's words echo in her brain, and dubby-trippy light trails in the air around her. The dark trails around Uncle Juan exit the kitchen and then so does she, but only after his final narrowed-eyed stare of hate has burned onto her retinas. She scans left and right to avoid facing him again. Her stuff's in Inmaculada's room; with a galloping heart she goes to retrieve what she can. Then she has to walk through the living room. Juan's in there, laughing. And Inmaculada too, her eyes wide.

"Bunty, what is wrong?"

"I'm sorry, Inma. I have to go."

"But what for?" Inmaculada looks like she will cry. Bunty holds her, but she can't speak, she might be sick. The room spins as she moves to the door, where finds her friend is with her. She's still there when she steps into the street. And she's still there when her arms, then her knees, hit the pavement.

Rest.

Besuited arms have her. Black-clad men with deep brown eyes gaze down, then they bump her head as they carry her up the stairs. She can't resist, there's nothing left to resist with, and as they bring her back into the apartment she starts to cry. Mourners in the living room part as she processes past, the normally-loud conversation reduced to a hush. "Yes, in my mother's room," she hears Inmaculada say, and her body meets silky covers. Inma ushers the bearers outside and shuts the door.

Bunty's trying to tell her friend that she's sorry for causing a fuss, but all she can do is cry.

"You are sick, I think?"

"Juan… said I had to go…" she manages between sobs.

"That hijo de puta…" curses Inmaculada, her eyes narrowing. "Me cago en la leche…"

The obscenities coming out of Inmaculada's mouth make Bunty start to laugh, which stems the flow of tears. But when she realises how serious Inma is in her hatred of her uncle, she goes quiet.

"Don't listen to that fucker. We need you here. I need you. You care for us, but do you care for you? Did you eat?"

Bunty tries to think of when she last had a meal and is drawing a blank. Ronda, it must have been Ronda. But what day was that?

"You are going to eat, and you are going to sleep, okay?"

Bunty does the second thing she was told to do until her host returns with a bowl of soup. Inma sits with her until Bunty eats it all.

"Bunty, stay here as long as you need."

"But – your mother's room…"

"Yes. You stay here." Inmaculada is firm, and Bunty isn't strong enough to keep up her side of the argument. She stays slumped on a big pile of pillows, and Inma fetches a blanket which she tucks around her limp form.

"I pray for you." She kisses her forehead. "I have to go now."

Bunty smiles and lets her eyelids drop. When she opens them again, the apartment is in sleeping silence. She gets into bed for real, into Lola's sheets, and thinks about the family – what they're going through, how she can repay them, and how they should have justice. Would money help? But money isn't something she has a handle on. Even if she could cross the border, could she bring back enough to make a difference?

She recalls the conversation with Martina and Marisol, and the strategy the girls mapped out with her and Asif. Lola's gone, but if this could never happen to anyone else ever again – that would be the greatest thing.

Plans swirl around her mind; M and M told her to think about what the people need.

What do people need?

We need food, water, shelter. We need to breathe.

Chapter 40 – Dance This Mess Around

Fever keeps her down all the next day. In the evening she feels well enough to get a shower, and days of grime come off her. Squeaky and towel-dried, she wanders into the kitchen in her pyjamas, looking for something to eat. Inma arrives as she's sinking her teeth into peanut butter-smothered toast.

"Bunty, you look better!"

"You're my hero!" Bunty hugs Inmaculada, putting greasy toast crumbs on her blouse. "Yes, I feel human again."

"Come to rosary tonight?"

"Like this?" Bunty looks down at her PJs.

Inma nods. "And do not worry, Juan will not be here."

Bunty makes it through several minutes of chanting before her head drops to the arm of the sofa. Loud conversation wakes her – it's over, and cups of coffee are being passed around the room. Could this be a good time to test the water?

Inmaculada's next to her, and her aunt Paloma is at the other end of the sofa. "This is my mother's youngest sister," Inma tells Bunty, by way of introduction.

"I'm so sorry for your loss."

"Thank you. I will miss her too much," Paloma replies sadly.

"I have an idea, but I don't know if it's a good idea, and I want to ask you both. What do you think of having a vigil for Lola outside the refinery? To show pictures of her, and to let them know that they've caused this, and so many other deaths?"

Inmaculada looks at Bunty and nods slowly, but Paloma answers straight away.

"You can't do this. We need this place for work. My husband works there, and many people in La Línea. They see us do this, he lose his job."

"Okay, I'm sorry..."

"It is a bad idea," Paloma continues, waving her finger at Bunty. "It is not possible."

She enunciates the last two words so powerfully that Bunty dare not disagree. She pushes herself back into the sofa. Inma squeezes her hand and smiles at her, but only when Paloma isn't looking.

When she returns to Lola's room she sees a missed a call from Asif. She dials him back.

"Hey! What's happening?"

"A lot, actually. I don't know where to start."

"That sounds serious." A pause. "Want me to come over?"

"You can? On a weeknight?"

"I'm breaking all the rules these days!" He laughs. "Why not?"

"Well, I've got more space now, but that's not as good a thing as it sounds..."

"No? I can be there in half an hour. Want me to bring anything?"

"I could use some food." Bunty realises there's a void in her stomach, and assesses the size of it. "Chinese food!"

"Okay! Make it forty minutes."

They sit at the table in the living room with tin foil trays of noodles, fried vegetables and tofu. Inma and Carlos don't want any and are chilling together on the sofa in front of the TV. The ceiling lights are switched off and the table is lit by orange streetlights. Bunty's broken the news to Asif about Lola, which killed his appetite, but hers is running away with her and she's eating his food too. When the film ends there are quiet hugs as the siblings leave for their respective rooms, and Bunty and Asif take over the sofa. They sit facing each other, knees bent in front of them. Bunty's filled him in about the other key events of the last few days, and he's looking worried.

"I can't believe Juan did that to you. And poor Inmaculada and Carlos. Why didn't you let me know?"

Bunty can't explain.

"What are your plans now – where are you going from here? Have you given up on getting your passport?"

"All I can think about is what these guys are going though, and how loads of people here have to experience this exact same thing. I want to do something about it."

"Like what we were talking with M and M about – a protest?"

"Yeah, but my head's all over the place. I'm not sure I can pull it off in a foreign country. My Spanish is shit, apart from anything else."

"Bunty, I believe in this and I want to help, if you'll let me. And I'm sure there will be people who'd work with you." He reaches for her hand. "I know what you mean about the language barrier, but loads of people here speak English. Do you want me to talk to the environmental group in Gibraltar?"

"Thanks Asif!" She breaks into a smile. "Yeah, that'd be amazing. But I don't know if it's even ethical; Inma's aunt says people here rely on jobs at the plant."

"But it's killing them – and the ones who don't work there. You can't call that ethical."

"People need work though – what would you do if you couldn't get a job?"

"True... But you're not trying to shut it down though, are you?"

"I want to! I'm not into using more fossil fuels and making more plastic at the best of times. But if we could get them to limit their emissions to legal levels, that would be a start..."

"I like it. They might even need to employ more people to bring it about. You could demand that they choose local people for that!"

They high five. Oh, how she wants to jump him right now. He's so gentle and pretty and has such excellent ideas. But would it be rude to do that in Inma's living room? Probably yes, and especially now. She sighs. "I gotta crash, but thanks for coming round, and for the food!"

"Will I see you again soon?"

"Tomorrow night?" she finds her mouth saying before her brain stops her.

Asif looks delighted. "Pick you up at eight?"

Chapter 41 – The Towers of Doom

It's not exactly the date he'd been hoping for

"Bunty, I've never done anything like this before."

"I know, but we have to find out."

"Find out what?"

"Exactly what's going on there. We need to look inside."

"Is this really the best way to do it though?"

"M and M said I should find out as much as I can. It makes sense to me."

"But not to me. This is dangerous, Bunty. I don't want to have the Spanish police in charge of me."

"Me either. They won't be."

"What makes you so sure?"

The Polvo CD that's playing on the car stereo gives her courage. Her breath is hot and the windows are steaming up. She winds hers down; the handle's stiff and it takes some effort.

"You've got to have faith."

"Faith?" Asif sounds vaguely outraged. "It's just – there are other ways of getting information. Less scary ones."

A light breeze is blowing in off the sea. They're driving by the tall wall now, the one covered in reassuring images of dolphins and space. "Anything to distract from what's really happening," Bunty mutters as she stretches her hand outside. It breaks her heart to think of local people creating this art to improve their area, summoning all the optimism in their souls, just to hide the thing that kills their families. And it doesn't even hide it very well – nothing conceals the chimneys that tower over them.

They pass the plant's main entrance and Asif pulls the car over by the beach. Bunty jumps out and he follows. He sighs and stares out to sea. The lights of Algeciras twinkle to the west, and to the east Gibraltar's Rock looks like a massive squashed hat.

"I'll be fine by myself." Bunty's facing the bay; it's hard to hear her.

"You're kidding, aren't you?"

"I'm not. You don't know me very well."

The water laps at the scrubby land by the road, and a cargo ship sounds its horn. Bunty strides away.

"Wait up, Bunty. I'll drive us."

She stops and turns to face him. "Let's go in via Karpeia."

"I'm kinda wishing I'd never brought you there."

"I'd have found it."

"I know."

They pull into the tourist centre's car park. There's no lighting, thankfully, and Asif parks sideways to the fence so his license plates won't be visible to any passing patrols. When he gets outside the thick, gravelly air hits his throat.

Bunty's already opened the boot. She takes out a large bag and walks towards the fence that encloses the archaeological site. Asif follows; he can't protect her unless he goes in with her.

"Can you hold this torch please? I need both hands."

She takes out a pair of bolt cutters from the bag and begins snipping though the fence at ground level. A few twists, and she's opened up a hole. She keeps cutting in parallel lines. Asif looks about for lights, any evidence of security guards. There are none. His heart's racing and he feels sick. He watches her roll up a small area of fence; it comes up easily from the ground.

"Right, this should do," she gasps. "Hold this up for us?"

He grabs the section and she slithers underneath it. Then she holds it up for him.

"Only if you want to."

"Oh, what the fuck."

He climbs through. It takes longer cos of his height; he's half a foot taller than she is.

"Thing is," she whispers as he straightens up, "all we've done is broken into an archaeological site. We've hardly even broken the law."

"Ummm..."

Asif doesn't have time to explain the niceties of the legal system; he's just trying to keep up and hold the torch steady.

"Over here!"

He remembers the way. Crunching gravel, they go up a slope and through a grove of tall trees till they reach the low section of ruins which Pedro had told them was probably the circus. From there they turn left to the huge theatre site where they can hear the spitting, churning noises of the refinery. It seems that much louder in the dark.

They climb the bank of the theatre into the wooded area behind. Then they're right up against another fence, this one much bigger than the last. It's laced with razor wire, both at the top and the bottom, but that's on the other side. They can easily touch it from here, which means they can cut it.

They both drop down. They've still not seen a security patrol, but that could change any minute. Bunty's got the cutters out again, and this time she's slicing fence at waist height. She cuts a horizontal line then makes vertical cuts underneath. When it's complete she pushes the wire forward and down, letting it fall over the glistening roll of razor wire that Asif's been eyeing anxiously. Then she reaches for her bag and pulls out something large and cylindrical, which she unrolls and places over the lower cut. It's a fluffy rug, borrowed from Inma's bathroom.

"Sorted."

She glances at him, and he sees the determination in her eyes. All he can do is follow. She's putting one leg through the hole, holding onto the sides. Her leg's on the rug, and it holds her. Then the other leg, so she's sitting on the roll.

"It's quite comfy," she whispers. And then she's on the other side.

Her heart's racing like never before. It's only bloody-mindedness that's keeping her together. Asif's struggling; he has to bend a bit more around the middle than she did, but with a little wriggling he limbos in with just a scratch on his face from a stray piece of severed wire to show for it. He lands on his knees, clambers up and touches his cheek, and there's a small dark patch on his finger.

She speaks at normal volume against the racket of the refinery. "Are you okay?"

"Fine."

He looks terrified.

"Come on then." Bunty takes him by the arm and they head for a bank of massive steel containers. She's starting to feel guilty for her initial fervour. What will they really find out, what can they really understand from snooping around this place?

He stays by her side. The torch is off; they can't afford to attract attention. Red and orange lights shine and flash everywhere. They're on the edge of a city of industry, with most of a Roman one hidden underneath, standing in the shadow of two huge cylindrical tanks that look like massive flying saucers. She pulls Asif's arm to navigate him. They're edging towards stainless steel structures with chimneys rising from their rooves when she sees two moving lights. Headlights, on high beam. A car.

Shit.

She pulls Asif to a low building set back from the road. There's an alley down the side, between that and an identical unit. They barrel in, but it's too dark; Bunty drops his hand so she can run with both arms in front. They squeeze into a tiny gap at the end, their backs pressed to the rear wall. She focuses on the corner of the corridor they've just turned from, and on trying to breathe as quietly as possible. Small. Still. Shhh.

The car sounds like it's gone past, but a moment later it's back. Two doors slam. There are voices, deep and Spanish, and rapid footsteps. Bunty thinks they might be moving away, but they get louder, and a beam of torchlight flashes next to Asif's shoulder.

No breathing at all now. Eyes the widest they could ever be. All the games of musical statues she ever played are serving her well. She's just a stick with a heartbeat. Can they hear it pounding? Will it give them away like fox scent to hunting dogs?

The light moves up, down, and away. Footsteps retreat, doors slam, the engine revs. They drive off quickly, continuing their patrol.

Bunty and Asif wait until the engine noise dissolves into the refinery's din, then they wait a few moments more.

"We're gonna have to run."

"I didn't sign up for this." Asif's voice is jagged.

They creep back along the corridor. There's no-one to see, but that car could be anywhere. Another signal, eye to eye, and they run. Asif's better at this than she; he sprints ahead, then holds back for her. They're not far from the fence, but terror stretches the time out until they reach their exit point. The rug's still in place; Asif almost pushes her through. He follows, one leg, then the other, and they're back in the remains of Karpeia.

Stumbling over ruins, Bunty trips on the string that demarcates one part of the excavation from another and falls forward, grazing hands and knees on ancient stone. Asif picks her up and practically carries her. She shakes herself free and carries on, limping now, and indulges in the luxury of a look behind. No-one's following, but there could be someone waiting at the other side.

They hurry along the path under the trees and emerge into the bathhouse area, then bolt for the hole like trained seals. Asif's in the lead and he shimmies straight through. When Bunty crouches down to follow, he's getting in the car, and by the time she's clear of the fence, the vehicle's growling softly in front of her. She jumps in, slamming the door.

"Fuck."

"Where to now, madam?" Asif asks gruffly.

"Far away from here?"

He's already on the move, speeding up the road along the west side of the plant that seems to go on for ages, flanked by sparkling flaming chimneys pushing steam clouds into the night sky. At the motorway he turns left, away from Gibraltar, his car joining a thin flow of traffic.

"Asif. Are you okay?"

He's staring straight ahead. "Let's just get out of here."

He doesn't seem like he wants to talk, and she gets it. She feels bad about what she's just put him through, and for what?

He drives on for half an hour. They're going uphill on a coastal road and there's a constellation of windmills up ahead, red lights on huge swinging arms. Then he pulls into an empty car park, switches off the engine and slumps forwards.

"That... was just so incredibly stupid."

"Asif, I..."

"It's just," – he pulls himself back up and turns to face her – "there are other ways of doing things. Like I said. Other ways of getting information."

"I really wanted to..."

"But it's so old school!"

Bunty tells him about her aunt who used to go to Greenham Common. "She always said that was the time in her life when she felt like she was really making a difference."

"You need to be focused, and know what you're trying to achieve. Those sorts of heroics don't necessarily apply in another country. Or another decade... another millennium. I mean," he sighs, "what do you even know about the Spanish police?"

"Not much... But I know what you're saying."

He doesn't come back with a smart-arse comment, and she likes him more for that. "Asif, I'm really sorry. But I'm also really glad you took me there."

"Why??"

"Because I had to see it, close up. To understand. To hear it and smell it... it's hard to explain."

She's exhausted and leans towards him. It's uncomfortable, but the idea of holding him is irresistible, and suddenly nothing else matters. He puts an arm around her and his touch ignites a fire that rushes up her torso. Despite the weight of her contrition, she wants him now more than ever. But what does he feel? She's really pissed him off tonight – she might be pushing her luck.

141

Pushing my luck should be my middle name.

She lifts herself up to sit astride him on the driver's seat, and gazes down into his eyes. He doesn't fight her off; his pupils are so wide that they're almost obliterating the brown of his eyes. But she hesitates...

Then he's kissing her. She's kissing him back.

And they can't stop.

Somehow, later, they drift into sleep, Bunty's legs swung over his lap, her shoulder under his arm. The first shrieks of the dawn chorus alert her to the world, and she tries to see through a windscreen misted with breath and sweat.

Asif stirs, and turns his head to kiss her. He looks so cute, sleepy and happy at the same time.

"What do you think's going on out there?"

Asif grins. "Shall we have a look?"

They crawl from the car, and as they unfold, they see a pinky-orange light breaking across the sky, underlined by the brilliant blue of the Atlas Mountains.

She gasps. "The mountains are close. We could swim to them... I don't even know where we are!"

"Near Tarifa – we're almost at the southernmost point of Europe."

"Wow..."

"I just wanted to get away from there last night."

"That's understandable." She feels terrible, thinking of what she put him through. And then she had the nerve to get off with him. Jesus, she's probably just gone and wrecked their friendship, and she really needs friends right now.

"Bunty! Look!"

Asif points to the eastern horizon, where a sliver of intense luminosity has appeared over the sea. They stand and stare at a searing, glowing pink globe that slowly ascends from the edge of everything there is to see. It balances on a horizon of silver-blue water in a miracle of beginning.

And he's holding her hand.

Chapter 42 – Ready

Carlos is about to leave for school when she arrives home.

He looks at her sideways. "Where were you last night?"

"A couple of places."

"Tell me."

"I can't." Bunty notices he's wearing a Slipknot t-shirt and jeans. "Why aren't you dressed for school?"

"It's the last day before the holidays. I don't have to."

"Cool. Listen, will you meet me after school? I want to ask your advice about something." Then she recalls her own after-school antics. "Unless you're meeting friends?"

"No. Yes. Yes I will meet you."

He's smiling when he leaves the apartment.

Inma's not home, so Bunty spends the day online and on the phone. She's already done what Stephanie told her to, and now she's free to work on her plan.

She has coffee and cake ready for Carlos when he gets in, but all he wants is to know what they're going to be doing.

"I want you to take me to the shops."

"Is that it?" he asks with a scowl that speaks of mega-anti-climax.

"Not quite. It's the sort of shop that you know about and I don't. You are a painter – where do you get your paint?"

He stares down at his feet. "It's not that kind of paint..."

"No. But I think it is. Your kind of paint. Take me to where I can get some."

"For real?"

Bunty nods and puts her trainers on. When they're in the street it's hard to keep pace with him, he's so excited to show her his secret. They walk for a while into the north part of the city where the streets are sketchier, but he knows his way round. He stops at a large garage door with a smaller door set into it, and bangs on that. Shouts come from within, and the door opens.

"¡Carlitos! ¿Qué tal?" A man in overalls around the same age as Bunty greets him with an elaborate ritual handshake. "¿Quién es la chica?"

"This is my English friend. I tell you about her!"

"I thought she was in your imagination!" The man laughs and kisses Bunty on both cheeks. "I'm Luis."

"I'm Bunty. Encantada. Carlos says you can sort me out with some paint?"

"Oh yes. Come this way."

They step through the door into a yard full of cars-in-progress, cars in not-so-much progress, and bits of cars. The garage doors that line the yard are covered in brightly graffiti'd murals. "Look, Bunty, this is mine!" Carlos shows her proudly, indicating a huge dragon surrounded by flames and multicoloured clouds.

"That's amazing, Carlos! Do your teachers know how talented you are?"

"Fuck them!" he declares. "I don't need them to say what I can do."

She laughs at his nonchalance as they follow Luis, who's waiting at another door. He leads them into a storeroom where there's a cupboard full of cans of spray paint.

"They've all been used on cars so it's just what is left in each can. What colours do you want?"

"One of each? How much are they?"

"Cerveza. You can pay me in beers," Luis grins, filling up a carrier bag with sticky-looking cans, and handing it over to her.

On their way back, Carlos is determined to find out what she's up to. "I want to do some art," is all she feels ready to tell him.

"Then I help you! Art is... in my heart!" he laughs at his newfound ability to rhyme in English.

"Okay, maybe you can help me. But I'm hesitant cos it's illegal, and I don't want you to get into trouble. Inma wouldn't forgive me if you get arrested because of me."

"Inma will forgive. She is like the Virgin Mary."

"Yeah, I don't think she is," grins Bunty.

Carlos splutters with laughter. "I will paint you a big wall, yes?"

"The thing is, it's not just one wall..."

"¿Qué es eso? What is it?"

"All of them."

"No way, man!" Carlos yells, with a jump in his step. "You are very lucky, mi amiga inglesa. I got all summer!" And he dances ahead of her on the narrow pavement, pointing out the tags of friends and heroes as they make their way home.

Carlos is making stencils when Inma comes back from work. There are pieces of cardboard all over the floor. Bunty looks up guiltily – what has she started?

"Bunty is helping me with a school project!" Carlos tells his sister, excitedly.

"But you finish school tomorrow?" Inma looks confused.

"I am ready for next year!"

She sighs and lets it go. "It is good to see him happy," she whispers, as she sits down next to Bunty on the sofa. "Thank you."

Inma goes to bed early, and Bunty messages back and forth with her new friends in Gibraltar and Spain. And she sets up a Facebook event called *Bunty's Leaving Party*.

The next day is crazy. Bunty and Carlos start work early, making posters and flyers, and when night falls he prepares to leave the house with his backpack jangling.

"You sure you'll be safe, Carlos?"

"I am safe always. Tranquila." He kisses her on both cheeks, like an adult.

That gives her an idea. An adult. She makes a quick call to Abbo, summoning him from the beach.

"Sure thing Bunty – glad to help! I like that kid!"

Once Carlos and Abbo are gone she can concentrate fully on that task at hand, assured that her young charge has a worldly-wise chaperone.

144

Everyone knows the time and place. She just needs to work out the details. When Inma comes back from work she looks sad and exhausted.

"How was your shift?"

"It is shit, today. Rude people."

"Aww, Inma, that's all you need. I wish you could take some time off."

"I am away now for the weekend. What is happening Bunty, you are so busy?"

Bunty lets Inma in on her plans. Inma gasps. "But it is too soon! You know Spanish people – we do not do anything, how you say, in a hurry!"

"I know, but I'm not here for very long, so it's now or never..."

"I wish you will stay." Inma looks down at her hands. "But if you want to do it this way, I will help you."

"Are you sure? I could send you the text message I'm sending out to everyone..."

Inma sits down and starts to forward the message to her contacts. Her phone's beeping non-stop when they hug goodnight.

But Bunty can't sleep. Inma's right, it really is short notice, and there's so much to organise. And she won't rest until Carlos and Abbo are back; she's relieved to hear them finally come through the door.

She jumps up. "How did it go?" she asks quietly, so as not to wake Inma.

"Well, we had help..." Abbo replies with a grin. "Carlos has a lot of friends, did you know?"

Bunty looks at the teenager in delight. "All okay?"

He's beaming. "All okay!"

"Alright!" She high fives him, then tilts her head. "You both look wide awake. Wanna help me with something else?"

"Yes, but for us to do any more work we are going to need take out," Abbo explains. "Carlos seems to have a serious pizza deficiency. I think I do too." He rubs his belly and feigns a pained expression.

Bunty laughs. "I have a budget for that." She calls a shop that does two for ten euros; it's the first time she's used any of Stephanie's cash.

After they've eaten, they get down to work.

Chapter 43 – Steady

Inma gets up to find a mess of beer cans, shredded paper and crashed out bodies on the living room floor.

"What the fuck happens here?" she laughs, tiptoeing her way through to the kitchen. Bunty opens an eye.

"Uh, sorry Inma..."

"Tranquila. We clean later."

Abbo raises his head. "It's like an explosion in a charity shop... I need water..."

They look at Carlos. He's sleeping blissfully, arms folded behind his head.

"Let's leave him," smiles Bunty. "Go out for coffee?"

It doesn't take much to persuade Inma to join them. The apartment door closes lightly and their feet trickle down the stairs. Out in the street strong sunlight is flooding down as usual, and they choose a café in the nearby plaza. With coffee and tostada on the table, and shielding their eyes from the sun, they discuss their plans for the day. Fine details are nailed down. Bunty stretches in her seat, and looks around.

This is the way to do it.

When they return to the apartment to shower and get everything together, Carlos is up and ready to go. Bunty thought they were going to walk, but Inma shows her on a map that it's further than she'd realised.

"Oh no! I messed up!"

"It's okay cariño, we go on the bus."

The four of them walk to the bus station laden with bags. Bunty's suitcase has been repurposed as a wheelbarrow for the day.

"I didn't think it through about how to get everything there, and get people there too. They're not going to walk that far."

"People round here don't like to walk, do they? You ask them directions to a place that's a kilometre away and they're all like 'muy lejos' – very far," Abbo observes, eliciting a punch in the arm from Inma.

"Maybe we have better things to do!"

"Yes, like having a siesta!"

They playfight in the street and Abbo's bag falls off his shoulder onto the ground.

"Careful!" Carlos chides them. It's strange to see him caring about something so much, thinks Bunty. And he's looking so thoughtful...

When they reach the bus station Bunty, Inma and Abbo slump down on a huge stone-slab bench by the bus bays. There's a slight breeze and abundant shade, and the bench cools their legs. Carlos remains standing, then announces that he's going.

"Why?" demands Inma. "Where you go?"

"It's okay. You go on the bus. I see you later."

He sprints out of the station before they can stop him

Inma grumbles about his absence – "I don't know what he is doing these days..." – and Bunty doesn't know what to think. He had seemed so committed. She worries in case she's overstepped her limits and might be causing problems for this little family, rather than alleviating their troubles.

Abbo, on the other hand, is slumped on the bench grinning to himself.

"You look like you know something?"

"Ah no – not much," he smiles.

Bunty realises that's all she's gonna get from him.

Their bus pulls in and they join the back of the queue. Bunty pays their one euro fares out of her special fund. After ten minutes Inma calls the driver to ask him to stop, and that's when it hits her – she's freaking out.

"I feel like the lion from The Wizard of Oz," she tells the other two as they stand at the side of the road, the bus smoking its way into the distance. "I'm shitting myself."

"What do you think got you this far?" Abbo asks, squeezing her shoulder. "Anyway, you're in good company. I'm the scarecrow cos I'm such a scruffy fucker. Oh, and I don't have a brain, of course."

"That means I am the Tin Man," says Inma, wide-eyed. "I don't have a heart!"

"You gave it to everyone," Abbo tells her, kindly. "Ask them to bring it back."

The sun shines brightly on the tarmac as they walk towards the plant. Are we off to see the fucking Wizard?

They set up using the stuff they've brought, but it's a very quiet party.

"What if no-one shows up?"

"We can riot on our own," grins Abbo.

Inma points to an approaching security guard. "We are four now!"

He's tall and wears a fluorescent orange jacket with Bajamonde printed across the back in red. "¿Qué pasa? You cannot be here."

"It's okay, señor, we're having a small party," Abbo explains.

"This is not possible. You have to leave."

"Don't you think that it's good to examine the limits of possibility, sometimes?" Abbo asks. "Maybe they're not quite as rigid as you think. Certainly in this case it's more than possible, given that we are here already."

Bunty giggles, and the man walks away, speaking into his radio. "Hay un problema, sí, tres personas están invadiendo la refinería."

Inma's busy setting up her table. She's brought a table cloth, framed pictures of her mother, and a candle. "I will save this for later," she whispers.

"What music shall we have?" asks Abbo, pulling the speakers out of his bag.

"My mother loves Vivaldi, we could play it for her?"

"Of course." Abbo looks it up on his phone.

Bunty's worries about the whole thing falling apart are dissipated by watching these two just getting on with it. Maybe it doesn't matter if there are only three of them after all. Or four, when Asif gets here. She sends him a message. "We're all ready to go here. Hopefully it's not a completely stupid idea. See you soon? X"

She looks up to see a taxi arriving, and a man in black leaning over to pay the driver. Four people get out – the priest, and three women that Bunty recognises from the rosary services. They greet Inma with hugs and kisses, and she looks delighted. "Gracias, thank you for coming!"

The newcomers greet Bunty in the same way. They don't seem to know what to do with Abbo, but he offers each of them his hand. "I'm the prodigal son," he tells them with a smile, which seems to confuse them all the more.

"It's quiet, shall we say the rosary now?" suggests the priest, and the three ladies agree. There's a small flight of concrete steps near to where Inma's set up her table; they settle on these and begin chanting.

The security guard returns with two more of his kind. "I have to tell you..." he begins, and then goes quiet when he realises a service is taking place. He looks thoughtful; sad even.

"Ave María," one of the other guards says. "I think this is not a problem for us?"

"No," agrees the first, and they nod to the priest and the three ladies before walking back into the building. It's an amazing feeling to see them retreat. Bunty relaxes, closes her eyes and thanks the goddess. When she opens them, there's a minibus, marked Gibraltar Environmental Group, turning into the car park. She counts eight people climbing out of it, and when she goes to greet them she's delighted to see that they've brought banners – and refreshments.

"Asif told us about the event," a red-haired lady tells her. "I'm Michelle."

They kiss faces, and Michelle introduces Bunty and friends to the rest of her team. "We've been campaigning about this place for twenty years," she explains. "Let's get set up, and I'll tell you more about it."

Banners go up, the chanting continues, and bottles of water are passed round. Brian, one of the Gibraltar group, has even thought to bring parasols so they can shelter from the worst of the afternoon sun.

Their new friend the security guard comes back, on his own this time, perhaps having lost the faith of his colleagues when he called them out to investigate people saying the prayers that their mothers taught them.

"No, you can't do this here. Prayers yes, but not signs..."

But nobody's taking any notice. They're all looking straight ahead, trying to work out where that noise is coming from.

That beautiful noise – a screech of guitars, a death-rattle of drums, and -

The Ace of Spades!

The Ace of Spades!

The driver and co-pilot are frenetically head-banging as they bring the battered van right up to the steps. Carlos climbs out, grinning like a maniac, followed by Luis. "I brought some friends," he tells Bunty proudly.

Luis pops the back door open and seven teenagers jump out, dusting off their jeans and t-shirts. Five girls and two boys, they gather closely and talk amongst themselves, looking over nervously at the priest.

Bunty approaches the huddle. "Thanks for coming. We need you because everyone else is too quiet. And we don't have anyone who can shout."

"I can shout!" one of the girls exclaims. "Arrrggghhhh!!!!"

Her scream gets the others going till they're drowning out the Motörhead that's still howling from the van's stereo.

"How about 'Bajamonde NO!'? Or do you wanna come up with some rhymes?"

The kids get to work on their chants, belting lines at each other in a fragmented rap battle.

Michelle comes by with information packs in both English and Spanish. Individual sheets detail the history of the plant, its illegal pollution record, accidents that have happened over the years, the absence of certain safety measures, and maps and graphs indicating the unusually high incidences of cancer in the area. "This is what we've been working on; we're constantly petitioning the EU to demand that the emission levels go down to legally established levels."

"This is brilliant."

"I don't know how much good you can do with this action, but we're happy to support it. We're all suffering so much with the poor air quality here."

Has she stepped on this woman's toes? She's wondering what to say when Carlos taps her on the shoulder.

"I wanna show you something!"

He points to a crappy looking wooden chair; Bunty goes with him to investigate. "What is it, Carlitos?" She's so happy he made it after all, and with so many reinforcements.

"Print your own T-shirt," he tells her. "Give me yours!"

"I can't! I've not got anything on underneath it!"

"Go inside the van, there is a jacket you can change into."

She does as she's told, and comes back wearing a tracksuit top. She hands him her yellow t-shirt. "It smells a bit."

"Gonna smell worse in a minute!"

He stretches it over the back of the chair, holds the stencil he made the other night in front of it, and picks up a spray can. "Black okay?"

"Sure!"

He presses the nozzle and waves the can in front of the stencil for a few seconds. Then he pulls the t-shirt off the chair back and hands it to her. Bunty hugs him, and waves her newly-decorated shirt in the air to try and lose the fumes.

Abbo's come over to see. "That's amazing, I want one."

Her shirt is now emblazoned with a splodgy image of a gas mask. She climbs in the van to change back into it, and when she emerges she sees that the rosary group are handing out corn snacks to Carlos's gang, and Luis is in the front of the van, about to drive off.

"You're leaving already?" Bunty asks.

"For a while. Here." He hands her his business card. "If you need anything today you call me, okay?"

He beeps at incoming vehicles as he exits the car park, and Inma rushes to greet the new arrivals. Bunty recognises several of them from the tanatorio. They've brought their own tables and are setting them up next to Inma's, and putting up framed photos of people she doesn't recognise. Some of the photos are of children.

"They are some of the other people in the town who have died from cancer," Inmaculada tells her. "This is my father, and these are my mother's sisters..."

Bunty squeezes her hand.

"I'm okay." Inma assures her. "I'm going to take some photos for Facebook."

Bunty leaves her to it and goes to rest on the steps. A bunch of kids run past her, chasing a balloon bouncing on the breeze. This has to be the most organised disorganised thing she's ever started. There's so much grief here, but so much positivity too. She feels grateful to everyone who's showed up, but their presence only exacerbates her anxiety; what if she's wasting their time?

I come here, a foreigner, and raise their hopes, when they have countless tragedies that I haven't experienced... Am I being an arrogant dick, like I was with Asif the other day?

Is that why he isn't here?

Chapter 45 – The Sound of the Police

Her stinky new t-shirt is making her cough, but it looks amazing. She straightens it out and looks for Michelle. There she is, sitting on a fold-up chair, shielding her eyes from the sun.

Bunty walks over. "I'm sorry about that interruption."

"No – what? It's okay."

Michelle doesn't look okay. Bunty drops down next to her. "Are you alright?"

"Yes, it's just..." she makes a choking noise.

Bunty touches her shoulder. Michelle coughs and sniffs.

"It's just, it's not only people on this side of the border who are affected. Did you know we have the best cancer doctors in Gibraltar? But they can't save us..."

"This means a lot to you," Bunty suggests, softly.

"My husband..." Michelle's voice cracks up again. "He was everything to me. He supported me in my work, he encouraged me..."

Bunty lowers her head, and her eyes fill with tears.

"He died of leukaemia. He was Gibraltarian. This is our curse too."

She flings her arm in the air. Bunty knows she means the refinery, and what comes from it.

"Then we have to fight together."

"It's all I can do. If I can prevent this pain for one other person..."

Bunty gets an idea. "Do you want to keep in touch with the people here? Maybe add them to your mailing list?"

"Would they want to? Even if it's in English?"

"We could ask them."

Michelle nods, and dries her eyes with a handkerchief. They walk together, asking everyone if they want to join the Gibraltar group's list. Only the older ones without email addresses don't join. "My English is not good, but this is practice for me," one man tells them, and his friend offers to make a Spanish translation for Michelle to use.

Bunty goes to check on everyone else. Abbo's rhyming with the teenagers; the freestyle rap battle is raging on. The plant's security team have the police involved now; two police officers are chatting with the guards. They seem to know one other, and they're sharing jokes. A rhythmic tapping sound makes her turn her head. An old woman, leaning on a walking stick, is staring at her.

"Bunty! It *is* you! I haven't seen you in ages – your hair's getting longer!"

"Nancy!" Bunty embraces her. "You made it!"

"I had to come to your leaving do," Nancy smiles. "Nice venue! How did you manage to get yourself embroiled in *this*?"

Bunty catches her up – the flight from Pandorina's place, how Inma took her in, and the tragedy that befell her family. Nancy listens intently, but at the end of her story only wants to know what happened to the boy she met on her first day in Gibraltar. "Ajit, was it?"

"Asif. You know, I don't know." Bunty looks downcast. "Something seemed to be happening with him, but now I can't get hold of him. He said he was gonna be here today."

"Hmm. I hope he's not a player."

"I don't think he is, but I'm starting to doubt myself today."

"There's still time!" Nancy says brightly. "Now, where shall I put my banner?" She unfurls a large sheet with marker-penned writing all over it.

BAJAMONDE REFINERY – WORST POLLUTER IN EUROPE

"Ace banner! Maybe we can hang it from the branches of these trees?" Bunty rummages in a box for gaffer tape and string.

"This is a great protest, Bunty."

"It's not my work, I only thought of it, but it seems like people were waiting for something like this. I'm amazed at how many've come out."

"You've got a few more now," Nancy replies darkly.

Bunty follows her gaze towards the mouth of the car park, where two vehicles are pulling in – police cars. Eight cops join the two already here, and she sees the security guards directing one, presumably the boss cop, over to her.

"Erm, hi..." She tries to smile at him but it's probably coming out weird.

"Okay, we have to stop this now. Please tell everyone to leave."

The guy sounds quite certain about this and Bunty doesn't feel she can argue. She nods, and goes to look for Abbo. Maybe she can tell everyone really slowly and string it out for a while at least. He's still with Carlos's friends; they've set up a barbecue and are cooking burgers. This makes her laugh, it's so brilliant, but she has to talk to him about the police.

"We have a slight pig-related problem, I'm afraid. They seem to want us to go..."

"Do they?" He smiles. "We're about to have our dinner. Tell them to come back later – unless they'd like some?"

Abbo's having too much fun to take this seriously. She looks over and sees the head cop talking to the priest. The priest's nodding – are they going to pack up and leave? But he's gesticulating to the tables; there are more of them than there were earlier. She finds Inmaculada.

"Inma! I'm stressing cos the police want us to go!"

"But everyone is arriving now. You know what I tell you about the Spanish, we have our own times."

Bunty exhales, and looks around. The space is crowded with shrines.

"I put the photos on Facebook," Inma tells her, "and everyone wants to come to remember their relatives now. I can't say they go home."

A cop approaches them, and Inma says something similar to him. Bunty hears sympathy in his voice. "I lost my mother and my brother too because of cancer. I would like to make a shrine for them too."

Fuck! The police might be on our side...

But then Bunty sees something that could shift the balance of power once more, though she's not sure which way. A huge coach is easing its way into the car park.

She stands, uncertain about what's going on or how to handle it, and waits to see what the deal is. The door opens and a girl jumps out and starts running towards her, followed by another girl.

"Martina! Marisol!"

They hurl themselves at her, yelling incoherently.

She hugs them both. "What's happening? Is everything okay?"

"We got lost! This is a stupid place!"

"Wow, you're here now! But...?" She looks at the coach. Dozens of people are spilling out of it.

Marisol's eyes are shining. "These are people from our village. They are here to give support. Now, did you think about all the things we told you?"

"Yes, but I haven't had time to do everything yet."

"Okay, let's see what we can do."

The three of them sit on the steps and start to plan.

Police officers mosey around talking to friends and neighbours at their shrines, while the Marinaleda posse starts to set up tables and chairs for a large group meal. From the looks of the abundant spread that's appearing in the centre, everyone's brought a dish.

There are people are flooding onto the site, though it's hard to see exactly what's happening in the now-crowded car park. And Luis is back. He's setting up a sound system but getting it a bit wrong; the screeching feedback makes everyone gasp and cover their ears. Bunty wants to help him but she's busy with Martina; the sun sets behind them as they talk. Families are lighting candles around their shrines and Bunty hears the murmuring of prayer. Sounds like they're getting a few rounds of the rosary in before the music starts.

"So, this is what we need to do..." Martina is busy writing something down. "And then I need a gang of about six..." She looks at Marisol. "Necesitamos seis voluntarios, ¿de acuerdo?"

Marisol nods and runs over to the Marinaledans, who pass her a plate of food. She puts it on the table and talks and waves her arms, until a small group of people are assembled around her. They follow her back to the steps.

"This could involve getting arrested, is that okay?" Martina asks Bunty.

"Actually, I'm hoping to go home in a few days..." She feels bad that she can't offer herself in this way.

"I understand. You do not want to get arrested in a foreign country. I won't do it either; it is much harder in that system if you are a foreigner. But we have a group here. Also you are the organiser, you must stay free!" She smiles at Bunty, and then starts to explain the task to the group of villagers.

Martina and Bunty watch as they march to the front door of the reception building. It's closed and locked, so they bang on it. A security guard shows up to see them, and the group members speak in unison.

"Hola, my name is" and then there's the sound of seven names at once, 'Marisol' being one of them. "We are here to collect information about the emissions of this refinery. Access to information is basic to democracy. Without that information we

153

cannot have a meaningful public debate. We ask the police to do their jobs and help us search for the data. Please let us through."

"I am sorry, I cannot help you with this. You are illegal here, you must leave." The guard talks into his radio as the group stands strong in their now-silent demand for information. Two more guards appear, and then the police officers. Martina and Bunty watch as the head cop approaches the Marinaledan rebels. He asks what they want, and they recite their demand again. "I have to ask you to leave the front of the building now," he tells them.

The gang stays put, and he radios for reinforcements. In minutes they're surrounded by a dozen police. "We have to arrest you now," the chief cop explains.

"We just want information. It is our right," Marisol argues.

"I know, but I must do this." He gives the order, and the seven are cuffed and escorted to a waiting van.

They go peacefully, but Bunty is horrified.

"Are you okay?" Martina asks her.

"I feel responsible! This was my idea!"

"No, that was my idea," Martina corrects her, "and they all knew they would probably get arrested. We will wait for them tomorrow, I think they will go free. You cannot make an impact without confronting all the systems. That's why we will carry on like this. Did you bring the large banner?"

"Yes, but I don't have anywhere to hang it. It's too big!"

"Leave that with us." Martina goes back to the group to find more volunteers.

There's more intermingling now; the rest of the Marinaledans are chatting with the La Línea families. Inma comes to tell her that there are now families from neighbouring town San Roque in attendance, and some from Algeciras. The tables are now lined up at the top of the flight of steps, filling up the forecourt. It's a moving sight. Bunty goes to each one, greeting the people who are tending to them. Most of the shrines support several photos, evidencing the number of family members lost. Then she sees an old man sitting by a table with just one picture frame on it.

"My wife." He rubs his brow. "She used to walk by the bay every day. We have no other family."

Bunty sits down next to him. There's nothing she can say. She imagines him going back to his empty house, senses his desolation, and wishes she could turn it into something happy. They watch the crowds together, and the children running between various family groups.

"It is good to be here," he tells her after a while.

She smiles at him, and hopes he'll find a sense of family in this community somehow. When Inma comes by she introduces them, and Bunty finds out that this man is called Ignacio.

Luis fires up the sound system with some gentle Spanish pop, and Bunty's glad he's chosen something that isn't metal. Many of the kids run across to dance, and the teenagers gravitate towards the PA speakers where they stand in groups and shout at each other. The boss cop guy approaches her again.

"We are going to have to close it down now, there is a fire risk with people burning barbecues."

"There's a bigger fire risk behind us," Bunty retorts. "Why don't you close *this* down?" She didn't know she was going to say that; the collective grief of the local people has got under her skin.

"I know, but I have my job," he says sadly.

"Just following orders, huh?"

He walks away.

Erm, diplomatic much? Anxiety churns her guts. She looks for Nancy, who she discovers chilling in a deckchair near the sound system, tapping her foot to the music and devouring a burger. "Hey Bunty! Nice party!"

"Yeah, the filth wants to shut it down though."

"What are they going to do? Use force?" Nancy gestures around her. "These are their own people, their relatives and neighbours." And it's true – the police have joined in. She even sees one of them dancing a bit, but he stops when he notices her looking at him.

"Ha! Yes."

"Bunty, you are not in charge. You started it, but what happens now is not under your control. Have a beer?" Nancy holds out a bottle.

"Fuck it. Alright."

The priest and many of the other families left around half ten, and Inma and Carlos departed in a taxi with their relatives before midnight. but most of Carlos's friends are still here. The Marinaledans are sticking around too, some of them drinking and smoking, others resting on their bus; they have to wait till tomorrow for the release of their seven. Bunty knows Spanish people like to party late, but she didn't realise how much. At one point she finds herself dancing with a cop, and they end up chatting.

"You lot have been quite cool with us."

"Well, we have sympathy for your cause. But this is not normal. You have to be careful."

Bunty raises an eyebrow. "How do you mean?"

"Just don't do anything else illegal, okay?"

She nods, and goes to see Abbo. He's sitting on the floor smoking a roll up.

"Erm, I think we might have pulled it off."

"Yeah, we did!" He high fives her.

"Wanna call it a day? I'm knackered!"

"What time is it?" He checks his phone. "Half four. Sure."

"What's up Luis?" Bunty shouts over the noise. "Shall we pack up now?"

Luis's eyes are red and he looks about ready to give in – but not quite yet. "I play one more song," he tells her, rummaging through his record box and pulling out a battered piece of vinyl with an excited flourish. "This is a very special artist for us," Luis tells her. "Camarón de la Isla. He is from this province. We have a statue of him by the sea. He died of lung cancer…"

155

The needle goes down and Bunty tunes into rhythmically strummed strings and handclaps at intervals she can't compute. An acoustic guitar is plucked and chimed, and when the singer's voice powers out it's like nothing she's ever heard. It arrives on the night breeze like an insurrection. Everyone gathers around the sound system; people raise their drinks, some clap along, some dance. A woman's voice joins in so powerfully that the whole thing becomes a storm that nothing can stand against.

Luis appears beside her and whispers some of the words.

I can't stand it

And I can't even live this way

Because I can't, because I don't want to, not even if God wants it

Because I can't do it anymore, because I can't do it, because I can't live without it.

I am a Gypsy and I come to your wedding,

To tear my shirt,

Which is the only shirt that I have...

And that's how the party ends, on a high of refusal, of kisses and embraces, and promises to never give up.

Chapter 46 – Way Home

Bunty and Abbo stay to help Luis take down the sound system and pack it up. When they finally drive out of there Luis tells her to look to the left. That's when she glimpses her banner hanging across the front of the petrol station forecourt. How the fuck? So now the Bajamonde garage is displaying the words

BAJAMONDE = HELL
Let La Línea Live

Luis pulls up the van and they take photos, whooping and cheering as they do. One click, and it's out there.

Even that doesn't prepare her for what they see next. They appear, one by one, on billboards, street furniture, recycling bins and walls all along the way back to Inma's; the entire town is covered in gas masks.

"Woah!"

Bunty turns to Abbo, her eyes massive.

"Is this what you and Carlos did the other night?"

"One or two of them, yeah. But you remember I said he has a lot of friends?"

"I do remember..."

"I think they've been busy."

Luis pulls up on Calle Aurora, and Bunty turns to him. "You're a star!"

"It is strange, we needed one lady from England to help us do this."

"It was you guys who did it! I just had the idea! But," she looks at him hopefully, "Do you think you'll do it again?"

"I hope so. Then I will be there with my protest bus."

He smiles and they kiss goodbye. Bunty and Abbo trudge up the three flights of stairs; she couldn't send him back to the beach, and she's sure Inma won't mind. He crashes on armchair cushions on the floor, and she has the sofa. The last thing she does before her head hits the arm rest is check her phone for messages or missed calls from Asif.

There's nothing.

Chapter 47 – Irish Stew

Bunty rises late, and the apartment is silent, so she takes a shower and heads out. There's only one thing on her mind: she doesn't know if she's crazy or stupid, but she just wants to know what happened to Asif.

It's Sunday – maybe the border will have fewer staff than usual? There were no consequences from her last attempt, and she feels confident today. In a few minutes she's at Focona. She hangs back for a while, squinting at the first corner – Spanish passport control – until a German family in matching white shorts strides past. In an attempt to replicate the sort-of success she had last time she files into the security booth with her newly-adopted family. Maybe this group of white-dressed white people isn't the best Trojan horse. The security guard glances at her, then his eyes flash in recognition.

"Un momento, señorita," he commands, one hand reaching under his desk. "I need to see your passaporte."

Shit. Of course he does. Her stomach drops.

"Oh sorry, let me find it."

She rummages in her bag, hoping she can somehow deflect whatever's going on. Her new mum and dad have disappeared into the distance, unaware of her existence, and she wishes she had her real parents here right now. A door opens behind the desk and two more cops appear; in a moment they're beside her. A tall fella with a Morrissey-esque quiff grabs her by the left arm, but there's no vegetarian tenderness here.

"I am arresting you."

"What for?" she demands, terrified yet furious. She flinches as a second cop places a metal bracelet on her right wrist. He pulls her arms behind her back and closes the other side on her left. Snap, snap.

"For travelling without documentation. This is not legal in Spain."

No no no no no.

The officer behind the desk shouts that "no pasa nada", nothing is happening, as he tries to herd the pedestrians in the room towards Gibraltar, but several have stopped to stare. Suddenly she's a figure in a drama; she hears a woman shouting "Esa chica!" pointing Bunty out to her friend. Her bag's been caught under her arm and they're hurting her as they push her through the door. Once outside they march her away from the building. She feels like an animal chosen for slaughter.

"Where are you taking me?" Her voice squeaks as it comes out.

"The police station, of course."

Morrissey states this with a satisfied certainty in his voice, but there's tension there too. They don't do this very often, she senses. Yet they'd seemed so prepared, like they were waiting for her.

A Guardia Civil car is parked outside and more officers are standing around it, watching keenly. They sport black uniforms, laid back demeanours, stubble and guns. She's expecting to be shoved into the car, but instead they walk her to a nearby building. It's part of the border complex, but it's not one she'd noticed before; a brand-new police station, all white and shiny. Bunty can smell the paint as they manhandle her inside. They uncuff her to free her bag, and drop it on the counter.

"I need that. It has my inhalers in; I'm asthmatic."

"If you need medicines, we ask the doctor first," the guy behind the desk tells her. This one looks just like George Michael in the video for 'Outside'; he has slicked-back hair, and aviator shades cover half his face.

Why am I being arrested by Spanish cop versions of eighties pop stars? she wonders, as they take away her belongings, her rights, and her freedom.

"You go to the cell now."

The shock and terror have done a number on her guts; she has to shit.

"I need to use the bathroom."

George Michael looks confused. "You want a bath?"

"Servicios," she corrects herself. "Por favor."

George shrugs. He and Morrissey guide her round the corner into a disabled toilet. Are they gonna stay here in with me? But Spanish Morrissey mutters something and goes to wait outside. Thank fuck they don't take their job *that* seriously.

She raises her arms towards him. "I can't..."

He removes the cuffs, then lets her have the room. Afterwards she washes the sweat of fear from her face. When she looks in the mirror there's a line on her forehead she's never seen before.

The men escort her to a corridor that hasn't been painted yet. At the furthest door she knows this is where she must go; they don't need to push. It's just a dark room with a bench in it, nothing else. Once she's inside, a striplight flickers on.

The door closes to the sound of their muttering voices. Dizziness pushes her onto the bench. Deep breaths might help; she drags the tang of disinfectant deep into her innards, then feels sick. She presses her back up against the wall, quelling the urge to cry, then gives in, leans forward and sobs.

All those times I thought I was trapped, and now I really fucking am...

But when I tell them what's happened with my passport it'll be okay, won't it? They'll understand I'm trying to sort it out and get a new one? And I'll be able to get legal help, make a phone call...?

The door opens and she jerks her head up. Maybe they've realised how stupid this is, and they're letting her go. But it's a copper carrying a tray, which he places at the end of the bench. "For you. To eat."

Eating is the last thing she wants to do. Bunty inspects the offerings – two slices of ham, a hard bread roll and an apple, pitted and bruised. She puts the tray on the floor so she can lie down. The strip light hurts her eyes; she turns onto her side. Her hip presses uncomfortably against the bench so she bends her knees to take the pressure off. It doesn't help much.

How long am I going to be here?

She feels panic rising. Don't go there.

I wish I could speak to Sofia.

I wish I could switch my mind off.

I'm scared.

I'm so fucking angry.

How can they arrest you for not having a passport? I know you're meant to have ID with you in Spain, and of course it's dodgy to try and cross a border without it. But is this how they treat you for doing that? All I'm trying to do is get mine back! But then I got distracted, wanting to change things... maybe I went too far. Will they take Inma and Abbo in too? Who should I speak to when they let me make my call? Nancy, or Inma – but what if that gets her into trouble? Or Asif, but what's even happened to him? Or my parents? No, I can't call them...

Bunty paces the cell. The questions in her mind won't shut up, and there's nothing she can do to get answers right now. She decides to engage her internal jukebox, mentally unpacking her favourite tracks in the hope of quieting the tumult within. Where to start? Sleater-Kinney's back catalogue is the obvious way to go, but the second track of their first album chokes her up straight away.

When I look and I can't find you
Feels like you have gone away...

Chapter 48 – No Hospital

She lies awake listening to the rumble of traffic as it crosses the border. Martina had been confident that the Marinaleda Seven would be out on bail the next morning – this morning – so Bunty supposes that overnight is the normal length of time that one would expect to languish for minor offences. The thought relaxes her enough that she can use some of her solitary time to process the events of recent weeks.

The ship was a nightmare, but then I ended up being trapped in Gibraltar... Escaping to Spain felt so liberating, like I could think again, and learn so much, and act, and now I have friends here and it's started to feel like home. But when I leave, what do I go back to? Futile job searches, more pressure, and what if I give in this time and take a zero hours contract doing something I hate? Job prospects are so much worse here though... Any day now I'll have my passport... I just need out of this cell!

She wonders why she feels trapped most of the time. And then, how she can possibly feel empowered, in a system like this?

But yesterday... shit, was it yesterday? That was powerful. All those people, making a noise, taking a stand, realising they could get up Bajamonde's noses, at least a little bit. Not as much as Bajamonde has been up their noses, all their lives, but it's a start. I really hope it's gonna have an effect, that it will make people's lives better here – that they'll do more actions, keep the pressure up. There were so many there, it was frickin' awesome. It might have been the best day of my life...

But where was Asif though? Her mind switches between worry for him and indignant rage at him for going AWOL, for letting her down, for not caring – for not liking her anymore. And for pretending to like her in the first place.

She tries lying on her side again.

Damn, thoughts are painful in here. And this bench...

The door buzzes and clicks open.

"Come outside."

She has no idea what the time is. In the doorway are two men she hasn't seen before; Morrissey and George must have gone home. Her latest guards walk her down the corridor.

"Are you letting me go?"

"No. Vamos al hospital," one of them, an older guy, tells her. "Para tu medicamentos."

Shit. Why are they making such a big deal about this, when I'll be free in a few hours?

It's dark and quiet outside. There's a car waiting, and they guide her into it. From the back seat she stares at orange-lamp-lit empty streets. It seems late, or early even. She glimpses the dashboard clock: 02:50. When they stop it's 03:03.

Wow, I'm being escorted by police into La Línea hospital. Could my life get any less glamorous?

They're parked in front of the main doors for Urgencias. Her bodyguards give curt instructions for her to get a move on, and they stay close, one on either side. The hospital looks grim, but it's quiet at least. Is this where Lola was... where she died?

At the front desk, an understandably cheerless woman in a pale green uniform addresses the officers. In the waiting room an old man perched on the edge of a row of seats shuffles anxiously when they enter. The cops tell her to sit, but they stand. She tries to read the notices on the board.

"Boonty Maguweer!"

It's hard to know where the voice has come from. It turns out it's emerged from a nurse in a small room at the side of the waiting area. They all pile in.

"¿Tienes asma?"

"Sí."

"¿Qué medicamentos usas?"

Bunty reels off the details of her inhalers, and their doses.

He tells her to wait outside, and they bumble back into the waiting room. The old fella's still there when, ten minutes later, Bunty is called again. Her chaperones walk with her into a corridor lined with numbered doors. A doctor sticks his head out of one of them, and calls her inside. Her friends come too. The same questions, but this time there's an examination, a cold stethoscope on her chest. The cops look away as the doctor feeds the listening end of the device down the front of her t-shirt. This has to be the weirdest night of her life. The doctor writes a prescription, the older officer leans over and takes it from him, and then she's being bundled back out to the street.

They seem more relaxed on the way back. Mission accomplished. But Bunty needs to know what's going on.

"How long are you keeping me for? Can I go in the morning?"

"It is not our decision. You have to go to the court."

Does it have to be so complicated? All she did was walk into an office without a little booklet with her picture in it. It's hardly the crime of the century.

"I think I should have a lawyer?" She's vague about this shit. Should know better.

"We will get you a lawyer," says the older one, somewhat ominously. What's that tone of voice for? His younger counterpart is smirking. What have I got into here?

Bunty sits back, feeling mega uneasy as the prospect of a morning departure appears to slip away. She looks out at the street. If I wave at passers-by, maybe they could spring me out? She considers banging on the window and shouting that she's being kidnapped, but there's no-one out there. The streets are empty, these windows are smoked, and no-one's going to intercept a cop car for me...

Back at the station her rubbish new friends take her by the arms, returning her to the cell without so much as a 'hasta luego'.

I could do with a drink, guys, she says to herself. And some pizza or something. Fuck.

She groans, lowers herself onto the bench, and weeps.

Chapter 49 – Caught

Exhaustion took her and wrapped her around its haggard finger, spinning her into a darkness that obliterated pain and confusion. But the door click has no mercy; it comes when it comes, and there's still no light at the high window. What now?

"Come with us."

Maybe this is it, after all – time to leave. But she remembers the talk in the car.

"Where to?"

"The court."

The car seat yields to her form. She sinks into it, closes her eyes and tries to work everything out. I guess this is normal procedure, just what they have to do? And this must be Monday morning, so that's the soonest they could do it. Maybe everything's under control.

But it doesn't feel that way.

Bunty opens her eyes and looks out at the bay; they're about to drive by the refinery. Will her banner still be there? They move along quiet roads, passing commuters heading into Gibraltar. There must be a court in La Línea? But we're leaving town…

Petrol station signage glows in the distance. Her guards talk in low voices, something about 'Bajamonde' – so they *do* know about her role in the protest the other day. As they pass, Bunty sees that there's nothing suspended from the forecourt roof; her banner's been taken down, of course.

There's a sign for San Roque. Maybe the court's here? But they turn onto the motorway.

"¿Qué tribunal? ¿Qué cuidad?"

"Algeciras," the younger of the two responds.

Her heart sinks even further and she wishes she could reach her nails to bite them. They enter Algeciras as dawn illuminates the eastern sky, casting an orange sheen on shabby apartment towers. It looks like a city without a soul.

The handbrake cranks up in front of another police station. She's ordered out of the car, escorted inside, and handed to a new pair of guards. Bunty eyes them anxiously. These two seem quite perky, and have coffee breath; she guesses they've just come on duty – unlike the last pair, who must be yearning for their beds by now. They take her to a basement corridor lit by harsh strip lights. The taller of the two unlocks a cell door and looks at her like she should know what to do.

Bunty steps into a windowless cave, and the door closes behind her. Scared to move, she waits for her eyes to adjust to the darkness. The smell of damp, mould and sweat threatens to overwhelm her. She makes out two beds, but there's no-one on either. She doesn't want to touch anything, let alone sit down, so she freezes, imagining rats cavorting around her feet.

"Any room service in this place?" she says out loud, but then stops. It even feels wrong to speak; germs will get in her mouth.

I thought I was going to court...

She paces the tiny space between the beds in frustration and disgust. Her knee catches the corner of a bed and she falls forward, palms to the wall; now her hands are sticky.

Eww.

How long am I going to be in here?

The words of the rosary prayer appear in her mind. She mouths them under her breath:

Dios te salve, María. Llena eres de gracia.

I'm not going crazy... I'm not going Catholic...

There's a noise behind the door. She turns to face it. Clattering, clunking, and it opens. Stark white light and the same pair of coppers. "Fold your blanket. We go now."

They can't see enough to know that she didn't lie down, and they don't know her well enough to understand that she wouldn't touch one of their stinking blankets. She steps into the light and they escort her to the ground floor, into a room that looks like all the interrogation rooms on all the TV cop shows.

"Sit, here." They indicate a plastic chair on one side of the table, and the shorter geezer places himself opposite her. His mate leans against the wall. There's a sheet of paper on the tabletop.

"You sign here," the one facing her says, indicating a dotted line at the bottom.

"What is it?"

"This is the legal paperwork you have to sign before you go to court." He hands her a biro.

"Okay, I'll read it."

He looks up at the lanky one, who is now standing at the side of the table, and raises his eyebrows.

"No time to read. Just sign," he tells her.

"I'm trying to concentrate," she responds irritably, her finger tracing along the lines of Spanish. Some words she knows, others she can guess, but a lot of the terminology is beyond her.

This is to certify that I do not require a lawyer... I do not require a telephone call... something something... Embassy will not be informed...

"I'm not signing this."

"You have to sign it now, then we go to court. You not sign, you do not go to court."

"You can't hold me without going to court."

"Do you know the law in Spain?"

Both men laugh. Then the shorter one scrapes back his chair and gets up to lean over her. "Sign!" he shouts, banging his fist on the table.

Bunty jumps in her skin. Her heart's pounding, and her mind is greying out. She hugs herself, and finds she's shaking.

"We have work to do," he continues. "You are selfish to take our time like this."

164

His colleague crosses the room and kicks the wall behind her.

Bunty chokes on a sob.

"Tranquila. Calm down. You will have a lawyer. He is waiting for you upstairs. But we cannot go until you sign this." He sighs. "Now, please."

"I don't believe you."

"I shit in the milk..."

His Spanish swearing almost makes Bunty laugh, but he doesn't notice as he's now speaking into his radio. "Yes, problem with detainee. Come down."

Bunty watches the men shuffle and grumble, and wonders if this is a dream. In which case, how interesting: she observes details about the room; the clock behind his head, which reads five to ten. The calendar, illustrated with a painting of a matador and an elaborately decorated bull. The door of the room opening, and another man coming in. He's not police. He's wearing a white shirt and a black tie, and his grey hair has thinned on the top of his tanned head.

"The problem?"

"She not sign."

The man huffs, puts his hands on the table and leans towards Bunty. She looks at his stretched-out eyebrows. He has an age spot on his cheek.

He straightens up. "She is sick?"

"The La Línea office took her to the hospital. All okay. Just asthma."

He breathes out heavily. "Señorita... Magooeeray..."

She looks up; that's an interesting pronunciation.

"You must sign this now, so that I can represent you in court. I am your lawyer."

"But the paper says I don't want a lawyer. So I don't want to sign it."

"It is difficult to understand because it is in Spanish. It only means that you will not choose a different lawyer. Because the police cannot provide another lawyer. And we want for you to have a lawyer."

Bunty stares at him. Is this true? If so, it would make some sort of sense...

"If you sign it now, we can go up to court and I will be able to get you out of here."

She likes this one better than the other two. He hasn't hit or kicked anything close to her; he's the least of three evils.

"I can tell you that it is safe for you to sign it, because I am a lawyer!" He laughs gently.

"But it says that I can't have a phone call or... something about the Embassy."

"Tranquila – we will arrange those things after the court session. But now we must go. The judge waits for us."

"And if I don't?"

"Can you represent yourself in court without a lawyer? Your Spanish is this good?"

"Yeah... No."

"Let me help you. Is my job." He smiles.

I don't know. I don't fucking know.

All their eyes are on her. She doesn't want to give them the satisfaction, but all she can do now is trust this lawyer guy. She signs. The cops breathe out in unison, and the lawyer beams. "I'll see you upstairs," he says, but not to her – and leaves the room.

The officers take one of Bunty's arms each, squeezing more than they need to, which would be not at all; she winces as they walk her to the lift. In the moments of weightless suspension between floors she absorbs their contempt, and examines their footwear. Police and their shiny shoes; they tick all the boxes. She's checking their jackets for doughnut crumbs as the door opens at a floor marked 'Planta 1'. Shit, we're really getting out and about today.

They enter a well-lit room that actually has windows. She can see bright blue sky and the crown of a tree outside. At the far end there's an old bloke with grey hair sitting behind a big desk. Is this the court? Could they not have let her use the bathroom first, or given her a drink? She could really use some food as well – anything with calories in it would be just fine. The taller of her cops walks over to the old bloke and puts some papers on his desk. He scans the sheets, raises his eyebrows. The other cop tells her where to sit. This means she's facing the old fella, who must be the judge. But she's more interested in the woman next to her; Bunty guesses she's from Morocco; a scarf is covering her hair.

"She is the interpreter," the shorter officer tells her.

"Thank you!" she whispers to the woman. "I'm so glad you're here!"

"I sorry, my English no good," the woman tells her anxiously.

Bunty's mind explodes in a cascade of interrobangs. She stares at the woman. "But you're the interpreter?"

"I try with you," the woman answers kindly.

Tears spring into Bunty's eyes. She looks for the lawyer. He's up at the front, talking with the judge in hushed tones. Is he supposed to be doing that?

She feels like she's falling down a rabbit hole. Her hands are sweating, pressed flat on the table; she searches her mind for something that will help her. An image of the Virgin Mary appears, and Bunty tells it to fuck off.

"What did you say?" The lawyer's standing in front of her, looking perturbed. "You are certain you are okay?"

"I'm not really okay," she tells him. She wonders if she should retract her signature.

"This won't take long, and then you can leave here."

"Okay."

"Don't worry, I will tell you what to do."

The proceeding starts, and she can't follow much of what they're saying; they're all talking so fast. The lawyer goes to speak with the judge again, then the judge reads something out loud, and looks at her.

"Say 'Sí' now."

"I didn't understand what he just said."

"That's okay. Just say yes."

She looks around – they're all looking at her expectantly. She wants to run away. The lawyer nods.

"Sí." She breaks down in tears.

The two policías converge on her. "Stand up."

166

"Can I go now?"

"Yes," the tall one tells her.

She does as she's told, and the shorter one puts something cold and heavy on her hand. It snaps in place. She looks down at the chained metal bracelet, one end on her, the other on him.

"Come with me."

Chapter 50 – The Mouth

"What's happening?"

"You are going to the jail."

"What for? I don't understand!"

"It is the decision of the judge." He shoves her into the back seat, slides in after her.

"But I didn't know what was happening in there!" She's tenses herself, leaning forward as though she could somehow push herself out through the middle of the car.

"This is something you must say to the judge. We cannot help you." He secures his seat belt. "Your belt. Close it."

She obeys, and stares blankly as the city slips by. For the first time since she got here the sky is obscured by storm clouds. They move between charred fields, where skeletons of torched trees stand motionless, and soot coats the ground like black snow. She hears her guards say "fuego" – fire – and then "bota fuegos" – boot fires. It makes no sense, until it does, as they enter a lane signposted 'Cárcel de Botafuegos'.

A security guard steps reluctantly from his booth into the drizzle, and the driver-cop shows him some papers. He nods and returns to his shed. A huge gate opens and swallows them.

"Welcome to your new home," Her backseat companion shoves her from the car.

Bunty's guts grind like gears as she's frogmarched through a door marked 'Ingreso'. The cops give her to a prison guard who wordlessly ushers her into a large, glass-walled room. There's space for her to move in here, to get the blood flowing in her limbs after a night and morning of confinement. She rubs her wrist and swings her arms and watches as the police car exits the compound.

Through the transparent walls she watches a man in an office doing paperwork, and another mopping the floors. Is anyone going to come and see me, or are they just going to leave me here? She paces some more as people and vehicles come and go outside. Can't they at least give me something to eat, or a drink? She feels like a cat waiting to be fed – the pet that everyone forgot. These people shouldn't be allowed pets, it should be illegal! This is no way to treat anyone, but it's how she's being treated, and this time there's no way out that she can fathom. These fences are taller even than the ones at the Bajamonde plant. Could she crawl through them like she did there? But she doesn't have bolt cutters, and she can't get anywhere near.

There's nothing to do, no music, no phone, no book, no pen. Just her mind, and that's a mess. Rage and tears get her nowhere, yet time passes somehow. Where's it even going? How can it go, when she can't? Doesn't time only exist in relation to motion? She draws a graph on the glass, but her finger grease is barely visible; she can't see the axes. Can she not even get a wash? In her mind she composes a review for TripAdvisor:

Lack of en suite facilities. No breakfast included. Uncommunicative staff. Uninspiring views. No WiFi. No kettle. The decor is very tired.

Zero stars.

Why aren't they coming to get her?

Then she finds that, if she goes to a certain window and stares into the office across the hall, she can see a clock. It looks like it says half past two. Have they forgotten her? Maybe this is this what a goldfish feels like; all the fish in all the tanks are probably swimming around shouting "Help me, I'm trapped in here!" They'd be banging on the glass too, if they had hands.

The guy in the office looks up, and then back down at his work.

Later she lies down and squints at sunlight breaking through the silvery storm clouds as it wends its way towards the west. Time disappears for a while. She snorts at the man standing over her. "Get up," he snaps, as though she's been keeping him waiting all day.

In his office, he indicates an orange chair. She sits on it, and looks at him expectantly. There must be a reason why they kept her here all day. They've realised they've made a mistake, and they're letting her out. Maybe someone from the UK has been in touch, or someone from the Embassy? They must have been told them what's happened to her. Maybe it's been taking all day to sort out the paperwork. She watches intently as he flicks though what must be her records. Then he holds up her bag.

Hey, my phone! She smiles. I really need to make some calls.

He turns to a shelf and picks up a grey bin liner and a cardboard box, then tips everything that was in her bag out onto the table. He picks the items up one by one and starts tossing them into the box or the bag, seemingly at random. Her tampons, her Shopping T-shirt, her phone and shades go to the box, followed by the little scrap of paper on which Asif wrote his number, and her wallet. He counts the money in it, writes something down. She starts to cry, her body trembling against the plastic chair. The man looks up, having finished dividing her things.

"Why are you crying?"

"I... This..." She doesn't know how to answer.

He shakes his head in disgust, makes a huffing noise, and passes her the bin bag. It suddenly strikes her that this man is a prisoner here too. He isn't going home tonight, and neither is she.

She wipes her eyes. "I get to keep this?"

"Take it with you to your cell. The other things you get when you leave. And you need this." He hands her a folded blanket, brown and bobbly with age.

She accepts it, and follows the man's glance to a figure leaning on the wall outside the office. A prison guard. He exchanges a few words with the man in the office, and turns to Bunty.

"Come with me."

The guard leads her along a grey walled corridor. They take a lift, and ascend one floor in silence. Bunty couldn't be more spaced out. She's beyond hunger, thirst, beyond feeling even. There's nothing left of her, and maybe that's what all of this was for.

Corridors and doors. Many of them, and at the very end, a big room. It's very loud. It smells bad. And inside there are loads and loads of women.

Chapter 51 – Independence Day

Bunty tries to take in the scene, but it's overwhelming. Many of the women are staring at her; others glance up, then look away. The guard from reception leaves her with one of the guards on duty in the canteen, who asks if she has eaten.

She shakes her head, and stares at the counter where she can see that food is being served. He takes her over there, and as they pass women lean, leer and huddle to discuss her arrival. The guard points to a shelf underneath the glass-fronted food display; she reaches into it and pulls out a brown plastic tray that's divided into sections. He indicates she's to hand it over, so she passes it to a woman in an apron, who winks at her and pours something into one of the sections. The tray then goes to three other women, each of whom place something on it; she follows it along to the last one, who gives it back to her with a grim "aproveche". Bunty turns and gazes at the rows of tables. The guard must realise how out of it she is because he leads her to a table where two young women are sitting, and points to a spot on the bench. She shuffles onto it, and he returns to the wall to resume his leaning duties.

One of these young women is very thin; she leans her knobbly elbows on the table and gazes straight at Bunty. This is not conducive to eating. Bunty's consumed so little in the past two days that her stomach's shrunk, and she's so stressed that she's not even sure if she'll be able to digest anything anyway, but she picks up the bread roll and presses her teeth onto it. Shit; her teeth don't work either. She looks down at the rock-like bread, then up at the staring woman.

It's the one sitting next to her who speaks. A regular-looking Spanish lady, in her mid-thirties maybe. She could be a school teacher or a secretary. "Bienvenido. Welcome. I hope they don't expect us to show you round." Through narrowed eyes she peers at the guard, who doesn't look back at her.

"I don't know," Bunty tells her. "He didn't say."

"She'll work it out. She's a smart one," decides Skinny Girl.

"She's gonna have to," says the normal-looking lady, and laughs at a volume that strikes Bunty as unreasonably loud. Skinny Girl joins in with a granular chuckle. Bunty examines the contents of her tray with grim curiosity. She tentatively tastes a bit of something brown and mushy, but decides not to continue; she can't tell if the stuff is meat or vegetable in origin. Should she ask them whether the prison serves vegetarian food? Mm, maybe not. So much for a welcoming committee.

They have questions for her though.

"Stealing?" Skinny Girl asks her, twinkly eyed. The way she says it though, it's almost like a statement.

Bunty stares at her.

"Drugs," asserts Normal Lady.

Bunty's about to tell them both to fuck themselves when a bell rings and her voice is drowned out by the cacophony of benches scraping the floor. The women at her table get up and walk towards the door, along with most of the others in the

171

room, throwing the remains of their food in bins as they go, or pocketing items for later.

She doesn't have time to process the stereotyping. She looks down at her tray and decides to keep the half-orange and the bread, and takes a sip from her cup. It's some kind of watered-down juice, and it tastes gross; she goes to the bins to drop most of her meal into it. A shout comes from behind her. "Oi! Guapa negra! Hahaha!" She turns to look into Normal Lady's beaming face.

"You forget your blanket. You want I look after it for you? Mmm, nice clean blanket," she purrs, rubbing it on her torso.

"No. Wait." She holds her bread and orange in one hand and walks back to claim her blanket. The woman relinquishes it. Prison's not as hard as they make out, thinks Bunty; I had worse teasing than this at school. Then she hears another shout, a male voice this time. She swings round to see the guard. "Don't leave your tray like this. Put it away properly," and he points towards trolleys where the other women have stacked theirs. She crams the blanket under her arm and carries the tray in her left hand, food in her right, sensing that it's better not to put anything down around here. He's shouting again. "Don't leave your cup." She looks at him in puzzlement, and he opens his eyes wide. "Cup," he repeats, so Bunty grabs the vessel with her now free hand.

"I take you to your room."

Room now? She follows him unsteadily from the canteen to another corridor lined with identical, heavy looking doors. Halfway along he stops and opens one of them with a card. The door springs open, and she follows him inside. She looks around the 'room' in dismay. Their two bodies take up most of the space. There's a bunk bed and, behind a low wall, a shower, a sink and a metal toilet with no seat.

"You will meet your neighbour soon."

And he's gone.

Bunty stands on tiptoe to look out of the window, which is small and predictably barred. There's a concrete covered yard and another wing of the prison, long and grey; she guesses that's how this one looks from the outside too. She turns back to the room and inspects a small shelf built into the wall opposite the bed. There are a few pieces of clothing in it, and a historical novel in a language she doesn't recognise. On the bottom bunk a hairbrush and a mirror rest on top of a neatly folded blanket, so she guesses that the top one is hers. She puts her things on there.

How long will I be here? Just a few days, right?

'Just a few days' though. That was what she'd thought about Gibraltar – and then Spain. So *this* is what the bottom of the rabbit hole really looks like.

"Oi!" An old lady has entered the cell, and is shouting. "What the fuck you want?"

"I, err... live here now?"

"Zeu!" invokes the woman. "All I need! You leave my things!"

Bunty stares at her, but is repelled by the fury in the woman's eyes. There has to be another cell I can stay in...

She grabs her bin bag, blanket and cup, and moves to the doorway where she looks both ways like a cat that's not sure whether it's safe to go out. Women are pouring into their cells. Who should she ask? There's a male guard positioned at the end of the corridor. She walks along slowly, uncertain of her rights – does she have any? Women bump past her, regarding her curiously, or purposely avoiding her. She's about to call to the guard when a short-haired woman steps out from her cell and grabs Bunty by the elbow. "What are you doing?"

"Erm, I just got here..."

"I know that! Look at you!"

"The woman I'm sharing a cell with is really not happy about it."

"Well fuck her. We don't get to choose these things."

"I was going to ask the guard..."

"Him? Nooo." She looks across at the bony, grey-haired, uniformed guy. "Don't ask him anything. Not if you want a peaceful life. Listen," and she starts to push Bunty back in the direction she came from. "Get back into your cell. You must be there in time for inspection."

"Okay," Bunty answers dully. The combined lack of food, drink and sleep is really getting to her. "When?"

"Now!" she whisper-shrieks, as a buzzer sounds and the last of the women run into their appointed spaces. She pushes her again, and Bunty half-runs, half-trips down the corridor and back into her cell.

"Son of a bitch," mutters her cell mate, on seeing her return.

Bunty sighs, throws her things onto the top bunk once more, and begins to climb up.

"What you think you're doing? Is cell inspection!" caws the old lady.

Bunty freezes. She has no freaking idea what to do. The old woman's also standing still, next to the bed, so Bunty goes to the corner by the window just to put some space between them.

A tall blonde guard enters the room and looks around. Her eyes settle on Bunty, then on her bunk.

"Put your things away! Stand by the bed!"

Huh? In what order? "Wh... where should I put them?"

"You have a shelf. Can't you see?" She huffs. "Always this trouble with new girls!"

Bunty looks from the guard to the old woman, who is smirking. She picks up her bin bag and squeezes it into the shelf space in the wall, on top of the items that are already there. Her cell mate makes a low growling noise. The guard's eyes move from Bunty to the bed; Bunty goes to stand by it.

"Tidy it later. You are in prison now, you must learn. No more lazy ways." And she turns and walks out of the room.

Straight away the old lady starts bitching about the bin bag on the shelf, so Bunty grabs it and puts it back on her bunk. "No privileges for you now!" gripes the woman, and Bunty wonders what privileges she's been experiencing so far that could now be taken away. This is exhausting. The best thing to do is to hide in her bunk. First though, she needs to pee. But with this woman watching her? She steps squeamishly into the bathroom area, and when she looks back the lady is watching her, eyes lit up with glee. At least the old one's cackling obscures the sound of

Bunty's urine hitting metal, as she squats – but does not sit – over the bowl of the toilet.

A fragment of a song spins into her head:

How low can you go?

She has a theme tune now, at least.

Bunty washes her hands using the bar of soap at the edge of the sink, which attracts more snarking from her roommate. And then, since there's nothing else for it, she strips out of her grimy clothes, squirrels them in a pile at the foot of her bunk, and climbs with bare feet up the metal rungs.

She lies down, so that less of her can be seen. "What's your name?" she ventures, eyeing the old lady as she shuffles around the miniscule room.

"Doina!" the woman replies, brightly enough. "What they call you?"

"Bunty."

"Bunky. Buna Bunky!"

Bunty sighs. "Where are you from?"

"Romania. You English?"

"Yes."

"London? I wanna go to London."

"The North. Leeds."

The woman grunts, and Bunty shuts her eyes. She pulls the blanket over her head to screen out some of the light, and hopes she can ignore her cell mate's chuntering and the yelling coming from neighbouring cells, and get some sleep. It's proving difficult though cos Doina is stood right next to her, nudging her shoulder and grinning like a loon.

"You have happy Independence Day?"

What the freaking fuck. Bunty checks her mental calendar: Shit, it is. July the sodding 4th. She groans as Doina spins around the room, warbling an evilly off-key version of 'Star Spangled Banner'.

Chapter 52 – Schoolyard

Bunty sits up with a start. There's bright light shining in from the corridor, and cooler air. The door's open, and she's exposed, naked but for her blanket, but Doina is dressed and standing by her bunk.

"Bunky! Inspection! You screw it again. Stupid girl!"

Christ. Bunty grabs her dirty clothes from the end of the bed and starts to pull them on. But she's not quick enough – there's a guard looming at the door. He does a double take, and Bunty thinks she sees something like compassion in his eyes.

"I come back. Five minutes."

Bunty breathes out. A show of mercy! She carries on dressing, grossed out by her dirty clothes, and lowers herself to the floor.

"Fold!" hisses Doina, pointing to her blanket.

Bunty obeys; Doina knows the score.

When the guard re-appears it seems that everything is ship-shape. He nods once, and passes by.

"Likes you! Someone likes you!" Doina squeals.

Maybe that's what privilege feels like, Bunty thinks. A moment later the door closes, seemingly by itself. She feels lost.

"What happens next, Doina? What do I need to know?"

"Oh, nothing, you know," Doina responds cheerfully; she seems pleased to have been asked. "Breakfast in half an hour."

"I can shower now?"

"Yes, you can do it now."

Doina is kind enough to give her some space by sitting in her bunk with her back to the bathroom area, while Bunty strips off again and gets under the weak stream of warm water that emits from the shower head in the corner. It takes ages to remove the layers of scum and sweat that have accumulated since whenever it was she last showered. When was that? The morning she left Inma's, looking for Asif... She emerges, her hair dripping, and looks around for a towel... fuck.

"Erm, can I use your towel?"

"No." Doina is resolute. "I only got one. You can't use."

Bunty stands and drips. She could dry herself with her t-shirt, but then she'd have to wear it, and that's not the look she wants on her first morning in the women's wing of Algeciras jail. The blanket then...

It's gross, and it takes ages to render her skin merely damp. She pulls her filthy clothes on again, and hangs the blanket on the hook where a towel should be.

"Doina, how can I get my clothes clean?"

"You wash them."

No. Fucking. Shit. She draws breath.

"In the laundry. I show it you later."

175

"And what can I wear when I wash them?"

"I dunno! You work it out, Bunky!" she laughs, eyes sparkling.

The door clicks once more, and this time it swings fully open.

"Breakfast!" declares Doina, getting up and marching from the room.

Bunty sniffs the armpits of her t-shirt, makes a face, shrugs, and follows Doina. They join a river of women heading into the dining room. Bunty's presence is still attracting attention. She can see women studying her then talking guardedly to one another. The short-haired woman from last night appears at her side.

"Morning, you!"

"Hello! I don't know your name."

"Otsana."

It sounds Basque. "You're from Euskadi?"

"Very good!" But the woman eyes her darkly. "Look, you need your cup with you for breakfast, and your knife and fork..."

"Oh! I forgot the cup, but I don't have a knife and fork..."

"They will issue them to you. Go get the cup. I'll wait."

Bunty rushes back, not knowing how much time she's got. On her way she notices the other women are carrying little bags, presumably with their cutlery inside. Otsana smiles when Bunty returns and they walk across the dining room together, which attracts some whistles and whoops. Otsana joins the queue in front of Bunty so that she can observe the procedure, which is similar to last night, just with less food. She comes away with a piece of bread, some jam on a saucer, and coffee. They sit together, and Otsana offers Bunty her knife. Bunty spreads the jam and returns it.

"What happens when people are allergic to gluten and they can't eat bread?"

"They can have the same thing, but without the bread," Otsana answers. "This is not a good system, I am sorry to tell you."

It's been a few days since Bunty's had anything resembling a meal, and the bread she's trying to chew isn't making the grade. "I could do with an egg, and another egg, and some veggie sausages," she confides.

"You're vegetarian?" Otsana looks shocked. "Shit."

"They don't...?"

"They don't know what that is. You're in the south here. If you come to Bilbao you will be fine."

"Not much chance of that..."

"Not today."

Bunty drinks up her lukewarm coffee. "Where can I get some water?"

"From the tap over there. But..."

"What?"

"Well, I wouldn't..."

"Seriously?" Bunty's starting to think she shouldn't ask any questions at all. She walks to the small sink and draws some water into her cup. Despite the lurid yellow of the plastic, she can see that the liquid inside is brown. She lifts it to her face, then pulls back. It smells like something really bad. Back at the table Otsana puts her hand on Bunty's shoulder, but doesn't speak. Bunty uses this support to help her

176

pull her emotions in, to somehow squash them, and to definitely not cry. It's working, until someone crashes into her back. She looks up to see a chubby face, jam-smeared and grinning. Behind her is a tall woman, with typical Iberian features: pretty face, brown eyes, serious looking.

"Watch who you spend time with, new girl," the woman warns her.

Otsana tuts and shakes her head. Bunty looks fiercely at the serious woman, but holds her tongue. She's done fighting with homophobes and every other ignorant fucker. Got to rein it in now. She thinks again about school, but actually this seems a hundred times worse, and she never did work out how to deal with bullies back then. She lowers her head, and the woman leaves them. Time to train in a new art, the suppression of feelings. It seems to involve breathing less – kind of like the opposite of meditation. That can't be good...

"Look, you'll find your way," Otsana tells her, leaning down to catch her eye. "And I have some bottled water I can share with you. When you get your money you can buy it here."

"A shop?" This is a promising development. "But how do I get money?"

"Usually your family sends it..."

"My family don't know I'm here – I wasn't allowed to telephone anyone."

"Typical. They do that to foreigners..." Otsana sighs. "Well, family, or a friend, anyone can put money into your account. And then you can make phone calls as well.

"How do I tell someone so that they can do that, if no-one knows I'm here?"

"We can talk to the officers."

"What else do I need to know? Doina hasn't been much help."

"Oh Doina," Otsana laughs, grimly. "Well, you probably don't know about the privilege system."

"No, I don't think I do..."

"Okay, there is a teacher who comes almost every day, only not at the weekend, to teach people to read and write. Don't get excited, it's not going to be very interesting for you – she was a teacher of infants before she came here. But if you go to school, they give you points for it, and those points help you to get advantages. I go there, anyway."

"Okay." It sounds kind of shit, but she tries to see it as a positive.

"She doesn't speak any English, but there might be a book you can look at."

A book. "Okay."

"You can either go to those classes, or you can just hang around."

"What about work?"

"Most of the work in the prison is done by prisoners, but they only let us do jobs like cleaning and laundry. The men can be guards, or work in sick bay, or in Ingreso..."

"That's so sexist!"

"I thought that too. But there are sixteen different departments here, and just one for women, so there are a lot more men. And most of the time when you put the women and the men together..." Otsana makes a face.

"It's chaos?"

"Right."

They've left the dining room, and are in the room with the chairs and the TV.

"So, what do we do now?"

"Whatever you want!"

"I don't get it. I don't feel like I can do anything here."

"Well, there is a gym, or you can sit here..." She gestures around the room; all the chairs are empty.

Bunty looks out of the window; it seems like all the women are out there. "Outside! I wanna go outside!"

Otsana nods. "Of course."

The glass doors – so well cleaned and with only a little bit of jam streaked on them – creak open, and the stench of cigarette smoke smacks Bunty in the face. She stares at the women; they're all doing the same thing – walking, slowly, heads down, in circles, around the concrete patio. It's like some bizarre religious procession, and it makes her feel nervous. Their grim march is soundtracked by low conversation and intermittent coughing.

"What's going on here?"

"We have to move," Otsana explains. "Most of the time we are lying down."

"Well... I get it. I want to too. It just looks so freaky!"

"Come on then!" Otsana holds out her arm as an invitation to promenade with her. Bunty smiles and takes it, and, to the jeers of some of the inmates, they join the procession. She wants to walk at a normal pace – or what she thinks of as normal; it's clearly not the norm here, where the women move at a painstaking trudge. Each circuit involves getting engulfed in clouds of cigarette smoke and in no time she's chorusing along with the coughing contingent, but she doesn't want to stop walking. Out here is infinitely better than being stuck inside.

They're like this for an hour or so. Otsana gets Bunty up to speed on prison culture while they contend with a volley of tuts, dirty looks and giggles. Doina is actually being friendly to her, and seems to be getting some of her buddies on board too; others pester Bunty repeatedly about what she's in for. She ignores them, but comments to Otsana about their enthusiasm.

"It's because they are new. Only new ones ask this."

"Why? Isn't it something everyone wants to know?" She looks quizzically at her mentor. "Or is it something you shouldn't ask?"

"The longer you have been in here, the less you want to know. The less you care, in fact. It's a survival thing. But the new ones, they haven't learnt it yet."

Bunty considers this. She does want to know about all the other women and their crimes, whether real or framed, but she's hesitant to ask. It's like a fear of heartbreak.

"Could I ask you...?"

"No. Don't. It is best for you to learn this quickly."

"Oh..."

They walk in silence for a while, but Bunty's bursting with questions and fears.

"Can't I tell those women what they want to know? I'm not ashamed of why I'm here."

178

"It's your choice. But maybe don't give too much away. It can be used against you."

This makes logical sense to Bunty, but it doesn't match her reality. How could they use her organising a protest, or not having a passport, against her? Yet she knows her understanding of human nature is limited. She's clearly made mistakes, these last few weeks...

The procession fragments as women drop out to play games, or chat in small groups. Bunty's legs have had enough too, but she doesn't want to go back inside. They lean on the wall, and keep talking. Otsana describes her childhood in San Sebastian; Doina's friends come by to hound them for cigarettes. They seem to think Bunty might have some, and her insistence that she doesn't smoke has little effect.

"Bunky has nothing!" Doina tries to persuade them, and in the end gives them a reassurance: "I tell you when her money comes!"

Bunty crinkles her face into a frown. "Thanks Doina."

A guard shows up, the one that brought her in yesterday, and addresses her. "Come with me."

Terror quakes in her guts. "What did I do?"

"You have a visitor."

"But no-one knows I'm here..."

Then she notices Otsana gesturing for her to shut the fuck up. Of course; any visitor is better than none. *Anything* here is better than nothing.

She follows the guard and he takes her back down in the lift, to her old home, Ingreso, and along a corridor to a room with rows of chairs and tables. That's when she sees him.

She can't help shouting across the room. "Asif!"

"Quiet," the guard warns, and guides her between the tables to where Asif is practically jumping up and down. She rushes into his arms and he holds her tight. It feels amazing, like fire and snow at the same time. Happy chemicals explode in her veins.

He unfolds her, but keeps hold of her shoulders.

"Bunty! What the fuck? Are you okay? I've been so worried!"

"I'm okay. Well, you know, they caught me and I'm in here. But how did you know? They wouldn't let me call anyone!"

"I couldn't get hold of you, and Inmaculada didn't know where you were, and so in the end I called the police."

"You didn't!"

"They told me you'd been arrested so I just had to work out where you were. This is the nearest jail. Thank fuck you're here. I mean, no..."

"I know what you mean! Thanks for coming to see me!"

"Well of course I would!"

He gazes at her intently, and it hits her that she definitely has a thing for him. Why didn't she realise it before? She feels confused and crazy.

"Arghhh!"

"What? What's wrong? Are you in pain?"

"No, it's just, emotions... I thought I'd stopped having them..."

"Jeez, I mean, what is it like in here? How do they treat you?"

"It depends what you mean by 'they'. There's a lot going on, with everyone."

"It sounds intense."

"It is, considering how no-one's allowed out..."

"Do you need anything?"

"I don't think you can bring me anything? When I get money in my account I'll be able to buy soap and stuff."

He nods. "Well, just tell me if I can do something."

"Thanks Asif."

"No, it's the least – you shouldn't even be in here..."

"I'm not even sure what I've been charged with."

"What's the situation with that, have you got a lawyer?"

"Well, they made me sign something that waived my right to a lawyer and stuff like that, when I was arrested."

"Made you?"

"They were pretty insistent."

"Fuck..." Asif shuts his eyes. "I know a lawyer in La Línea, I'll get hold of him and see what he can do."

"Oh! Cool! That would be ace."

"Is there anything else?"

"I don't know whether to tell my parents... it might be too scary for them... and Inma..."

"Inma knows. I told her – I hope that's okay."

"Yes, sure. Is she alright?"

"She's been better, I think, but she's coping. She said she's missing you. And Bunty," he says, stroking her shoulder, "I think you should tell your folks, cos they need to know, and maybe they can do something from the UK. You shouldn't be here," he repeats.

She looks at him uncertainly. "I guess so, if you think... I just don't want to worry them."

"This is a time when people *should* be worrying about you. I mean, how are you? Are you eating okay? You look a bit skinny. And tired, I think."

"It's not exactly The Hilton, ya know?"

"Have you got any friends in here?"

"Well, I'm sharing a cell with a scary old Romanian lady, she seems kind of harmless... I mean I don't know what she's done..."

Asif looks like he might cry. Bunty decides to try and cheer him up. "I've made a friend, Otsana, but everyone's being shitty about it cos they think we're having a relationship."

His face drains, and he gulps. "Is... are...?"

"No, they're just being homophobic. She's helping me out a lot."

Asif continues to look discombobulated.

"You're not a homophobe too?" Bunty's beyond dealing with this shit.

"NO!" he practically shouts. "It's just..."

"What?"

"I'm... I..."

Her heart melts, and she stops being angry with him. Is this him trying to tell her he has feelings for her? And how can she reassure him that's she's not hooking up with Otsana? Bunty too is struggling to formulate words...

"Tiempo. Time." The guard is stood over her.

"Oh, shit!" She looks alarmed. "I never got to ask you where the fuck you were on Saturday. Why didn't you come?"

"There are some things I really need to tell you," Asif gulps. He grabs her hands and looks as though he wants to put them to his mouth, but the guard marches Bunty away, and her fingers slip away from his.

The distraught look on his face stays imprinted on her mind.

I'm not supposed to cry. I'm not going to cry. It's her new mantra; she bites her hand and stares at the plastic wall. Then she's back in the recreation area where she collapses into a chair, puts her head down, and covers her face with her hands.

"Fun visit?" It's Otsana.

"It's... that was harder than I thought." Not that she had much time to think of it before it happened. She feels like a jelly baby, softening and hardening in alternating climactic extremes. But mostly, she realises, it's gonna be cold. She'd better harden up.

Chapter 54 – Bootless In Fire

Everyone's moving to the dining room, and Bunty joins the flow. She's mechanical now, standing in line, holding out her tray. Sitting with Otsana, she peers at the items she's been given. An apple, but half of it is brown and soft. Another bread roll. A soupy thing. And something yellow and spongey that she's guessing is from the egg family, but when she presses it with her fork, oil comes out of it. She puts her spoon in the soup and fishes out three pieces of vegetables. They taste like salt. She looks at Otsana in confusion.

"This is the main meal babe. Make the most of it."

"How do you survive on this?"

"You just do. Or you get skinny. Or you get sick. It depends how strong you are when you come in. You look strong enough though," she says, assessing Bunty's physical set up.

The serious woman comes by to gloat and tut.

Bunty watches her as she saunters away. "What's her problem?"

Otsana doesn't answer; she looks towards the window. Maybe the homophobia is too much for her to handle, Bunty thinks. I shouldn't have probed. She picks through her food in silence, wondering what the rest of the day will bring. When a bell rings and the scrape of the benches merges with the cacophony of voices, Otsana speaks again.

"Siesta time."

"Really – we go to sleep?" Like kids?

"Maybe, or just lie down, read…"

"I don't have anything to read."

"I can show you the library tonight. Come on, we go."

They climb the stairs, both locked in their own thoughts. Bunty has been deterred from asking her friend anything at all, and she can't talk about what's happening to her, about the shut down in her mind. Otsana bids her a quiet goodbye, and then Bunty's back in the cell with Doina. When the door shuts Bunty tests it just in case, but it really is locked.

"Buna Bunky," Doina grins. "Nice day?"

"Yes Doina, nice day," she answers flatly.

"You get used to it," the woman tells her, and pats her arm.

I'm never going to get used to this. And I'm never going to put an animal in a cage, not even a rabbit. Not even a rat.

"What time do we get out now?"

"Three hours, then we eat supper." Doina beams, evidently enjoying her role as the dispenser of prison facts.

She tries to work out if three hours is enough time to dry her clothes, realises it isn't and decides to wash them anyway; they smell too minging. She takes her t-shirt off and runs water on it. "Doina, I need soap. I'll pay you back when I get my money."

"You pay me back and a euro more."

"Sure, whatever."

Doina rummages under her clothes on the shelf and comes up with a piece of soap, brand new, wrapped in plastic. "Here."

"Oh, you could have given me this before!" But she's glad to have it. She rubs the perfumed bar on her t-shirt, before rinsing, wringing it out, and hanging it up on the towel hook.

I still need a frigging towel!

Bunty takes off the rest of her clothes, washes them, then gets under the shower for a celebratory wash with actual soap. She climbs naked up onto her bunk to drip dry in the afternoon heat rather than rub the blanket on herself again. Doina has her nose in her novel; thank fuck, she can get some time to herself. She pulls the sheet off the mattress so there's something to cover her. No-one's looking, but she feels vulnerable; the door could open at any minute. Under the sheet the mattress is stained with myriad yellow marks, and she shudders at having to rest her bare butt on it. She needs distraction.

So she thinks about Asif. He said she should tell her folks she's here but it's the last thing she wants to do, even if she could. Is that irresponsible? What's better – telling them their daughter's in a Spanish jail, or letting them think she's on holiday? Her chest feels loaded with guilt – she kept things from them out of a sincere wish to be independent, and ended up here, in the most horribly dependent state, chained up like a Spanish guard dog.

After this realisation she can't stop thinking about them. Maybe she can somehow tune in to them, pick up their signals, or transmit one to them. She thinks about where they'll be, what they'll be doing. Mum in the café, laughing with the customers, the smell of spices rising from the cooker behind her. Dad upstairs, pottering around, making too-strong tea, playing his records. She loves talking to him about music – well, listening to him, really... She can almost hear his voice as her mind drifts back to the things he used to tell her.

"Before I came over I listened to John Peel on the World Service, he had a show once a week, but when I got to London he was on every night. I was in fuckin' heaven. Come in knackered after work, crack open some cans, feet up – he played everything. That's how I got into reggae, electronic stuff, hip hop, African bands, but mainly indie stuff, lots of yer US melodic hardcore like Hüsker Dü, and tonnes of weird British bands who sent him tapes..."

Then he'd start playing her his favourite tracks. It was clearly such a magical time when countless musical treasures were revealed to him by Peel, who he revered as some sort of a god.

Jimmy honed in on one particularly obscure band called Eyeless In Gaza. "Look, I have their album," he told her excitedly, flicking through shelves stacked full of vinyl. "Ah she's messed it up again!" – her mum would never obey the rule of the alphabet – "Nah here it is – hang on, the first track's crap..." And he lowers the needle to a spot one centimetre in from the edge of the spiral of grooves.

The turnstile swallows and regurgitates her ticket, and the ramp leads her to the embarkation port. "They sounded weird. I mean, really beautiful music, but the singer has this queer old English accent," he explained – or warned – as the ululations of a male voice warped by over-exposure to folk emerged from the grooves. No-one sings like that! Yet his tones are flexible, replete with tenderness, and they're backed by a pristinely treble-y electric guitar. It was so melodic, and so strange...

"Were they popular at the time?" she asked, trying to work out their place in the scheme of things, at a time before she was born.

"No, not at all. And you couldn't play it to your mates, cos his voice, it was uncool even then, ya know? It was all about the post punk then – the new wave. Everything was harsh, artificial, like machines – it was all synths and bristly guitars..."

She was fascinated by this band that didn't even fit in at a time when it had seemed that everything was possible. She ripped the album 'Rust Red September', from his vinyl copy – except for the first track – and carried it with her on her old MP3 player. That was one of the few things they'd let her keep. Listening to it was a seasonal treat, a guilty pleasure that she'd save for the autumn. What would happen if she plays it in the scorch of the Iberian summer, whilst trapped in jail?

Bunty dares to select it now, and her mind is flooded with its beauty and yearning. But the yearning they wrote it with is mounted by her own – her wish to be home – and it rides the music like a helpless passenger, clutching it round the neck. These songs, extended meditations on the slendour of the English countryside, are like nature poetry, enhanced by deeply expressive instrumentation. And she's back home, walking in the tree-gorged Gledhow Valley, scarfed up, breathing the nippy air. Feelings of longing, helplessness and guilt burst in her chest with a force that pushes tears from her eyes. She lets out a jagged sob, and convulses on the bunk, her mind reaching for another world, the kinder, much more beautiful one she used to know. When the final track crescendos and subsides, she's racked with homesickness. She stares at the ceiling of her cell. How is she going to tell them?

Chapter 55 – Got To Get Down

She drifts awake blissfully, emerging from golden light, like a flower being born, like... her eyes crack open to the cell's antiseptic glare. No... Not like this...

She turns to the wall. How do I switch it off?

At breakfast she asks Otsana: "How do you do it? How do you cope, how do you shut yourself down in here?"

"I don't know." Otsana shrugs. "It's natural."

"There's always something in me that bounces back, I'm like a balloon."

"You can't do that here." Otsana shakes her head and sips her coffee, making a face. "I never get used to this shit!"

"That's what it is – something in you that always thinks it should be better, or it could be better, or it's going to get better. You believe in real coffee still. That part of you isn't dead."

Otsana laughs and hits Bunty on the back of her hand.

"I'm not joking though. I'm serious about this."

"Well, maybe if you knew you were here for a reason, you could just think about that."

"What do you mean?"

"Say if the thing you did was something you believe in, then it doesn't matter if they jail you forever, you would always do it again. It doesn't matter if they put you away or not."

"Mmm, I dunno." Bunty fights with her stale bread. "I believed in the cause I was working for, but I didn't plan to go to prison for it, and I don't think that's why I'm here anyway – not officially."

Otsana looks into Bunty's eyes. "I don't know what your deal is. But you have to work that out for yourself."

She doesn't feel any closer to learning the secret of the shutdown. When she's tried meditation or yoga it's been about opening up; no-one ever trained her for this, for being in a place where it's dangerous to be aware, but you have to stay awake. In the yard, everyone walks like zombies. She still wants to walk at a regular speed; she can't tone it down. Maybe it'll come in time, and the anxiety will subside. Not that she wants to be here for any time at all...

"Oww! Fuck!"

It's Jammy Hands again, banging into her. Maybe that's how she shows affection, like the way cats give you little fluffy headbutts.

"Bunky, hey," she cries, pawing at her.

"That's not my name." Fuckin' Doina...

"Bunky, oi," her voice is quieter now. "You want smack? I get you some." She grins at her sideways.

"Hell no! Fuck off!" Bunty pushes the girl's hands away from her and breaks the circle to walk away. It means leaving the air and going back inside. Otsana comes after her, laughing.

"Uh! No!" Bunty's wriggling like someone's put spiders down her top.

"You'll get used to this..."

"You're kidding! I don't wanna be involved with that at all!"

"Erm, hello? Prison, drugs..." Otsana does her best 'duh' voice.

"So that's how people do it..."

"Some of them, yes. Come back outside, we're losing time."

Bunty follows her out again. She eyes Jammy across the yard, and shudders.

"This is no place for snowflakes, I'm afraid."

"Oh fuck off, Otsana." Bunty looks up at the sky. "Don't give me that bollocks."

Otsana pats her on the back and laughs again. "You'll be okay. The first few weeks are the hardest."

"First few weeks? I'm not gonna be here for weeks!"

Otsana looks up to the sky now too. "Oh, I'm sorry, I didn't realise. Look, is this your helicopter come to pick you up? Out the way everyone!"

Bunty has to laugh, but she feels sick inside. They walk in silence then, and she listens to the dull chatter, the coughing and the cackling of the other women. Did they all feel like she does now? How many of them still do?

Otsana interrupts her reverie. "Coming to school today?"

"Umm, okay."

"Good. I think it will help you."

Bunty looks at Otsana, trying to weigh her up. She can be sarcastic, but she's also genuine. She decides to forgive her for not being sensitive; she's been here much longer, after all. And isn't sensitivity exactly what she's trying to lose right now?

Otsana walks with her to the classroom. On the way Normal Lady passes them, hissing at Bunty. "What I tell you?"

Shit, she's in the class as well? Bunty puts her head down. She can't cope with this stupidness. When she walks into the classroom the teacher looks up, and greets her warmly. But when she sees Otsana following her in, her expression changes.

The teacher too? Really?

They choose adjacent tables, and Otsana goes to take a book from the top of a cupboard. It's a thick Spanish-English dictionary. "You can use this."

Bunty starts off by following what the teacher is saying, but gets bored after a short while cos it really is basic literacy and numeracy. She distracts herself by reading the dictionary, looking for words she doesn't know and writing them down. It's a happy way to spend two hours. Otsana looks pissed off, but she doesn't interrupt Bunty's studies until a bell goes off and the other women start to move.

Lunch is barely edible again. Today it's something resembling meatballs, so she swaps hers for Otsana's salad.

"I think I got the best deal," Otsana grins, pointing at Bunty's still-small portion of crap lettuce and tomato. "You should tell them you're vegetarian, you might get something else."

"Who do I tell?"

"Try that guard."

Bunty scrapes her bench back and goes over to the blonde guard by the door. "Excuse me, I'm vegetarian..."

"Nice for you!" The woman smirks at her. "Good luck with that."

"Can I get some sort of alternative food?"

"I'll make a note of it. We'll let you know."

Bunty's not sure whether this is a positive response. She goes back to her leaves and bread roll.

"Some women say this prison is like a really good weight loss programme. It's notorious for not giving enough food."

"I like eating," she responds glumly. "I don't care if it makes me fat."

"I have some snacks in my room, I'll get you something later," Otsana promises.

Bunty smiles and thinks how she's fallen on her feet meeting this woman, but her ruminations are interrupted by the arrival of a guard with a prisoner at his side.

"New one," Otsana mutters. "I think she was here before."

The woman saunters in to the cheers of some of the inmates. She raises a hand in the air and smiles, like she's doing a lap of honour. Then she spots Bunty.

"Ooooh!!" She rushes over. "I know you! You're the girl on the posters!"

Bunty stares back blankly. This is confusing.

"You're Bunty, no? From La Línea! You are the girl who made the protest."

"Yeah, but – posters?"

"All over town. They love you there!" The woman beams. "I get your autograph later!"

Then she goes over and joins her friends, who absorb her into their group with kisses, hugs, and endless questions about life outside.

Chapter 56 – Farewell Innocence

At school the next day the blonde guard drops by to speak with the teacher. They look over at Bunty, and the teacher beckons her to the front.

"Would you like to teach English?" the guard asks.

"I don't know." This is a surprise. "I haven't before. I'm a sound engineer."

"Unfortunately, we don't have any openings for sound engineers," Blondie tells her snidely. "But if you want to teach you can try. The teacher says you can do that in the back of the classroom here, with one woman at a time."

Bunty agrees to what seems like a daunting task. Her mum brought her up to believe she can do anything – and what else is she going to do here anyway? She might as well try and help some of the women.

"Gracias," the teacher says, gently. "You start mañana."

The first in the queue for an English lesson is Normal Lady. She sits opposite Bunty, who passes her a handwritten sheet about pronouns. Normal Lady ignores it.

"I try to say you, her is not good person," she hisses, in an urgent whisper.

Is this jealousy?

"I am trying to tell you," says Bunty.

Normal looks at her blankly.

"She is not a good person."

"Yes, is what I say you!"

Bunty sighs, and takes the lesson back to basics. I, you, he/she, us, them. Normal plays with her nails and fidgets till her half hour is over.

Well, that was worthwhile. Bunty looks up to see who the teacher has in store for her next. It's Doina.

"Doina, we can do this in the cell, we've got so much time together already."

"I get extra points for English lesson. Tell me about you life in London."

And so the morning is wasted.

"Are you going to the cinema tonight?" Otsana asks that evening.

"Yeah, sure. I'm going for a drink with my friends afterwards, so don't wait up."

"I'm not joking. It's what they do here on Fridays, twice a month."

"What do you mean? Where?"

"At the sports hall. There are men there – you'll be able see the straight women going crazy."

There's a sports hall? "When do we get to play sports?"

"Ah, sometimes. They don't have the staff to go very often."

"But the men?"

"Yes, they can go. It's like I told you before; easier for the men."

"I still don't get why though?"

"Well, I told you there's one section here for women and twenty, twenty-one for the men. So there's one section that's mostly Moroccans, one for guys who are into sports, one for junkies, one for guys with other problems, and so on. But here, the women are all mixed up." Her hands move as if she is drawing a diagram on the wall they are leaning on. "So you have women who transport drugs, murderers, thieves, people traffickers, junkies of course, prostitutes... I mean you know there are women here with HIV?"

Bunty shakes her head, suddenly stricken with fear.

Otsana seems to take in her reaction, but warns her anyway. "You need to be careful here, always."

"I'm gonna need time to properly process that." She looks around anxiously. "Where do we go though, how do we get to the cinema?"

"You go and wait in the recreation room. I won't go."

"Why not?"

"I'm not allowed. Some rules," she says, in such a way that, even though it's setting off Bunty's injustice detector, makes her feel she shouldn't ask. Not just yet, anyway.

Bunty's silent as they walk, in a large group, to the sports hall, accompanied by a column of guards. Some of the women are preening and flirting with men they pass on the way, others hoot and crack lewd jokes. There's some bickering over seating in the brightly lit room; Bunty keeps out of the way. She takes a blue plastic chair in the back row, breathes in the sweaty, dusty air, and gazes expectantly at the screen.

The film that comes on is an old one about people living in rural Spain, in the north, she thinks. It's hard for her to follow the dialogue, though she picks up some of it. Normally she could never watch something as slow-paced as this, but in here it's a diversion, helping her forget the grey-walled monotony.

Afterwards they're ordered to get moving back to the women's section. There's grumbling and swearing, and further attempts to communicate with the male prisoners on duty in the hall. She wonders why, if the problem is scale, they can't just have a women's prison with the appropriate facilities. And she knows what the answer would be.

But what she really wants to know is why Otsana isn't allowed to watch the films. She bumps into Normal. ¿Por qué Otsana no puede ver las peliculas?"

"Because she has special rules. Because of the thing she did."

"What... what did she do?"

"You not know? Oh!" and she makes a beeline for a group of women, who gather round Normal and gasp and laugh, looking over at Bunty as they do so.

Shit, what did Otsana do that's so sensational? What did Normal do? What did anyone do?

Otsana's waiting for her when she gets back. Bunty tells her what happened.

"I'll tell you," she says sadly, "if you really want to know. But first you should know about the other people around here."

Bunty wants to tell her to stop, but her curiosity wins.

"Okay. What about Normal?"

"People trafficking. Forcing women into prostitution."

She's stunned. "I heard about things like that, but it never seemed real..."

The wall takes her weight. So now she knows what evil looks like; it looks normal. And remorseless.

"Her skinny friend killed and cut her boyfriend into pieces and put him in the boot of the car and set it on fire," Otsana continues.

"Oh..." Bunty can't speak.

"And your cellmate Doina..."

"Don't – I don't want to know!"

"She killed an old woman for ten euros. She bashed her head in from behind."

Bunty needs to get away. She needs to be sick. Her cell is nearby, but that's the scariest place to run to. She moves a few feet and bends double, retching. Otsana holds her hair back as Bunty vomits on the floor.

The buzzer sounds for eight o'clock inspection. Otsana pulls her up straight, guides her to her cell, and walks away.

She steps in to see Doina, standing next to their bed, grinning. Bunty's shaking and sweating. She washes her hands and face, and gets into position just in time. The guard peers in.

"All okay?" he asks her. She guesses he heard about her being sick. Or saw it, most likely.

She nods her head weakly. He accepts her answer and moves on. The cell door closes, sealing them in for the next eleven hours.

Doina potters around the cell, tidying, muttering and singing. Bunty shrinks as far from her as she can, into the edge of her bed, her back pressed against the wall, and watches her.

They say travel broadens the mind, but my world has shrunk down to this; I'm locked inside a tiny room with a crazy murderer. What the fuck did I do?

She retraces her steps, trying to work out where she went wrong. She takes it back to getting the job on the ship. Then further back, to the Job Centre adviser pressuring her, then to the Department of Work and Pensions policy of quotas for sanctioning people who don't get jobs quickly enough – or anyone who makes the smallest mistake when they're applying for help. Back to the Tory government, imposing the cuts, creating the policies. She thinks of politicians like David Cameron, using their privilege to support their rich mates while everyone else falls through the net. And she's been falling and falling. She thought she'd hit bottom before, but that was a false floor, and it disintegrated...

And all of these women are here due to combinations of conditions just as complex – poverty, poor education, mental illness – all worsened, or unaided, by other governments that also work to support the rich. And fuck the poor. She contemplates individual responsibility, what it means when people choose to do evil shit to each other. How does it even function amongst all the social pressures from family, school, religion, economics? She looks at Doina and doesn't see an evil person. A stupid one, maybe, who's been misled – or a crazy one, she's not sure –

but not evil. Yet, the thing that she did – killing a poor old woman to rob her of almost nothing – is an evil act that can't be ignored. She wonders what could have led her to do it. And is jail helping? Is she learning anything, or making any progress psychologically? There isn't much of an education programme here, and no counselling that she knows of. Yet Doina seems to be enjoying herself; Bunty wonders what sort of life she could have come from, to find this place so much fun. The whole system stinks. But this new knowledge of her cellmate's crime is unbearable. There's no way of knowing whether or when she might feel like doing something like that again – and that's terrifying.

Chapter 57 – Reciprocity

Bunty chooses to sit alone at breakfast. Her fan girls call her over, but she's not interested. She finds a table near the window, far from Otsana. She keeps her back to the wall so she can observe; the more she can learn here, the better the chances of survival. And she needs to repress her natural tendency to trust people; it's not safe to do that here.

She looks at the women, at the ones she knows something about and at the others that she doesn't. Some of them may be innocent, others guilty, and there's no way for her to know the difference.

I wish I could go back to not knowing what Otsana told me; to somehow rewind time so I don't have to keep turning the implications over in my mind. How do they all do it? How the fuck do they stay sane?

A guard and a guy who looks like a nurse have showed up in the canteen and stationed themselves with a trolley by the door nearest to her, and women are forming a queue. It's an event she hadn't noticed when she was sitting on the other side of the room with Otsana; this must be for women who are ill and need meds.

"Metadona!"

The guard hardly needs to shout – most of the takers are already lined up, or are mooching in his direction.

Methadone. Jesus. That one word is the last piece of the puzzle. The shuffling walks, glazed eyes, the subdued temperaments; now it all falls into place. *This* is how they cope. She sees Doina in the queue, tapping her foot to music only she can hear.

A wave of nausea rises in her, but she knows she has to eat. She forces little pieces of bread down her throat, softened by the milk that she chose today instead of coffee. It's all about keeping going now, staying strong so she can work out how to get out this place.

Jammy runs over and tries to headbutt her. She's being playful, but it makes Bunty feel cornered and panicky. The girl's obviously crazy, but she's dangerous too. Bunty's ears squeal with tinnitus; she puts her bread down. Tears emerge against her will, so she lowers her head. When she raises it she sees Normal walking towards her. Fuck, not her – not now.

"What's wrong, Free Bunty?" she smirks. "Why you cry?"

Bunty shakes her head. "Nothing."

"How long are you in for?" She jeers. "They give you a sentence yet?"

Skinny has just joined her, fresh from the front of the methadone queue, so Normal has an audience to embolden her. "You only been here a week and la princesa is crying!" The pair cackle in her face.

She hasn't asked for this... she hasn't asked for any of it. But Normal keeps going.

"You should fuck off," she spits. "Go back to your terrorista." Then she stomps away with an air of satisfied pride.

Bunty leans back against the wall. Terrorist? What the fuck?

She can't bring herself to go outside; she doesn't trust a single person here. Under Otsana's sheltering wing she'd briefly felt a semblance of safety, but not now. She lurks in the dining room till the guards throw her out. The recreation area is deserted. She hunches in a chair, working on her anti-meditation technique, but feelings still seep through. They hurt.

If I had some fucking money I could take up smoking...

A woman enters the recreation room and sits near her. "My husband came to visit," she tells Bunty with a grin. Bunty's heard about the room that's available for conjugal visits and imagines she knows the reason for the Cheshire cat smile.

But she's wrong.

The woman opens her thighs, reaches her hand in between them and makes a face as she pulls something from her vagina. Bunty watches in horror as she produces a condom filled with something lumpy. She checks it, moves her legs to the side again, then pushes it back inside.

"You say me if you need anything," she tells Bunty with a wink, and saunters out to the yard.

Bunty can't believe what she's just seen. She tries to make herself smaller in the chair, to shrink from the onslaught of fucked-upness that this place seems to be made of.

That's when Normal comes by to gloat.

"Princess is sad? Princess wanna cuddle?" she gurns, and emits a sharp laugh.

A guard stops by. "Everything okay?"

"Yes, no problem," Normal smiles at him. A very nice smile.

The guard turns to Bunty. "Come with me. You have a visitor."

Normal starts to coo sarcastically, but Bunty's struggling to stand up. Her legs have stopped co-operating with her brain. She falls forward. The guard puts out a call on his radio, and the tall blonde one rushes in from the station.

"What's wrong here?" she demands.

"The prisoner fell. She has a visit now."

"Trying to avoid someone, huh?" Mean Blondie sneers. "Come on, get up."

Normal watches in amusement as the two guards each take an arm and yank Bunty from the floor. She doesn't resist, and they manhandle her out of the room.

"If this is real, she has to see a doctor," Mean Blondie tells the other guard, as they put her in the lift. Bunty tries to get it together. The lighting is too bright, but she manages the rest of the journey with the male guard's support. He sets her down at a table. The gabble of voices overwhelms her, and she closes her eyes.

"What the fuck? Bunty, what's wrong?"

It's Asif. He's come back. She slumps forward.

He puts his arms out, holds her, touches her face.

"You're sick. What's going on? Can I get help?"

"I dunno," Bunty slurs. "Prison?" And then realises she hasn't explained herself. "I'm in prison."

"Yeah, you are..." he says gently.

"I mean, it's not like that... It's not like anything you know."

"Jesus, what are they doing to you?"

193

"Nothing. It's just... hungry... scary..."

"You're hungry? You've lost weight again." He rustles in his bag and pulls out a Snickers, passes it to her. Somehow it goes under the guard's radar as Bunty tears the wrapper and stuffs the whole thing in her mouth. She chews and tries to thank him at the same time, but it doesn't come out right. The lights flicker back on in her brain.

"They're starving you!" Asif looks alarmed.

"No, just, normal. Bad food. Not vegetarian."

"Oh..." A wave of comprehension spreads across his face. "How do I get food to you?"

"You need to have money in your account for extra food."

"You don't have any money?"

"No..." she looks down. "They took it off me when I came in."

"Fffff..." Asif lets out all his breath. "You should have said. I can sort that for you."

"No, I can't ask you."

"Why can't you ask? What's your problem with asking, Bunty? Surely this isn't your style?"

She stares at him for a moment, then almost growls "How do you know what my fucking style is?"

"No... I'm... "

He's never seen her angry like this before.

"Bunty, you know everyone has to ask for help sometimes." He furrows his brow, working out how to get this over to her. "If you're the one who always gives, other people have to be the ones asking or in need." He holds both hands towards her, like he's yearning for her to hear. "Does that mean they're weaker than you, that you're better?"

"No..." She's calming down, the ferocity dissipating from her throat. "I grew up not asking, you know? I knew not to. My folks were struggling, exhausted from working hard, and there wasn't enough cash to go round. And with my friends, it was always the same. Who would you ask? Who had anything more?"

"But you did support each other,"

"Of course."

"So there had to be asking, for there to be giving."

"People would just notice. They'd pick it up when you didn't have the money for lunch, they'd see you sitting there with nothing to eat."

Asif slides a hand right across the table. "I understand. I mean, I was lucky, it wasn't like that for me, we didn't go short of anything. What you say makes sense. But," and he speaks with more urgency now, "it's really important you reach out and ask for what you need right now. It's critical. Do you get me?"

"Mmm hmm."

He's asking her to change in a big way, and she isn't sure she can, even though it sounds perfectly logical. She doesn't want to prolong the argument by telling him she has other reasons too – that she won't depend on another person, won't depend

194

on a man and subject herself to dangerous power imbalances. She's seen that in others' lives; she saw it happen to Sofia.

But it's Asif who changes the subject.

"How's it going with that woman, Otsana?"

Bunty blanches, and turns away.

"Bunty?"

"I don't know. I'm frightened..."

"What do you mean?"

"I don't know who she is."

Asif gets eye contact with her. "It sounds like a nightmare in here. Listen, I got hold of that lawyer." He rustles in his pocket and produces a card. "Here, this is him, he's going to get in touch with you this week, I hope that's okay?"

Bunty takes the card. José Jesús Ruiz, Abodago, San Roque. "Thanks Asif." She smiles, and it's like the sun's come out.

"And I wanted to tell you why I wasn't at the protest."

"I'm listening." This is her big question; she sits back, ready to hear whatever the fuck stupid reasons he has for letting her down so badly, and watches sternly as he produces something from his bag.

They're papers. A big fuck off pile of them.

"I found the true emissions data for the plant."

"What?!" she shrieks, alerting the guard's attention, who signals for her to shut it. It's Bunty's turn to lean forward now, to loud-whisper-interrogate him. "How the fuck did you do that?"

"Well, it took all that day and night. I hacked into their servers. Then I leaked the data." He says all this under his breath, looking anxiously at the closest guard, who's being distracted by a toddler that appears to be a contraband-smuggling suspect, judging by the number of plastic bags in her anorak. Asif relaxes and sits back, better to savour Bunty's long-overdue reaction.

"Jesus, Asif. That's... amazing! But you – are you safe? Can't they get you for that?"

"I think so. You know how it is. Schwarz, Manning, Snowden, Assange..."

"And you!" She beams at him proudly.

"And many others!" he qualifies. "What I meant was the sort of sentences, or the type of treatment they got – or are still getting."

"Understood – and," she connects with his eyes and sends a beam of love, "Forgiven."

"I didn't know I was ever not forgiven." He pauses as it sinks in. "Oh, I was so shit! I didn't answer your messages..."

Well duh! It's only now the remorse is kicking in? She doesn't want to have to say that's how she got arrested, trying to cross the border to find out what had become of him.

The guard announces the end of the session. Asif embraces her and kisses her head. "I will be back very soon Bunty. I love you."

The guard is taking her away; Asif goes out of view. She stumbles, in shock and not knowing how to respond to his declaration. The guard saw and heard it all. "You can get conjugal visits, you know," he informs her.

"Euww! We're not married!" Way to cheapen what just happened.

But when she thinks of it, an hour alone with him sounds like the best thing ever.

Chapter 58 – Phone Home

She's improving her ability at blocking out what the women did. Her teaching role means she has to, most of the time anyway.

First thing Monday morning, and she's got Normal again, though she can't figure out how she's worked her way back to the top of the list so quickly.

"Wassap, druggy girl?"

WTF. I'm like the least on-drugs person here! "What's up, people trafficker?"

"Fuck you, bitch."

"Right back atcha."

"It is shame for you," Normal says, folding her arms and sitting back.

"It's *a* shame for you."

"You no have amigas and nobody help you."

"You have no friends, and nobody is helping you."

"I serious. You are in the bad situation."

"I *am* serious. You are in *a* bad situation."

"Is no wonder they don't want to help a black bitch like you," Normal spits, losing patience with this teaching technique.

There's nowhere to take that one. "What the fuck are you talking about?" Bunty hisses. "Who won't help me?"

"You know the guards are racistas. They won't help foreign womens, they won't help black ones. You ask them special food?"

"Yes."

"And telephone calls, and to get money in the account?"

"Yes, I tried."

"They give it to the other women who need."

"So what can I do?"

"You need have better friends."

"You need *to* have better friends."

She's not buying this crap.

That night she gazes at the bars separating her from the night sky, wishing she could hack away at them and fly away, before she loses her mind in here. The job gives her something to focus on, at least, a puzzle to work out in the long hours between supper and breakfast. It's better than sitting around feeling guilty about not having contacted her folks, and the frustration of not being able to. But it's hard to concentrate on lesson plans when homesickness is pummelling her. Thoughts of her mum's café are overwhelming; the warmth inside those steamed-up windows, the smell of brown stew chicken, the loud talk and the laughter. None of it seems real, now, here.

"Good news Bunky!" Doina's back and she's practically skipping around the cell. "You got money! Now you pay me back for soap! And some..." She grins toothily.

Oh, thank fuck. Bunty sits up. "When can I go?"

"After breakfast. I show you."

The next morning Doina finds her in the dining room, and they join the queue for the shop. It's a little hole in the wall with a sliding tray at the bottom, like they have in petrol stations at night. Doina's chattering about what she wants in addition to soap, by way of interest.

"I'm only getting you one extra thing," Bunty tells her. And then she starts to feel anxious. Now that I have money, is she going to kill me for it? But the funds are stored in her account; she doubts they would go to Doina if she got murdered in the night.

When her turn comes, the male prisoner on the other side of the screen fetches two bars of soap, cigarettes for Doina, three bottles of water, two bars of chocolate, a big bag of crisps, and then she sees the thing she needs most of all – a phone card.

"Do I have enough for one of those as well?"

"Sure."

She walks away with her arms full of stuff. It feels like Christmas.

After downing half a litre of water, she heads to the phones and waits for someone to finish a call. She's gripped by anxiety but can't put this off for a moment longer. The woman in front of her hangs up. Bunty takes a deep breath, and taps in familiar digits.

"Mum."

"Bunty!" Precious is screaming. "Christ Jesus! Jimmy, it's our Bunty! What are you doing in prison?"

"How do you know?"

"Your boyfriend phoned us!"

"What, Asif?"

"Yes, that's him! Are you okay, baby?"

"Yes Mum, I'm alright," she lies – a familiar habit. She's grown up knowing it's better to reassure them than to confide.

"Here's your dad!"

Jimmy's grabbed the phone, and she can hear him breathing hard, like he just ran up from the cellar.

"Bunty, for the love of God, are you alright?"

"Yes Dad, I'm fine."

"Will we come and visit? I've been looking at flights but they cost an arm and a leg."

"Don't." She's trying not to choke up. "I'll be out of here soon. I'll be home as soon as I can."

"How the Bejeezus did you end up in jail – in fucken' Spain?" he bellows.

"It's a long story Dad. I think it's cos I didn't have my passport. I left it on the ship."

"Since when do they put you in jail for that? Fucken' hell..."

"It was hard to tell what they sent me down for," she sighs. "My Spanish wasn't good enough."

"Do they not have translators there?"

"Well, there was, but she didn't exactly speak English..."

"Christ on a fucken' bike! I'm callin' the fucken' Embassy."

"Okay Dad. Thanks." She can hear Precious shouting in the background.

"Yer mam's sayin' somethin', hang on – are ye eating alright?"

"Pass me back to her?"

"Listen, love, we'll get you out of there."

"Okay, but don't worry, please..."

There's a muffled goodbye from Jimmy, then Precious is back on the line.

"Are they feeding you baby? What's the food like?"

"It's okay," she lies again. This is breaking her heart. "How are you and Dad?"

"We're..." she starts crying. "We just want you back."

Bunty leaves the phone area in tears. Talking to them hasn't assuaged her guilt at all; it's installed itself heavily in her gut.

I promised them I would get out. How do I do that?

She remembers the lawyer Asif told her about. She goes back to the cell to pick up his card – there might be enough time before work to make another call.

"¿José Jesús Ruiz?"

"Sí, soy yo. Dígame." Talk to me.

"I'm Bunty Maguire – my, erm, friend Asif has spoken to you about me. I'm in Botafuegos."

"Asif who?"

"I, err..." Why did it never occur to her to ask his surname?

"I think I remember. A tall young man from the gaming industry."

"Yes! Do you think you can help me?"

"I can try. Shall I come to see you?"

"Yes please."

"I will be there tomorrow. Wait for me."

Like she's gonna go anywhere else.

It's Skinny's turn for an English lesson.

"Hola, terrorist lover," she sneers.

"Hello, racist." Bunty glares back at her. "What do you want to learn today? How about how to not stereotype people?"

"But I know what you are like. I seen girls like you."

"I have seen girls like you. But you haven't. You might as well say that my African blood makes me run fast."

"Do you?"

"I'm shit at running. I have two left feet – do you know this phrase? It means not well co-ordinated." Bunty does a mime to suggest lack of balance.

"Two left feet." Skinny looks under the desk, at Bunty's shoes, and laughs.

"I work as a sound technician. I like punk rock music. These are not characteristics shared by all black or mixed-race people. It's just who I am. Tell me about you – what you like doing, the things you enjoy."

"I like musica trance. I like big mens."

"I like trance music. I like big men. Is every other Spanish person the same as you?"

"No!"

"Do you like paella and bullfighting and flamenco?"

"Yes – no – no."

"So I won't stereotype you. Please don't do it to me." Bunty grimaces at having to educate her so blatantly. But, here we are... And maybe Skinny can educate her in return.

"Listen, María," – because she does have a real name after all, and Bunty really ought to start using it. "Why do you call Otsana a terrorist?"

"Because is true. That is why she is here."

"Because it *is* true. What do you mean though? What did she do?"

María blanches.

Shit shit shit, do I really want to know?

"She is from ETA. She bomb trains in Madrid, kill many people."

"She bombed trains in Madrid," Bunty says, as the tears jump into her eyes. "She killed many people."

Bunty's voice has trailed away to nothing, remembering some of the things Otsana said to her – about being true to your convictions, and how that makes it easier to be here. She clearly believes what she did was right...

This is the person she was friends with; this is what Skinny and Normal have been trying to tell her all along. She couldn't trust Normal, so clearly corrupt, operating with vested interests, but Skinny – María – doesn't seem to have an agenda. Could it be true?

María watches her with soft eyes. She touches Bunty's forearm, squeezes it.

"You trust too much."

"Maybe I do." I need to find someone I can trust. I think that means getting out of here. "She seemed so nice..."

"Very nice, yes. Very nice dangerous bitch."

Bunty finds there's nothing to correct.

Walking back from school she hears women singing in the yard. When she gets closer she finds they're part of a larger group, clapping out arhythmic flamenco beats and shouting words of encouragement at intangible intervals. Some women are stomping their feet and bucking their hips to the singers' soulful wails, exhibiting a passion that has no outlet in regular prison life. Bunty leans on a wall, taking in the patterns of sound and movement that unite the group. This is the local culture, their folk music, and it's so alive! Their voices express the sorrow and anger that come with incarceration, and although they're trapped deep inside this prison, somehow they are liberating themselves. The tears she's been holding tip forward, and streams flow down her cheeks. For a moment, she is free.

Chapter 59 – Waiting for The Man

The lawyer's coming today. But when? After breakfast she checks out the procedure with one of the guards.

"You wait. We call you if a visitor comes."

She paces the yard.

"Free Bunty!" one of the girls cries. "Got cigarette for me?"

"I don't smoke."

"But you get me cigarette?"

When's this freaking lawyer coming?

All the women turn to watch as a guard walks out among them. He approaches Bunty.

"Maguire. Visitor."

She practically skips away with the guy, to a soundtrack of low grumbles. Maybe her visits are attracting too much attention. But not for much longer...

"Lawyer. Wish me luck," she whispers to María, who winks at her, and she's buoyant on her journey down to the hall.

"Bunty!!!"

A woman's voice. Fuck, Inma's here! But how can she see two people at once? She looks at the guard in confusion. He nods towards Inma. This is her visitor.

"I'm waiting to meet with a solicitor," she tells him.

"Not today."

Inma gets hold of her hand and pulls her into an embrace. It's so good to see her, but her guts are churning with disappointment.

"Bunty, how are you?" her friend asks gently.

"I'm alive. Are *you* okay?"

"We are very sad, you know, but we are okay. We worry about you."

"And Carlos?"

"He wants to come here but I am not sure to bring him. He is very busy though – did you hear?"

"No?"

"He make the posters about you – Free Bunty – and a Facebook group. He has found a lot of your friends in the UK too."

"Woah!"

But that means *everyone* knows?

"And he does this." She hands Bunty a sheet of paper. On it is a series of photos of spray-painted gas masks, but each one has the letters LLLL running underneath.

"What's LLLL?"

"Let La Línea Live. It is his Twitter tag too."

Bunty gasps. "Genius!"

"Asif is helping him. You see Asif, yes?"

"Twice! And he put me in touch with a lawyer who said he'd visit today, but he hasn't..."

"It is like this with people in Spain. They say one day, but it is another day. Try not to worry."

"I need to get out of here."

"Yes. We want you to be free. Many of us." Inma clutches Bunty's hands. "Did Asif tell you about the data? He leaked it, and the newspapers and websites are writing about it."

"It's in the news?"

"Yes, is very exciting. I think something will change. They must free you because the situation is claro now. Is clear."

"Something will change..." Bunty repeats, feeling dazed yet excited.

"Also we have a protest each Saturday, for you, and because of the emissions, and all the victims."

"That's amazing, Inma! Oh..." A doubt crosses Bunty's face. "Did my passport arrive?"

"No," Inma enunciates gently.

"Stephanie told me she would send it – that was before the protest – I think it was two weeks ago..."

"You know how the postal service here is not fast? It can be a month to receive something from abroad. Carlos has this problem when he buys things on eBay..."

Anxiety about every area of her life is overwhelming her, but she mustn't waste this short, precious visit. "Tell me more, Inma. What have you been doing? Have you been to the beach with Carlos? How is work?"

"Just coping. We go sometimes. With work, Jorge is still an asshole. Jasandra asks for you, and Javier joined your Facebook group..."

But their time is up. Inma reaches over to her. "Can you take this?"

Bunty feels something cool in her palm. She looks down at green cut-glass rosary beads.

"To help you!"

"Thank you," Bunty mouths as she's walked away.

I need all the freaking help I can get.

At lunch she makes the mistake of telling Skinny that she's waiting for her ID to arrive in the post. Skinny finds this hilarious; "Your life is in the hands of Los Correos!"

"What?"

"You know what it means? They are called runners – but they should be called lazy stealers! Sit on their asses and steal your shit!"

"Thanks, that's really helping."

"De nada."

Bunty goes back to her oily rubber-egg with some lettuce leaves. Shit... I don't have any support here, no real friendship. Only people on the outside. Great people, but they're not here. And what about that fucking lawyer?

She rushes to the phones to call him before afternoon lockdown.

"Yes, yes, I come tomorrow. You wait, I will get you out of there."

She's heard *that* before.

The cell door closes and locks; that's it for today. The boredom is driving her mad, and there's nothing she can do to hasten her release. She turns over the pretty beads Inma pressed into her hand. What the hell? It can't hurt. She tries to remember the words they chanted, but only fragments come to mind. She translates them into English, but not all of them, so she's left with even less of a prayer. She fills in the gaps herself.

Hey, Mary, full of grace. God thinks you rock, which is cool cos it suggests you're a remnant of a matriarchal culture. You are blessed among women apparently, but we all need a leg up so please help us crush the patriarchy and all its implements, like this fucking jail. You had that nice baby who was into peace and being non-judgemental, but everyone got into him and turned him into an emblem of war. Not your fault. Pray for us, though I don't think it's as much that we are sinners as that the system is biased against us. Unless sin is like having fun, in which case fine.

Please help Doina and Jammy and all the others get off smack.

Please help Normal-Laura become an alright person.

Please help Otsana stop thinking that bombing people in the name of nationalism is righteous.

Please get me out of here.

A-women.

Chapter 60 – Terror Upgrade

The days run into each other, characterised by tedium, conflict, and waiting for that lawyer guy to get his arse over here.

She's still not mastering the shutdown technique, but at least she knows not to talk to anyone about how she feels. Crying's the worst thing she can do; Normal-Laura catches her at it one day and starts lecturing her:

"Everyone here got their problems. Everyone the same. Everyone miss their family, everyone miss the outside. Everyone scared." She's shouting down at her. "No-one wants to know about your feelings, how you sad, you scared."

"I didn't even say anything!" Bunty snuffles. "Fuck off."

"Shut up your crying. You make it worse for everyone."

"Since when are you bothered about other people?"

"I know how it is in here," she answers sharply. "I'm not a selfish little bitch like you."

At this she turns on her heels and is gone before Bunty can tell her to fuck off again. She feels like punching something, so she bangs on the wall in fury. Guards rush into the room – shit, is that all it takes? But they're not after her. With them is some medic-looking guy and they're heading toward the cells. Bunty follows them round. Fuck, they're in her cell! By the time she gets there they're carrying Doina out on a stretcher. She's pale, and her hands are on her chest. Bunty tells her 'Hey', but Doina doesn't respond.

Later they find out it was a heart attack, and that Doina's staying in the infirmary. Bunty has the cell all to herself; such unspeakable luxury – it's the first time she's been alone for weeks. When they lock her in that night she dances around naked, singing and laughing to herself. Get better soon Doina – but maybe not too soon...

The next morning after inspection, Mean Blondie returns to Bunty's cell.

"Get your things together now. You're moving."

"What? What's happening?"

"An upgrade."

Blondie walks with her to a corridor near the entrance of the section, and shows her into a new cell. There's only one bed in there! Bunty places her things on the shelf – a whole shelf to herself – and turns back to the guard uncertainly.

"Is this... I mean, how is Doina?"

The guard shakes her head. "Not good." And she exits, leaving Bunty to her new home.

She trips down to breakfast with a brand-new emotion, something like exhilaration mixed with smug, and only a smattering of guilt that concern for Doina's health is not more dominant in her mind. Her need for personal space is irrepressible, and it's rare for any of her needs to be met these days, but the flipside is that in the canteen, and in her whole life, there's no-one to share this happiness with. She sips nasty coffee and contemplates how much she's looking forward to the siesta lock up.

Instead of yard time Bunty goes back to her latest pad. It doesn't take long to explore, so she snoops around the corridor like a cat with new territory to mark. The cells opposite look different; their doors are locked, but she gets the feeling they are inhabited. Guards enter and leave, but there's no sign of any prisoners.

Until that night, when the peace she anticipated is broken by howling. The voices sound like they belong to men, which makes no sense here. She lies awake and anxious, and in the morning she asks Maria about it.

"It is men in the isolation cells. For when they fight, or if they are very bad."

In the evening there are women hanging around the end of the corridor closest to hers, calling out to male staff. One woman with bleached orange hair is yelling through the double doors at a prisoner on duty.

"Give me your name and number. We can write!"

He shakes his head, but she persists with her request. Bunty shrugs and walks into her cell, looking forward to when they'll all be shutting the fuck up, but dreading the noises that will replace them later.

Bunty's still not seen the other inmates on her row, but the following day one of them sends a signal. She's returning to her cell for siesta when she smells smoke; it's pouring from one of the isolation cells and the stench of burning plastic is filling the corridor as well as her room. She watches from her doorway as guards run, yelling. When the first one opens the door flames burst out; evidently someone's managed to set their mattress on fire. More guards arrive – she never imagined there were this many in the whole place – and three of them attack the blazing cell with fire extinguishers. The cylinders roar and in minutes they've put the fire out. A pair of guards extract the prisoner from the foam-filled cell; he's convulsing with coughing and his wet clothes are dripping grey soot water onto the tiled floor. A cohort of male guards sets on him. Bunty sees one of them bend his arm behind his back. He screams and goes out of view as they lunge at him with feet and truncheons.

"You crazy motherfucker!" one of them bellows, before smashing him in the face with his fist. Bunty hears a sound she'll never forget – the cracking of bone followed by a screeching so horrible that she backs into her cell to escape it. The guards are commanding him to stand up, but he can't anymore. He's still screaming as they drag him along the floor, past her doorway.

"Walk! Now!"

Blood is pouring down the man's legs, as he grunts "Lo siento, lo siento." I'm sorry.

Someone closes Bunty's door. She lies foetus-like on the bed, blanket over her face to protect her lungs from the smoke that clouds the room. She's shaking. And she misses Doina.

The next day when they tell her she has a visitor she's still hoping it will be the lawyer, but it's Asif. She isn't sure she can face him like this, but she can't just leave him down there, so she follows the guard.

"Bunty, hey," he greets her, trying to catch her hands as she flops onto the chair opposite.

She bites her lip and tries to open her eyes a bit wider. Making an effort.

"Shit..." He's staring at her. "What's going on?"

She can't find words, but then his arms are around her. She gives up trying to mumble something into his chest. It feels nice here, and she's glad he doesn't keep talking.

Some time later she works out what she needs to say.

"A fire... a man got smashed up... the guards..." The last phrase is whispered; an armed one is watching them.

"I don't know what to say..."

Bunty sees he's crying, but doesn't know how to respond.

"We have to get you out of here. I spoke to José Ruiz."

"He said he would visit me! He never did. I keep trying to call him."

"He seems like a busy guy, but it's no excuse. I'll call him again as soon as I leave. Pin him down to a day."

"It's Friday today, right?"

"Yeah."

"So there's no chance till next week..." Bunty voice cracks into a sob. And she hears herself uttering a familiar refrain. It's all taking too long. A reasonable voice in her head is talking to her about this and she listens and relaxes.

"What's happening?"

"Sometimes... I get this voice telling me things. Like when I was in Madrid, it said I could fly..."

"Okay..." All the stress on the last syllable.

"You think I'm nuts?"

"No! Stressed maybe. I don't like what's happening to you in here." He looks thoughtful. And then remembers something. "I brought chocolate!" And out of his bag he spills a variety of goodies onto the table.

"Oh, fuck! Wow!" Bunty picks up a Boost and peels back the wrapper. She's eating it and trying to say thanks at the same time, which is creating a mess on the table. Then she grabs a Twix. It's a similar performance.

"This is better than the monkeys!" Asif laughs.

"Fuck off!" She bats her hand at him across the table.

The guard calls time and indicates that she can't bring any chocolate with her, so she stuffs an Aero in her face and gives Asif a gross, chocolatey kiss whilst trying to enunciate a goodbye. He squeezes her, kisses her head, then looks into his eyes. Bunty realises he isn't going to risk another unrequited declaration – it's her turn.

"I muv moo," or something similar, is what comes out. Asif looks like he doesn't know what to do with his face. Even the guard is smiling.

Chapter 61 – Breaking Spell

They call her into the supervisor's office; it's the first time she's seen the inside of it. The supervisor guy is speaking rapidly in Spanish, and she hears him say something about "el tribunal."

"¿Cuándo?"

"Friday."

"This week?" In four days!

He nods, and hands her some papers. She receives them like a priceless tapestry.

"You go now. Lunch."

Bunty steps out of the office in a daze. She moves slowly towards the dining room, reading the precious paperwork as she goes. 'Indocumentado' – she really is in here for being without a passport, not for organising the protest. Seeing the row of payphones, she wishes she could call Asif and the lawyer now, but the phone's out of bounds during mealtimes.

Just cos I don't have ID... How can this be real?

She's still staring at the papers when Skinny María calls her over. She lets her read them.

"Ohhh. Sin identificación. Is not a big problem. Just a few weeks, I think, is usual."

"I don't know what to do to prepare for court."

"I not know. Laura is smart about these things, you can ask her."

"Yeah..." No. She goes to get her meal.

But when Bunty returns to the table, Laura's there; Skinny's told her the news. Laura chews her food contemplatively. "They normally transfer to the detention centre in this case," she murmurs.

"Detention centre?"

"For the immigrants."

"But I'm from the UK – part of the EU."

"Do they know this? You can prove it?"

"Well, obviously not without a passport. But there must be a way of proving who I am..."

Someone's screaming. They all look up. And then down at the papers again. Bunty realises how she's changed; she used to be the first to help someone in need. Laura glances up from the notes once more though, her curiosity winning out. A guard is attempting to escort a woman from the room.

"She not want to leave."

"Hmm?" Bunty looks up.

"This girl. It is her time to go free."

That's when Bunty tunes in. The woman is crying and shouting "Leave me here!" over and over while the guard talks into his radio.

"What the fuck? Why does she wanna stay here?"

"Maybe she has a very bad life outside..." Skinny guesses.

Three more guards enter the dining room. They approach the woman and pick her up between them. At least they're being gentle this time. The woman leaves the hall in their arms, wriggling and crying as she goes.

"Addict. It is easier for her here," Laura comments. "She will be back soon."

"Does that happen often? I can't wait to get the hell out of here."

"Sometimes. Usually if they have been here a long time, and no longer know how to live outside."

"I can remember! It's all I think about."

"You only been here two, three weeks. You have not lost your mind, you don't do drugs."

"I'm glad you acknowledge that, now."

"Yes, I misjudge you."

"You pre-judged me."

"Okay señorita princess, you shut up now or I shut you up."

"Yeah whatever. What do you think about this court thing then?"

"You need to see your lawyer."

"No shit. He keeps saying he'll come. I'm gonna call him now."

"First let me show you something."

"What? Why?"

Laura goes to clear her tray and beckons for Bunty to follow. "Just something to help you leave and never come back."

Bunty trails Laura out of the hall and down the corridor by the side of the kitchen. There's a doorway there that she's never been through. Laura kicks it, and they hear groaning and shouting from the other side.

"Is Laura. Open up."

The door opens a crack and Laura forces her way in. Bunty, stood behind her, sees that it's a tiny room, maybe a storeroom. Three pallid faces look up at them – ones she recognises from the methadone queue.

"What's up, coño?"

"Fuck you, Laura," says the greyest of the cupboard gang. "What you want?"

"Just wishing you good day. And see what the dirty girls are doing today."

What they are doing makes Bunty's stomach lurch. This seems to be some sort of beauty salon, but a gross prison version of such. One of the women is piercing the ears of another using a pen, and there's blood running everywhere.

"This is Bunty. She goes to court in a few days. I bring her round to show her what she will miss when she leaves here."

The woman with the pen wipes a bloody hand on her trousers and offers it to Bunty. "Nice meeting you."

Bunty waves back. "Encantada." She wants to be sick.

"I gotta make a call."

"Good Bunty." Laura leans against the door frame with her arms folded.

Bunty races to the phones and is the first one there. She dials José Ruiz's number. No-one picks up.

Chapter 62 – Caught (Again)

Two guards escort her down to the ingreso where she's transferred into the care of a pair of bodyguard cops. She smiles to herself; she kinda misses these rituals.

The gate spits them out and they head to the city. Bunty is chained to a silent, uniformed man, but her eyes are all over everything: dusty earth, gnarled olive trees, the blue blue sky. And people – random assorted people, in other cars, and in the city streets, walking around. Women, men, kids, little dogs – everyone's just living their lives. But how can this be, when some people are stored away in containers in the countryside? Why does the world carry on when some people can't? Her head buzzes with anxiety. After the shitshow of the last six weeks, when pretty much everything that could go wrong did exactly that, it's hard to rely on a sense of justice or sanity about the way her life is heading. Will this hearing set her free, or send her down for more time in that crazy place, or even some other jail? If so, how much time, and when will she see her folks again? Will she survive with her mental health intact? The total absence of legal representation is agonising. After three weeks in Botafuegos her head is in no great shape... She's not ready.

She's certainly not ready for the scene outside the court building. First off there's the shouting, like the din of a demonstration. Are they chanting her name? Then the crowd comes into view and she sees the placards. Yep, that's definitely her name. Insane! There are TV station cameras; she watches a young woman addressing one of them, a boom mic above her head. She spots Javier, then Nancy, Asif, Inma, and Carlos – the last three have seen her too and are waving. They seem excited, and a team of police is busy trying to keep them, and the rest of the crowd, in check. Bunty roars at her friends, and the driver cop raises the electric window, telling her to shut up. Then they're round the side of the building, being swallowed by the dark of an underground car park. The cops seem more tense than usual, and she doesn't know what to do with her face when they're all in the lift. Then they're taking her up a wooden staircase into an enclosed space at the front in a large room. The dock. From here she can see her friends as they file into the room. Asif smiles and winks at her, and Carlos does some sort of gangsta salute. Inma is grinning crazily, and Nancy mouths "Good luck." She puts her elbows on the side of the box that's holding her and rests her head on her hands, just for a moment. When she looks up it's a different picture – Asif is frowning uncertainly and Inma's face is creased with concern. Shit! This is too much. Her concentration's out of order, and it's not as though she even knew what was going on to begin with. She's falling apart.

There's a line of people sitting separately from all the others in a section under the window. Are they the jury? What kind of trial is this? They're studying her, and when she checks them out in return, all but one appear white. She hopes to fuck they're not racist.

A man approaches her with a messy-looking folder under his arms, papers spilling out of it. "I am José Ruiz, your lawyer."

"Oh! Good to meet you, at last." She glares at him. "You never came to see me, or answered the phone…"

"Is okay, I have your case ready. You will admit to the judge that you were travelling without ID, and I will explain the rest."

This sounds well shonky. "What's going to happen then? Will they let me go or are they gonna send me to the immigration detention centre, or…?"

"There has been some pressure on your behalf, so it is important…" He looks around suddenly as the judge enters the room.

"What?"

"We start now." He straightens his paperwork and turns to walk away.

"What's important?"

"I tell you later."

Bunty gazes out at her friends, who are winking and gesturing to her, and wishes more than anything that she was on the other side of this box, on the other side of the room, safe with them. If she gets torn away again, sent back to that jail again – or even worse, to a detention centre – it will break her.

She's rubbing anxious tears from her cheeks while the judge addresses the room. Then another guy starts up, the prosecution lawyer, she guesses. He's asking her a question, something about a 'manifestación'. She looks around for some sort of guidance. Should she answer in Spanish? Her lawyer stands and speaks to the judge, and the guy sitting next to him gets up and leaves the room.

For fuck's sake. This is horrible.

She's biting her nails when the assistant returns with another guy, who steps over to her. "I am the translator," he announces.

He speaks English!

The other lawyer repeats his question, and the translator relays it to her.

"Were you involved in organising a demonstration in La Línea de la Concepcion on the second of July this year?"

What should she say? She doesn't have another story about this, and the lawyer's told her nothing, so the truth is all she has left.

"Yes."

The prosecution guy talks some more; he seems to be saying that the protest was dangerous – 'peligroso' – and that she should be detained for months, or years. But shouldn't she be charged for that separately?

He's passing some papers to the judge and she glimpses a colourful photo – it's some of the graffiti that Carlos and his friends created.

The judge asks her "¿Lo has hecho?" – did you do it?

That's an easy one. "No." She's glad he didn't ask the question differently, as she's certainly responsible for it.

The prosecution lawyer keeps talking, and her lawyer seems to be raising an objection, which the judge accepts. A couple of jury members are writing notes. And then he's finished. It's over to her guy.

He introduces her case to the judge, and then the translator asks her something.

"What, sorry?"

"How did you lose your passport?"

She grips the wooden bar around the balcony of the dock to steady herself. "Um, I was working on a cruise ship – I had a job as a sound engineer, but I needed to leave the ship – I didn't feel safe there, so I got off in Gibraltar. They kept my passport..."

She trails off, feeling stupid, as the translator relays this information to everyone in the room. All her mistakes.

"What steps did you take to try to recover your passport?"

It's hard to talk without choking up but she holds on and gets the words out. "Erm... I tried getting help in Gibraltar but they gave me the wrong forms, and then I went to Spain and tried to get help from the Consulate in Madrid, but it all went wrong and I didn't have enough money to stay in Madrid. And I contacted the cruise company to ask them to send me the passport, but they wouldn't do that. Then a friend offered to recover it from them and send it to me, but I've been waiting for it to arrive in the post." Her voice disintegrates into a sob.

For some reason, Inma's waving what looks like a package above her head, but Bunty has to look away so she can focus on what the translator's saying.

"Can you explain why you organised the demonstration?"

"It's because..." Fuck. She's not prepared for this at all, so has to search her heart and trace it right back to the start. "I met a Spanish girl and she was so kind to me, but members of her family were sick because of the pollution from the plant, and it caused the death of her mother and other relatives. I was staying with her around that time, and I wanted to do something to help her and her family, and the other families in the area."

Her lawyer nods, and says a few more words before sitting down.

Then the prosecution guy's up again. She hears him saying stuff like 'criminal', 'dangerous' – he's even using the words 'extremist' and 'terrorist'. Bunty folds her arms around her chest. He appears so confident in his use of these disturbing words; Bunty's alarmed to see members of the jury taking notes.

Then it's up to José Ruiz to summarise, then the judge says something, and the jury file out of the room. One of her bodyguards taps her on the shoulder and says she has to go too. She waves to her friends, and then they're moving down the stairs. They put her in a small bright room with one other person, a young woman.

The door slams. Bunty nods at the woman and sits on a bench in the corner where she rests her head on her knees. She needs to process what's just happened. Everything depends on what this jury does; there's nothing she can do about it. And that prosecution guy has just likened her to – or even called her – a terrorist.

This is terrifying. Would a terrorist be terrified? She wants to shit, but the hole in the ground in the corner of the cell looks horrendous, and she can't let rip in front of this other person. So she holds it in, and holds it together.

¿Qué tal?

"Bien," the woman answers, unemotionally. She looks care-worn, tired.

Should she ask why she's there? What would Bunty say if asked back? Such fun conversations: "Hi, I'm a prostitute." "Hi, I'm a terrorist. Allegedly."

211

The door opens, it's her fellas again. "Buena suerte," she says to the woman, who nods forlornly back at her. In the lift Bunty examines the cops' faces, as though they could tell her something, but of course they don't know. No-one knows yet.

What's next in this comedy of errors? Some sort of crazy sentence for terrorism would fit right in with her entropic run of bad luck. Time slows down as they approach the court room, but eventually she's back in the dock. She makes a scared face at Asif and Nancy. Carlos forms a heart shape with his hands, which makes her cry a bit more, and Inma holds up something that glints in the light – ah, rosary beads. Alright, Virgin Mary, please pull a trick out of the bag for me this afternoon. I promise to join your fan club or something.

The judge speaks for a few moments, then one of the jurors, a middle-aged woman, walks over and hands him a piece of paper. Her expression is grim; this could be really fucked. What if she's some sort of Francoist throwback, the kind of woman that gives you the evil eye in the street for not being the right kind of feminine? Bunty watches the judge as he opens the paper and reads it. His brows go up. He says something to the lady, 'Gracias' it looks like, and she goes and sits back down. She looks pleased with herself. What did she just do?

The judge coughs and begins to speak. The translator stands to Bunty's side, where he can watch the judge and relay the news in her ear.

"He says that the jury have found you guilty, and he has to sentence you."

There are gasps from the room, several voices saying "¡No!" Bunty looks around, but the sight of Asif's crumpled face is too much for her. The translator's speaking again.

"He is sentencing you to three weeks in prison."

"Wha...?" She's been in there for almost that long: two weeks and four days...

There is laughter from the back of the room, and she looks up to see that her friends' smiles have been restored. Inma is beaming and holding up three fingers, mouthing: "¡Tres días!"

"See you Monday!" Asif has both his hands in the air, as though he could grab her from all the way back there.

Tears are rolling down her face. She takes one last look at her friends as the cops pull her towards the stairs.

Chapter 63 – Inside Out

She's back in time for the film.

The women clamour round her when she shows up in the dining room. "How long you get?" "You gonna get transferred?"

"Three days."

There's a chorus of 'What the fuck?'s. Laura laughs, and demands more details.

"The verdict was guilty, and judge said three weeks. I've been here two weeks and four days already."

"The fucker."

Bunty looks around, startled. It's Otsana.

"It is just a show of power. He could have let you go today."

"But then I don't get to say goodbye!"

And there *is* someone she really wants to see.

"How is Doina, does anyone know?"

Suddenly, they're all quiet.

"What? Is she...?" Bunty looks at their sad faces, aghast.

It's Skinny María who speaks up. "She die."

"What? When?"

"Last night. They tell us today."

The walk to the sports hall is sombre, but some women are still trying to cadge fags, and a bit more, from the men on duty. She sits with Laura and María, who explain the parts of the film that she doesn't get, but her heart's filling with grief and shock, and she's impatient for the movie to end.

"What happens now? Do we have a funeral?"

María shakes her head sadly.

"But she must have a funeral?"

"The state will burn her body. We cannot go."

"We must be able to do something for her?"

Blank faces all round.

"Like what?" asks Laura, harshly.

"Erm, a party? We could have drinks and talk about what we remember about her."

Some of the women nod and murmur.

"I go ask the guards."

"Thanks Laura."

Saturday night at Botafuegos – the recreation room is buzzing. They've got orange squash in plastic beakers, dishes of corn snacks, and some peanuts that Bunty had stashed away. A guard comes in, sets up a battered radio cassette player, and places a box of cassettes next to it. María runs over to scrabble through it and emerges with a tape of cheesy Spanish pop. The other women go crazy; Bunty just smiles. Jammy's running around excitedly, bumping prisoners with her behind. Some sway to the music, and others wave their arms in the air. A small group of prisoners are slumped in a corner, talking – probably this is too much for them now, and it's a long wait till their breakfast methadone.

"Do you have happy memories of Doina?" she asks María and Laura.

"Remember that time she farted in the lunch queue? The guard had to come over because people were running away!" Laura cracks up laughing. "She was a crazy bitch,"

"That's a beautiful eulogy."

Laura elbows Bunty in the ribs.

Otsana chips in with something about Doina being a victim of a broken Europe, and the Romanian situation. María lets out a "Yeah, whatever," between slurps of orange squash. "I'm gonna dance!"

María and Laura join the dancers in the middle of the room and Bunty leans on the wall with Otsana.

"Gonna miss you."

Bunty looks at her. "But we hardly hung out, and not for ages."

"At least I could see you, in the dining room, in the patio..."

"Oh, Otsana..."

Bunty doesn't know what to say. But when Otsana leans towards her, she knows what to do.

"I gotta go!"

And she races from the room. *The last thing I need now is an affair with a gorgeous mass murderer.*

She can hear the music from her cell. She rubs her eyes and smiles. *I'm gonna miss these bitches.*

Chapter 64 – Freedom Fire

Bunty's walking in a way she's not been able to for a while – at the correct speed, and right out the fucking door – and no-one's stopping her. Sunlight greets her like a long-lost friend, caressing her arms and face. She screws up her eyes, recalls the existence of shades, and rummages through the bag of her stuff that they've just handed to her. She puts them on as the guard unlocks the gate. They enter the outer enclosure, and Bunty feels more excellent by the moment, like she's busting through the rings of hell. At the final gate, a guard gives the customary advice:

"Take care, guapa. Keep out of trouble."

And with those words she's free. She doesn't hear the sound of the gate being locked from the inside, cos she's already running down the road. Her feet smack on cracked asphalt. The force of each blow through her tatty Converse hurts her prison-soft feet but she doesn't mind. Asif was supposed to be here, and he's not, and she doesn't even mind about that either. He's unreliable as fuck, but she's out! And home soon. Home!

Now that she has her phone, her trusty little friend that she's missed so much, the first text has got to be for Sofia.

Sof I am outta jail! I busted out just now! And I have finally thought of the perfect title for our album.

Sofia's right back at her: *OMG Buns I am so glad to hear from you! I am so glad you are out! Fuck!!! YAY!!! What's this LP title then?*

Bunty smiles as she holds down caps lock: *QUIME.*

Oh my fuck, Bunty, that's perfect!

There's a noise up ahead, and a billowing of smoke; a metal thing is glinting in the sun, getting bigger by the second. It's green. Lime fucking green.

"Asif!"

He stops the car in the middle of the road and jumps from it, runs at her.

"Hello, you fucker," Bunty roars, grabbing him round the waist in a beast-like hug.

"Thank god you're out!"

As the car picks up speed she howls at the wasteland, and to everyone trapped inside the perimeter fence. Asif joins in the primal screaming.

"Where are we going?" she asks when she's quietened down enough to speak.

"Lap of victory?"

Bunty's halfway out of the window, giving her arms to the breeze, waving at people in other cars, and generally going nuts. Some wave back, others look bemused. Every now and again she lets out a yelp, and then remembers she can do anything she likes. She leans over and kisses Asif.

"Easy, tiger!"

They pass the place where the remains of the ancient city were found, and move beyond, to the bay. It seems like too long since she's seen the sea, and even this mucky corner of it is beautiful to her eyes.

"I wanna sleep on the beach!"

"You can! I think? The police wouldn't have an issue with that, would they?"

"Fuck tha police!"

She's yowling at the sky again. Asif reaches across to hold her down as if she could fly out of the window.

"This is what I want to show you – hang on..."

They're going around the front of the plant, past the entrance, to which Bunty yells a friendly "fuck you", and then they're by the wall of murals.

"I saw this before!" she bellows. She feels like a rapidly expanding lion, about to fill the whole sky.

"Yeah. But you haven't seen *this*." He slows the car right down. And then she sees. In each painting, every single animal, fish or person is wearing a gas mask.

"What the – who???!"

"Your protégé."

"Carlos?"

"And friends."

"Woah..." Bunty's mouth is hanging open, and her eyes are sparkling.

"I was worried about you in there, but they clearly didn't kill your spirit. Looks like they didn't get anywhere near it."

"They hurt me, but they can fuck themselves... and they can fuck off while they're doing it!"

Asif squeezes her shoulders.

"Where we go now?"

"I know you like surprises..."

"No, what, where? I don't wanna go far. I had too many bad surprises in there."

Asif picks up her anxiety. "Don't worry. Inma's? Is that okay?"

"Yes!!!" She's happy again. "That's exactly where I wanna go!"

She settles back into the seat, to relax, to take it all in. Everything looks wonderful today. The Rock shocks her almost as much as it did the first time she saw it – that preposterous mass of jagged darkness jutting so suddenly above flat land, flat sea. Even La Línea's apartment blocks and tumbledown streets make her coo with delight.

When Asif stops the car she jumps out to press the intercom, but no-one answers. Moments later there's the pounding of feet: Carlos appears on the other side of the door and yanks it open. Inma's right behind. He's yelling an incoherent greeting and hugging her. Inma lands next, embracing them both.

The siblings seem desperate to tell her everything; Inma starts by asking Bunty how she is. "You got free! How do you feel?"

"Just, so happy," Bunty beams. "To see you two, and Asif, and to be outside! I wanna stay outside forever!"

"I hope you do," smiles Inma. "I don't want you to go back there."

"I mean outside outside. I want to sleep on the beach! I want to breathe the real air, all the time!"

"Can you bear to be inside for a short time? We have something we want to show you…"

She assents to this, and they start up towards the apartment. "We didn't have to climb stairs in there," pants Bunty. "My muscles have forgotten how to do it." They pause with her after two flights, and soon she resumes the race towards the front door. It feels great to be back in a place that smells normal and not like cheap detergent. But she can't see what it is that they might want to show her.

"What is it? What am I meant to see?"

"Sit down, Bunty," Inma tells her, pulling out a chair in front of the computer. She flicks on the screen and they're looking at a Spanish news site, El País. It's an article about a new EU directive limiting the plant's emissions.

"No! Freaking! Way!"

"Yes way," Asif corrects her, looking more than a little pleased with himself.

"This is because of you?"

"No, because of you. You started the protests, and then you were our equivalent of Pussy Riot, in jail for no sensible reason."

"It was you guys! Oh, Carlos, I saw all the gas masks! I saw them on the animals!"

He laughs delightedly and she pulls him into another hug.

"And Inma, you kept the protests going... And you all did the Free Bunty thing..."

"It was all of us, together" whispers Inma, stretching her arms around the three of them. "We fucking changed the world!"

Chapter 65 – Sleepy Beachy

When she said she couldn't bear to stay inside, she meant it.

"Let's go out! Let's drink booze!"

"Can you remember how to drink booze?" teases Asif. "You've not had it in a while."

"It's like falling off a bike – I think I'm gonna remember!"

"You should eat first." Inma's inspecting her. "Look at you!"

Bunty looks down at herself. There's less of her than there used to be. "Prison food isn't very nice," she admits.

"Come on!" Carlos is beckoning them excitedly from the doorway. They head to a nearby bar that serves food, to kill both birds. As they go to sit down, a man taps Bunty on the shoulder.

"You are Bunty?"

"Huh? Yes?"

"You are out of the jail!" He looks delighted, and kisses her confused face on both cheeks. "I buy you a drink!"

"Alright!" she laughs. Then she overhears Inma talking with Asif.

"She really wants to sleep on the dirty beach?" Inma has her dubious face on.

Bunty interrupts. "Yeah, I really am gonna sleep on the dirty beach!"

"Can I come with you then?" Asif asks gently.

Bunty smiles a yes at him, biting her bottom lip.

"Me too!" It's Carlos. He's too excited to pick up any subtle goings on.

Inma looks at Bunty, who is laughing some more. "That would be awesome!"

"Really, are you sure?" Inma again.

"All of us! We can all sleep on the beach!"

Inma looks uncertain, then breaks into a grin. "Okay, what the fuck!"

Bunty and Asif crack up with laughter. Bunty's emanating warmth like the sun. It reminds her of someone who's not here.

"Has anyone heard from Abbo?"

"I not seen him for weeks!" exclaims Carlos, looking wounded.

Bunty taps out a quick text.

I busted out of jail. Where you at?

The food arrives, along with a response: *Skipped over to Morocco. Imma explore The Continent. Congrats on the escape!*

Bunty smiles at the thought of her friend's adventures, and in a few moments her belly rediscovers joy.

They return to the apartment and gather the things they might need – blankets, music, food and drink. As they arrive, the sun sets behind them. Carlos collects driftwood and Asif helps him set it on fire. Bunty lies on her back staring up at the sky, watching the colours change. The luminescent afternoon sun, bouncing back

218

off the whitewashed walls of the apartment blocks, gives way to the oranges and reds of the sunset, while in the eastern sky the prettiest pink blush adorns the horizon. The sea is that impossible hue, or mix thereof: an undulating mesh of silver and all the colours of the sky. Finally, the night blooms, deep and dark.

Quietly, Inma asks Bunty how she's feeling.

"I'm mending." She turns over in the sand and looks at her. "I need to breathe air and see sky and be with you guys. It's all so perfect."

The wood is crackling, and some smoke catches Bunty in the throat. She sits up, coughing, and Inma passes her a drink.

"You know we have another surprise for you. Something we did not give you before."

"Oh yeah? Like what?" So many surprises today!

Carlos and Asif watch keenly as Inma takes something out of her bag. It's a brown envelope, about twelve centimetres long. She passes it to Bunty, who tries to bend the contents, testing its tensile strength.

"Noooo!" She looks at them all, her eyes expanding.

"Well, aren't you gonna open it?" Asif suggests, with atypical impatience.

"Open! OPEN!" Carlos is smacking his hands on the sand.

Bunty takes the edge of the envelope between her teeth and rips it away. Dips two fingers into the envelope and pulls out a small, thin, burgundy coloured book.

She opens it book, sees the little picture of herself, and begins to sob.

Asif holds her shoulders. "Bunty?"

"I just never thought... I mean I thought all the time... but..."

"It didn't seem like it was going to happen, did it, at times?"

If it wasn't for Asif she'd have fallen sideways into the sand. The three of them watch her, silently. She stops crying long enough to speak.

"I can go home!"

They're looking at stars, drifting off to sleep.

"Do you know what?" Bunty interro-announces. "I am really fucking hungry! Can we get pizza on the beach?"

"Yesss!" yells Carlos. "I will get it!"

They hand coins and notes to Carlos whilst arguing about who pays – everyone wants to.

"We can get lots of pizzas!"

"And beer!" Bunty instructs. "Erm, can you buy beer?"

"I try!"

And he's gone. The three of them lie quietly, listening to the water lapping the sand.

Asif is the first to speak. "What do you think you'll do?"

"Hmm?"

"Now you have your passport."

"Well, it'd be crazy to go straight back when I can stay here and lie on the beach... but I gotta go, for my mum and dad at least. I think they probably need to physically see me, so they can know I'm okay."

"Makes sense."

"But what about us?" It's Inma. "We will miss you too much!"

"I will come back. And you'll visit me – won't you?"

"I hope so." She squeezes Bunty's hand.

"There are cheap flights. And you can stay with me, wherever I am. I want to pay you back for taking me in."

"You already did! Because of you the plant will be safer. The air will be better for all of us."

"We're a crack environmentalist team." She puts up her hand and Inma and Asif high five her clumsily from their supine positions.

"Yeah, and what about me?" Asif's tone is humorously sulky.

"What about you?" Bunty mumbles back in babyish tones, and turns her face to snuzzle his. "You will visit me, won't you? You go back sometimes to see your folks and stuff?"

"Yeah, but that's only like three times a year."

He's not hiding his sad very well, but Bunty isn't taking it on. She knows what she has to do.

"You're both amazing. I'm so happy to be here. And I'm so glad I can go places. My passport means shit loads more to me now." She caresses the cover, with its garland of European Union stars. "Even though it looks like they're gonna be downgrading it pretty soon... At least I can get an Irish one."

"Yeah, you can do that! What can I do?" asks Asif.

"Ask Bunty to marry you and then you can have the Irish passport too, no?" laughs Inma.

Asif goes quiet. Too quiet. Bunty punches him.

"Asif, you're being silly. You have your own mission. More truth to leak. Whistles to blow."

"Yes, sir. I will be brave." He's messing, but he sounds morose.

There's a slapping noise on the sand. They turn to see Carlos, laden with bags and boxes, racing towards them. He skids to a halt and lands on his knees next to Bunty.

She pats his shoulder. "Congratulations on your underage beer purchases!"

He's out of breath and victorious. They sit in a circle around the boxes and cans, and share out slices and beer.

This is it, thinks Bunty. It doesn't get better than this.

Chapter 66 – Out The Gate

Saying goodbye to Inma and Carlos was awful. Everyone was crying, and in the end the only way she could deal with it was by running up the escalators to the departure gates, turning at the top for a final wave, and then step, sob, step along the glass-walled corridor away from them. Maybe forever?

The worst of it was, Asif didn't show. After everything they went through, and what he – unknowingly – put her through, and even after that glorious beach party a couple of days ago, he couldn't even come and say goodbye. She's sick in her stomach at him, and relieved they never made it more serious, never put a name on it. Better to be pissed off for eternity.

She's slamming her bags onto the conveyor belt at Security, and a man is telling her that she has to take liquids and electronic devices out of them, so she's rummaging and swearing and tears are still dripping out of her as she recovers a shampoo bottle, which the man then confiscates cos it's too big. Bunty glares at him in messy indignant rage, but this is just one more thing she has to leave behind if she's going to get home.

She walks through the metal detector and scopes out the departure hall. Three gates, that's all there is to it, so she can't get lost, however upset she is. Beyond the ends of the queues are vast floor-to-ceiling windows, and there's even an outside balcony that you're actually allowed to go and sit on while you wait for your plane. She trails her stuff out through the door, finds a metal bench, and plonks herself down to commune with the crazy Rock one last time. This is the north face, grim and looming. Asif's somewhere on the other side of it, on slopes that would melt into the sea if they could. He's embedded in that shiny nest of tower blocks riddled with gambling companies, fleecing the poor, deceiving the desperate. If that's where he wants to be, if that's what he thinks is right, then it's correct that she's leaving him to it. I need to go now, more than ever.

She peers over her shoulder as the lights go off in the departure lounge shops. A woman is locking the glass door of the Duty Free, and it makes her feel even sadder, somehow. Everything is ending – even the airport is closing. How does it feel at night when there's no-one here to race and wait and grumble?

Bunty notices that the queue at her gate has vanished, as a voice over the Tannoy announces the final call for boarding. She jumps up and races into the hall, pulling her passport from her pocket, and runs with it in her outstretched hand. The airline clerk takes it from her like a baton in a relay race.

"Bunty!!"

Someone is yelling in the near-empty hall. What the...? She swivels round.

It's Asif.

"Fuck! How did they let you up here?" She's scowling and shouting at him and he's dropping bags on the floor and trying to hold her. "It's too late to say goodbye now Asif! I have to go!"

"Bunty! Listen!"

He's out of breath, but she doesn't care about his obvious discomfort. Pleased about it even. Furious!

His eyes are brimming.

"I just quit my job."

"Good for you," she spits.

"You're mad at me..."

"You didn't say goodbye." She glares at him.

"Don't you see, Bunty? I didn't want to say goodbye. That's why I'm here. I'm not saying goodbye. I got a ticket for this flight! It took ages – I'm sorry – but I wanted to surprise you."

Her brain cannot compute. She just stares.

"I couldn't let you go. I mean, I have to let you go. So I thought maybe I could come with you? I... is it okay?"

Bunty stands with her hands on her hips and a crease in her brow. "Hmm..."

The flight attendant is getting antsy. "Do you want to board this plane or not?"

"Fuck yes!" she tells her. "I think this dude wants to get on it too."

Asif laughs inanely as the attendant scans their boarding passes, and Bunty thanks her with one last "Gracias." They stumble, tumble and race down the stairs, giggling like eejits. When they hit the tarmac Bunty takes one last look at the shadowy face of the Rock, then turns to Asif, takes his sweaty hand in hers, and raises both their fists in the humid, noisome air.

He grins at her. "Let's go?"

"Yeah. Let's go home."

Universal Acknowledgements

This book arose from myriad confluences; it might be easier to say who didn't help - and on that count, no-one springs to mind.

In 2015 a friend took a job trial as a sound technician on a Mediterranean cruise liner. In a social media post he described the toxicity of the onboard culture, rife with racism, homophobia and misogyny, and I suggested he disembark at Gibraltar and come to stay with me in Spain. His response? I can't, they've got my passport. Many of the indignities that Bunty experienced on the ship came from Danny Wolfe's account of his brief time in that role.

The project was initially going to be a fanzine, called The Oddness of Gibraltar. It transmorphed into a novel as the rock loomed into view during a bus ride one typical bright blue afternoon. I credit the switch to fiction to the influence of writers' groups I was attending at the time. They tolerated my pieces about music, but soon the peer pressure kicked in and I was away on an adventure of a hundred thousand words, and several years, without a paddle.
The last bit isn't true. I enlisted paddling help from a number sources and ended up rowing myself around in circles for much that time.
Thanks are due to three Writers' Groups – Estepona, with Lorraine Mace at the helm, Sotogrande, run by the ever-supportive Tracy Thomson and Jo Ward, and Gibraltar, especially to Jackie Anderson, who also gave assistance with my attempted rendering of Llanito.

To fill the gaps in my creative writing education I joined several courses with Gotham Writers, made accessible online due to the SARS-CoV-2 pandemic. Thanks to all tutors and fellow students including Susan Breen, Carmen Bugan, Bob Silber and John Catalinotto. I also benefitted from Ariel Gore's Winter 2021 Intensive course.

My thanks go to all the following:

The late Ingrid de Leeuw, who spent fifteen months in a Spanish prison, and gave me an interview in which she vividly described experiences I could not otherwise imagine. Her own story of betrayal and tragedy deserves to be told.

Christopher James Brereton, who helped by leaving me alone for days or weeks at a time, but also by listening to many sections of the text, contributing to plot brain storming, and creating two excellent character names: Pandorina and Jasandra.

For assistance with local research: Janet of the Environmental Safety Group in Gibraltar, Ana Sanchez, Vivienne Wilson, Karl Jones, Sue Manning, Jane Howard, Mac, Jane Hart, Jill Kearney, Jean and Amy, and Alva.

Lucy Cage for the typo that became Bunty and Sofia's band name.

Joanna Howard, Darren Lockwood, Delia Sparrow, Eleanor, and Cassie Fox for knowing things about kitchen work, cruise ship music and sound engineering respectively.

To Catherine Kemp, for asking "How's Bunty?" every day.

Harry Dewulf, who wrote a thorough, inspirational and at times contentious editorial assessment, and Kelly Townley for her scathing reader's report.

To the many beta readers who steadied my nerves. Simone Ivatts, who also helped me with the editing process and a great deal of support, Anne Grange, Patrick Courtney, Ngaire Ruth, Tabitha Bast, Mitzi Waltz, Louise Woodcock, Justine Railton, Nicola Jay Burgess, and Emmett.

To sensitivity readers Nila Kamul Krishnan Gupta (may they rest in power), Erin Fuller, Aisha Ali who gave input about racism and Indian and Pakistani heritage, and Sophia Howard who also provided insight into Irish and Jamaican dual heritage as well as contemporary Black British experience.

Inge Beaujean and Baldo Gordillo, who corrected my Spanish.

Bela Emerson, Mandy Newman and Ian Cockburn, who proofread the book to near perfection.

Pascale Hutton for being the most understanding book cover designer an overly-precious author could wish for.

To the many friends who assisted me in my final deliberations over the book's title and cover design, including Rachel Mary Lawson, Reb Jane, Melanie Barnes and Elizia Volkmann, and to Kirsten Ivatts, Rachel Holborow, P.P. Priestley and Jasmine Beau for assistance with design conceptualisation.

Finally, I would like to thank the album Fire Dances by Killing Joke for being the aural equivalent of strong coffee, and the bar of Hotel Patricia in Torreguadiaro for being a fine place to write, with the sound of waves crashing on the beach below, or spraying the old wooden-framed windows during a storm. Sacarello's and Modelo in Gibraltar and many establishments in Seville also permitted me to sit for hours with a cup of tea by my notebook.